K **Sinclair**'s first foray into writing romance was for a
hi ol English assignment, and not even being forced
to e Scotland-set historical aloud to the class could
d er enthusiasm…although it definitely made her
bl e sold her first book to Mills & Boon Blaze
in nd has enjoyed exploring relationships, falling in
lo happily-ever-afters since. She lives in North
A with her two teenage daughters and their ever-
en ng bernedoodle puppy, Sadie. Kira loves to hear
fr ers at Kira@KiraSinclair.com

K **ooth** is a Midwestern girl transplanted in the
So ised on '80s music and repeated readings of
Fc oy Judy Blume. When she takes a break from
th f romance, she's listening to music with her
co aged kids or sweet-talking her husband into
ma her a cocktail. Learn more about Karen at
ka oth.net

Also by Kira Sinclair

Bad Billionaires
The Rebel's Redemption
The Devil's Bargain

The Risk-Taker
She's No Angel
The Devil She Knows
Captivate Me
Testing the Limits
Bring Me to Life
Handle Me
Rescue Me

Also by Karen Booth

Once Forbidden, Twice Tempted
High Society Secrets
A Christmas Temptation
A Cinderella Seduction
A Bet with Benefits
A Christmas Seduction
A Christmas Rendezvous

Discover more at millsandboon.co.uk

THE SINNER'S SECRET

KIRA SINCLAIR

ALL HE WANTS FOR CHRISTMAS

KAREN BOOTH

Version: FSC C007454

This book is produced from independently certified FSC
paper to ensure responsible forest management.

For more information visit: www.harpercollins.co.uk/green

Printed and bound in Spain
by CPI, Barcelona

MILLS & BOON

First Published in Great Britain 2020
by Mills & Boon, an imprint of HarperCollinsPublishers,
1 London Bridge Street, London, SE1 9GF

The Sinner's Secret © 2020 Kira Bazzel
All He Wants for Christmas © 2020 Karen Booth

ISBN: 978-0-263-28009-8

1120

MIX
Paper from
responsible sources

FSC

THE SINNER'S SECRET

KIRA SINCLAIR

There would be no Bad Billionaires without my amazing editor, Stacy Boyd. She believed in me and this project from the very beginning. I'm grateful for her support, guidance and vision that helped make this series amazing. Thank you, Stacy!

One

The last two weeks had been surreal, culminating in this moment. Blakely Whittaker stood behind her new desk, staring at the persistent log-in screen waiting for her to input something on her standard-issue laptop.

She had no idea what to do next.

A box of personal belongings waited in her car, which was parked in the basement deck. There was a folder of HR paperwork that Becky had handed her after a quick tour of the building. Blakely should probably read it all.

But her body wouldn't move. Instead, her head kept swiveling between the closed door of her own private office and the huge windows at her back with a view of the city.

A far cry from the dingy, cramped cubicle she'd called home for the last few years.

The people here were so different, too. Everyone she'd encountered, from Finn DeLuca—the charismatic guy who'd approached her about the job—to the receptionist and HR staff had been upbeat, personable and genuinely happy. A huge shift from the depressed, downtrodden lot she'd been working with.

Sure, it was a nice change. One she'd desperately needed, along with the raise that came with her new position as lead accountant for Stone Surveillance.

But something about the whole thing felt off.

Which was why she was still standing, unwilling to take a seat in the very expensive and, no doubt, very comfortable chair waiting beside her.

Blakely could hear the voices in her head—sounding strangely like her parents—fighting like an angel and a devil. Her mother on one shoulder, wary, practical, cynical, warning her that if something looked too good to be true then it most likely was. And her father on the other, eternally optimistic, opportunistic and not to mention criminally inclined, telling her that if someone wanted to give her the world, it was her obligation to take it and run before they figured out their mistake.

Which left her stuck in the middle, a product of both and often paralyzed by indecision.

No, that wasn't true. The decision had already been made. She was here, in her new office, which meant the only path was forward. After pulling out the chair, Blakely dropped into it and let out a deep sigh when her assumptions were confirmed. The thing was real leather. Hell, her last chair squeaked every time she stood up and the underside of the cushion had been held together by duct tape. And not the cute, decorative kind.

Opening the manila folder, she began reading through the packet of information on company policies, leave accrual and insurance plans. She was halfway through when the door to her office opened.

She expected to see Becky walking back in to give her more information, or maybe IT bringing her log-in info so she could access her computer.

But that wasn't who'd come in.

Blakely's belly rolled and her skin flushed hot as she took in the man lounging, bigger than some Greek god, against the now-closed door. Unfortunately, no matter what she thought of him personally, her physical reaction to Gray Lockwood had always been the same. Immediate, overwhelming, bone-deep awareness.

Today, that familiar and unwanted response mixed with a healthy dose of "what the hell?"

Because the last person she expected to saunter into her brand-new office was the man she'd sent to prison eight years ago.

"Bastard."

Gray Lockwood had been called much worse in his life, and probably deserved it.

Hell, he deserved it today, although not for the reasons Blakely Whittaker assumed. She no doubt thought he was a bastard for the past, which he wasn't. He *was* a bastard for maneuvering her into a corner today, though. Unfortunately for her, she hadn't fully realized just how tight a space she was in.

But she was about to learn.

"Is that any way to greet your new boss?"

Incredulity, anger, resentment and, finally, understanding washed across Blakely's face. Gray wanted to be thrilled with the reality he'd just crashed down over her head—like the farce that had rained down over his, the one she'd been an integral part of.

But none of the satisfaction he'd expected materialized. *Dammit.*

It was wholly inconvenient. Especially since he still wasn't certain whether Blakely had been an unwitting participant in the deception that had landed his ass in jail, or a willing partner in the fraud.

Eight years ago, he'd been aware of Blakely Whittaker. She was an employee at Lockwood Industries. He'd passed her in the halls a time or two. Seen her in meetings. Been attracted to her in the same distracted way he'd regarded most beautiful things in his life back then.

All that changed the day he sat across from her in a courtroom and listened as she systematically laid out the concrete evidence against him. Blakely had provided the prosecution with a smoking gun.

One he'd never pulled the trigger on. Although, he hadn't been able to prove that. Then.

He still couldn't prove that now, but he was bound and determined to find a way to exonerate himself. It didn't matter that he'd already paid for a crime he never committed. He wanted to get back his good name and the life he'd had before.

And Blakely was going to help him do it, even if she wasn't aware that's why she'd been hired by Anderson Stone as the newest employee at Stone Surveillance.

Stone and Finn had both asked Gray why he was pursuing the investigation. He'd served his time for the embezzlement and was free to live his life. He had enough money in the bank to do anything he wanted—or nothing at all.

Before he'd been convicted, he hadn't given a damn about the family company. And, yes, it stung like hell that his family had disowned him. His father had barred him from Lockwood and refused to speak to him. His mother pretended she never had a son. But he'd learned to live with those facts.

Back then, he hadn't much cared what people thought of him. He'd been lazy, uncaring, spoiled and entitled. Prison had changed him. Connecting with Stone and Finn on the inside had changed him. Now, it bothered him that people whispered behind his back.

Mostly because he hadn't done a damn thing wrong. He might have been a bastard, but he was a law-abiding one.

Blakely shot up from the chair behind her desk. "I work for Anderson Stone and Finn DeLuca."

"No, you work for Stone Surveillance. Stone and Finn are two of the three owners. I happen to be the third."

"No one told me that."

"Because they were instructed not to."

Blakely's mouth set into the straight, stubborn line he'd seen several times. She might be petite, gorgeous and blonde, but she could be a pit bull when she wanted to be. He'd seen her determination firsthand. And not just in the courtroom, when she'd hammered the last nail in his coffin.

He'd watched her in meetings, impassioned about some piece of information she felt to be important. The way her skin flushed pink and her eyes flashed... Gorgeous, enticing and entertaining.

But she was also the kind of woman who placed that same passion into everything. And back then, Gray had been too lazy to want to take on that kind of intensity.

He'd appreciated it from afar, though.

Reaching into a drawer, Blakely pulled out her purse and looped the strap over her shoulder. "Why would you hire me? You hate me."

Gray shook his head, a half smile tugging at his lips. "*Hate* is such a strong word."

"I helped put you in prison. *Hate*'s probably the correct word."

"I wouldn't stake my life on it." Because as much as he wanted to hate the woman standing just feet away from him, he couldn't seem to do it.

Oh, sure, she was an easy target for all of his blame. And, it was still possible—no, probable—that she was up to her eyeballs in the mess that had taken him down. But he wasn't going to learn the truth without her. And she wasn't likely to help him if she thought he blamed her.

"No? What word would you use then?"

Gray tipped his head sideways and studied her for several seconds. "I'll admit, you're not my favorite person. However, I'm not sure you deserve my hate any more than I deserved to be sent to prison."

Blakely scoffed. The sound scraped down his spine, but her reaction wasn't unexpected.

Shaking her head, Blakely scooted around her desk and headed for the doorway. Gray shifted, moving his body between her and the exit.

She stopped abruptly, trying to avoid touching him. Gray didn't miss the way she flinched. Or the way her hand tightened over the strap of her purse.

Smart woman.

Gray had spent the last several years biding his time. Not to mention beating other prisoners in an underground fighting ring that Stone, Finn and he had built. He'd needed a physical outlet, one that didn't constantly land him in solitary.

Those fights had taught him to measure and watch his opponents. To pick up on the subtle physical cues that telegraphed a thought before it became action.

Although, Blakely's intentions were far from subtle. She wanted out of this room and away from him.

Too bad for her.

They were going to be spending a lot of time together in the coming weeks.

"Get out of my way."

The way her eyes flashed fire caused an answering heat that sparked in the pit of Gray's belly. There was something enticing and intriguing about her show of bravado. Even if he didn't want to be impressed.

Gray let his lips roll up into a predatory smile. His gaze swept down her body. It was damn hard not to take in the tempting curves. The way her skirt clung to her pert ass and how the jacket she'd paired it with cinched in at her tiny waist.

A part of him wanted to refuse. To see what she'd do if he pushed a few buttons. Would she put her hands on him? Would his body react with a physical rush at the contact?

Not smart to play that game. Instead of standing his ground, Gray slid sideways, clearing a path for her to exit.

Because he didn't need his body to stop her.

"You're welcome to leave anytime, Blakely."

Her eyes narrowed as she watched him. "Thank... you," she said, her words slow, as if she was sensing danger, but was clearly unable to identify the jaws of the trap.

He let her get one step forward before he hit the pin.

"Although, it isn't like you have anywhere to go. I've taken the liberty of informing your former employer of some questionable activity I recently discovered."

"What questionable activity? I've done nothing questionable."

"Of course you haven't, but that's not what the evidence suggests."

Blakely sputtered, her mouth opening and closing several times before she finally whispered, "Bastard."

"You've already said that. Doesn't feel real great to have lies used against you, huh? Either way, you have no job to go back to. And we both know how difficult it was to find that one after being released from Lockwood."

Blakely's skin flushed hot and her ice-blue eyes practically glowed with fury. God, she was gorgeous when she was pissed.

"What do you want?" she growled. "Is this payback?"

In an effort to keep from doing something stupid, Gray crossed his arms over his chest. "Hardly. I want your help in proving my innocence."

"I can't do that."

"Because you're unwilling?"

Her voice rose in frustration. "No, because you're hardly innocent."

"Maybe you're wrong, Blakely. Have you considered that at all?"

"Of course I have," she yelled, leaning forward and punctuating the words with indignation. "Do you know how many nights I've lain awake, wondering? But I'm not wrong. The numbers and evidence don't lie. I saw proof, with my own eyes, that you embezzled millions of dollars from Lockwood's accounts."

"You saw what someone wanted you to see." Or what she'd maneuvered so that everyone else would see.

"I'm leaving. I'll find another job."

"Sure you will…eventually. But the question is, will you find it here in Charleston or in time to pay your sister's tuition? Or cover the mortgage payment for your mom? Or, hell, your own car payment? It's a little difficult to get a job if you can't drive to an interview."

"Bastard."

"Maybe you should invest in a thesaurus. The job here is real, Blakely. And despite everything, I'm fully aware that you're an excellent accountant. We want you to work for the company. We simply want you to accept another assignment before you begin that work. And we'll pay you handsomely for both."

"For how long?"

"What?"

"How long do I have to work at proving your innocence? Because I think this could turn into a never-ending story."

Gray watched her. It wasn't an unfathomable request. In fact, Finn had asked him much the same question. How long was Gray willing to put his entire life on hold to chase a ghost of a possibility?

"Six weeks."

Blakely growled in the back of her throat. Scrunched her nose up in distaste. And then said, "Fine," before walking out.

Blakely had no idea where she was going…but she needed to get away from Gray before she did something stupid.

Like start to believe him.

Or worse, give in to the invisible tether that pulled her to him whenever the man walked into a room.

The ladies' room down the hall offered her an escape.

The man was walking, talking sin. And always had been. He'd carried the reputation of being hell-bent on pleasure for pleasure's sake. Sex, adrenaline, fast cars and the jet-setting lifestyle.

Gray Lockwood's picture would appear next to the word *sinner* in the dictionary.

Seriously, it wasn't fair. The man had hit the lottery when he'd been born. And not just because he'd been part of a prominent Southern family with good breeding and lots of money. His parents had passed on some amazing genes.

The man was gorgeous, and he knew it. Eight years ago, the most important decision she'd ever seen Gray make was choosing which of the women throwing themselves at him that he would take to bed. He had a confident demeanor, an outgoing attitude and Greek-god good looks.

Sure, Blakely had found him attractive, as did every other female in his vicinity. But he'd been easy to resist because he'd been ungrounded, spoiled and entitled. The man had thrown around money like he was playing *Monopoly*. He had a reputation for buying expensive cars just to drive them fast and crash them. He'd loved to party and had been known for paying for twenty people to have a wicked week in Vegas or Monaco or Thailand. And during the trial, the prosecution had brought into evidence that he'd racked up millions in gambling debts.

Now, he was...different.

The beautiful body had been hardened, probably by some time in the prison gym if she had to guess. And she'd been hard-pressed to miss the puckered skin of a scar running down his left eyebrow into the corner of his deep green eye. Somehow, the imperfection made him even more appealing. Before, Gray Lockwood had been too perfect.

But the biggest change was in his demeanor. While he still had the ability to command any room he walked into, his force was quieter.

The question was, could she work with him for the next six weeks without either wanting to kill him or being tempted to run her hands down his solid body? Or, even more, could she work on a project she didn't believe in simply for money?

She had no doubt, then and now, Gray Lockwood had plenty of secrets to hide. She'd uncovered one and it had derailed her life. Did she really want to risk uncovering more?

Blakely groaned, rubbing her hands down her face before washing them. Leaning over the sink, she stared hard into her own reflection. She'd spent her entire adult life doing the right thing. Because integrity was important to her. As someone raised by a criminal and con artist…you either joined the family business or became straighter than an arrow.

Watching her father bounce in and out of jail her entire childhood, that decision had been a no-brainer. She despised people who took the easy way out—anyone who took advantage of others' weaknesses or misfortunes. As far as she was concerned, Gray Lockwood was the worst kind of criminal.

Because he hadn't needed the money he'd embezzled.

Sure, he'd owed some nasty bookie a few million. But his net worth had been close to a billion. A lot of that wealth had been tied up in assets, but instead of liquidating, he'd decided to dip his hands into the family cookie jar. Probably because the spoiled rich boy thought he'd been entitled to it.

He'd never understood how taking that money had jeopardized the financial position of the company, not to mention the livelihood of all Lockwood Industries employees.

So the question was, could she spend the next six weeks pretending to work on a project she really didn't believe in, in exchange for a salary that she desperately needed?

A knot formed in the pit of her belly. It wasn't like she was lying to Gray. He knew full well she didn't believe him. He had to be aware she wouldn't exactly be the most motivated employee. Not to mention, he'd obviously maneuvered her here—which was something she'd have to talk with Anderson Stone and Finn DeLuca about, the assholes. So, really, she didn't owe Gray anything.

At the end of the day, the question was, could she go to sleep at night with a clear conscience if she stayed?

Today, the answer was yes. She might not like where she was standing, but she had no doubt Gray had backed up his statement and she'd have a hard time finding another job right now. He couldn't blackball her with every company in the country, so eventually she'd find something. But that might entail uprooting her life and moving. And while that didn't necessarily bother her, she couldn't do it right now.

Not when she was concerned her father was back to his old habits.

God, how had her life come to this?

Taking a deep breath, Blakely straightened her spine. She'd stay, take Gray's money and work the six weeks. At least that would give her a cushion to line up something else.

She pulled out a paper towel and dried her hands, then pushed open the door. Two strides out, she jolted to a stop.

She didn't even need to turn her head to know he was there. Her entire body reacted, a riot of energy crackling across her skin. So inconvenient.

Slowly, she turned her head, anyway. Arms crossed over his chest, Gray leaned casually against the wall right between the doors to the restrooms.

"Feel better now?"

Two

Blakely watched him with wary eyes. "No, not really."

He shrugged, dismissing her statement. Because it didn't matter. He wasn't really worried about her comfort.

"Follow me," he said, pushing off from the wall and striding past her. Her tempting scent slammed into him—it was something soft and subtle, but entirely her. Gray remembered it from before.

The one time he'd gotten close enough to pull her enticing scent deep into his lungs had involved a clash in the break room over some creamer he'd "borrowed" from her. After that, he'd purposely kept his distance. She was a vixen, and he'd had to fight the urge to shut down her tirade by kissing the hell out of her. Not smart.

Blakely might be beautiful, but she had a remote, standoffish manner about her. She'd been cordial with her coworkers, but not overly friendly. She wasn't one of the women invited to a girls' night out after work. Everyone appreciated her dedication. However, she didn't exactly give off warmth.

And back then, Gray hadn't just been looking for warm, he'd been looking for red-hot. With no strings. Everything about Blakely screamed serious.

So it hadn't mattered that he couldn't keep his gaze from tracking her whenever she walked down the hallways. Or that he would fall asleep with the phantom scent of her tickling his nose if they'd passed in the lobby.

Hell, he needed to get his head back in the game. Because now, Gray wasn't so certain that the wall she'd put up between herself and everyone else wasn't to hide her own nefarious intentions.

At the end of the hallway, Gray paused. He waited for her to decide what she was going to do. When the click of her heels sounded against the marble floor, he continued to the right.

"Where are we going?" she asked from several paces behind, in no hurry to catch up once she'd made her decision.

Without turning around, he answered, "I've got all the records from my trial in another office. You're going to walk me through the evidence you presented against me."

"Why? You were there in the courtroom."

Yes, he had been. Watching her every move. The way she'd tucked a golden strand of hair behind her ear each time she looked down at the documentation the prosecution was using against him. Or how the sharp tip of her pink tongue would swipe across her lips each time she needed to pause and gather her thoughts before answering.

Had those pauses been her organizing thoughts, or her making certain she told the right lies?

Turning into the empty office beside hers, Gray waited

until she brushed past him, then closed the door. "I sure was, but I didn't know then what I know now."

"And what do you know now?"

Oh, there were so many answers to that question. Most she wouldn't understand or appreciate. Several he had no intention of sharing with anyone, ever. But the only answer he was willing to give her right now was "Let's just say I used my time in prison to broaden my education."

Blakely made a buzzing noise in the back of her throat. "You're one of those."

"One of what?"

"People who go to jail and use the taxpayers' money to get an education they couldn't otherwise afford."

Wasn't that rich. "We both know I could—and did— afford a rather expensive Ivy League education before going to prison." He'd graduated from Harvard Business School. Sure, he'd barely made the cut and hadn't taken any of his classes seriously, but he had the damn degree.

"Little good it did you."

He wasn't going to refute that statement, mostly because he couldn't. "But, considering I'm innocent of the crime I was charged with and spent seven years imprisoned against my will because of it, the least the state owed me was an education in whatever I wanted."

"And what education was that?"

"I got a law degree."

"Of course you did."

At first, his plan was to figure out how to use his degree to help his own cause. Not surprising. However, it became obvious there wasn't much the legal system could do for him. His own attorneys filed every appeal possible, but they were all denied. Short of a call from the governor—not likely since the man had never liked Gray's father—that avenue wasn't going to help.

What he had used it for, though, was helping several of the inmates incarcerated with Stone, Finn and himself. Guys who might have been guilty, but had gotten screwed over or railroaded because they couldn't afford competent representation.

"That wasn't all I accomplished inside."

Blakely crossed her arms, her ice-blue eyes scraping up and down his body. "Oh, obviously."

Gray's lips twitched at her reaction. Her disdain was loud and clear. However, that didn't prevent heat from creeping into her cheeks or her nipples from peaking and pressing against the soft material of her shirt.

He wasn't stupid or oblivious to how women responded to him. He'd simply stopped taking advantage of the ones who shamelessly threw themselves at him. Funny how going without sex for seven years could make you appreciate it even more than having orgasms every day.

But he had no problem giving Blakely a hard time about her reaction. "And what, exactly, do you mean by that, Ms. Whittaker?"

"You know."

Gray hummed, drawing out the low, slow sound. "No, I don't think I do."

Blakely rolled her eyes, then pursed her lips and glared at him. Gray waited, silent, his gaze boring into hers. So he was being slightly juvenile by enjoying the way she shifted uncomfortably under his scrutiny.

Finally, she answered, as he'd known she would if he waited long enough. "It's clear you hit the gym whenever you could."

"How is that?"

She waved her hand in front of him. "You're huge. Broader, more muscular, than you were before."

"I didn't realize you'd noticed my physique before."

The heat in her cheeks deepened. "You made damn sure every woman at Lockwood noticed you. You wallowed in the attention from every female you could snag."

"But not you."

"No, not me."

"Is that because you weren't interested or because I didn't indicate that I was?"

Blakely's jaw clenched and her molars ground together. He could practically hear the enamel cracking from here. This was fun, but not very productive for the work he needed to get out of her. He could hardly expect her to be cooperative if he kept taking digs.

Shaking his head, Gray moved farther into the room. "I'm sorry, that wasn't very professional of me."

"No, it wasn't," Blakely quickly agreed.

"Let's agree that whatever concerns or animosity we had in the past, we both need to set them aside in order to work together right now."

Her eyes narrowed. She was damn smart and had no doubt picked up on the fact that he'd suggested they set them aside, not let them go. He wasn't ready to do that, not while he still questioned her role in the whole mess. Just as she wasn't likely to forget what she knew—or thought she knew—about him.

"Let's pretend we don't know anything about each other and start from square one."

She mumbled something under her breath that sounded suspiciously like "not likely." Gray decided to ignore it.

Pointing to a tower of seven cardboard boxes stacked in the corner of the room, he said, "Here's the data. I also have most of the files electronically, but we need any notes from the attorneys, as well. Why don't we start by tackling the information you presented on the stand and go from there?"

* * *

They'd started three days ago by going over the accounting records the prosecution had entered into evidence. The information she'd uncovered showed a pattern of behavior that had gone undetected for several months. Small amounts had been withdrawn daily from the operating accounts and transferred to a holding account. The amounts had been strategic, varied and below any threshold for automatic review or audit. The final two transactions were transfers of funds out of the company and into offshore accounts.

That first withdrawal was what had finally flagged Blakely's attention. Unfortunately, not until almost four weeks later, when she'd been performing her monthly audit.

The first twenty-million-dollar transfer to Gray's account had been flagged immediately since none of the proper paperwork had been completed. However, considering who was involved, Blakely just assumed he'd failed to follow protocol. At first. Once she'd started digging, she'd discovered a second transaction.

That transfer out had been different. On the surface, it had looked legitimate, with the proper documentation and supporting paperwork in the electronic files. But something about it had still felt wrong. Being a huge international organization, she wasn't always privy ahead of time to large transactions…but more often than not she was aware when the company made large lump-sum purchases.

If anyone else had been auditing, they might not have bothered to look deeper. But she hadn't been willing to let it go. It had taken her a while to pull the threads of the transactions to figure out what had really happened—and that the two transactions were connected.

What she hadn't understood then, and still didn't understand, was why Gray had covered his tracks on one withdrawal but not the other. It made no sense. Unless you took into consideration how lazy the man was. Maybe he just assumed no one would question his actions.

Blakely hadn't been impressed with Gray's work ethic and didn't care whose son he was. The man had stolen millions of dollars from the company. Money they hadn't been able to afford to lose.

She'd turned over the information, never realizing just how instrumental she'd become in the trial process. She'd been inside plenty of courtrooms in her life, all for her father. None of the experiences had been pleasant and neither was Gray's trial. She'd been nervous on the stand, not because she hadn't been confident about the information, but because she'd hated being the center of attention.

Reviewing the documents now brought back all of those emotions. She'd been on edge for days and it was wearing on her.

Or maybe that was being cooped up in an office with Gray. Any other time, she would have said the office was pretty spacious, but put a sexy six-foot-two, two-hundred-and-twenty-pound guy in there, too, and it turned into a closet with all the air vacuumed out.

Letting out a frustrated groan, Gray tossed a bound testimony transcript toward an open box. The sheaf of papers bounced off the edge and clattered to the floor. "I need a break."

Amen. "Okay," Blakely said, seriously hoping he'd leave for a while. Or the rest of the afternoon. Or the week.

Standing up, he put his hands at the small of his back

and leaned backward. The audible pop of his spine made Blakely shiver.

She tried to concentrate on the report in front of her. But it was damn hard not to notice every move he made. Each time Gray passed behind her chair, the tension in her body ratcheted higher. Her neck and shoulders ached with the struggle to ignore the physical awareness she really didn't want. Without thought, Blakely reached around and began pinching the muscles running up into her neck, hoping the knots would loosen.

They were starting to…until Gray brushed her hands out of the way and took over. The minute his grip settled onto her shoulders, Blakely bolted upright in her chair.

"Easy," he murmured. "Is this okay?"

Was it? Heat seeped into her skin. Her body tingled where he touched. Logically, Blakely knew she should say no. Move away. But she didn't want to and somehow found herself slowly nodding.

Gray's fingers dug deep into her muscles. At first, what he was doing hurt like hell…until her muscles started to relax and let go. Then it felt amazing.

Blakely was powerless to stop herself from melting beneath Gray's touch. Delicious heat spread from his fingers, down her shoulders and into her belly. A deep sigh leaked through her parted lips as she sagged against the back of her chair.

"God, you're so uptight."

"Don't ruin this," she groused.

"Admit it. You wouldn't know how to relax if someone gave you a flowchart."

"And you know nothing except how to relax."

Gray let out an incredulous chuckle, his grip on her shoulders tightening for a split second. "You know nothing about me." Then he dropped his hands.

Blakely bit back a cry of protest. Nope, she refused to beg him to touch her.

Scooting around her, Gray headed for the door. "I'm gonna go grab something to eat. Want me to get you something?"

It was well past lunchtime, but she'd been nose-deep in the report and hadn't noticed until now. At Gray's prompting, her stomach let out a growl loud enough for them both to hear.

A teasing smile tugged at the corners of his mouth. "I'll take that as a yes."

He was out the door before Blakely could tell him not to bother. Shrugging, she let him go, grateful for the reprieve so she could get herself back under control.

He'd needed to get out of there.

Never in his life had he gotten so hard from merely touching a woman's shoulders. Although, if he was going to be honest, his physical reaction to Blakely had little to do with actually touching her skin.

It had more to do with the way she'd softened beneath his hands. The way she'd relaxed, letting her head loll back against his belly. The soft sigh of pleasure and relief she'd made in the back of her throat. The way her eyes had slowly closed, as if savoring the sensations he was giving her.

If he hadn't left, he was going to embarrass himself. Or embarrass them both when she noticed his reaction. Food had been a quick, easy excuse.

He was two steps past Stone's office when his friend called out, "Gray."

He backed up, then pivoted inside.

"How's it going?"

There was no need to wonder what Stone was asking

about. The only case Gray was working on right now was his own. "Nowhere."

"I'm sorry, man. Is she cooperating?"

"Yeah." At first, Blakely had appeared to be shuffling papers around more than looking at them. But it hadn't taken her long to actually start reading and digging, which didn't surprise him. Blakely was the kind of woman who couldn't ignore a task once it was placed in front of her. She worked hard and did her absolute best no matter what.

"What are you going to do if there's nothing to find there?"

"Honestly? I have no idea. I mean, it's likely the files won't give us anything, but I have to look, anyway."

"I don't blame you."

"Joker's working his magic, too. Maybe he'll find something."

Their freelance hacker was one of the best on the east coast. Gray had cultivated an introduction through one of the guys he'd fought on the inside. He made damn sure not to ask what else Joker was working on because he didn't want to know. The guy had a reputation for being choosy about his projects and difficult to find.

"We can hope. Let me know if there's anything Finn or I can do."

Stone's offer was unnecessary since Gray already knew the two men would do anything he needed without question. But it was nice to hear, anyway. Especially when he had no one else in his corner.

"Thanks, man," he said, starting to back out of the office.

"A little advice?"

Gray paused, tilting his head and eyeing his friend.

"Don't be a dick," Stone said.

"What?"

His eyebrows rose. "She's gorgeous and I can practically see the sparks you two are striking from my office. You've spent too much time getting her here to screw it up simply because you haven't gotten laid since you've been out."

"I've gotten laid." Okay, that wasn't true. But he wasn't about to admit that to Stone, who'd just give him hell over the fact. Sex wasn't exactly high on his priority list right now. He couldn't move on with his life until he figured out just who had screwed him over. And why.

Because there was no way of knowing when or if it would happen again until he did.

"Not nearly enough."

"I wasn't aware there was an orgasm quota I needed to fill. Perhaps you should put that in my personal development plan."

"Asshole," Stone countered, no heat behind the word.

He was about to make another snide comment when a commotion sounded down the hall.

"Sir, you can't just walk back there," Amanda, their receptionist, hollered down the hall.

Both men headed straight for the doorway. Gray hit it first, fists balled at his sides, his body strung and ready for a fight. Stone was right behind him, no doubt also prepared.

Several of their employees crowded into the hallway, but Gray and Stone both started telling them to get back into their offices and lock their doors. Considering their line of business, it paid to be careful. It wasn't that long ago that Piper, Stone's wife, had been kidnapped and held against her will.

Halfway down the hall, Amanda was chasing after a

man stalking down the line of offices. "I'm just looking for my daughter. I know she's here."

"Sir, if you tell me who she is, I'll be happy to get her for you."

The gentleman waved his hand, dismissing Amanda. "I don't have time for that. They'll be right behind me."

From behind, the man appeared disheveled. Although his clothes were obviously of good quality, his shirt had come untucked from his slacks, the tail of it hanging down past the bottom of his suit coat. The hems of his pants were splotchy with mud and water.

It had been raining earlier in the day, but had stopped several hours ago. However, this guy looked like he'd been tromping through mud puddles and fields.

It didn't take long for Gray to catch up to Amanda. Wrapping a hand around her arm, he pulled her to a stop. "I've got it from here."

"Sir, *who's* going to be right behind you?" Gray asked, his deep voice loud as it echoed against the hallway walls.

The guy glanced over his shoulder, but shook his head instead of answering.

"Who are you looking for?"

"I've already said—my daughter."

At that moment, the office door at the end of the hall, the one he and Blakely had been using for the past several days, swung open. Blakely stepped straight into the path of the man.

Gray cursed under his breath and sped up. He didn't think this guy was dangerous—he didn't appear to be holding a weapon or have one tucked into a holster anywhere on his body—but Gray really had no desire to test that theory with Blakely's safety.

"Get back inside," he said at the exact same time Blakely said, "Dad?"

Three

Oh, God. What was her father doing here? Blakely wanted to scream or curse or both.

"Dad?" Gray's dark, smoky voice floated to her from down the hall. Squeezing her eyes shut, Blakely prayed for strength. And wished her face wasn't currently going up in flames. Which it obviously was, since her cheeks felt like they were on fire.

Of course, he would be right there to witness her father at his absolute worst. She was never going to live this down.

"Baby girl, I don't have much time." Her father was completely oblivious to the people hovering in the hallway, gawking at the spectacle he was making. Or, more likely, he just didn't give a damn.

Her father had never cared what kind of stir he left in his wake, or whether it bothered the people closest to him.

Blakely threw a glance toward Gray, who'd stopped

several feet away, hands balled into fists on his hips and the fiercest scowl scrunching up his handsome face. An unwanted thrill shot through her system. There was something attractive about him, like he'd come ready to swoop in and save her.

Yeah, right.

Not wanting to deal with that thought, Blakely's gaze skipped down to Stone, who was lingering behind Gray, a quizzical expression on his face. She didn't have time to handle either of them right now. Not with her father spouting gibberish.

"Much time before what?" she asked, directing her attention back to her father.

"Before the authorities arrive to arrest me."

Damn, it was worse than she'd thought. *"Dad."*

"I didn't do it."

If she had a dollar for every time she'd heard that... "Uh-huh. What are you being arrested for this time?"

"Conspiracy to commit murder."

Blakely blinked. Her mind blanked. Everything went silent for several seconds before a roar of sound rushed through her. "Excuse me?"

Her dad was a lot of things. A con artist, an idiot, a dreamer and a thief. What he wasn't was a murderer.

"I'm being framed for this. But there's not enough time to explain. I need you to get in touch with Ryan and tell him to come fix it."

Blakely bit back a groan. If she ever heard that name again, it would be too soon. Ryan O'Sullivan had been part of her life since the day she was born...and a thorn in her side for just as long.

"Dad, you promised."

The hangdog expression on her father's face didn't make the pang in her stomach ease any. She was seriously tired of feeling like the parent in their relationship, especially when he gave her that misbehaving, little-boy-caught-with-his-hand-in-the-cookie-jar expression.

Life wasn't supposed to be like this.

"He's my best friend, pet. What was I supposed to do?"

"Stay away from the man who is single-handedly responsible for landing you in prison several times." It appeared, despite everything she'd done to stop the cycle, the man was going to have a hand in sending her father right back. "We agreed when you got out that you were going to cut all ties with Ryan O'Sullivan."

"I tried."

Blakely was quite familiar with the obstinate set of Martin Whittaker's jaw. She wanted to scream. And cry. But neither reaction would help the situation.

"Not hard enough, and now look at what's happening." Blakely flung her hands wide to encompass the Stone Surveillance offices. Other people were now sticking their heads into the hallways to eavesdrop on the juicy gossip.

Wonderful. She might not be thrilled to be working here, but that didn't mean she wanted her family's dirty laundry aired for everyone to judge. "This is where I work, Dad."

Martin let out a sigh and stepped closer, the petulant expression morphing into true regret.

Dammit. That was always how he got her. If there was a single shred of hope, Blakely just couldn't turn her back on him. Her mother and sister both called her ten kinds of a fool. And a softy.

She was probably both.

But when Martin reached for her, Blakely couldn't force herself to stop him. Although, she didn't hug him back. This wasn't the kind of problem that could be solved with some trite Irish quip and a pat on the head.

"I didn't do this, Blakely," he murmured. "I promise. Please, just contact Ryan. He'll take care of everything."

Sure. She wouldn't call that man if he was the sole survivor of the apocalypse. Instead, Blakely started mentally flipping through names of good attorneys. She didn't know many. Her father hadn't ever been able to afford representation, so he'd always stuck with whomever the court appointed. But this time, thanks to Gray and his maneuvering, she had the means to pay for someone who might actually be able to help.

Although, she couldn't quite shake the feeling that it wouldn't make a difference. Her father might not think he was guilty of anything, but that didn't mean he wasn't guilty in the eyes of the law. Especially with a charge like conspiracy.

Who the heck could he have been accused of trying to kill?

Blakely shook her head. One issue at a time.

Before she could open her mouth and ask, another commotion started at the end of the hall. Two officers were stalking toward them, followed by Amanda. They didn't have their guns drawn, but their hands were on the butts ready to pull at the first sign of concern.

In a loud, stern voice, one of the officers demanded, "Mr. Whittaker, put your hands in the air."

Slowly, her father's arms rose over his head. Staring straight at her, his soft blue eyes filled with regret and remorse.

Blakely's throat grew tight and a lump formed. Her body went ice-cold with fear, sadness and frustration.

There was nothing she could do but watch.

One of the officers took another step down the hallway, but before he could reach her father something unexpected happened. Gray moved between them, blocking his path.

"What is Mr. Whittaker being charged with?"

The officer's gaze narrowed. His eyes raked up and down Gray, sizing him up. But that didn't seem to bother Gray. He was perfectly relaxed, his body loose and hands open by his sides.

"Conspiracy to commit murder."

Hearing the words from her father had already sent a shock wave through Blakely. But hearing them from an officer, hand poised on a gun, made her downright terrified.

Because her father wasn't known for being smart or cooperative.

"Now, please step out of the way."

Gray stood exactly where he was, feet unmoving, for what felt like forever. The hallway was silent, the only sound the whoosh of air through the vents in the building. Everyone waited.

Her father was connected to one of the most notorious crime families in Charleston.

Everyone knew Ryan O'Sullivan, mostly because he was the kind of man you wanted to avoid, if at all possible. At least if you were a law-abiding citizen.

There was a time in his life when Gray would have avoided any association with the man. But now... O'Sullivan didn't scare him. He might have connections, but then, so did Gray.

He'd never had any personal experience with the man, or any of his associates. However, the minute they were done here, he'd be making a few phone calls because he was absolutely certain one of his contacts knew O'Sullivan.

And while information on Martin Whittaker might be interesting, what he really wanted to know was just how deep Blakely's ties were to the O'Sullivan family. Because from the sound of things, she knew the man pretty well.

O'Sullivan was definitely connected enough to pull off the kind of theft and cover-up that had landed Gray in jail. Especially with the help of an inside man. Or woman. And twenty million was a big incentive. Especially with a ready-made scapegoat.

Gray folded his arms over his chest, sizing up the officers in front of him. He could continue to block their path, but there wasn't value in doing it. Not only would it not prevent Martin from being arrested and taken in, but it could also potentially land Gray's butt back behind bars.

Nope, not worth it.

However, there might be information to gain and some goodwill to bank. Without glancing behind him, Gray raised his voice and said, "Martin, are you going to leave peacefully with the nice gentlemen waiting to take you downtown?"

"Yes."

Cocking an eyebrow, Gray held up a single finger to ask for a moment, then turned his back to the officers so he could face Blakely and her father.

Gray's gaze skipped across her, as he tried to find a clue that might help him determine something about the state of her mind. But all he could see was a jumbled mess of fear, irritation and determination.

That didn't tell him much, other than that she was a good daughter who loved her father.

"Martin, I'm going to follow the officers and meet you at the station. Take some unsolicited advice and keep your mouth shut until the lawyer I'm about to call gets there."

Blakely made a strangled sound before she opened her mouth to say something. Gray held up a hand, silencing her before she could get out a single word.

Both she and Whittaker shut their mouths. Gray waved behind him for the officers to come forward and then moved out of the way. He didn't bother to watch the commotion in front of him as they cuffed her father. Instead, he watched Blakely.

And because he did, he was probably the only one who noticed the way her body flinched at the sound of the cuffs snapping together around his wrists. Her mouth thinned with unhappiness at the same time her teeth chewed at the inside of her cheek.

Gray didn't even think she was aware that she was doing it.

She started to take a step to follow the officers as they led away her father, but one of them called out behind him, "Stay where you are, ma'am."

Everyone waited and watched. The sound of people shuffling uncomfortably where they stood was like the unsettling scratching of leaves against a window in the middle of the night.

Once Martin was out of view, in unison, all of the spectators turned toward Blakely. And that's when her face flamed bright red.

But Gray had to hand it to her—she didn't bow under the weight of the embarrassment or scrutiny. Instead, she let her gaze travel slowly around the hallway, as she looked each and every person square in the eye. She practically dared them to ask a question or make a snide remark.

No one did.

Dammit, he didn't want to be impressed with her backbone.

Walking up beside her, Gray grasped her arm. She tensed and he could feel her about to jerk away from him.

Pressing close, he murmured low enough so only she could hear, "You probably don't want to make an even bigger scene."

The sound of her breath dragging deep into her lungs shouldn't have had any effect on him. Neither should the way her body brushed against his with the motion. And yet, it did.

"Do you really think I care about making a scene?" she whispered back.

"Yes, I do."

He was close enough to hear her teeth grinding together. But she didn't refute his statement. Because they both knew it was true.

"Now, be a good girl—walk quietly down the hall with me and I'll take you to your father."

A low, growling, frustrated sound rolled through her. "I really don't like you."

Gray laughed, the sound filling the space between them. "Sweetheart, the feeling is mutual."

Propelling her down the hallway in front of him, Gray chose to ignore the pointed expression on Stone's face as they walked past him. No doubt, he was going to hear about this the next time he and his friend were alone.

So Gray would simply avoid Stone for a little while.

Gray and Blakely were both silent as they headed out of the building and into the parking garage. Blakely took the first opportunity to speed up and break the hold he had on her. Which was fine with him. And, no, he didn't flex his hand because it was tingling where he'd touched her bare skin.

Several paces ahead of him, it was clear Blakely intended to take her own car. He could have redirected her, but decided to wait and see how long it took her to realize she didn't have her purse or keys.

She was halfway there when she came to a sudden halt. Her head dropped back and he didn't need a clear view in order to know she was squeezing her eyes shut and probably asking a higher power for strength.

Not that she needed any. For all her faults, Blakely Whittaker was one of the strongest women he'd ever met. Not that he was going to tell her that.

It only took her a few seconds to gather herself, turn and head back toward the entrance to the building.

"Don't bother. I'll take you."

"No, thank you." Her words were formal, but there was no real appreciation behind them. Not that he particularly cared. He wasn't letting her drive. Not because he was worried about her state of mind—or not just because. He wanted to make damn sure he was a fly on the wall.

"Look, you can waste precious time going back inside or you can ride with me to the station. Either way, I'm heading there, and if you don't come with me, I'm going to get there first. And something tells me you'd prefer me not to speak to your father without you."

"Why are you doing this?"

"Doing what? Being nice?"

"No, being a pain in my ass."

"I didn't realize helping your father could be viewed as being a pain in your ass."

Blakely's eyes narrowed. A string of expletives flowed from her lips, some of which were quite inventive. He was impressed and, considering he was a convicted felon and had heard a whole hell of a lot, that wasn't an easy feat.

Stalking past him, Blakely headed straight for his car,

parked a few spaces from the door. It didn't escape his notice that she knew exactly which one was his. Intelligence gathering or something more?

Standing beside the passenger door, she glared at him over the hood. The tap of her foot against concrete rang out, a perfect staccato of irritation and impatience.

If there wasn't a reason to hurry, Gray would have slowed down on principle alone. And because he knew it would bother her. But he wanted to reach her father as quickly as she did. Maybe more.

The drive to the station was silent, the air between them thick with tension and the familiar scent of her perfume. Sweet and exotic. Floral, yet somehow spicy. It had been tempting him for days. The office they were using wasn't exactly small, but when that scent filled the space...

The front seat of his Bugatti was even worse. Normally, it was his sanctuary. The car was the one frivolous, flashy and over-the-top thing he'd allowed himself once he was out of prison. Today, with Blakely so close beside him, it felt just as much like a prison as the cell he'd been assigned.

He couldn't help but wonder if her scent would be stronger if he buried his face between her thighs?

Gray willed away his response. Nope, he wasn't going there.

He might not be naive enough to believe he had to actually like someone in order to be physically attracted to them. But he *was* smart enough to realize his situation with Blakely was complicated enough without adding mindless sex. And that's all that could be between them.

The fifteen-minute drive felt like an eternity. As soon as he pulled into a space in front of the station, Blakely shot from the car. She was halfway across the lot before he'd even turned off the ignition.

Not that her haste would make much difference. She wasn't going to get very far with the officers inside.

Tucking his hands into his pockets, Gray strolled leisurely after her. Once he entered the station he could hear her voice, already raised in frustration.

"I just need to speak to him for a minute. That's all."

"Ma'am, your father is being processed. You can't see him right now."

Gray bypassed the commotion, choosing to approach another officer at the far end of the counter who was protected by a half wall of bulletproof glass.

"Excuse me," he said. "I'm Gray Lockwood, here to see my client, Martin Whittaker. He's just been brought in."

The desk sergeant barely glanced up from a stack of papers. "Are you his attorney?"

"Yes."

He shuffled a few more things. "I'll let them know you're here. Take a seat. Someone'll get you in a few."

"Excellent."

Gray gave the man a polite smile, even though he wouldn't notice it, and turned to sit in one of the chairs lining the far wall. They were hard plastic—no doubt, the cheapest thing the city could buy. The metal legs had been scratched to hell and back. Clearly a lot of people had spent time waiting in them over the years.

With a huff, Blakely collapsed into the chair beside him.

"They won't let me see him."

"Really? How surprising."

Blakely gave him a grimace, her only response to his obvious sarcasm.

"Why did we come here if we weren't planning to see him?"

"I have no idea why you decided to follow your father. And I have every intention of seeing him."

"You do?"

"Yes."

"Oh."

Gray knew exactly what wrong conclusion Blakely had just jumped to. And he had no intention of disabusing her of the notion. At least not until it suited his purposes.

Several minutes ticked by. There was motion and activity all around them, but Gray was content to wait. He'd done a lot of that in his adult life. And he'd learned quickly it was a waste of energy to wish things were different. He'd gotten very good at accepting situations as they were, not as he'd prefer them to be. It saved heartache and disappointment.

Blakely, however, was a bucket of nerves and energy. She couldn't settle and constantly shifted in her seat. Crossed and uncrossed her legs. Cracked her knuckles.

Unable to take any more, Gray reached out and placed a hand on her knee. Blakely immediately stilled. In fact, she stopped moving entirely, not even taking a breath.

Her heat seeped into his skin, making his entire arm hum with unexpected energy.

Shit.

"Mr. Lockwood, please follow me."

Thank God for small favors. Gray looked up at the officer standing at the far doorway. He pushed up from the chair and was halfway across the room before he realized Blakely was following him.

This was gonna be good.

Gray gave the officer a polite smile as he walked past.

"Ma'am, I'm sorry, you're not allowed back here."

Pausing in the hallway, he turned in time to catch Blakely's pointed gesture. "I'm with him."

"Are you part of Mr. Whittaker's legal team?"

"No, I'm his daughter."

The officer shook his head. "I'm sorry. Mr. Whittaker is being questioned. Only legal counsel is allowed into the room."

"Then why is he going back?"

"Mr. Lockwood? Because he's acting counsel."

Blakely stared at him, her gaze narrowing. Gray shrugged. "I mentioned that I have a law degree."

"You don't practice."

"No, I'm fortunate enough that I only take the cases I want to. I'm taking your father's." At least for the moment. Gray had every intention of calling in a few favors to get someone else to actually take Martin's case. While he could do it himself, he had other concerns at the moment and didn't need the distraction.

However, he was going to take this prime opportunity to learn everything he could from Martin about Blakely and her connections to the O'Sullivan family. And whether that could have played into how Gray had found himself framed for embezzlement.

"Tell him I'm with you," Blakely demanded, pointing at the officer standing between them.

"Ah, but you're not."

Four

Blakely wanted to scream. Or find something hard to throw straight at his head. Probably not smart, considering there were at least half a dozen people standing close who could arrest her for assault.

Gray Lockwood was as frustrating as he was sexy. That knowing smirk twisting his gorgeous lips… How could she want to kiss the hell out of him at the same time she wanted to shake him?

What was wrong with her?

Blakely watched him disappear down the hallway, irritation churning in her belly. Dropping back into a hard chair, she stared at the door. And waited.

Conspiracy to commit murder.

God, how could this get any worse? Her father was about to go to jail for a very long time. Sure, he'd been in and out her entire life, but for small crimes. Ten months here, two years there. This would be different.

She wanted to believe him when he said he wasn't guilty…but she just couldn't kill that last spark of doubt taunting her from the back of her brain. Her father had a habit of bending the truth.

And Gray… She didn't trust him further than she could throw him. Like every other criminal she'd ever met—and plenty had marched through her life—they all insisted they were innocent.

She'd yet to meet one who actually was. Especially her father.

But a bigger part of her just couldn't believe he could be responsible for anything close to murder. Her father might be a con man and a thief, but he'd never been violent. Hell, he didn't even own a gun.

Gray, on the other hand, was dangerous as hell. Only he didn't need a gun to be that way. The hum in her blood proved that point nicely. She didn't even like him, but he had the ability to make her body react.

Blakely didn't need the details to know he'd been through a lot. The scar through his eyebrow and the rock-hard muscles he now sported hadn't been earned by doing bench presses and back squats. But there was more to him than his physically intimidating presence. He was quiet and observant. Gray saw too much.

She'd watched him over the last several days, not just as he interacted with her, but with others at the office. He watched and cataloged. Almost as if he was gathering intel on everyone who moved through his existence, even if they only touched his life in the most minor way.

He hadn't been that way when she'd known him before.

Clearly, he brought value to Stone Surveillance. On several occasions Stone and Finn had come to consult Gray's opinion on a case they were working.

She didn't want to see anything good in him. She didn't want to believe he was helping her father. She wanted to see him only as the criminal he was. Without that concerning history, it would be so much more difficult to keep her distance. To pretend she hadn't noticed the layer of humanity and honor. She definitely didn't want to like him. Because right now, she was having a damn hard time keeping her awareness of him in check.

Lucky for her, watching him walk through that precinct door without her was just the reminder she needed.

When she saw him again, he was going to get an earful.

Selfish bastard.

Gray walked into the room and immediately flashbacks assaulted him. A shiver of apprehension raced down his spine, but he refused to let it take hold.

He wasn't the one being questioned here.

Although, being in the small, nondescript, uncomfortable room made it difficult not to let bad memories take over. The barrage of questions he hadn't understood or known the answers to. Feeling blindsided and out of his element. Cut loose without a safety net.

Those first few hours of being questioned had been disorienting because he didn't have a clue what any of the investigators were talking about. And since he'd been innocent, he'd waived his right to counsel. His first mistake.

The detective sitting across the table from Martin glanced up as he entered the room, but didn't say anything. Martin's eyes skipped distractedly over Gray, a puzzled expression filling his face. "Why are you here?"

Gray's first impressions of Martin weren't great. He was the complete opposite of Blakely—scattered, loud and obnoxious. Or at least he had been so far. Although, he also appeared to know exactly who Gray was, which wasn't surprising considering the role Blakely had played in the well-publicized, high-profile trial that had completely turned Gray's life upside down.

"I'm part of your legal team—why wouldn't I be here?"

Martin quirked an eyebrow, but he didn't vocalize the obvious question. Smart man, considering a detective was sitting across from him.

Gray turned to the officer. "I'd like a few minutes with my client, please." The statement might have technically been a request...but it really wasn't.

A frown crunched the corners of the detective's weathered and weary eyes. He stood without saying a word and the door squeaked shut behind him as he left.

Martin opened his mouth, but before he could say anything Gray shook his head. He assumed they were being recorded and watched, and intended to act accordingly.

Taking the vacated chair, Gray folded his hands on the table between them.

"The rest of your legal team should be arriving shortly."

"Why are you doing this?"

An expected question for sure, but one Gray wasn't prepared to answer. At least not here. And not entirely honestly.

"Blakely works for my company and we take care of our own."

Martin scoffed. "Blakely might think I'm gullible, and maybe occasionally I am, but I wasn't born yesterday, son."

Maybe not, but something told him Martin Whittaker wasn't entirely smart when it came to the world, either. Or that was the impression Gray had gotten from Blakely.

And he might not trust her, but she was smart as hell and rather aware of what was going on around her.

"Let's just say I have a vested interest in keeping your daughter focused on a project she's working on with me. I won't have her full attention if she's concerned about you. Money isn't important to me, but right now her assistance is. Buying peace of mind by providing your legal team is a smart strategy for me to get what I want."

Martin slowly nodded. "You could have easily accomplished that without lying to the officers and coming in here to see me."

"Perhaps, but I don't know you."

"True."

"And had no idea whether you'd be smart about what you said until the lawyers I've retained arrive. Besides, I didn't lie. I have a legal degree and specialize in criminal defense."

"But you're not taking my case."

"No, I don't have the luxury of splitting my focus right now, either."

Martin hummed in the back of his throat. "Still doesn't explain why you came all the way down here."

He might be gullible, but Martin Whittaker clearly had enough street smarts to go with his naivete.

"I have a couple questions for you."

"About the charges against me?"

"No."

Martin tugged at the cuffs wrapped around his wrists, rattling the chain connected to the ring bolted to the table. The movement had been instinctive, a gesture he couldn't quite complete.

"Then what?"

"Tell me about your relationship with O'Sullivan. How long have you known him?"

Martin's head tipped sideways as he considered for several seconds before carefully answering. "Ryan and I grew up in the same neighborhood. I've known him for the better part of fifty years."

Interesting. Gray was surprised he'd never heard Martin's name before, all things considered. "And how well does Blakely know him?"

"Not very well." Martin's answer was a little too quick and adamant for Gray's taste.

Perhaps he'd asked the wrong question. "How well does Ryan know Blakely?"

Martin gave him a knowing smile that made Gray wonder whether his scattered persona was all an act.

"Ryan's been in Blakely's life since her birth. Although, my daughter would prefer that not to be the case. He's her godfather and helped put her through college."

Right. Gray stared at the other man, wondering just how to use the information he'd been given to find out if Ryan and Martin had used Blakely's connections at Lockwood Industries in order to steal twenty million dollars and frame Gray. Martin wasn't likely to admit it, especially in the middle of a police station.

And asking outright would tip his hand. Better to have Joker do some digging. The problem they'd run into before was having no real direction to start looking.

Gray began to push up from his chair, but the next words out of Martin's mouth stalled him halfway up.

"My daughter, however, is completely unaware and she'd never speak to me again if she found out Ryan paid for her education. My daughter is proud and honorable to a fault."

While most fathers would say those words with pride in their voices, Martin's tone conveyed disappointment. Gray had to shake his head.

"If Ryan was on fire, Blakely wouldn't cross the street to spit on him. She would, however, cross to throw some gasoline."

Well, that was pretty definitive. And left little room for the idea that Blakely would do anything to help Ryan O'Sullivan. Although, if she really had, no doubt her father would be the first to say whatever he could to deflect suspicion.

So this conversation had done rather little to help Gray decide whether Blakely had been involved in framing him, or had just lucked into information that had been planted.

A knock on the door prevented him from asking any more questions, even if he'd had any.

The detective stood in the open doorway, a very pissed off Blakely glaring from behind him.

Blakely stormed out of the station. She was halfway to Gray's car when he grasped her arm and jerked her to a stop.

Turning to glare at him, she ripped her arm from his grasp. But instead of turning away again, she leaned forward into his personal space and growled, "Don't touch me."

Her blood whooshed in her veins. The sound of it throbbed through her head, along with the tattoo of her elevated breathing.

Seriously, she needed to get a grip.

Logically, she realized the emotion directed at Gray was not entirely his fault. Everything that had happened today was simply coming to a head, crashing down over her at once. And he made a handy target.

But realizing that didn't do her much good.

Glancing around them, Gray frowned. How was it fair

that the man could still manage to look like a Hollywood heartthrob even while irritated?

Ignoring her snarled words, he grasped her arm again and urged her ahead of him and around the corner of the building.

He maneuvered them both into a dark patch of quiet shade. Using his leverage, he set her back against the brick wall and then let her go.

He backed away, putting a few feet between them. "Now isn't the time to lose it, Blakely."

"No joke."

Gray cocked a single eyebrow, silently calling her ten kinds of stupid for doing exactly what she shouldn't be doing.

It stung that he was right. Blakely groaned. Dropping her head back, she let her body sag into the rough surface of the wall. The sharp edges scraped against her skin, but she didn't care.

"I'm pissed at you. I'm pissed at him. I'm just—"

"Pissed. Yeah, I got that."

"He promised me. And I'm such an idiot for believing him because it's not like he hasn't broken a million promises before. But I couldn't stop myself from hoping, even when I knew I shouldn't."

God, she knew better. But it was so difficult to cut those ties. And that's what it would take in order for her to be free of her father's drama and messes. The only way to avoid it all would be to avoid him. And she wasn't to that point yet.

Or she hadn't been.

Her mother and sister had given up on him years ago.

"Perhaps he's being honest and really is innocent."

Blakely stared at Gray, the echo of his words slightly eerie, all things considered. Was he saying that because no one—including her—had believed *him* when he said he was innocent? Was he being just as naive as she was?

"I've heard that before, Gray." And, no, she wasn't just talking about her father.

"Well, I believe him. I've called in a few favors and arranged for a friend to represent him."

"Why would you do that?"

"Funny, he asked me the same question. And I'll give you the same answer. Because I need you fully focused on helping me prove my innocence, and you won't be as long as you're worried about him. I have the money and connections to afford the best representation for Martin."

Blakely shook her head. "No, I won't let you do that. We don't need your money or your help."

The statement, vehement though she tried to make it sound, was a complete lie. She did need his help. And his money, in the form of the salary he was paying her to help him on this wild-goose chase.

"We don't want your charity."

"Too bad, you're getting it, anyway."

"I refuse to accept your help, Gray." There was one sure way she knew to get him angry enough to back down and agree to leave her and her father alone. "You're a criminal, just like Ryan. I won't go to him for help and I won't accept it from you."

Gray's expression went stone-hard. His mouth thinned and his eyes glittered a warning it was too late to heed.

He took a measured step, closing the gap between them. Blakely swallowed even as a frisson of awareness snaked down her spine. Nope, she refused to give in to it.

He shifted. The soft brush of his body against hers made her skin flush hot and a molten center of need melt deep inside her. His voice was low and measured as he leaned close and murmured, "I'm nothing like Ryan

O'Sullivan, although you already know that. Don't get me wrong—I'm ten times as dangerous as he is, only because I have very little left to lose. The difference is I have standards and morals."

The heat of his breath tickled her skin. His lips were so close and she wanted them on her.

No, she didn't.

Blakely tipped her head backward. She tried to crowd into the wall, but there was nowhere for her to go. Nowhere to get away from him. Or get away from her own unwanted reaction.

This close, all she could see were his eyes. His expression. The desolation and hope. The pain and the heat. The intensity centered squarely on her.

The spot at the juncture of her thighs throbbed. The breath in her lungs caught as the warmth of his body invaded every pore of her skin.

Gray Lockwood *was* dangerous. To her sanity. Her peace of mind. The very foundation of her personal morals. She'd spent her entire life avoiding men like him. And she wasn't just talking about his criminal past, although that surely should have been enough to give her pause.

But it was more.

Gray Lockwood was a force to be reckoned with. He was intelligent, observant, dynamic and demanding. In his youth, that combination had manifested in an entitled attitude that had been less than attractive.

Now, those same qualities had the ability to make her panties damp. She shouldn't be turned on by his confidence and domineering attitude. But she was.

Blakely stared up at him, her lips parted. Waiting. Although for what, she wasn't entirely certain.

Gray seemed poised, as well—on the edge of something neither of them wanted to want, but couldn't stop.

So close to her, Blakely could feel the tension coiled in every one of his muscles. He was like a tiger, waiting to spring.

The moment stretched between them. On the far side of the building, a police siren went off. A couple exited the building and chatted, although Blakely couldn't have said what their conversation was about.

She breathed in, filling her lungs with the tantalizing scent that had been taunting her for days. Him.

"To hell with it," he finally murmured right before his body pressed in against her.

All the air whooshed out of her lungs, as if he'd slammed her against the wall, although he hadn't. Excitement flashed through her as his mouth dropped to hers.

Blakely's gasp backed into her lungs as he kissed her, swallowing the sound.

Gray's arm snaked around her, settling on the small of her back as he pulled her closer. His other hand found her face, cupping it and angling her just where he wanted.

The first touch was light, but that didn't last long. Seconds later, Gray was opening his lips, diving in and demanding everything from her.

His tongue tangled with hers, stroking and stoking and driving the need she'd been ignoring into a raging inferno she couldn't deny. Seconds—that's how long it took for him to steal her resolve and leave her a shaking mess of desire.

Her own hands gripped his shoulders, pulling him closer even as her brain screamed that she needed to push him away.

But she couldn't make herself do it.

The angle changed. The kiss deepened. He demanded more. And Blakely didn't hesitate to give it. Going up on her toes, she met him force for force. Need for need.

Somehow her leg raised, hooking up over his hip as she made demands of her own. The overheated center of her sex ached. Blakely moaned in the back of her throat as she undulated against him, looking for relief.

The sound seemed to snap him out of whatever had tangled them together.

Hands gripping her arms, he pushed away, unraveling their intertwined bodies. She leaned into his hold, unconsciously pushing against the invisible barrier he'd placed between them.

"I'm sorry," he said.

"I'm not." Blakely wanted to slap a hand across her wayward mouth, but it was too late. This was his fault. He'd obviously fried her brain.

Shaking his head, Gray gave a soft chuckle. "Thanks for being honest. But I shouldn't have done that."

Blakely wasn't going to argue with him. "You're right."

She expected Gray to walk away, leave her there and let her figure out her own way back to the office.

Instead, he reached out, soft fingers trailing lightly over her cheek. "I've wanted to do that for days." His heated gaze skipped across the features of her face, following his teasing fingertip.

His honesty unnerved her, although it also settled her. It was reassuring to know she wasn't the only one fighting against urges she shouldn't have.

But she also couldn't pretend. "This can't happen." Blakely tried to make the words sound adamant, even if a huge part of her didn't want them to be.

Gray nodded, but his words contradicted the action. "Why not? We're both adults."

"Yes, but you don't like me and I don't like you."

Gray's eyes jumped back to hers, staring straight into her. "That's not true. I like you just fine."

Blakely couldn't stop the scoffing sound that scraped through her throat. "Yeah, right. You hate me. I was instrumental in putting you in jail."

"Maybe."

There was no *maybe* about it. Her testimony had been key to his conviction.

"I'm attracted to you, Blakely. We're working closely together, which makes ignoring the physical pull difficult. You tell me you're not interested and I'll do just that. But knowing you are..."

Blakely understood completely. Her body still hummed with the memory of their kiss. "It's going to be hell to put that genie back in the bottle."

Five

It had been two days since the kiss. Since he'd grabbed her, pressed her against the wall and gotten the first intoxicating taste of her mouth.

Nope, the feel of her hadn't been haunting him.

Gray sat on the opposite side of the room from her, trying to concentrate on a stack of evidence, just as he had for the last two days. Honestly, if Stone walked in right now and asked him what he was doing, Gray couldn't have told him. He hadn't actually absorbed anything he'd read for hours.

This wasn't good. Or productive.

For her part, Blakely had chosen to pretend the kiss never happened. When they'd walked away from the police station, Gray hadn't been entirely certain what her reaction would be. The fact that she hadn't slapped him was promising. And there was no way she could deny being just as into that kiss as he'd been.

But by the next morning, her stiff, perfect facade had been back in place.

Honestly, he preferred Blakely when she was energetic and emotional. Real and authentic. He'd seen the evidence that she could be more than just a disapproving robot who followed all the rules because she was scared of what might happen if she didn't.

His conversation with Martin had been rather enlightening, though. Discovering Blakely had grown up on the outskirts of a major crime family shed some light, for sure.

But after his little meeting at the police station, one thing had become crystal clear—neither Blakely nor Martin were sitting on twenty million dollars. First, if they had been, Blakely wouldn't have been worried about paying for her father's lawyer. She would have called up the best defense attorney money could buy. Second, if they had that kind of money, neither of them would still be in Charleston.

Gray was convinced Martin might act the fool, but was far from it. He used that facade to his advantage. But the man wouldn't stick around near the scene of the crime if he had the means to disappear and live the good life.

While that didn't precisely mean Blakely hadn't been inadvertently involved in the frame job that had sent Gray to prison, it did, at least in his mind, clear her of intentionally setting him up.

Blakely had been just as much a pawn in the whole scheme as he'd been. It was possible that whoever had placed the trail of financial information in the Lockwood Industries books had simply banked on *someone* finding the crumbs.

It really wouldn't have mattered who that someone was. In fact, it might have played better if the someone was completely innocent and unconnected. If the police had done a thorough job—which Gray wasn't willing to concede—they should have investigated every witness just to be certain of their character before they took the stand.

Squeezing his eyes shut, Gray shoved away the file he'd been looking at and dropped back into his chair.

He and Blakely had been pouring over testimony, evidence and notes for a week. And so far, they'd found absolutely nothing.

The only thing Gray had to show for his effort was a growing certainty that Blakely had been unwittingly involved. Which benefited him not at all. It would have been easier if she had been purposely involved. Because then he wouldn't have felt guilty for the way he'd maneuvered her into helping him.

Or for the way he wanted to cross the room, pull her out of her chair, wipe everything off the desk and kiss every inch of her naked skin.

Opening his eyes, Gray glanced across the office. It probably wasn't smart to have his desk facing Blakely's if he wanted to ignore the awareness pulsing beneath the surface of his skin.

Not that it really mattered. He didn't need to be watching her to know she was there. Gray could feel her presence the minute she walked into the room.

Right now, though, it made his lips pull down at the edges to watch her. Because bent over a file spread open on her desk, one hand lodged in her hair and her forehead crinkled with a frown, she looked just as frustrated and unhappy as he was.

And despite everything, he didn't want her to feel that way.

"Let's get out of here." The words were out of his mouth before he even realized he'd meant to say them.

"What?" Blakely looked up at him, blinking owlishly. Her entire body stayed poised over the file, which only made him want to take her away from here even more. It took several seconds for her gaze to clear and focus on him.

"Let's get out of here."

Her head tilted to the side. He was starting to learn she did that when she was weighing things. What she should do against what she wanted to do. Or what everyone else expected of her against what her instincts told her.

He was tired of seeing her calculate every step before taking one. Sure, there was a time in his life when he didn't calculate anything because he knew there were a pile of safety nets—not to mention billions of dollars—to save him if he fell flat on his face.

Trust him to land in a mess that would rip the safety nets out from under him and make his billions worthless in getting him out of the jam.

However, that didn't mean Blakely's approach to life was any better. If there was one thing he'd learned, it was that life was short. You never knew what was going to happen or where you were going to end up. It was your responsibility to make the most of where you were while you were there.

He had a feeling Blakely rarely allowed herself that pleasure.

Gray also knew that if he gave her enough time to come up with a valid excuse, she'd decline his offer simply because he made her nervous. Not because she was scared of him, but because she didn't want to like him.

Or want him.

Well, that wasn't going to work for him anymore.

He wanted her and he wasn't going to let the mess they were trying to unravel stop him from getting what he wanted.

Standing up, Gray walked around to her desk. "Let's go."

"Go where?"

"Does it matter? We both need a break. I haven't seen you eat anything today. You've got to be starving."

She paused. Gray's stomach knotted with nerves that he really didn't want to acknowledge or investigate. And to his surprise, Blakely offered him a small half smile.

"I am pretty hungry."

What the hell was she doing?

For the second time in a few days, Blakely found herself riding in the passenger seat of Gray's low-slung sports car. The leather cupped her body, making her feel snug and safe even as he tore through the city at break-neck speed. Apparently, he wasn't concerned about getting the attention of an officer...or a speeding ticket.

She should have said no and stayed at the office. Not just because avoiding small, enclosed spaces with Gray was just smart. But because she was seriously starting to think the man was innocent of the charges for which he'd been convicted.

And that left her with a nasty taste in her mouth.

They'd spent a lot of time together in the last week. In that time, one thing had become obvious. The man he was now was nowhere near the man he'd been back then.

And, yes, that did nothing to prove he'd been innocent. Gray's reputation back then might have been difficult to surmount. But, honestly, had he really been that terrible?

No. He'd been an entitled prick who'd had everything handed to him on a silver platter, but even as he'd partied and gambled and gone jet-setting around the world, he'd been generous to a fault.

Blakely had also discovered that while he'd been blowing millions on random and pointless things, he'd also established a foundation to assist underprivileged children with college scholarships. He'd been involved in a local fine-arts program, paying to keep art and music in schools that no longer had funding. He'd donated millions to drug-rehabilitation programs and randomly provided money to just about every charitable organization that approached him for a donation.

The information had been brought up in court, which was how she'd discovered the truth. But the prosecutor had implied it was easy to write a check, especially when one needed the tax write-off.

Blakely couldn't dispute that, but something told her the donations had been more than some accountant telling him it was a good money move. The amount he'd donated in the three years leading up to the embezzlement had been significant. In fact, it had been almost half of what he'd been accused of stealing.

Which made no sense. Why would he steal money only to donate it?

He wouldn't. Which had been his argument all along. He didn't need the twenty million. The prosecution had argued need wasn't the only motivation to explain his actions. But Gray hardly struck her as the kind of person who would steal simply to prove he could.

The attorneys also detailed a contentious relationship with his father. Several Lockwood employees testified to arguments and tension between the two in the office. Gray's father was fed up with his irresponsible ways and wanted him to take on more responsibility within the company. Their implied motive for the theft was revenge against his father, but Blakely couldn't see how stealing twenty million from Lockwood had harmed Gray's father. Certainly, the company had struggled for several months, but they'd pulled through just fine.

It all circled back to the fact that Gray hardly needed the money. Which was honestly how she found herself sitting in the seat beside him.

She was starting to like him. Starting to realize the man she'd forced into a round hole was really more complicated than she'd given him credit for.

She'd misjudged him, then and now.

The question was, what was she going to do about it?

"Where are we going?" Blakely finally asked, filling the charged silence stretching between them.

"A little place I know."

That really didn't answer her question. "Where?"

Gray swiveled his head, studying her instead of the road for several seconds. Normally, especially at this speed, that would have made her nervous, but she had no doubt Gray had complete control of his car.

"Do you trust me?"

What a loaded question. Did she? No, but then she didn't really trust anyone. And while she was beginning to think she'd misjudged Gray, that didn't mean she was ready to place her life in his hands.

However, that wasn't necessarily what he was asking.

"To pick a good place to get food? Yes."

Gray's mouth tipped up into a lopsided, knowing grin. He understood precisely what she was saying.

"Excellent. We gotta start somewhere."

Did they?

Blakely's stomach flipped at the idea. She wanted to, that was clear. Even sitting this close to him was doing crazy and unexplainable things to her body. Her skin tingled and heat settled deep in her belly. Her panties were damp and he hadn't even touched her.

He drove her out to a little place near Rainbow Row. It was quaint and small, not exactly what she'd expected him to pick. But even more surprising, she hadn't heard of it.

"I've never been here," she said, staring up at the front as she climbed from the car. Better that than stare at him as he held open her door. Or get tangled up in thinking how easy it would be to lean into the hard planes of his body, press her lips to his and drown in another mind-bending kiss.

Was it her imagination, or did he linger a little longer than necessary before moving out of her way?

"I'm not surprised. It's fairly new, but the food is amazing."

"I guess I'll find out."

It was past the normal lunch rush, but there were still a handful of occupied tables. Mostly older women with their makeup and hair done, obviously out for lunch with friends. There were several affluent neighborhoods close by, so not altogether surprising.

The hostess was pleasant and nice, even if she did stare at Gray a little longer than necessary. But who could blame her? Take away the criminal element and the man was a walking fantasy. Polished, but still with the hint of a few rough edges. He carried himself with a confidence that was both attractive and enviable.

But Blakely wouldn't allow herself to be jealous. Mostly because she had nothing to be jealous about.

The perky hostess showed them to a table in the far corner, beside a window that overlooked a lush garden. The empty tables surrounding them created an illusion of privacy, which might not be a good thing.

Gray held out her chair, brushing his fingers over the curve of her shoulders as he pulled away. All this time, Blakely had assumed holding chairs was simply a polite thing for men to do. Now she realized it was a perfect excuse. That simple touch had sent a low hum vibrating through her body and she was going to spend the next hour fighting to turn it off.

How could she manufacture a reason for him to touch her again?

Nope, she wasn't going there. Picking up the menu, Blakely studied it rather than Gray. After a few moments, the words actually started to make sense.

Their waitress was friendly, and she obviously knew Gray, judging by their conversation. But she was also efficient, as she took their drink orders and highlighted the day's specials. Blakely ordered a pecan-crusted chicken salad that sounded amazing. Gray ordered pimento cheese and homemade pork rinds, followed by pan-seared tuna and asparagus.

Once the menus were taken and some soft rolls appeared on the table, there was nothing left to keep her distracted. Which wasn't necessarily a good thing.

For the first time, Blakely realized Gray had positioned her in a chair with her back to the rest of the room…filling the spot right in front of her with nothing but him. Sneaky man. Had he done that on purpose?

Blakely was trying to decide whether to ask him—because maybe she really didn't want the answer—when Gray's cell, sitting facedown on the table, buzzed. Frowning, he flipped it over. The frown went from a mild crease to full-blown irritation as soon as he read whatever was on the screen. Glancing up, he said, "I'm sorry, I need to get this."

Blakely waved away his apology. They weren't on a date so he didn't need to justify his actions to her.

She expected him to get up and walk away, to gain a little bit of privacy. Instead, he just answered the call, so she could hear his side of the conversation.

"Hello, Mother."

If Blakely hadn't been able to see Gray's expression, the tone in his voice would have clearly conveyed his displeasure. She wondered if that was his normal reaction to his mother, or if there was something specific going on between them. Not that it was any of her business.

Hell, she could identify. It wasn't like she rejoiced whenever her father's name popped up on her cell screen. He never called her when things were going well.

"Calm down." Gray's eyes narrowed, the irritation quickly morphing to something more. "I have no idea what you're talking about." He paused, listening to something on the other end before letting out a sigh. "I'll be there in a few minutes."

Hanging up, he dropped his phone onto the table with a loud clatter that made her concerned for the safety of the screen. "I'm sorry to cut this short, but I need to run over to my mother's house."

"So I gathered."

Waving over their waitress, Gray didn't bother asking for the check. He slipped a hundred into her hand and then stood, holding out an arm for Blakely to go in front of him.

The walk to the car was silent, mostly because she didn't know what to say.

What she didn't expect, once they got inside, was for Gray to head in the opposite direction of the office.

Apparently, she was about to meet his mother.

Six

Gray wasn't looking forward to this confrontation at all. And part of him felt like an ass for dragging Blakely along for the ride. But his mother had been spouting an irate tirade of nonsense and he was afraid to take the time to drop off Blakely at the office, which was in the opposite direction.

With any luck, he could calm his mother and they could be back to work in less than half an hour.

Although, he wasn't holding his breath.

It had been just about eleven months since he'd last spoken to or seen his mother. Before that, it had been seven years. He'd stopped by the estate after getting out of prison. Although he hadn't exactly expected the fatted calf to be slaughtered, an acknowledgment of his place in her life would have been nice.

Instead, she'd followed his father's line and refused to even let him inside the front door.

Who knew if she'd let him inside this time, either. Not

that he particularly cared. His mother hadn't exactly been a warm and loving example of motherhood to begin with. The minute his father disowned him she'd taken that as permission to pretend he didn't exist.

There was a spiteful, vindictive part of him that enjoyed knowing her friends talked about her behind her back because of him. If nothing else, being wrongly convicted of a crime gave him that perk. Although, it hardly outweighed the cons.

It took about five minutes to get to the estate on Legare Street from the restaurant. Not nearly long enough.

He climbed out of the car and headed for the front door. Blakely slowly followed. He purposely hadn't asked her to either stay behind or come with him, instead leaving it as her decision.

He figured, after meeting Martin, she could most likely handle his mother in one of her states, anyway.

Gray didn't bother knocking. Why would he, when the estate had been his childhood home? But it did feel weird walking through the front door after such a long time away. The place looked exactly the same—not a single mirror or piece of artwork on the wall had been changed in almost eight years.

Not surprising, either. His mother was a creature of habit. When given an option, she'd take the path of least resistance every time. One reason she'd made such a perfect trophy wife.

After striding down the hallway, Gray bounded up the wide, sweeping staircase to the second floor and the rooms his mother had claimed as her own long ago. Opening the door to the sunroom, he wasn't surprised to see her pacing furiously back and forth.

She didn't turn when he opened the door, apparently so deep in her own discourse that she hadn't heard him enter. But the minute she spotted him, he became the object of her obvious rage.

Charging across the room, she yelled, "Who does this bitch think she is? Blackmailing me after all these years? I had nothing to do with this, dammit! Nothing. And I'm not paying her a single dollar, let alone twenty million."

Gray shook his head, trying to make sense of his mother's words.

But her rant didn't end there. The words continued to come, punctuated by her slamming fists hitting into his chest and rocking him back on his heels.

Well, that was unexpected.

And so was the way Blakely shot between them, shoving into his mother's face and pushing her backward. "What do you think you're doing?"

"I don't know who the hell you are, but get out of my way."

"Not on your life. Whatever's going on, it doesn't give you to the right to physically assault your son."

His mother laughed, the bitter sound of it sending a shiver down his spine.

"He isn't my son."

"Excuse me?" It was Blakely's turn to be knocked backward. She collided with his chest.

Distractedly, Gray wrapped an arm around her waist, holding her tight against him.

His mother's words startled him, but Gray locked down his reaction and refused to show it. This woman had abandoned him long ago and didn't deserve anything from him.

"What the hell do you mean?"

His mother's eyes jerked up to his. The blind fury clouding them slowly faded. "Shit."

Yeah, that pretty much summed up this whole situation.

Waving a hand in the direction of the sofa in front of the floor-to-ceiling windows, she indicated he should sit. Gray didn't bother following her request. But for the first time, he realized she was holding a piece of paper in her hand.

"What's that?"

Frowning, she waved the thing through the air. Just by sight, it appeared to be cheap copy paper. The shadow of several lines of text could be seen through it, so it wasn't very heavy. "This? This would be a blackmail demand."

"Who sent it?"

"You probably should sit."

"I'm good."

"Your father's going to kill me."

"Since he disowned me several years ago, I find it hard to believe he'll care what you say or do."

His mother shook her head, sadness washing over her expression. "That's where you're wrong."

Somehow, he didn't think so. Not only had his father ignored Gray's insistence that he was innocent, but his father had also gone so far as to cut Gray out of his life entirely. What loving parent did that? Gray had always been nothing more than another pawn to the man. Someone his father could control and move at will. And when Gray became a liability instead of an asset, he was sacrificed.

Unlike Stone, whose parents had stood by him, even before they learned the truth—that he'd murdered their friend's son because he'd walked in on an attempted rape. His friend had kept the details to himself for years, protecting the woman he loved. His family had supported him, accepted him. Hell, they'd thrown him a lavish party when he finally got out.

But despite being innocent, *Gray's* family had disowned him, cut him out of the family business and left him alone in the world.

Sure, he could tell himself that he was better off without his mother and father in his life. And, logically, he realized that was absolutely true. But it still hurt like hell when the people who were supposed to have his back had abandoned him.

His mother gave a grimace. "Oh, don't get me wrong. He wouldn't care because *you* know. But he will care that someone else is privy to the dirty laundry he's so desperate to keep hidden."

Now that sounded more like his father. "Well, then, by all means, tell me. I'd really appreciate having something I could hold over his head."

Especially once Gray had proof of his innocence. Even sweeter to demand access to the company, and also have the means to control the strings on the man who viewed himself as the puppet master.

Blakely, who had taken his mother's suggestion and sat on the sofa several feet away, piped up. "I'm going out on a limb here, but reading between the lines, I'm going to guess that Gray isn't your son, but he is your husband's."

His mother glanced over at Blakely, her gaze moving up and down, taking stock.

What was wrong with him that he wanted his mother to approve of her? Childhood impulses he couldn't control? Wasn't he too old to need parental approval for anything? Especially considering he and his mother hadn't particularly had that kind of relationship to begin with.

Finally, his mother said, "Nailed it in one. She's a smart one."

Yes, she absolutely was. The more time he spent with Blakely, the more he appreciated her quick mind. And he was starting to understand her rock-solid sense of honor, too.

"That note. It's from his biological mother? Demanding money to keep the secret?"

"Pretty much."

"Twenty million. That's what you said earlier?"

"Yes."

Blakely turned her gaze toward him. "Coincidence?"

He knew exactly what she was asking. Was it a coincidence the blackmail demand was the same amount of money that was still missing from the embezzlement? Maybe. It was a nice round figure. Not to mention, the media had been linking that number with his name for years.

But while his release last year had prompted a new flurry of media attention, that had died down in the months since. Partly because both of his friends had taken some of the heat off his back with their own releases and high-profile antics.

But what if it wasn't? They were still looking for that missing twenty million. Maybe his birth mother thought she deserved it? Or maybe she was somehow involved and never got the money she was supposed to get?

"Who is this woman?"

"I don't know."

Yeah, right. That was a lie if ever he'd heard one. His mother might have never gone to college and spent most of her time involved in several charitable organizations coordinating glitzy events, but she was far from ignorant. In fact, she was quite brilliant at gossip and knew exactly how to dig up dirt on just about anyone. There wasn't a snowball's chance in hell she hadn't done—or paid for—a full investigation of her husband's fling. Especially if the woman was the mother of her "child."

He wasn't the only one skeptical. Blakely scoffed. "Please, you don't strike me as stupid."

"Why, thank you, dear." His mother's voice practically dripped syrupy sarcasm all over the floor.

Blakely ignored it. "You know exactly who your son's mother is. You wouldn't be foolish enough to let that important piece of information go until you discovered who it was."

A half smile tugged at his mother's perfect lips. "I like this one. You should keep her around."

"I'll take that under advisement. In the meantime, why don't you answer her question?"

"Fine. I know who she is. Your father wasn't exactly as discreet as he'd like to think."

Gray wasn't entirely certain what to say to that. Sorry? How convenient? So he simply kept his mouth shut and waited.

"She worked at the club. One of those girls that drives a cart around and brings drinks out to the men playing golf. At least, until your father set her up in a nice town house and provided her a monthly stipend to be at his beck and call."

Great, his mother sounded like a winner.

"When she got pregnant, he was pissed. Supposedly, she was on birth control, but the hussy forgot to take it. However, as he always does, your father found a way to make that work in his favor. We'd been trying for years to get pregnant, but couldn't. The doctors weren't hopeful and fertility treatments weren't as advanced back then as they are now. He convinced me that he'd found a woman who'd agreed to a private adoption."

"But you knew."

His mother grimaced. "I knew. I was aware of the affair already. It wasn't the first one and, clearly, wasn't the last. But as long as he was inconspicuous I didn't particularly care."

"You agreed to accept the baby as your own."

With a sigh, his mother walked over to the chair across from Blakely and sat. "I did."

"But you knew," Blakely said. "It wasn't simply that he wasn't yours. It was that he was hers."

His mother looked up at him, regret filling her eyes. "Yes. Every time I looked at you, it was a reminder of your father's infidelity. It was one thing to live with it in the background, but…you look like her."

"I do?"

She nodded. "And him. I tried. I really did, Gray. I wanted you to be my son. And you are."

"But I'm also not."

"It was so hard not to allow you to shoulder the blame for something you had no responsibility for."

Gray nodded. What else could he do? Argue with her? Tell her she should have tried harder? That it wasn't fair for her to agree to accept him as her own, but then not follow through with actually being his mother?

Speaking those truths aloud would change nothing.

"Who is she?"

"Now? She's a showgirl in Vegas. My one requirement was that the adoption be closed and the mother agree to leave the state. Your father paid her a huge sum and she left."

Clearly, his birth mother had been more interested in the money than in her son. And if the letter was any indication, she still was. That was something he'd have to deal with later.

"Do you know how to find her?"

His mother nodded.

"Give me the letter and her information and I'll take care of this."

Reluctantly, his mother handed the letter to him. Without looking, he held it out to Blakely, knowing she'd grab it and keep it safe. When they returned to the office, he'd send it to their forensics team to be analyzed. He'd also contact Joker to see what information he could dig up before heading to Vegas.

Holding out a hand, Gray indicated Blakely should follow him out of the room. She rose, heading in his direction. He stood still, waiting for her to exit first.

And was surprised when her palm landed on his chest and stroked down across his body as she passed. Somehow, that simple touch helped settle the chaos rioting inside him.

He followed her through the house. His mother's footsteps echoed behind his. But before they left, Blakely paused at the front door. Turning, she glanced around him to his mother. "Why did you call Gray instead of your husband?"

"Because Malcolm's indiscretions are the reason we're in this mess in the first place. And I know Gray is part owner of a security firm. I assumed he'd be better equipped to handle the situation than his father."

Blakely nodded. "That's what I thought."

Gray was surprised when she grasped his hand and headed down the wide front steps. Squeezing his hand before she dropped it, Blakely rounded the hood of the car and slid into the passenger seat.

He loved the smooth, graceful way she moved. It was becoming more and more difficult to tear his gaze away from watching her whenever she was close.

Gray slid down into the driver's seat, but before he could put the car in gear, Blakely placed a staying hand over his.

"Are you okay?"

Was he? Gray honestly didn't know. Certainly, his

mother's revelation should have rocked his foundation. But it really hadn't. It wasn't like she'd ever been the demonstrative, loving type. Actually, learning he wasn't her real son added context to his childhood. It helped him understand things that had never made sense before.

And he'd actually lost both of his parents long before now, so learning this new detail changed nothing, although it provided another possible motive for what had happened to him.

Which was a good thing.

"Yeah, I'm good."

Blakely stared deep into his eyes. She didn't try and tell him he wasn't okay. She simply searched for clues that he really meant what he'd said.

After several moments, she gave him a sad half smile and squeezed his hand again. "I'm going with you."

Gray's eyebrows arched up in confusion. "Where?"

"Vegas. Don't pretend you're not going. I'm going with you."

"No, you're not."

"Yes, I am. What would Stone think about you gallivanting off to Vegas by yourself to meet the biological mother you didn't know existed until twenty minutes ago? A woman who may or may not be involved somehow in your embezzlement conviction?"

Oh, she really was good. "That's playing dirty."

Blakely's smile morphed into a megawatt one. "What can I say? I'm learning."

Blakely never expected to find herself sitting across the aisle from Gray on a private plane. Sure, she'd half expected to fly first class for the first time in her life, but this…? Totally unexpected. She was completely out of her element, although tried not to show it.

"Relax."

And she was apparently failing miserably.

"I'm relaxed."

"No, you're not. You're wound tighter than a top. What's wrong?"

Wrong? "Nothing."

Gray arched an eyebrow, silently calling bullshit.

Not that she was going to tell him the truth. When she'd insisted she was going with him, she hadn't completely thought through the implications. It was one thing to be cooped up in the same office with him for ten hours a day, but to be a shadow at his side for the next several days...

At least back in Charleston she had the ability to go home and clear her mind of him. Or attempt to.

"Remind me again, why are we staying so long?"

Another expectation blown to bits. She'd assumed they'd fly up, track down his birth mother and head home. A day at the most. Instead, Gray had told her to pack enough for three or four days. Considering they already had a full rundown on his mother's information, including where she worked and lived, Blakely wasn't entirely certain what he expected to take so long.

"There are a couple other people I want to pay a visit to while we're here."

Blakely couldn't help the suspicion that snaked through her system. She'd been reading enough about Gray's history before he'd gone to prison to know that he'd spent quite a bit of time in Vegas before. And most of that time revolved around gambling, sex and outrageous benders that went on for days.

None of which she was interested in being a part of.

Sure, Gray hadn't done any of those things since he'd been out—at least not to her knowledge—so she didn't think that's what he had in mind, but...

"I'm not down for some wild Vegas weekend, Gray. I'm not interested in the lavish parties or high-roller games."

"Good, since neither of those things are on the agenda. I simply want to check in with some people I used to know."

Blakely's eyes narrowed. Gray looked entirely sincere, his steady gaze holding hers as she watched him. Every fiber of her being wanted to believe him. But she couldn't completely shut down the sneering voice in the back of her head.

She finally shrugged and said, "Great, then I'll leave you to it and take a commercial flight home after we've talked with your mom."

"Nope. I need you here for my meetings."

"Why?"

"Because I'm talking to my former bookie, Surkov."

Nope, that did not sound like something she wanted to be involved with. "You don't need me to gamble."

"Do I look like an idiot to you?"

Blakely didn't understand the question, and seemingly unconnected segue, but answered, anyway. "No."

"Apparently I do if you think I'm here to place a bet. The main reason I spent seven years in prison is because I had a gambling habit. By no means was I an addict, but I wasn't exactly careful, either."

"Why'd you do it? The prosecution's biggest argument was that you were up to your eyeballs in debt to some bad people and didn't want to confess to Daddy to bail you out."

Gray's eyebrows rose. "And what do you think about that now?"

Blakely cocked her head and considered her answer for several seconds. What did she think? At the time, the only information she'd had about Gray was either what the media had told her or based on the limited interactions she'd witnessed at Lockwood Industries, which hadn't exactly painted Gray in the best light.

There was no doubt in her mind the man she knew now wouldn't have hesitated to do or say anything he needed to, including talking to his father, even if their relationship was strained.

But that didn't mean the man he'd been before would have reacted the same way. In fact, she was pretty certain the time he'd spent in prison had fundamentally changed him. And maybe for the better.

"I think I don't know who you were back then, so I can't really say. But I have a pretty good grasp of who you are now, and I don't think you'd be concerned about your father's reaction to anything."

"That's very true."

"However, after pouring over your personal financial records for the last week, I'm well aware that you had more than enough assets to cover the gambling debts without consulting your father."

"Also true."

"But that does raise the question—why did you routinely take out loans in order to gamble?"

Gray frowned and looked away for several seconds. "Because I was young, stupid and lazy."

"Well, doesn't that just explain all sorts of decisions we've all made."

Gray chuckled. "I was spoiled and used to getting what I wanted immediately. On several occasions I found myself in Vegas, enjoying some high-stakes games, and ran out of liquid cash. It's easier to take out a high-interest loan in the middle of the night than contact my portfolio advisor to liquidate assets. Especially when I knew I had the ability to pay back the principal before the interest skyrocketed."

"But the last time…you didn't pay it back immediately."

"No, I didn't. Because my life got blown to bits when officers barged into my home to arrest me for embezzlement. I was a little preoccupied with clearing my name to worry about the latest loan. If I'd known it would be used against me, I would have taken care of it immediately. But, once again, I was spoiled and didn't give a shit. Not even when the gentleman who'd loaned me the money sent an envoy to impress upon me the need to make good on it."

Was he really saying what she thought he was? "They sent someone to rough you up?"

Gray's laughter filled the cabin. "You've been watching too many movies, Ms. Whittaker."

"No, I grew up around organized crime, Gray. I've seen plenty of despicable men do despicable things. Beating someone up over money would be mild in comparison."

Gray's sharp gaze cut to hers and Blakely realized just how much personal information she'd revealed. Personal information she hadn't meant to share with anyone, especially Gray Lockwood. The last thing she wanted was for him to feel sorry for her. Or, worse, ask for more details.

But he didn't. "They actually did just come to have a conversation. At the time, I thought because they knew I was good for the money. I'd paid in full before. But now…"

It wasn't hard for Blakely to connect the dots to what Gray might be thinking.

"Do you really think they had something to do with the embezzlement?"

Gray shrugged. "Logically, it doesn't make much sense. They knew I was good for the money."

No—no, it didn't. But then sometimes crazy people did asinine things.

"It's worth double-checking, though. Especially since we're in town. Turning over all the stones…"

Eight years too late. The guilt she'd been fighting for the last several days swelled inside her. The more she learned about Gray, the more certain she was that he was innocent. Which meant she'd played an instrumental part in sending an innocent man to prison for a significant chunk of his life.

And there was nothing she could do to make up for that.

It was her turn to apologize for something she couldn't change. "I'm sorry."

Gray shrugged, not even attempting to pretend he didn't know what she meant. "Not your fault."

That's where he was wrong, but she wasn't going to argue with him about it. She was going to protest staying, though.

"Considering you don't really expect it to be anything, you don't really need me here for this." Which meant she could escape, and maybe, just maybe, prevent herself from doing something stupid.

Like throwing herself at him and begging him to kiss the hell out of her again.

"Talking to my bookie? I don't."

Well, she hadn't expected him to agree with her. That was easy. Too easy.

Reaching across the aisle, Gray ran his fingers down a strand of Blakely's hair, sending a cascade of tingles from her scalp down to her toes.

"I want you here for me."

Seven

He'd made her nervous, which was actually a little cute. Mostly because from his observations, not much made Blakely Whittaker nervous. He was learning that she might appear small and fragile, but she had a core of straight-up steel.

It was one of the most attractive things about her. Although, he wasn't thrilled knowing she'd built that tough core because of the things she'd seen and experienced in her life.

It was still cute. He liked knowing he could make her off-kilter. Because she certainly had the ability to set his own life on its head.

It might be seriously inconvenient to be dealing with this now, but if there was one thing he'd learned in the last few years, it was that one couldn't control everything. Sometimes, one simply had to roll with the punches, enjoy the experiences and find the lessons.

And like he'd said earlier, he wasn't stupid. When

faced with the opportunity to follow a couple of leads and spend several days in close quarters with Blakely... This was one of those times to take advantage of the opportunities.

Gray breezed through check-in at their hotel, going straight to the penthouse suite. It might have been several years since he'd visited, but the staff was fully aware of who he was and they'd been more than happy to accommodate his last-minute requests when he'd contacted them.

After punching in the code for the private elevator, he led Blakely into the small space. The minute the doors closed, he reached for her. Pulling her tight against his body, he backed them both up until she connected with the shiny chrome wall.

But he didn't kiss her. Yet.

Instead, his gaze raced around her face, taking in her wide, surprised expression. Her soft pink lips parted and a puffed gasp of breath caressed his face.

But she didn't move to break free. Instead, her hands settled at his hips, curling in and pulling him closer. Her pupils dilated as she leaned into him.

She wanted this as much as he did, which was all he needed to know.

Cupping a hand around the nape of her neck, Gray tilted her head and pulled her mouth to his. She tasted like peppermint and sin.

He tried to ease into it, to let them both sink into the connection, but Blakely had something else in mind. With a muffled groan, she rolled up onto her toes, trying to get more. One leg hooked over his hip, widening her stance so he could sink into the welcoming V of her open thighs.

Her heat and scent melted into him as she yanked him closer, grinding his hips against hers. Hers rolled, stroking his throbbing erection through the layers of their clothes.

She was hot as hell. And no doubt someone in security was enjoying the free show. As much as his body begged him to pull off all her clothes and take what she was clearly willing to give, he wasn't thrilled with the idea of having an audience the first time he stripped her naked and feasted on her delectable body.

Reluctantly, Gray put some space between them. But he couldn't make himself completely let her go. His hand still wrapped around her neck, he pressed his forehead against hers.

There was something calming and enticing about the way her body reacted to him. Labored breaths billowed in and out of her lungs, as if she'd just run a marathon instead of kissed the hell out of him. Which was good, since she made him feel the same way—as if he'd had the wind knocked out of him.

Her body arched, trying to find the connection again.

"Shhh," he whispered, nuzzling his lips against her forehead. "If I keep kissing you, I'm not going to be able to stop myself from pulling every stitch of your clothes off. And as much as I want that, the eye in the sky is always watching."

Blakely jerked and then stilled. After several seconds she whispered, "What are we doing? This isn't smart."

A puff of silent laughter escaped his lips. "Enjoying each other's company?"

"We don't like each other."

"You keep saying that. I like you just fine, Blakely. You're sharp, tough and resourceful. You're loyal to a fault and sexy as hell."

Brushing a strand of hair away from her face, Gray stared down at her as she stared up. Both of them paused, teetering on the edge of something. A choice. Potential. An opportunity that could be everything…or nothing more than a few stolen days of a good time.

Gray wasn't sure what would happen, but he knew without a doubt he was willing to take the chance to find out. He'd spent years without choices, without the option of doing and having what he wanted. Tonight, he was damned and determined to take the opportunity in front of him.

But only as long as Blakely wanted the same thing.

"When this elevator stops, I'm going into that room. If you follow me, I'm going to strip you bare, kiss every inch of your naked skin and fuck you until we're both blind with pleasure. If you're not okay with that, don't get off."

Blakely pressed a palm against the cold wall of the elevator. Gray didn't bother turning around to see if she followed when he exited. Was that because he knew she'd follow?

His words rang through her head. There was no question that she wanted what he was offering. Her entire body hummed with the aftermath of that kiss. She could feel the echo of his hands on her skin and needed more.

Following him wasn't smart. It wasn't safe.

But she was tired of being both. God, she'd been smart and safe her entire life. Played by the rules and watched as others who didn't were rewarded. Tonight, she wanted to feel. Real and raw. For once, she wanted to make a stupid, amazing, earth-rocking choice.

The aftermath would come soon enough.

The doors began to shut. Blakely's belly dropped to her toes, as if she'd already taken an express ride back to the bottom floor.

No.

Her hand shot out with inches to spare. The doors touched her skin and immediately bounced back. She slipped through the opening and into the entryway of an amazing suite.

A high ceiling soared above her head. And a massive wall of windows greeted her from the opposite side of the room. Taking several steps, Blakely surveyed the amazing view, a backdrop of light and action against the inky night sky.

Her breath backed into her lungs. Not because of the stunning view, but because Gray stepped up behind her.

The hard length of his body pressed against her. His arms wrapped around her and his palm found the edge of her jaw. Gently cupping her face, he eased her around until his mouth found hers again. The angle of his hold had her arching against him, a little off balance and dependent on him for stability.

Something about that felt uncomfortable and inviting all at once. Because she knew there was no way he'd let her falter.

He held her exactly where he wanted, commanding the moment in a way that made the blood in her veins thick with anticipation. His other hand was busy, as well, methodically popping open the buttons down the front of her shirt.

She'd been purposeful when she'd dressed this morning. Casual, but professional. Determined to set the tone of this trip from the outset.

Spreading open her blouse, Gray let her mouth go long enough to peer at what he'd revealed.

"Please tell me your panties match this bra."

A small smile tugged at Blakely's lips.

She might have been professional on the outside, but

staring at her lingerie options this morning, she just hadn't been able to make herself reach for anything plain. Instead, she'd chosen a mesh-and-lace bra that left almost everything except the bottom edge of her breasts naked. What was that saying? Something about sexy lingerie making a woman feel confident, even if no one else knew she was wearing it?

She'd embraced that school of thought for sure.

"As a matter of fact, they do." Maybe she was gloating. A little. But the appreciation and approval in Gray's voice was absolutely worth it.

"Let me see."

Setting her away from him, Gray took several steps backward.

Turning, Blakely did the same, increasing the space. Without the pressure of his body to keep it in place, the shirt he'd opened slithered off her shoulders to pool at her feet.

Normally, Blakely felt uncomfortable in these types of situations. She was typically a get-naked-get-in-bed-and-have-sex kind of girl. Focused on the end result, because that's what they both wanted, right?

Tonight was entirely different.

Probably because of the way Gray was watching her.

His hungry gaze tripped across her skin. She could feel it, as tempting as any caress. Clearly, he wanted her. Appreciated her. Which only increased her confidence.

"I'm dying here, Blakely. Show me."

Reaching down, she popped the button and zipper on her pants. Rolling her hips, Blakely let them follow the shirt down to the ground.

Gray's sharp intake of breath was worth a million words. His deep green eyes went hot. Kicking off her heels, Blakely stepped closer, standing before him in nothing but her bra and panties.

Her nipples ached and her sex throbbed. She wanted him to touch her. A cool draft of air kissed her overheated skin, sending a scattering of goose bumps across her body.

"Gorgeous. You're beautiful, Blakely."

Closing the space between them, Gray cupped the nape of her neck and gently pulled her up onto her toes. He eased her into the towering shelter of his body, fusing their mouths together.

The kiss was powerful, deep. Drugging.

Languid desire melted through Blakely's body. His clothes scraped against her naked skin, reminding her how vulnerable she was right now. A dangerous edge of anxiety swirled at the fringes of the heat he was building.

Pulling back, she reached for the hem of his shirt, tugging it out of his slacks. Gray let her, somehow sensing her need to even the playing field. Lifting his arms, he helped her work the shirt up and off. Blakely didn't even bother tossing it—she simply let it drop to the floor behind him.

His ruffled dark brown hair made her lips curl up in a smile. Gray Lockwood wasn't the kind of guy who let much of anything ruffle him. It felt intimate somehow, to see him that way. More intimate than standing in front of him in her underwear.

Reaching for him, Blakely let her fingers sift through it, smoothing his hair back down. She let her hands drift down his neck, shoulders, torso.

Everything about him was tight and hard. His body swelled with muscle that had not been built in a gym. But what gave her pause was the smattering of scars scattered across his body.

Blakely let her fingertips play over them, memorizing the way the puckered skin felt. Gray stiffened beneath her exploration, but didn't pull away. She wanted to ask the questions, but knew he really didn't want to answer them.

And now wasn't the time.

Turning her gaze up to his, she leaned forward and placed her mouth over a particularly ugly one just over the swell of one of his pecs. And then let her mouth trail downward until she found the tight, tiny nub of nipple.

Sucking it into her mouth, Blakely relished Gray's groan. His fingers tangled in her hair, curled into a fist. His hold arched her neck at the same time he pressed into her. Blakely responded with the scrape of her teeth against the distended bud of flesh.

But that patience didn't last long. With a growl, Gray grasped her around the waist and boosted her up onto a kitchen island she hadn't even noticed was there.

The cold surface of the countertop connecting with the warm curve of her ass made her gasp with surprise. Reaching behind her, Gray had the clasp of her bra popped open and his mouth on her breast within seconds.

She arched into him, relishing the way Gray's wet mouth sucked on her skin. His palm spread wide at the base of her spine, keeping her where he wanted. Waves of sensation built in her belly as he tugged and sucked and laved.

His mouth played across her skin. Tingles chased up and down her spine. Pressing her knees wide, Gray stepped into the open V of her thighs. His fingertips caressed the delicate skin at the juncture of her hip and thigh, tracing the edge of her panties. Teasing, tempting her with what she really wanted.

She writhed beneath his touch, needing so much more. "Please."

Gray obliged, slipping a finger beneath the barrier of her panties and finding the moist heat of her sex. Blakely gasped and arched up into his caress, silently demanding more.

"God, you're wet," he groaned.

Urging her down, Gray hooked his fingers into the sides of her panties and tugged them down her legs. Kneeling at her feet, he stared up at her. The expression on his face sent her reeling. Harsh, needy and sexy as hell. She'd never had a man look at her with such desire and intensity.

Naked, spread across the kitchen island, Blakely should have felt exposed. But she didn't. Instead, she felt empowered and sexy.

Hands to her knees, Gray urged her wider as he leaned forward to trail kisses up the expanse of her inner thigh. He licked and nipped, sucked and nuzzled. Until his wicked mouth found the very part of her aching for relief. Blakely's world went dark as his mouth narrowed everything down to that one spot.

His mouth was magic. Blakely groaned, dropping back on her elbows because her body just wouldn't stay upright anymore. Her eyes slipped shut, bursts of color flashing across her brain along with his lightning strokes of pleasure.

The orgasm slammed into her, rocking her entire body. Her hips bucked against him, but his hard hold on her thighs kept her in place. She rode out the relentless waves for what felt like an eternity.

Blakely was breathing hard, her entire body laboring to pull enough oxygen into her lungs. Her elbows were shaky, but somehow she managed to stay mostly upright. It would have been embarrassing to collapse completely onto the kitchen counter in front of him.

Although, he probably wouldn't have cared.

Gray rose between her spread thighs. His mouth glistened with the aftermath of her orgasm. His own lips curled up into a self-satisfied smirk. Blakely had the urge to do whatever it took to wipe that expression off his face.

Starting with stripping him of the last of his clothes.

Blakely curled her hands into the waistband of his slacks, using the hold to jerk him closer. Sitting up, she made quick work of his fly and pushed both the pants and boxer briefs over his hips.

Gray toed off his shoes and stepped out of the pile of clothing, kicking it out of the way.

God, he was gorgeous. Light spilled over his body, highlighting the peaks and valleys of pure muscle. Two grooves sat at the edge of his hips, leading with a V straight to the promised land.

His erection, long and thick, jutted out from his body. A tiny pearl of moisture clung to the swollen tip. Blakely's tongue swept out across her bottom lip. She really wanted to taste him.

A groan reverberated through the back of his throat. "Don't look at me that way."

Startled, Blakely's gaze ripped up to his. "What way?"

"Like I'm a chocolate sundae and you're starving."

A grin played at Blakely's lips. "You're better than a sundae, Gray, and you know it. You're hot as hell."

"You think so, huh?"

Shaking her head, Blakely gestured for him to come closer. "You're walking, talking sin. Shut up and come here."

Gray did what she demanded, stepping back between her open thighs. Blakely started to jump down from the counter, but the solid wall of his body prevented her.

Shaking his head, Gray said, "That's where I want you."

You'd think, considering she'd just had a mind-blowing orgasm, that she might have been a little more malleable and accommodating. Not so much. "Maybe I want to be somewhere else." Like on her knees with him in her mouth. That's really what she wanted.

"Too bad."

Perhaps if she told him her plan he would relent. But she never got the chance. Because the ability to speak left her the minute his fingers found her sex and plunged deep. A strangled sound stuck in the back of her throat and her hips jumped forward, pressing tight against his hand in an effort to get more.

"God, you're so tight."

She nodded, her brain unable to form any other coherent response. Gray's fingers worked in and out, stroking deep. Blakely's brain scrambled, emptying of every thought except for the pleasure he was giving her.

Her body went white-hot as her hips pumped in time with his fingers. She was so close…and then he simply stopped. With his fingers still buried deep in her pussy, he gave a come-hither motion with his other hand that had her eyes crossing.

"Holy…"

"My thought exactly," he said. "Lean back, open the drawer behind you and grab a condom."

Blakely blinked, but did as he asked. Rolling onto one elbow, she reached to the far side and pulled out a drawer. Sure enough, a pile of condoms sat there.

Grabbing one, she asked, "How'd you know?"

"Not my first time staying in this suite."

Blakely tried not to let his statement derail her. She

didn't want to think about him being up here with another woman. Or women.

"And I might have asked the concierge to stock all the
rooms with condoms."

Laughter and irritation bubbled up inside her chest.
"Asshole."

He shrugged. "I believe in being prepared."

Apparently. Sitting back up, Blakely ripped into the
package. Gray held out his hand for the condom, but she
shooed him away. This was something she wanted to do.

Reaching for his hips, she guided him closer. Wrapping a hand around the long shaft of his sex, she relished
the weight and size of him. Heat seeped into her palm.
Friction added to it as she slid her hand up and down the
length of him several times.

Blakely relished his groan and the way his hips thrust
into her strokes. The walls of her own sex contracted.
She wanted to feel him deep inside.

She rolled down the condom over his length and positioned him at the opening to her body. Hands on her
hips, Gray paused, holding them both still.

Looking deeply into her eyes he said, "I'm sorry."

"For what?"

"It's been a while. This is probably going to be fast."

"How long is a while?"

"Almost eight years."

"Nope." No way was that possible. Sure, she understood why he was celibate for seven years, but he'd been
out of prison for almost a year. Was it really possible he
hadn't been with anyone that entire time?

"Why would I lie about something like that?"

He wouldn't. There was no reason to. "That's not what
I meant. I just…find it hard to believe someone as handsome and sexual as you has chosen to be celibate."

"I was indiscriminate when I was younger. The past several years taught me what was important. And I haven't found anyone I wanted to be with…until now."

Blakely had no idea what to make of that, but she really didn't have time to consider because Gray took that moment to thrust home.

Blakely's head dropped backward. Her eyes slid closed as she savored the indescribable feel of him. Gray gave her a few moments to adjust.

Hands on her hips, he held her firmly in place as he thrust. In and out, Gray set a pace that had tension and pleasure building steadily inside her.

Sex on the kitchen counter in a penthouse suite should have felt decadent and dangerous. Something completely out of her normal life. And in some ways this moment with Gray did feel like that. Eight years ago, if someone had told her she'd be here with Gray, she probably would have laughed in their face.

But now…

Blakely's hands ran across his body, touching, memorizing, exploring. He was buried deep inside her, and still she wanted him closer. Needed more of him.

This wasn't just physical, although there was no doubt they generated plenty of heat together.

Gray's mouth found hers, fusing them together in a way that mimicked the connection of their bodies. His tongue stroked deep inside even as his sex sank deep.

She felt the flutter of another orgasm teasing at the edges of her senses. Gray's thrusts became harder and deeper, his grip on her hips holding her tightly in place.

And then the world burst open around her again. Just as he let out a roar of relief. His body shuddered against hers. And somehow she found the brainpower to wrap her arms around him and hold him tight. Together, they collapsed, the edge of the kitchen counter the only thing keeping Gray upright.

His labored breaths panted in her ear. The room around her slowly started to come back into focus. And, eventually, Gray pulled away.

She expected him to say something smart. To make some quip to cut the tension and make light of what had just happened between them. Because that's what she needed to keep her head on straight.

Instead, Gray smoothed a hand over her face. He cupped her jaw and brought her close.

"That was everything I ever imagined and more."

Blakely's chest swelled and something soft fluttered deep inside her belly.

But the feeling didn't last long. How could it when he looked at her, his intense gaze trained solely on her and filled with a heat that nearly singed her skin.

"But I'm nowhere close to done with you tonight."

Eight

One night was clearly not enough time with Blakely. Even if that one night had been the best sex of his life... and that was saying a lot.

As closed off as Blakely was in her regular life, she was just as open and free in the bedroom. It was a surprising discovery. One he was grateful for.

But as much as he'd love to take advantage of their surroundings by keeping her in bed all day, that wasn't an option.

Trailing his lips down the curve of her naked spine, Gray murmured, "Rise and shine, sleepyhead."

With a groan, Blakely buried her head farther under the pile of pillows she'd burrowed beneath. An unintelligible mumble floated up from the mound, but he got the gist of it.

"We don't have a few more minutes to spare."

He'd already let her sleep in. After grabbing the pillow shielding her face, Gray threw it onto the floor beside the bed.

Rolling his way, she cracked open a single eye and glared at him. "Go away."

Who knew she could be so cute in the morning?

Grabbing the mug of coffee he'd set on the bedside table, Gray waved it beneath her nose. "I will, if you really want me to. But I'm pretty sure you were adamant about going with me yesterday."

"What kind of monster sets a meeting for the butt crack of dawn?"

Gray chuckled. "It's almost noon."

Blakely bolted upright. If he hadn't acted fast, her elbow would have connected with the mug in his hand, sending hot coffee flying across the bed.

"You're kidding."

"I'm not."

"Why'd you let me sleep this late? I never sleep this late."

Which was one reason he'd done it. He hadn't needed her to tell him to know she wasn't normally the type to sleep in. Blakely was a meet-the-day-at-dawn-and-work-until-well-into-the-evening kind of woman.

But it was also clear she wasn't used to staying up until almost two having sex.

"Letting you sleep was the least I could do after last night."

Blakely's gaze narrowed. Obviously, what he'd thought was a cute quip had hit her entirely wrong.

"Sleep for sex?"

"Uh, no."

Her gaze ran up and down his body, a confusing mixture of heat and disdain filling her eyes. "You obviously didn't feel the need to sleep in."

He'd gotten up a couple hours ago, showered and been handling a few things. "I don't sleep much."

Normally, he would have left the statement as it was, but for some reason more words followed. "Before prison I easily slept until past noon every day because I was up half the night. In prison…everything you do is regimented and controlled by the clock. They tell you when to sleep, eat and even go outside. I have a hard time sleeping in now, even when I want to."

The hard edge that had tightened Blakely's features eased. She collapsed back against the pile of pillows, her mouth twisting into a self-deprecating grimace. "I'm sorry."

"For what?"

"Waking up defensive. I'm not used to this."

Well, that had been obvious without the confession.

"I don't know how I'm supposed to act or what you expect."

Gray set the mug on the bedside table. Shifting, he sat on the bed and settled his hip into the curve of her waist.

"Blakely, I don't expect anything. And the only way you're supposed to act is whatever way feels right to you. You and I get to decide what we're doing and what we want from each other. Nothing else matters."

Her head tipped sideways as she considered him. "You're not at all what I thought."

"You've said that before."

"But I keep getting reminded."

Shifting higher against the headboard, she grasped the covers and tucked them beneath her arms, leaving her shoulders and collarbone bare.

What he really wanted to do was pull them back down again, lean forward and feast on her ripe breasts. Instead, he grabbed the coffee and held it out to her again.

Grasping the mug between her palms, she held it up to her face and pulled in a deep breath. Her eyes closed in bliss, her expression making his half-hard erection stir. She'd looked the same last night when he'd put his mouth on her.

Clearly, she liked her coffee. The look of surprise she sent him when she finally took her first sip was totally worth the extra effort he'd taken to make it just the way she liked it.

"How'd you know?"

Gray didn't pretend not to know exactly what she was asking. Shrugging, he said, "We've been working pretty closely together for the last week. I paid attention."

Her lips twisted into a wry smile. "I didn't."

"That's okay."

"No, I'm starting to realize it isn't."

Leaning forward, Blakely set her mug back on the bedside table. Rolling up onto her knees, she let the covers pool at her waist. "How much time did you say we have?"

"Not enough."

Her hands roamed over her naked body, kneading her breasts. The tight bud of her nipples peaked between her spread fingers. "You're sure?"

Gray groaned. He wanted to be the one touching her. "Unfortunately, I am." Grasping her wrists, Gray pulled her hands away. Leaning forward, he laved one nipple, the rough scrape of his tongue across her soft flesh sending a sharp spike of need through him. "But, trust me, I have plans for you later, Ms. Whittaker."

"Oh, you do, do you?"

"Absolutely."

After a weird and unusual day, Blakely found herself back at the hotel, sitting on the couch with her feet curled up underneath her. She was reading through several emails that had come through on her Stone Surveillance account. Surprisingly enough, she was starting to feel like a real member of the team. In fact, one of the other investigators had sent her a request to review some financial documents on another case.

The case was simple and it had taken her less than an hour to look at what he'd sent…but it was interesting. And when she'd been able to send back a message with her insight, she'd felt like she'd contributed to something important.

That hadn't happened in a very long time.

She was just shutting down her computer when a loud knock on the door startled her. The sound reverberated through the huge suite, reminding her just how alone she was right now. After they'd returned from the meeting with Surkov—which had been unproductive, to say the least—Gray had left her in the suite to "run a couple errands," whatever that meant.

Unfolding from the sofa, Blakely padded across the room, the marble floor cool against the soles of her feet.

"Who is it?" she asked, looking through the peephole. Unfortunately, all she could see was a cart full of bags and boxes and a pair of shiny shoes sticking out from the bottom.

"Ms. Whittaker? Mr. Lockwood sent up some clothes for you from the boutiques downstairs."

Why would he do that? She had a suitcase filled with perfectly good clothes.

Opening the door, Blakely was already shaking her head. "I'm sorry to waste your time, but I don't need anything."

A petite woman stuck her head around the side of

the cart and gave her a disarming smile. "He said you'd say that."

"Did he now?" Blakely wasn't certain what to think about that.

The woman nodded, her bangs flopping into her eyes. With a puff of breath, she blew the hair back out again, uncaring where the strands landed or how they looked. "He also said I wasn't allowed to leave until you let me inside. And he promised me a huge tip. Like a-week-of-salary huge, which I really need. So, please? Let me in?"

Blakely eyed the other woman. She couldn't be more than five-two, a hundred and ten pounds. Her face was round, but skinny. Her features were petite and yet somehow inviting. Maybe it was the disarming, begging smile that stretched her wide mouth. Or the contagious sparkle of excitement in her brown eyes. Either way, she was hardly threatening.

And there were logos from the shops Blakely had seen downstairs stamped on all the bags.

With a huff, Blakely pulled back and swept her arm wide, indicating the other woman should come in. Far be it for her to deny anyone a chance to make some money.

The other woman was practically bouncing as she wheeled the cart past Blakely. "I'm Desiree." With a grimace and a roll of her eyes, she continued, "Yeah, I know. It's awful. My mom was an eighties showgirl, convinced I was going to carry on the family legacy. To her utter shame, I have two left feet and about as much grace as a cactus."

Desiree pushed the cart into the center of the living room, stopped and took a quick turn around. "Nice." With a clap of her hands, she dismissed the opulence of the space and the amazing view outside the windows in favor of the loaded-down cart.

Tapping a finger against her lips, her eyes narrowed as she studied the things. Occasionally, she'd flip a considering glance over at Blakely.

"Not much to go on—"

"Hey!"

Desiree dismissed her indignation with a flip of her hand. "That's not what I meant. You're gorgeous. I meant I can't tell much about your personal style based on the oversize sweatshirt and bare feet you're currently wearing. I'm going to assume that's not your norm."

"You assume right."

"Mr. Lockwood gave me a few parameters and suggestions for what he'd like to see you in, but I'd like to get your input. Sure, we dress to impress the important man in our life, but you should feel amazing in it, too."

Was Gray the important man in her life? Blakely wasn't sure. Her libido definitely wanted a repeat performance of last night. And over the last week she'd come to realize, despite everything, that she might actually like the guy. But it was a huge leap from sex and mutual respect to him being the center of her universe.

A leap she was hardly ready to make.

"He's not important."

Desiree flipped her a disbelieving glance. "Trust me, I know people. He's important."

"Fine, but not to me."

Desiree gave her another expression that said "yeah, right," and shrugged. "If you say so."

"No, really. There's a lot you don't know about him. It's…complicated."

"Sister, it always is. Complicated makes life interesting."

"Interesting is dangerous."

Desiree shook her head. "Interesting is just interesting." Zipping open one of the bags, she revealed a sleek black jumpsuit. "Mr. Lockwood suggested you tend to wear very tailored clothing. Pieces that convey a sense of authority and control."

Interesting. Who knew he'd been studying her wardrobe? And apparently forming many opinions that he'd never voiced.

"He suggested you'd be most comfortable in something tailored and classic. But he also mentioned he'd like to give you the opportunity to try something new. To come out of your shell."

Come out of her shell? What did that mean? Was he passing judgment on her clothing choices? Blakely stared at the cart of things Gray had decided she needed to try.

Embarrassment and anger began to climb up her neck. "There's nothing wrong with the way I dress."

"Oh, I don't think that's what Mr. Lockwood meant."

"And just what did he mean?"

"He said he didn't think you'd had a lot of opportunity to indulge and play in your life, not even as a little girl. Which made me sad. I mean, every little girl should have a chance to play dress-up."

"So he wants me to dress up like a doll now?"

Blakely was lost, uncomfortable and out of her element. But she was also surprised because Gray had pegged her pretty closely. She'd never been the type to play in her mother's makeup or clomp around in her heels. In fact, looking back, she couldn't remember a lot of laughter or happiness in her childhood.

It wasn't that she'd been miserable. Or mistreated. There were plenty of kids who'd had it worse than her, by far. But...

"I think he just wants you to have a chance to feel beautiful."

Blakely blinked at Desiree. She couldn't remember a single time in her life when she'd felt truly beautiful. The suits she preferred to wear to the office made her feel powerful and competent. Prepared to handle anything that came her way.

She hadn't even gone to her high-school prom. Thinking back, she'd never actually owned a ball gown. Or had a reason to want one. And she wasn't exactly sure she wanted a fancy dress now. "I'm not big on pink puffy dresses."

Desiree laughed, the warm, sultry sound surprising Blakely. She'd expected the tiny thing to have a tinkly little laugh. "Good thing I don't have any of those here, then."

With a twinkle in her eye, Desiree began to pull several more outfits from their protective bags. One was a dark red floor-length gown that would no doubt cling to every curve she owned. And make her feel like she was practically naked. Another emerald green gown had a trumpet skirt that kicked out with a row of ruffles.

Nope, neither of those were going to work.

Blakely's eye kept going back to the black jumpsuit Desiree had unwrapped first. It had a subtle sparkle to it and it had taken her several minutes to realize the satin material had iridescent threads running through it.

Desiree revealed a few more outfits, one off-white and another bright purple. There was no way she was wearing either of those colors. She swept her hands across the selection. "Pick your poison—which one do you want to try first?"

"The black one," Blakely stated without hesitation.

"Somehow I knew that's what you'd go for. Are you sure you don't want to try one of the others on just for fun?"

"Not on your life." Nothing about the others appealed to her.

"Okay." After pulling the jumpsuit off the hanger, Desiree handed it to her. "Just slip it on and I'll zip you up."

With a deep breath, Blakely disappeared into the bedroom. She pulled the sweatshirt over her head and dropped it to the floor. Turning her back to the doorway, she put one foot and then the other inside the garment. Pulling it up and over her shoulders, Blakely realized what had looked rather conservative on the hanger was actually sexy as hell. There was no back at all to the jumpsuit.

The waist cinched in, accentuating her hourglass figure. It rode high on her shoulders, cutting shallowly across her collarbone. The edge of the material fell away dramatically in a waterfall that pooled at the small of her back. The drape of the material hugged the curve of her ass and the deceptively long length of her legs.

Because the back was naked, she couldn't wear a bra. Her breasts swung free, brushing tantalizingly against the soft material with each deep intake of breath. She could already feel her body responding at the thought of wearing this in front of Gray.

Her nipples tightened and peaked, rubbing against the fabric.

Blakely reached up, covering both breasts and massaging in an effort to relieve the pressure.

"Well, that's a sexy sight to walk in on."

Blakely jumped and gasped at the sound of Gray's voice. She immediately dropped her hands as if she'd been caught doing something inappropriate.

"Oh, no, you don't. Put those hands right back where they were."

Blakely's gaze tore up to the mirror on the dresser across from her. Gray's penetrating gaze stared back at her, watching her with a predatory gleam that made the ache deep inside her ratchet higher.

He stood in the doorway, one hip propped against the jamb, head cocked to the side studying her. Both hands were tucked into the pockets of his slacks. He was deceptively calm even as his gaze ate her up. At some point he'd shed the suit jacket he'd been wearing earlier. The sleeves of his white dress shirt were rolled up his arms, revealing heavy muscle and bulging veins running up the length of his forearms.

He shut the bedroom door. "We're alone." A single dark eyebrow winged up, silently demanding she do what he'd asked.

Slowly, Blakely's hands rose, settling back over her sensitive breasts.

"What were you thinking about?"

"You." The answer was simple and easy. But that's not what he was looking for.

"What about me? What had that look of pure pleasure crossing your beautiful face?"

There was something freeing about having the conversation through the reflection of the mirror. An added layer of distance that allowed her to be more open than she might have otherwise been.

"I was thinking about you taking me out of this outfit. Your mouth tugging on my swollen nipples. The scrape of the material across them was torture, so I was trying to ease the ache."

"Did it help?"

"Not really."

"Why not?"

"Because it wasn't what I wanted."

A smile played at the corners of his lush lips. "And what is it that you want?"

"You."

He shook his head. "You can do better than that."

"I want you to kiss me like you did last night. Like I was the air keeping you alive. I want you to run your fingers over every inch of my skin. I want your length buried deep inside me, stroking in and out until we're both panting from the need for relief."

Gray pushed away from the door, but his hands stayed firmly where they were. Slowly, she watched him walk forward, closing the gap between them. Blakely's body reacted by drawing tight with anticipation. She wanted him to give her what she'd asked for.

Thinking that was exactly what he was going to do, she braced.

But he didn't. Instead, he sidled up behind her, bending his head down so he could rain kisses across the top of her shoulders. His hands settled on her hips for several seconds, holding her in place.

Slowly, his hands slid up her body, over her breasts and shoulders. One hand curled around her throat, his thumb placing pressure beneath her chin. The hold wasn't hard or demanding. In fact, it was soft and gentle.

He urged her attention to shift from watching his movements in the mirror to looking at herself.

At first, she was uncomfortable, her gaze continuing to slide away. But each time it did, the pressure of his thumb urged her back again. Finally, realizing the faster she complied, the faster he was going to let her go, Blakely gave in and did what he wanted.

"What do you see?"

"Me."

"Tell me more," he coaxed.

Blakely shrugged. "My hair's a mess. The jumpsuit is gorgeous, but not something I'd ever have a reason to wear again. I'm short and should have put on some makeup this morning. I look tired."

"You do look tired, but that's because you were up half the night having passionate sex, which should be a good thing."

"It is a good thing."

"Then why do you say that with regret?"

Because she didn't like looking like something the cat had dragged in. Especially next to him. "You look like you've just stepped off the front cover of some men's fashion magazine. It isn't fair."

Gray chuckled. "I'll take that as a compliment."

Of course he would.

"Would you like to know what I see?"

"Yes."

No. Blakely's shoulders tightened. Did she really want to know?

"You're absolutely gorgeous, Blakely. Your skin is pale and perfectly soft. Those ice-blue eyes draw me in every time I look at you. But it's not just the unusual color. They're so bright with intelligence, curiosity and integrity."

"You mean judgment."

"I meant exactly what I said. Your messy hair reminds me that last night I was the one responsible for making it that way. I remember grabbing a fist of it and holding you exactly where I wanted you. And I remember that you let me. You're a damn strong woman, Blakely. I've known that from the first time we met. But last night... you felt safe enough with me to let go. Which only makes me want to give you more opportunities to do that."

"Is that what this is about?"

"What *what* is about?"

"The clothes?"

"Something like that. And we were invited to attend a VIP event at an exclusive club tonight. I thought it would be fun."

"You were invited." Blakely hadn't been invited to much of anything in her life, let alone a VIP Vegas party.

Gray shrugged. "Only because no one here knows you yet. You're beautiful, intelligent and forthright. Qualities most people appreciate. And when you decide to let go a little, you're amazingly fun. You're going to be a hit tonight."

Blakely scoffed. Now he was just blowing smoke up her ass.

"And with you wearing that outfit, I'm going to have to post a sign of ownership over your head to protect what's mine."

Blakely's eyebrows rose. "Buddy, I'm not yours or anyone else's. No one owns me."

Gray's mouth spread into a wide grin that crinkled the edges of his eyes. "I know. I just wanted to hear your response."

Nine

He was playing a dangerous game, but something told him it would be worth it.

For the past week Gray had studied Blakely. Even when he'd been trying to ignore her, he couldn't help himself. Which meant he'd learned a lot in those days.

But he'd learned even more about her last night.

Watching her relax and let go with him had been… perfection. A gift.

But it had also made him realize he wanted more from her than a stolen weekend in Vegas. However, he wasn't entirely certain she'd be open to the idea of actually being with him.

He hadn't really had a meeting this afternoon, just a need for some space to clear his head. At some point he'd come to the conclusion that it didn't particularly matter what Blakely thought she wanted—it was his job to convince her they could be real and more than just a few stolen moments, even if those moments had been combustible and amazing.

So he was on a mission to seduce her, not just physically, but mentally. And the first step of that was hopefully giving her a chance to loosen up and enjoy herself, something he didn't think she'd had the opportunity to do nearly enough.

Because he wanted to see more of that sparkle in her eyes. The wonder and relief. That easy smile—hard-won, but totally worth the effort.

And right now was the perfect opportunity.

Gray watched Blakely's reflection in the bedroom mirror. She was beautiful even before the team of makeup artists and hairstylists showed up in a bit to do their thing. He'd picked out the jumpsuit himself, knowing it would be perfect for her. He'd also instructed Desiree to give her several other options, just in case he'd been wrong.

But he hadn't been.

He also wasn't wrong that it would look amazing on her.

The outfit was pure class and sophistication, but with a touch of drama at the back. And he couldn't wait to get his hands on the gleaming expanse of satiny skin left bare.

If he touched her right now, though, they'd never leave the suite. And as tempting as that idea was, he wanted to give her a night out first.

"Relax, Blakely, and enjoy the experience."

"Easy for you to say," she grumbled.

"No, it really isn't," Gray countered, his voice filling with wry humor. There was a time in his life that putting on a tux and attending some fancy party was the norm. No, not just the norm. He'd felt a sense of entitlement to be invited. Like the world and everyone in it owed him simply because of who he was.

However, it had been a long time since he'd bothered to enjoy the kind of party they were going to attend. Oh, it would have been easy to revert to old bad behavior once he'd been released. Especially after his father and mother had looked him in the eye and told him they'd be happy to never see him again.

But his time in prison had made him stronger than who he used to be.

That didn't mean he wasn't looking forward to bringing a little glamour and sparkle into Blakely's life. Something told him she'd been seriously lacking in those two things for a very long time.

She might be severely out of her element, but she deserved to have a Cinderella moment.

"You've got about thirty minutes before the rest of the staff shows up to help you get ready."

"Staff? What the heck are you talking about?"

"Hair and makeup."

"You think I can't do my own hair and makeup?" Blakely asked indignantly.

"Of course I know you can. But most women find it fun to let someone else do those kinds of things occasionally."

"I'm not most women."

Gray closed the space between them. Hands to her shoulders, he spun her around so she was facing him. "Of that, I'm keenly aware," he murmured before dropping his head and finding her mouth.

The kiss was deep and hot, a blazing inferno within seconds. Touching her always made him want. Gray let the connection pull him in and under—he relished the taste and feel of her.

It would have been so easy to just give in and let the moment spin out of control. But, somehow, he found the strength to pull back. "Can you do me a favor?" he asked, staring deep into her pale eyes.

Expression glazed with desire and need, she mutely nodded. When she looked at him that way…it was hard to think about anything else.

"Stop fighting me and assuming the worst out of everything I do and say."

"I expect the worst."

A tight band squeezed around his chest. "I know."

Reaching up, he smoothed her soft hair away from the edge of her face. It really bothered him that she'd been taught by everyone in her life to be so wary, including the people who were supposed to protect her the most.

"I have only the best intentions where you're concerned, Blakely. You're a remarkable woman and I simply want to show you how much I value your company."

"I don't need expensive clothes and people waiting on me hand and foot."

No, she didn't. Most of the women who'd been in his life would have accepted his gesture without comment. Hell, they would have expected it. But not Blakely. "Which is exactly why I want to give those things to you. Let me."

She blinked. Slowly, she nodded.

"Excellent. As much as I'd like nothing better than to strip you out of this outfit right now, that's going to have to wait until later. You have twenty minutes to shower before everyone gets here."

After spinning her away from him, Gray pushed her forward. She stumbled a step, but quickly found her footing. Shooting him a perturbed look over her shoulder, he couldn't help but take advantage of the perfect target in front of him.

Reaching out, he smacked her on the rear. "Hop to it."

Blakely yelped and glared at him. No doubt, he'd pay for that later, but he was looking forward to that, too.

Retracing his steps into the living room, he asked Desiree to leave all the accessories that matched the jumpsuit before dismissing her.

Dropping into a chair by the massive wall of windows, he ignored the spectacular view spread out before him. The city was alive with light and activity, but none of that interested him. Instead, he opened his email on his phone and began sifting through the business he'd been ignoring for most of the day.

The dead end with Surkov hadn't come as a surprise. And yet, he'd still left the meeting disappointed. Because he really was no closer today to figuring out who had set him up than he'd been months ago.

The longer he went without a credible lead, the more nervous he was becoming. Because without understanding what had happened, who had set him up and what their motive had been, the possibility that it could happen again lurked around every corner. The damage to his life had blindsided him. And he was willing to do whatever was necessary in order to make damn sure it didn't happen again.

And now, Blakely was involved. Which could potentially put her at risk. A reality he did not like.

With a sigh, Gray zeroed in on the email from Joker that had come in several hours ago. Opening it up, he was hopeful until he realized it was a report on his birth mother, not anything to do with the embezzlement.

Reading the details about the woman who'd given birth to him, basically sold him and then attempted to blackmail his mother did not give him a warm, fuzzy feeling. Apparently, she'd continued to live a high-profile life here in Vegas. At least until the last few years, when her beauty and talent had begun to fade and she couldn't trade on them anymore to support her excessive lifestyle.

She'd gone from having her name featured on the marquee to being a nameless face in the background. Without even meeting her, he had a feeling that hadn't gone over well.

Not to mention, she'd apparently had connections with some questionable people over the years. Joker had discovered that her long-term boyfriend was a well-known criminal.

After reading the report twice, Gray finally closed the document and tossed his phone onto the table in front of him. Nothing inside him wanted to deal with the situation right now. Tomorrow would be soon enough to confront his birth mother and tell her the blackmail wouldn't work; she was going to have to find another cash cow to bankroll her high-roller tendencies.

With a sigh, Gray sank back into the chair. He rubbed his eyes, realizing they were gritty with fatigue for the first time since he'd gotten up this morning. Not surprising, considering he and Blakely had been awake half the night.

He must have fallen asleep, because one moment he was contemplating getting up and taking a shower so he could be ready whenever Blakely was, and the next she was leaning over him, shaking his shoulder and murmuring his name. "Gray…"

Slowly, he blinked his eyes open, his vision bleary and unfocused. A halo of light shone around Blakely's head, like the ring of light depicted in paintings of Mary. Her entire being glowed. It wasn't a description he'd normally use for Blakely. She was many things, but maternally divine wasn't one of them.

However, there was no debating that the glow came from deep inside her. She was radiant in a way that made him want to worship at her feet.

"Gray, are you okay?"

Slowly, everything came into focus. He sat up and Blakely took several steps back, giving him a perfectly unobstructed view of her.

"You're breathtaking."

A deep blush crept up her skin. Clearly, she didn't receive enough compliments. He was going to have to remedy that.

But right now, he needed to get them out of this room, or all the effort the team he'd hired had put into Blakely's appearance would be wasted because they'd never leave the suite.

Standing, Gray texted their driver that they were on the way down, then slipped his phone into his pocket. He held a hand out to her and waited, slightly surprised when she actually twined her fingers with his.

He snagged his suit coat and led them out into the waiting elevator. Wrapping an arm around her, Gray used their joined hands at the small of her back to press her tight against his side. He loved the feel of her there. The way the lush curves of her breasts settled heavily against his arm. The subtle scent of her tantalized his senses. And he could feel the heat of her moist breath against his neck.

"Where are we going?"

"Excess—it's a club downtown."

"Sounds very Vegas."

Gray chuckled. "It's popular enough. I know the owner."

"Partied there often, did you?"

A wry smile tugged at his lips. "Something like that."

The ride in the car was quiet. Blakely would never be the kind of woman to fill a silence with chatter, which was something Gray happened to like about her. When she had something important or profound to share, she did it. Otherwise, she kept her thoughts to herself.

Which intrigued him. Because he really wanted to know what went on behind those intelligent, beautiful eyes.

The drive didn't take long. Less than twenty minutes later they were ensconced in the VIP area on the second floor, overlooking the bustle of the club and the main dance floor below. They had a private waitstaff, dancers and floor of their own.

Gray didn't bother to ask Blakely what she wanted, but ordered drinks for them both. His mission tonight was to get her loosened up enough to see her dance, something he'd hazard Blakely hadn't done much in her life.

A perfect reason for him to want to make it happen.

They'd been sitting there for about fifteen minutes when a heavy hand landed on his shoulder. Gray's heart raced and adrenaline shot into his system. He reacted, snapping a hand down over the wrist and barely checking himself before he could use leverage and power to break the person's arm and throw him over the back of the chair and onto the floor at his feet.

But he wasn't in the middle of a crude fighting ring.

Blakely sat forward, spilling her drink as she settled it on the table in front of them. She was halfway out of her seat, panic in her eyes, before he could stop her.

Shaking his head, he silently told her he was fine. Although, the hitch in his lungs suggested that might be a lie.

"Good to see you back here, my friend," a familiar

voice, clearly oblivious to just how close he'd come to having his arm broken, rumbled from behind him.

Pulling in a huge gulp of air, Gray willed his body to settle. Pasting a smile on his face, he turned and stood in a fluid motion, dislodging the heavy hold from his shoulder.

Clapping a hand across Dominic's shoulder, he said, "It's good to be back."

Blakely's heart was still in her throat as Gray turned to make introductions.

She'd seen the look of shock and involuntary reaction before Gray had shut it down. His body tensed, every vein popping into relief down his muscled arms. His eyes had hardened, turning to the most cold and deadly emerald green she'd ever seen.

A part of her had always recognized Gray had a hidden edge of danger, but there was no doubt she'd almost gotten a firsthand introduction to it right now. Luckily, he had impeccable control over his physical reflexes.

For the first time, Blakely realized she was standing. Her fingers were curled around the edge of the table. Loosening her grip, she held out a hand to the man now standing beside Gray.

"Blakely Whittaker, meet Dominic Mercado."

Dominic leaned forward into the space between them. He grasped her hand in both of his, giving hers a squeeze instead of actually shaking it. "Please tell me you're willing to dump this asshole and spend the evening with me instead."

Gray lifted a single eyebrow. "I'm the asshole? You're the man hitting on my date right in front of me."

Dominic's eyes twinkled as he offered her a wide grin. "I've learned in life, it's folly to ignore the opportunities in front of you. And I'd kick myself if I let this vision walk away without at least taking a shot."

"Too bad for you, she's already taken."

This time, it was Dominic's turn to cock an eyebrow. "Perhaps you should let the lady speak for herself. Are you going to choose this scoundrel over an upstanding citizen and business owner like myself?"

Blakely's gaze bounced back and forth between the two men for several moments. They were clearly friendly, but with an undercurrent of rivalry running beneath their exchange.

Gray simply watched her, waiting for her reaction. Although, his gaze did narrow when it slipped down to take in the way Dominic still had a hold of her hand.

Finally, Blakely turned to Dominic. Tugging gently, she pulled out of his grasp.

"I'm flattered."

Dominic sighed and shook his head. "No, you're not."

Blakely rolled her eyes. "Gray isn't a scoundrel. And something tells me 'upstanding citizen' might be a stretch."

Dominic's grin widened. "Perceptive, isn't she?"

Gray's entire body relaxed. "That she is. Smart as hell, too."

"Lucky bastard."

"You have no idea." Holding out a hand, Gray pulled her into the shelter of his body and she accepted. "Thanks for the info I asked for."

Dominic gave Gray a smile, this one actually genuine. "You're welcome. Anything for you, man, although I don't understand why you're looking into Vegas showgirls with questionable taste in men. Please tell me you're not looking to invest in a show or something stupid."

"Nothing like that. I'm part owner in a surveillance company and she's connected to a case we're working."

Dominic's mouth curled into a grimace. "Not surprising. Her boyfriend has a nasty reputation and I wouldn't be surprised to find out she's up to her neck in the bad shit, too."

"There's plenty of that to be found in this town."

Dominic's gaze scraped over the crowd around them. "Isn't that the truth? Well, I'm going to go back behind the bar and appease my wounded ego with an expensive glass of single-malt scotch." Tipping two fingers to his forehead, he offered them a salute, then said, "Enjoy yourselves. Let my staff know if you need anything."

Gray nodded, his grip around her waist tightening as Dominic turned to leave. Blakely watched as he melted into the crowd, stopping at several tables to speak briefly to people here and there.

From out of nowhere, a tall redhead in a flashy sequined dress stalked up to him. Blakely couldn't hear their words over the roar of music, but clearly the conversation was heated. And the affable, charming, slightly smarmy persona Dominic had been wearing disappeared. His entire body language changed.

Wrapping a hand around her upper arm, he pulled her in so they were practically nose to nose. And then let her go again when she used her other hand to shove him away. Spinning on her heel, the redhead disappeared into the crowd.

And Dominic simply watched her go. But his hands were balled into fists at his sides and his chest heaved as he tried to get ahold of his response.

"Well, that was interesting."

Blakely's attention turned back to Gray. "How so?"

"The redhead? That's his little sister's best friend. I

dated Annalise, his sister, for about two minutes when we were in our early twenties, which is how I met Dominic. Our friendship stuck when the relationship didn't. I didn't realize Meredith was still around."

Shaking his head, Gray's mouth twisted into a wry grimace. "I suppose a lot happened while I was gone. Not that it matters."

The techno music that had been blasting into the space changed. The tempo slowed, even though there was still a thump of bass running beneath the sounds. Several people streamed off the dance floor as others moved on.

Gray didn't bother to ask as he tugged her onto the dance floor.

Grasping her hand, he spun her out and then pulled her back in. Her body settled against the hard planes of his. Thanks to last night, she knew intimately what his Greek-god body looked like beneath the sophisticated layer of his suit.

And she immediately wanted to experience that wonderland again. Her hand snuck beneath his jacket, sliding along the rough texture of his tailored shirt. His body heat warmed her palm. And she loved the way he arched into her touch. Her fingers found the edge of his slacks and teased down as far as they could go. Unfortunately, she couldn't quite reach the bare skin of his ass.

However, his hands could find naked skin. One palm spread wide at the small of her back. His own fingertips tantalized as they dipped into the opening just above the dint of her ass. Pulling her close, he folded his other hand between their two bodies, strategically using the cover of the dance to hide the fact that he was running a fingernail across the distended bud of her nipple.

"I'm pretty sure that's not playing fair," Blakely gasped.

Her entire body began to tingle.

"No, I'm pretty sure this jumpsuit isn't playing fair."

"You're the one who picked it out."

"True. Who knew I was into torture? Knowing you're wearing nothing under this thing has been driving me crazy all night."

Pulling back, Blakely stared up at Gray. "Remind me, why are we still here?"

A grin played at the edges of his lips. "That's a good damn question."

As much as Gray wanted to accept the dare in her heated gaze, there was something they had to do first.

"We have one more stop to make…it's time I met my mother."

Ten

Getting backstage had never been hard for him. Money and notoriety provided access to more than most people wanted to believe. His conviction hadn't simply made the local news, but had hit the national media circuit. On the heels of several high-profile financial scandals, his was just another in a trend…or that's how the media machine had spun it.

Which had pissed off his father. That man did not subscribe to the any-publicity-is-good-publicity mentality.

Gray would admit that for most of his life, walking through doors locked to everyone else gave him a small thrill. A sense of power, right or wrong. Tonight, his stomach just churned when the guard looked at the cash he'd slipped into his hand and then swept them past without so much as a change in his facial expression.

Several steps down the darkened hallway, Blakely pulled him to a stop. Her calming hand rested on his arm as she turned to face him.

"You okay?"

No, he really wasn't. Normally, he'd have kept that confession to himself, but for some reason Gray let the confession free. "I'm a nervous wreck."

A short burst of laughter shot between them. Okay, not the reaction he'd expected.

"You certainly don't look it. I'm starting to realize the calm, reserved exterior you show the world might hide a whole lot."

It was Gray's turn to chuckle, but Blakely wasn't wrong. Long before prison, his father had taught him emotions were something that made you weak. The world rewarded strength, even if it was a facade.

Gray could count on one hand the number of people who recognized that about him, though. And those people were all the most important ones in his life. The idea that Blakely could join that group…made him even more nervous than knowing he was about to meet Cece, his mother.

Leaning back against the wall, Gray wrapped his arms around Blakely and pulled her tight against his body. His mouth found hers in a brutal kiss that gave him the strength he needed.

The feel of her settled him. Centered him in a way only getting in the ring had done before. The way she opened to him, melted against him, made him feel powerful and protective. He let the moment spin, allowing the connection he felt with Blakely to overshadow everything else.

She was the one to finally break the kiss. Pulling back, she whispered, "We need to go."

Shaking his head, Gray knew she was right. But a huge part of him wanted to stay in this dingy hallway with her. To freeze this moment and hold on to it. Hold on to her.

Pressing his forehead to hers, Gray let his eyes drift closed. "Thank you for being here."

Her hands, resting on his hips, squeezed. "I wouldn't be anywhere else. You're not alone in this, Gray."

Damn, it had been a long time since he'd felt that was true. His parents, the people who were supposed to support him and love him unconditionally, had turned their backs when he'd needed them most. They'd believed the lies instead of him.

Sure, Stone and Finn had his back. Of that he was one hundred percent certain. Not just because they said they did, but because they'd proven it time and again. But they both had their own lives. They were married and were hip-deep in building Stone Surveillance. No doubt they'd drop everything if he needed them, but their focus shouldn't be his problems and his life.

And Blakely… Right now, she made him feel like he mattered. She was the most amazing woman he'd ever met, and if she could care about him, maybe that meant he was actually a good person, worthy of someone else caring.

Gray was about three seconds away from saying to hell with it and taking her home without doing what they'd come here to do, when a wolf whistle sounded from down the hall. "Get a room!"

A wry smile lit Blakely's ice-blue eyes as she pushed away from him. Her hand slid down his arm until her fingers were twined with his. She didn't wait for him, but used their connection to bring him along behind her as they continued down the hallway.

The mountain of meat at the door had told him Cece was in the second-to-last room on the left. The closer they got to that end of the long hallway, the more noise could be heard. The tinkle of laughter and rumble of voices.

The ring of hangers against metal rods and the dull thud of things being dropped onto a wooden surface.

They passed one room that was occupied by a group of women. Glancing in, they were half-naked and didn't particularly care the door was standing wide open. Bright, naked bulbs ringed multiple large mirrors. Several women were leaning forward, applying makeup to their faces.

The cacophony didn't surprise Gray. It also didn't hold his attention for anything more than a passing glance. Blakely, on the other hand, slowed, her eyes glued to the sight. Her expression was blank and controlled, so he couldn't tell what thoughts were spinning behind her gorgeous eyes. If he had to guess, though, the thought of being half-naked in a room with twelve other women would give her hives. She wasn't exactly a prude, but she was fairly private.

Later, he'd ask. But right now, he was laser-focused on getting this over with. Something told him his mother wasn't likely to greet him with a teddy bear she'd been carrying around for the last thirty-four years hoping for the opportunity to give it to him.

He didn't live in a Hollywood movie. Not to mention, she'd sent a blackmail demand.

His nerves from before hadn't disappeared, but they'd been joined by a healthy ribbon of anger. Justified or not, it was there and if he wasn't careful, it might color the coming encounter.

The room that the security guy had directed him to was much different from the one they'd just passed. The door was closed, and there was no noise emanating from behind the solid surface.

Gray didn't bother knocking. He simply turned the old round knob and pushed.

The woman in front of the mirror on the far wall spun. Her face was ripe with surprise that quickly morphed into anger. Her eyebrows, clearly exaggerated with stage makeup, slammed down into an angry V.

Gray wasn't certain what he'd expected. Maybe to feel this cosmic connection. Or maybe experience a bone-deep recognition. But there was nothing. The woman looking back at him was a complete stranger.

Oh, certainly, he could recognize features of himself in her. The set of her mouth was familiar. The shape of her eyes, even if hers were brown while his were green. But that was it.

Dispassionately, Gray cataloged her as a woman. Clearly, she'd been beautiful once. Her skin was sagging and lined, but the array of jars behind her suggested she spent time and money to preserve what she could. Her hair was thick and shiny, and hung down her back in lush waves.

She'd also taken time and effort to keep her body in top physical shape. She was slender, and her collarbone jutted out.

Cece stood. The heavy wooden chair she'd been sitting in clattered to the floor. "What are you doing here?"

Gray reached behind him and closed the door. The quiet click reverberated through the room.

"You know who I am." Gray didn't bother to make the statement a question. It was clear from her reaction that she did.

"Of course I know who you are."

Gray huffed with sarcastic laughter. "There's no 'of course' about it, considering I didn't know you existed until two days ago."

"And whose fault is that?"

"I'm going to say yours since you sold me when I was just a few days old."

Her mouth twisted into a nasty expression, and suddenly, Gray realized she wasn't beautiful after all. It was a facade, like everything else about her. "Is that what he told you? Of course he made me out to be the bad guy."

"My father didn't tell me anything. How could he? He hasn't spoken to me in almost eight years."

Her eyes glittered with malice. "That bitch's account wouldn't be any better."

"I assume the bitch you're referring to is my mother."

"No, *I'm* your mother."

Her words made his stomach roll. Oh, he'd known they were true, but hearing her say them out loud, especially with a sneer in her voice, made him want to cringe. Or deck her. But he refused to do either.

"No, you're not. Neither is she, for that matter. But that's none of your business. I'm here to tell you the secret isn't a secret anymore. You can send threatening letters to whomever you'd like, but they're not going to do you any good. No one is giving you more money."

Cece slammed a container of makeup onto the table behind her. It exploded, a puff of powder raining over the surface. "I'm going to kill that little bitch if I ever find her."

Gray took a menacing step forward. Blakely's hand shot out, curling around his bicep and holding him in place. "Did you just threaten my mother?" She might not have been much of one to him, and certainly not when he'd needed her most, but he wasn't about to let this woman get away with threatening her anymore.

"No. I don't give a shit what your mother does. I'm going to kill your sister. Once again, she's managed to ruin everything and she isn't even here."

Out of all the revelations he'd gotten in the last few days, those words actually rocked Gray's world. He went backward on his heels, as if he'd just received an uppercut to the jaw. If Blakely hadn't been standing behind him, he might have fallen to the floor.

"What sister?"

He had a sister.

A sneer twisted Cece's lips. "Half sister."

He had a sister.

"Where is she?"

"That's a damn good question. I haven't seen her in about eight years."

Was it a coincidence his sister had disappeared around the same time he'd gone to jail? Warning bells clanged inside Gray's brain.

"Why?"

Cece stared at him for several seconds, then said, "Screw it." She collapsed back into the chair. "Not much you can do about it, anyway."

Something told him he wasn't going to like whatever she had to say.

"The worthless little shit disappeared the same night she moved twenty million dollars into your bank account. She was supposed to move another twenty million into my account, but obviously that never happened."

His *sister* had set him up. A sister he never even knew existed.

Why? Why would she do that? What had he done that she'd wanted to ruin his entire life? And was she still a threat?

Gray's stomach clenched tight. This conversation had just taken a severe turn he'd not been prepared for.

"Why would she frame me for embezzlement?"

"She wasn't supposed to. She was supposed to frame

your father. My guess is she screwed up and put the money into the wrong account. I didn't even know it had happened until the story hit the news and I realized the mess."

His father had been the original target? They did share a name. Gray was a nickname he'd used since he was a little boy. All of his accounts were obviously set up in his legal name, something he never thought of because he didn't actually use it.

"Why would she frame my father?"

"Because I'd hit a rough patch and he refused to help me out when I went to him."

"So you decided to rob him? What does that have to do with my sister?"

"Your sister is a computer genius. There isn't a system she can't access or a site she can't crash."

His sister was a hacker? And from what his mother said, a talented one.

"How'd she learn those skills?" That wasn't the kind of thing you were born instinctively knowing. Sure, certain people had an aptitude, but they still had to learn. Especially the illegal stuff.

"Michael, her father, recognized her talent when she was young. She was the kind of kid who'd spend hours taking apart the computer I bought her for Christmas just to see what the guts looked like and whether she could put them back together again. It didn't take long to figure out she was just as amazing at breaking codes." His mother shrugged her shoulders. "One puzzle is as good as another. He took her under his wing and trained her. She was seriously beneficial in his business."

His illegal business. Dominic had provided Gray with a bit of information about Michael when he'd passed along some details about Cece. While Joker had uncovered quite a bit, Gray had decided that getting insight from a local was just smart.

His mother had let her boyfriend use her daughter for criminal activity. Gray shouldn't be surprised, all things considered, but he was. "How old was she?"

"When she started?" She shrugged. "Seven or eight. When she screwed you? Sixteen."

Gray saw red. His mother had been exploiting his sister while she was too young to know better. She'd grown up committing crimes and didn't know any other life.

"Framing you was a mistake. She didn't even know you existed. But disappearing with my money—that was all planned."

No doubt. Gray couldn't help but be proud of his sister for her resourcefulness. Even if he'd been the one to pay the price with seven years of his life.

Although, that was assuming his sister wasn't aware of what she was doing. If she'd screwed him on purpose…

"You have no idea where she is?"

"If I did, do you think I'd have sent that note to your mom?"

No, she wouldn't.

Gray let his gaze drift up and down, taking in the woman who'd given birth to him. Even through the heavy makeup he could tell she was tired and worn. Her shoulders were slumped and the caked-on makeup had settled into the deep lines around her mouth.

The only word that came to Gray's mind was pathetic. She'd spent her life trading on her beauty to get what she wanted, but was clearly starting to realize external beauty faded. And now she was screwed because she didn't have a backup plan.

"Don't bother sending any more threatening notes.

You won't be getting any more money from anyone in my family."

"I'll go to the media."

Gray shrugged. "Go ahead. Do you really think a thirty-five-year-old sex scandal will matter to anyone?"

Cece laughed, the sharp sound scraping across his eardrums. "Your name is still big in the media. They'll eat up the story."

"No one will care. I've been out of prison for almost a year. Hell, my parole is finished in a couple months."

Blakely's fingers squeezed his arm again. She hadn't said a single thing during the exchange, but he'd known she was right beside him.

"Go ahead. See how far that gets you. You can only sell the story once."

Gray took a few steps backward. The expression on Cece's face left his belly churning—not because he was concerned, but because she looked utterly devastated and broken.

But that wasn't his problem. She was no one to him.

His sister, on the other hand, was someone he wanted to talk to.

From across the aisle on the plane, Blakely watched Gray. He'd been quiet and distant since they'd walked away from his mother. At first, she'd worried he was about to lose it and tear into the woman. But she should have known better. Gray Lockwood had tight control, even in the midst of utter turmoil.

Hell, she was still trying to digest the information bomb his mother had dropped and it had nothing to do with her.

She'd been quiet for a while, but at some point, they were going to have to talk about it.

"What are you going to do?"

Gray turned to her, his gaze distant and unfocused. "What?"

"What are you going to do?"

His gaze sharpened. He blinked several times. "Find my sister."

Obviously, she never expected anything less. "Are you going to tell the authorities about Cece and her role in everything?"

With a sigh, Gray let his head drop back against the seat. Reaching up, he rubbed his fingers into his eyes. "No, I don't have any proof."

"You have me as a witness."

"Sure, and considering we're sleeping together, that'll go over well."

"No one knows."

Gray's hands fell into his lap. He stared at her for a few seconds. "At the very least, everyone knows we've been working closely together."

"Surely there's a way to make your mother and her boyfriend pay for what they did."

"I doubt it. It's not likely there's a trail to follow, but I'll have Joker see what he can dig up. At least now he knows where to look, which should help. But I'm going to assume they were very careful about getting their hands dirty. And without the trail of money to trace back to them…it's going to be difficult to prove."

"Your sister is the linchpin."

Gray's body sagged against the leather. "She is. I need Joker to track her, as well. Same thing, knowing where to start will hopefully make the job easier."

Maybe, but his mother had said *they* hadn't been able to find her for the last eight years. And something told

Blakely they'd worked at finding her since the girl potentially had twenty million dollars.

Eight years of being missing—that was a long time. Blakely didn't want to say it out loud, but maybe she was dead. His sister had been sixteen, after all, when she'd disappeared. Even with twenty million, it must have been difficult to be on her own.

Blakely might have felt like her father had abandoned her, choosing his friends and a life that took him away from them, but at least she'd always had her mother to count on. To shelter and protect her. It sounded like Gray's sister hadn't had anyone to care about her. Blakely could hardly imagine the woman they'd seen tonight being anything close to maternal.

"When we get back, I'll tell Stone you're available for other assignments. I know he has a couple he could use your help on."

"No."

Gray's eyebrows beetled into a deep frown. "You're not still hell-bent on leaving Stone Surveillance, are you? Not only are you good at this kind of work, you enjoy it. Don't try to deny that."

Why would she deny it? "Yes, I really enjoy it. I enjoy putting the pieces together and solving the puzzle. I love feeling like what I'm doing might make a real difference to someone. But…"

"So why do you want to leave?"

"No one said anything about leaving. I'll stay as long as I have a job."

"I'm confused."

"My assignment with you isn't finished."

Gray shook his head. "Yes, it is. You agreed to help me figure out what happened. Now I know."

"Maybe, but the bread crumbs don't end there, do

they? I owe you a hell of a lot. The least I can do is see this through."

"You don't owe me anything, Blakely."

That's where he was terribly wrong. She owed him seven years of his life, but there was no way she could give those back to him. "You're wrong. My testimony was key to putting you behind bars for a crime you didn't commit."

Gray opened his mouth to protest, but Blakely wasn't having any of it. Holding up a hand, she said, "Don't even bother denying it. We both know it's true. How do you think that makes me feel? Knowing I'm responsible for you losing seven years of your life? Being disowned by your family and barred from the company and your heritage?"

Instead of smoothing out Gray's frown, her words had the opposite effect. Dark anger swirled in the deep green depths of his eyes. "Do you think I want your pity?"

"No, so it's a good thing what I'm feeling is far from pity."

"Ha." Gray let out a growling huff. "Guilt and pity are wafting off you so strongly I'm practically strangling on them. Blakely, what happened to me is not your fault. Nor is it your responsibility to atone for anything."

"Is that what you think? That I'm atoning for some self-assessed sin?"

"Isn't it?"

God, the man was infuriating and a major pain in her ass sometimes.

"No. I'm fully aware the only ones truly responsible for what happened to you are the people involved in framing you—your mother, her boyfriend and your sister."

Gray flinched, which made her regret the words, even if they were the truth.

"We started something. I won't abandon you or what we're doing simply because we got a few of the answers. Especially not when those answers raised more questions."

"Maybe I don't want your help anymore."

It was Blakely's turn to flinch. His words hit her straight in the chest, bruising her just as much as any real punch could have.

"Is that true?"

"Hell, no. I never could have gotten this far without you."

"So why are you trying to push me away?"

Gray closed his eyes. With a groan, he sank back into the chair. "Because you scare the hell out of me."

The confession was just as startling as anything else he'd said to her. "*I* scare you? That's impossible. I'm no one with no significance."

This time, when Gray looked at her with anger in his eyes, the emotion was clearly directed straight at her. "Don't ever say that again. Yes, you scare me. I've truly known you for a little over a week and in that time, you've become the most important person in my life. But my life is utter crap at the moment and I really don't want to drag anyone else into it, least of all someone I actually like and am starting to care a great deal for."

Blakely's mouth opened and closed. Words formed in her head, but wouldn't tumble out. Until she finally said, "Oh."

"Yeah, oh."

What the heck was she supposed to do with that? "I'm past starting to care a great deal for you, Gray. And you've quickly become the most important person in my life, too."

Apparently, she was going to be more honest with him than she'd meant to. Suddenly, a wave of heat washed over her body. What was she doing? Uneasiness filled her, not because she didn't mean what she'd said, but because the truth of her words made her vulnerable in a way she'd never let herself become before.

Relationships had never been her strength. In fact, she'd been accused of being cold and reserved by more than one boyfriend. And, no doubt, they'd all been right. Her father had taught her not to trust, a lesson that had been damn hard to unlearn.

Even now, the thought of letting Gray that close, letting him become important to her, had alarm bells going off inside her head. She was stupid for even considering it, wasn't she?

A week ago, she would have convinced herself that the fact he was a criminal meant he couldn't be trusted… but knowing what she did now, that felt like a cop-out.

But it also didn't make it any easier to let down those protective walls.

"You should take the opportunity I'm giving you and walk away."

Every self-preservation instinct inside her was screaming to do exactly as he suggested. But she couldn't make herself do it.

She didn't want to.

"No."

In the end, uttering that single word was the easiest decision she'd ever made.

Eleven

Gray couldn't decide if Blakely's decision was stupid or noble. Maybe a little of both. She should walk away. There was no doubt in his mind that would be the smartest thing for both of them.

A jumble of conflicting emotions churned in Gray's belly. Anger, frustration, hurt, apprehension. He couldn't shake the feeling of waiting for the other shoe to drop.

And that fear didn't dissipate two days later, when Joker gave them a rundown of what he'd uncovered about his sister.

"You said Kinley, your sister, was sixteen when she ran off on her own?"

Gray, Joker, Blakely, Stone and Finn all sat around the conference table at Stone Surveillance. Everyone who'd been instrumental in getting Gray to this point was there with him.

Why did it feel so monumental? Like another crossroads in his life. An unexpected one.

"That's what my birth mother said."

"I still can't believe you have a sister you never knew about," Stone grumbled. "This is an utter cluster, man. I'm so sorry."

That was Stone, apologizing for something that wasn't his fault. Taking the weight of the world onto his shoulders.

Finn, on the other hand, drawled, "Look on the bright side. At least this sister hasn't disowned you."

Gray laughed. He had to. "No, but she framed me for embezzlement."

"By accident."

So his mother said, but he wasn't convinced.

Joker chimed in, like he could read Gray's mind. "I wouldn't be so positive."

His stomach tightened, the muscles knotting into a tangle it felt like no one would be able to unravel. "Tell me."

Opening a dossier, Joker spread a bunch of papers across the table.

Blakely immediately jumped up, pulling several of them closer for inspection. Gray let her look. But he wasn't entirely certain he was ready to know what they contained.

"This chick is amazing," Joker said. "Who did you say trained her?"

"I didn't." Mostly because he had no clue beyond what his mother had shared. "My mother said she'd shown a natural aptitude at an early age and her father started teaching her."

"That makes sense. Sure, there are some young IT geniuses who could figure this stuff out on their own, but she's really damn slick for someone so young."

It hadn't taken Gray long to do the math. His sister was now twenty-four, give or take a few months. He didn't even know when her birthday was. And that made his stomach tighten even more.

Growing up, he'd desperately wanted someone in his life he could be close to. His father hadn't given a damn about him, unless he could be useful in some way. His father had been too wrapped up in his business affairs. And his mother had been happy to leave Gray's upbringing to anyone else she could pay to fulfill the role.

Maybe that was the problem. He'd gained a sister only to immediately lose her because she'd been instrumental in the worst moments of his life. Karma really was a bitch, although he still wasn't sure what he'd ever done to deserve her disdain.

"Yeah, yeah, she's brilliant. We get it," Finn groused. "Could you hurry this up? I've got things to do and places to break into."

Gray rolled his eyes. Trust Finn to be in a hurry for a little B&E. Luckily, these days his extracurricular activities were wholly sanctioned. Not to mention profitable for their business.

"No, man. I don't think you understand. I've never met another hacker that I couldn't track within a few hours. Everyone leaves a trail, even if they don't mean to. Bread crumbs are easy to follow when you know what to look for. This girl…" Joker looked chagrined. "She's the best. Better than me."

Shit. Gray sat up in his chair. *Joker* was the best he'd ever seen, which was why Gray had cultivated the relationship and convinced the man to work for Stone Surveillance. Joker had single-handedly uncovered information that had been instrumental in saving Piper's life and exonerating Finn from being set up by his wife's grandfather.

"Does that mean you can't find her?"

Joker glared at him. "Of course not. It just means it took me longer than I would have liked. But like I said, everyone leaves bread crumbs…even if they think they're sweeping them all up."

Gray sank into his chair. The comforting weight of Blakely's hand landed on the curve of his thigh. She squeezed, silently giving him her support. He hadn't realized how much he'd needed it until that moment.

Setting his hand over hers, he squeezed back, a silent thank-you.

"It took a while, but I traced her trail backward for the past eight years, right after she left Vegas. Most of that time, she bounced from place to place across the world. A few months in Paris, a couple in Thailand, Venezuela, Brazil, South Africa, Iceland. There was no rhyme or reason, at least none I could figure out."

He was damn good with patterns, so Gray would hazard a guess that if Joker couldn't find one, there probably wasn't one.

"She never stayed long in any place and she rarely came back to the States. She was here during your trial, though. One of her longer periods in one place, actually."

"Here, as in Charleston?"

Joker nodded.

"Why the heck would she be here?" It made no sense. They knew she was responsible for framing him. They also knew she'd stolen another twenty million. Why put herself in jeopardy by coming so close to his trial?

"To make sure it went as she wanted?" Stone mused.

"Or maybe because she felt guilty about what happened," Blakely countered, her eyebrows pulled down into a sharp V of irritation.

"We can speculate all day, but there's no way to know for sure. I think we can all agree it's suspect." At least, that was Gray's take on it. No matter what his sister's motives for coming to Charleston back then…they obviously hadn't been to see he didn't pay for a crime he didn't commit.

"It gets weirder," Joker said.

"Weirder?" Finn's dark eyebrows winged up.

"Once I was able to track her movements, it didn't take me long to uncover several accounts in her name."

"Let me guess—the balance started out at twenty million?"

Joker's mouth twisted into a wry grimace. "Yep."

"How much is left?"

"Just over thirty million."

"Excuse me?"

"And that's in one account."

A sly grin stretched across Finn's lips. "The little minx really is a genius. She's managed to evade everyone and grow her money."

"Oh, she's done more than that."

For the first time since they'd sat down, Gray realized Joker's voice was tinged with respect and pride each time he talked about her. The rascal was impressed.

"Explain."

"Kinley hasn't just been investing your money for the past eight years. She used a little, but each time would eventually replace it with interest."

"And how has she accomplished this?" Stone, who'd been silent and observant much of the time finally asked.

"By stealing money from other people."

Why didn't that surprise him? "Why haven't we heard about these thefts? Did she decide to change her tactics and go after smaller amounts to fly under the radar?"

"Actually, it's the opposite. Your twenty million is

small change. She's managed to steal almost a billion dollars from various people."

"Now I'm less impressed that her bank account has thirty million in it," Finn quipped.

"That's because she doesn't keep the money. Or doesn't keep most of it. She has another account with a few million in it that she appears to use when she needs to disappear again."

"So what's she doing with the rest of the money?"

"Giving it to various charitable organizations."

"Say that again."

"You heard me."

"She's stolen a billion dollars to give it all away?" Finn's incredulity wasn't surprising. The only thing keeping him on the straight and narrow was Genevieve. Without her, Gray's friend would be just as crooked as his sister might be.

"Not only that, but she's managed to keep the thefts out of the media because she's targeted people who can't afford to report the crimes."

"Because the money is dirty."

"Exactly. She's targeted some of the biggest crime syndicates in the world—Russian, Chinese, American, Central and South American. If the money came from human trafficking, selling drugs or trading in weapons, she's taken it."

No wonder Joker was verging on idolizing his sister.

"Let me see if I'm getting this right. My sister, a genius hacker, disappeared eight years ago after framing me for embezzling money from my family's company. She took that money, placed it in an account and hasn't touched it the entire time."

"No, she's touched it, but she treats it like a loan and always pays it back. With interest."

Right, because most criminals worried about interest when they committed a crime like stealing.

"She's spent those eight years targeting and stealing money from criminals around the world and donating the proceeds to charities."

"Most of it. She keeps some money, but not a lot. Not nearly as much as she could. And almost in every instance, the money she does keep funds the next target."

Gray stared at Joker, not really seeing him. Part of him had expected this endeavor would uncover things he might not want to know. Being targeted as a patsy for embezzlement didn't normally happen to people with squeaky clean lives. And he'd hardly been a saint.

But never in a million years had he expected to discover he'd been living a lie and his mother wasn't really his. Or that he had a sister. Who'd framed him, but now operated as the Robin Hood of hackers.

Honestly, he had no idea what to do with this information or how to feel about it all. The hits just kept coming. Like he'd been in the worst fight of his life and was losing, something he wasn't used to and didn't particularly like.

"Where is she now?" Blakely's soft voice filled the silence at the table, asking the question he was too numb to ask.

"Bali. She's been there ever since you were released. It's the longest she's stayed in one place since Vegas."

Gray was too stunned to wonder what that was supposed to mean.

"But there's more."

He wasn't certain he could handle more right now.

"She's been watching you."

That got Stone's attention. Before Gray could even react, his friend's elbows were on the table and he was leaning hard toward Joker. "What do you mean she's been watching him?"

"She has a back door into all of his electronics. She's been monitoring his email and internet traffic. My guess is she's also been listening in and watching through those same devices."

Which explained why Joker had told them to leave their cell phones and electronic devices outside before coming into the conference room. Gray had initially chalked it up to his friend's paranoia.

"You could have told us."

"I wanted to explain before you jumped to conclusions."

"What conclusions would those be? That my sister has been tracking my every movement since I got out of prison? For what purpose? To frame me again? Steal from me again?"

Blakely's hand moved to his arm, tugging. He hadn't realized he'd stood up until he looked down and discovered she was looking up. Slowly, Gray let his legs fold beneath him and he sat back down into his chair.

"I really don't think that's it, man. I think she's been saving the money and is trying to figure out how to give it back to you."

Wonderful. His sister had grown a conscience and was spying on him so she could make amends.

"Why didn't she just send a certified check?" Gray could hear the petty sarcasm in his voice, but couldn't stop it. He was pissed and she was the easiest target right now. Even if his brain told him she might not deserve it.

"Gray," Blakely said, her voice calm and soothing. "That's not going to accomplish anything."

Of course it wouldn't, but it had felt good. At least for a second.

But that feeling was fleeting. Logic, that's what he needed right now. And he knew just who would give it to him.

Turning, he focused squarely on Blakely. "What now?"

Her lips turned up at the corners into a sad, understanding smile that somehow managed to start unknotting the ropes in his belly.

"We go find her. I have a feeling she's waiting for you."

Was she? Gray wasn't sure he was ready for that encounter. But Blakely was right. It's what he needed to do.

This plane ride was much different from the last one. The flight was longer, but it hadn't felt that way.

The moment they soared into the air, Gray unbuckled his seat belt. Reaching across her, he did the same for hers. The metal edges clanged loudly against the seat as they dropped open.

"What are you doing?"

"Taking advantage of the time we have."

Grasping her hands, Gray urged her out of her seat and into the narrow aisle. He led them toward the back of the plane, past a small galley and through a doorway that she'd missed the first time they were on board.

Stepping into the room tucked away, Blakely thought, *Of course it has a full bedroom.*

Gray tugged her inside. And immediately found her mouth with his. The kiss was explosive, going from nothing to red-hot in mere seconds. It was easy to let herself sink into the craving that was always present when he touched her. But tonight, Gray seemed to need more.

Pulling back, he looked down at her, his evergreen eyes filled with passion, but something stronger. Something softer and more enduring.

Something that had hope and uneasiness twisting in her gut.

Slowly, he led her over to the bed. Without saying a word, Gray reached for the hem of her shirt and pulled it up and over. The rest of her clothes quickly followed until she was standing before him entirely naked.

Any other time, she would have felt vulnerable, but not now. Not with a look of such awe and need stamped across his face.

She needed to touch him. To feel him. Now.

Blakely quickly added his clothes to the pile at their feet. An arm wrapped around her back, and Gray urged her to the bed. The coverlet beneath her skin was soft and cool, inviting. But that thought lasted a nanosecond before the blazing heat of his body joined hers.

The drag and pull of his skin against hers made Blakely arch up, searching for more. Always more with him. She could never get enough.

His mouth found her, raining kisses across her entire body. He lingered here and there, nipping and laving, worshipping and teasing. Blakely did the same, letting her mouth and hands explore him with a languid urgency that was both breathtaking and compelling.

Words were unnecessary, but he whispered them, anyway. How beautiful she was. What he planned to do to her body. How he intended to make her writhe with desire, pleasure and passion.

And he was true to each promise.

Blakely's breath caught in her lungs, almost as if her body was too busy with other things to remember that basic function. She wanted to make his body hum with the same rich energy that he was building inside her.

Finding the long, hard length of him nestled between them, she wrapped her hand around the hard shaft and tugged. He growled, the vibration of the sound rumbling through her own body.

Rolling them both, Blakely positioned herself above him and used her hold to guide him home. A sigh of satisfaction and relief left her parted lips. Blakely threw back her head, relishing the joy of feeling him buried deep inside her.

But after a few moments, that wasn't enough.

She began to ride him, rolling her hips back and forth in an effort to get more. Gray's hands gripped her hips, guiding her, moving her, faster and faster until the world began to turn black around the edges.

Blakely's breath panted in and out. Her body burned, heat and need building higher and higher.

One moment she was upright, the next her back was bouncing off the mattress as Gray pounded in and out of her.

Somehow, as he'd flipped them both, he'd managed to find her hands. Twining their fingers together, he used the hold to keep her steady. His mouth found hers, the kiss as deep as the connection between them.

The orgasm exploded through Blakely. Gray's bark of relief was right behind as he thrust deep, once, twice, three more times, before collapsing onto the bed beside her.

Their limbs tangled, bodies sweaty and replete.

After several seconds, Blakely leaned up and stared down into his gorgeous face. His eyes were open, a self-satisfied smile stretching his lips as he watched her.

"Well, isn't it quite handy to have a bed at thirty thousand feet?"

Twelve

Blakely lounged against the pile of pillows. They should probably get up and get dressed, but she wasn't motivated to move, not after the multiple orgasms Gray had just given her. Honestly, she wasn't certain her legs would hold her, anyway, if she tried.

Gray didn't appear to be in too much of a hurry to go back to their seats, either. And she had to admit the view wasn't hard to look at.

He was sprawled across the bed, sheets tangled between his thighs, completely uncaring. Half of his delectable ass was on display. Blakely was tempted to tug at the covers just so she could see the rest. But she knew if she did, they'd end up having sex again, and as much as she enjoyed sex with Gray, her body needed a few more minutes of recovery.

Gray's fingers played across her skin, tracing mindless patterns over her hips, belly and ribs. He had her tucked beneath him, his head resting on the curve of her waist.

He was quiet and a little pensive, just as he'd been earlier when they first boarded the plane.

Threading her fingers into his hair, Blakely gently pulled until his eyes found hers. "Hey, everything's going to be okay."

"I know." His words said one thing, but the darkness lurking in his gaze suggested another.

"You've been hit by so much in the past several years, Gray. I really hope this is the start to everything changing. Your sister could help prove your innocence."

"Sure, but only by admitting to a crime herself."

There was a fly in the ointment for sure. As much as she liked to be able to think most humans were honorable enough to admit to a crime in order to save someone else from paying the price…she knew firsthand that wasn't likely. Most people were selfish and could only see the impact something like that would make on their own lives.

What struck her as surprising was that a few weeks ago she wouldn't have considered it possible at all. But Gray… He was starting to make her feel like there were good people still left in the world.

Maybe his sister would be one of them.

"Why do you think she's been watching you?"

"No idea."

"But you have a theory."

A frown crinkled the corners of his gorgeous green eyes. "Yes."

Blakely smoothed his hair away from his forehead so she could see him better, waiting.

"I'd like to think her guilty conscience means she's been trying to figure out how to fix what she screwed up. But the rest of me…"

Blakely's stomach dropped right along with Gray's voice.

"I keep thinking she's had plenty of time to act if she wanted to. However, if she's been waiting for another opportunity to take from me? To ruin my life some more?"

Blakely shook her head. Something deep inside told her that wasn't what his sister wanted. Maybe she was being naive—a state she'd never been afflicted by before—but it didn't add up.

"To what purpose? You don't have access to the company anymore. Sure, you have plenty of money of your own, but we both know she could have taken that at any point."

"True."

"And the people she's been stealing from have been terrible human beings."

"I'm a convicted felon."

Frustration tinged Blakely's voice. "Because she *framed* you."

Gray's gaze dropped back down to stare at a spot on the bed. He continued to trace patterns on her skin. Goose bumps spread over her arms and legs, but she ignored them.

"You know, going to prison saved my life."

Blakely's own fingers traced across his shoulders, paying special attention to the puckered skin under the ridge of his shoulder blade. She hadn't asked, but assumed he'd gotten the scar during his time inside. He'd told her he'd gotten several others that way.

She couldn't understand how anyone could feel a situation that had left multiple marks across his body had saved him.

"How?"

His mouth twisted into a wry grimace. "I was aimless and spoiled before I went inside."

Blakely couldn't dispute that statement, because it was clearly true.

"I spent my entire life being given everything. I never had to earn anything, not truly. Inside, I had to earn everything. But the most important thing I learned how to earn was respect. Respect for myself and respect from others."

Blakely's stomach clenched. She wanted to wrap her arms around him and hold him close, but something told her this wasn't the time.

"Don't get me wrong, at first I was pissed. Angry at everyone and everything. I was still entitled, wearing the idea that life had treated me unfairly like a chip on my shoulder."

She was surprised he wasn't still pissed. He'd lost seven years of his life because someone else had screwed him over. And no matter how hard she tried, Blakely couldn't forget the role she'd played in putting him there, either.

"But then I met Stone and Finn. Separately, we were vulnerable to the other gangs and groups that formed inside. But together, we had power and quickly discovered how to demand deference from the other inmates.

"The experience stripped away my entitled lifestyle and made me realize I didn't like the person I'd been very much."

That must have been a difficult moment. Not many people had the fortitude to truly evaluate themselves and admit they weren't proud of who they'd become.

"That takes real strength, Gray."

He huffed out a reluctant laugh. "I don't know about that. But it definitely wasn't a comfortable experience.

Stone helped me, though. He's one of the most honest men I've ever met."

Blakely could see that. She'd only had a few dealings with him so far, but he'd seemed very fair and concerned for her comfort and safety.

"It wasn't an easy process. There are things about my time inside I'll never tell anyone, because I'm not proud of them, but also because unless you've been there you can't understand."

Her fingers traced the white, puckered flesh again. Part of her wanted him to be able to share anything with her, but she understood. There were things about her past—her childhood—that she had no intention of sharing with anyone, including Gray.

At the end of the day, the details didn't matter, anyway. What did were the lessons and growth that had come from them.

"It didn't take Stone, Finn or me long to realize in order to stay on the right side of the other inmates, as well as the guards, we needed something that both sides wanted. Inside, boredom is a serious problem. Hours and hours of idleness is a breeding ground for serious issues."

She could absolutely understand how that would be true.

"We ended up running an underground fighting ring. A perfect solution for everyone. Stone managed and arranged things. He handled the details and ensured the guards' buy-in."

"So, basically, he worked the connections and people?" It was the role Stone appeared to fill for Stone Surveillance, as well. He was the face of the company.

"Exactly. Finn handled the books, worked the betting pools and ran the numbers. He also used his charm and personality to stoke friendly rivalries and build hype for whatever fight was coming up."

Blakely had a feeling she knew the answer to her question, but she had to ask it, anyway…even if a huge part of her didn't necessarily want the answer. "And what did you do?"

Gray's mouth twisted into a self-deprecating smile. "I fought."

Of course he had. Blakely's stomach clenched uncomfortably. A spurt of fear shot into her system, as if he was preparing for a fight now.

"I'd never been in a fight before walking into that prison. I was too soft. I'd always used money and status to get myself out of any difficult situations."

"So why did you take on that role? Why couldn't you have been the bookie and let Finn fight?"

Gray's burst of laughter tickled across her skin. "Yeah, right. Finn is a lot of things, but he's too soft to fight. Besides, his dexterous hands are a valuable commodity."

Blakely's eyes rolled. Sure they were. He'd been a jewel thief.

"I was good at it. The training gave me something to focus on outside of my feelings of anger and injustice. I discovered discipline. I finally had to work for something…or risk getting my ass beaten."

"How often did that happen?"

His lips twitched. "A few times in the beginning. By the end…no one could beat me."

Blakely wasn't surprised. Gray might be many things, but the man she knew was driven and determined.

"I learned a lot about myself in the process. But most of all, I grew into a man I could be proud of."

Blakely shifted, using her leverage to roll them both.

He dropped onto the bed, his large body sprawling. Blakely's hips settled over his, their legs tangling together.

The hard ridge of his sex stirred between them, making her own sex pulse with a reminder and demand.

But there was something she wanted to say first.

Wrapping her hands around the base of his skull, Blakely brought her face close to his, making sure she filled his entire gaze.

"You are one of the best men I've ever known, Gray Lockwood. You're honorable, strong, quiet and resourceful. I hate that you went through a terrible time in your life to become the man you are, but the man you are is amazing."

His eyes sharpened, going hot and hard.

His fingers buried deep into her hair, holding her steady as he surged up and found her mouth.

Apparently, words weren't necessary anymore.

They landed in Kuta. Gray was certain the city was gorgeous—they were in Bali, after all. Surprisingly enough, in all his travels during his younger years, Bali had never made it onto the list. Perhaps because he'd been more interested in wild adventures than calming, peaceful vistas.

Unfortunately, the view was still lost on him since his mind wasn't on taking in the sights. Apparently, neither was Blakely's, which shouldn't have surprised him, but did.

She was efficient and focused as they followed the man who greeted them as they disembarked the plane. Striding before him across the tarmac, *that* was the sight Gray couldn't tear his gaze away from. The compact, lithe movements of her body. The lush, rounded globe of her ass hugged by well-worn denim. Hell, he hadn't even realized Blakely owned a pair of jeans until she'd pulled them on when they'd finally decided to climb from the bed.

He liked seeing her relaxed and casual. Something told him not many people got to experience that side of her. He tried not to convince himself it was important she felt comfortable enough to let him in...but it was.

They reached a dark green Jeep, clearly set up for off-roading adventures. The top and doors were off, roll bars showing. Several men who'd followed behind with their luggage quickly stowed everything in the back. Blakely didn't hesitate, but grasped one of the bars and boosted herself up into the lifted vehicle.

Reaching into her bag, she rummaged around until she found a hair band and quickly pulled it into a knot at the base of her skull. Shaking his head, Gray followed her. Beneath his breath he murmured, "Always prepared."

"What?" Blakely turned to him, her eyebrows beetled together in confusion.

"Nothing."

But that was Blakely to a *T*. She hadn't questioned or hesitated. She'd simply seen the vehicle they were taking and adjusted accordingly. It never would have entered her mind to complain and request something else. There had been plenty of women in his life—before—that would have stood outside the Jeep and pitched a fit, refusing to get in because it would mess up their hair.

Climbing up, Gray settled into his seat. Reaching over, he grasped Blakely's hand and pulled it into his own lap. He simply needed to touch her right now.

The drive across the island was beautiful. But the closer they got to the villa he'd rented, the more his stomach churned. After some digging, Joker had finally been able to send him an address. His sister had apparently rented a small place on the beach not far from where they were staying.

In less than an hour he might be confronting the person responsible for his imprisonment. And she was his half sister.

Was he ready for this?

They pulled up at the villa. It was gorgeous, but Gray didn't particularly care. He was used to staying in beautiful places. Often took it for granted.

Blakely didn't.

She hopped out of the Jeep, her feet hitting the ground with an audible thud. And she simply stood there, staring at the place.

It took several moments for her reaction to catch Gray's attention. But when it did, he decided then and there they were coming back to Bali the first chance they got. He wanted to put that look of wonder and surprise on her face every chance he could.

After handing off a bag to the staff that had come out to meet them, Gray walked over to her. Wrapping his arms around her, he pulled Blakely against his body. She willingly went, leaning into him without hesitation.

"It's beautiful."

"Wait until you see the view from the bedroom." The master suite opened out to the pool, which overlooked a stretch of private beach. They could lie in bed and watch the sunset…and sunrise.

Twisting around, she looked up at him. "You didn't have to get a whole villa, Gray. It's just the two of us. Surely they have hotel rooms on the island."

"Of course, but I thought we might want privacy."

Her gaze sharpened. "Because you intend to make me scream your name repeatedly or because you expect things to go badly with your sister?"

Gray huffed out a laugh. "Both."

A smile teased the corners of her lips. "I'm in for the first and I'm going to hope the second doesn't happen."

Gray was going to, as well, but he wasn't holding his breath. Nothing added up where his sister was concerned, so he really had no way of making an educated guess as to how this encounter was going to go.

He was about to say as much when the cell in his pocket buzzed. Pulling it out, he glanced at the number on the screen. His belly tightened, but he answered the call, anyway.

"Joker."

"She's there right now, but she's not planning to stay long. She started moving money a couple of hours ago. Looks like she's getting ready to run."

Because she'd figured out they were close?

Gray had purposely left all of his electronics back in Charleston, including his personal cell. This one was a Stone Surveillance burner he'd grabbed on their way out of town. Not only had he needed to evade his sister's scrutiny, but he was also still on probation technically, and not allowed to leave the country without approval.

"How did she figure out we're here?"

Joker grumbled something unintelligible, but clearly he wasn't happy. Finally, he said, "She didn't. Someone else found her."

Gray let out an expletive. Shitty timing. "Who?"

"A Russian mob boss she screwed over about two years ago."

Perfect. "It going to be a problem?"

"Not if you get to her first."

Grabbing Blakely's hand, he started pulling her back to the Jeep. Whistling to get the attention of their driver, Gray pointed at the Jeep. The guy nodded, then passed off the piece of luggage he'd been carrying. Jogging over, he launched his small frame into the driver's seat.

Gray didn't wait for Blakely to pause, but grabbed her around the waist and boosted her up into the Jeep. Rounding the vehicle, he showed their driver the address before following.

He'd expected to have a little time to prepare for this encounter. But maybe this was better.

Thirteen

Blakely was patient and simply went along for the ride. He hadn't even bothered to tell her what was going on until they were already speeding away from their villa. The whole time Gray's mind raced with what would happen if the Russian muscle arrived first, anxiety gripping his gut.

No one deserved that.

The drive up to his sister's place was severely different from the drive up to theirs. Wild vegetation obscured the view of the house, not just from the road, but from the long, winding drive. Their rental had been meticulously landscaped—the lush vegetation had been tamed to give a sense of tropical decadence.

The house itself was also much different. Small and old, clearly it had seen better days. Their villa screamed affluence and attention, not because Gray cared about stuff like that, but because he could afford the comforts it provided.

His sister could afford the same things. But something told him she'd chosen this place on purpose. Not only because it was well hidden, but also in order to not draw any undue attention.

Before they actually reached the house, Gray leaned forward and tapped their driver on the shoulder, telling him to stop. She might have already heard the Jeep, but in case she hadn't, he didn't want to spook her.

Jumping down, he walked around to help Blakely from the vehicle. Grasping her hand, they quietly walked the rest of the path up to the house.

It was silent and dark. No lights on inside, which made a tight band constrict Gray's chest. Were they too late? Had they missed her?

Rather than knock, he tried the knob, but wasn't surprised to find it locked. No one who made a habit of screwing over powerful people left the front door unlocked. Not if they were smart, and from everything he'd learned, his sister was extremely intelligent.

He could pick the lock, a little skill Finn had shared. But his friend had also imparted another piece of wisdom—don't make a simple job harder than it has to be.

Urging Blakely to follow behind him, Gray circled the house. It might not have much to offer in the way of luxury, but the view was breathtaking. Like most villas here, the back of the house had a huge outdoor area. The living space was open to the breezy outdoor sitting area and a path straight down to the water. There were doors that could be closed for security, but right now they were standing wide open.

Which told him that either his sister had left in a hurry, not bothering to secure the place, or she might be somewhere inside.

Taking a chance, Gray stepped up onto the back deck and raised his voice. "Kinley."

Her name reverberated against the terra-cotta tiles. His instincts hummed. A sound echoed from deep inside the darkened house. A muffled curse.

"Kinley, I'm not here to hurt you. I'm just here to talk."

Slowly, his eyes adjusted to the dark. Moonlight high above washed everything with a ghostly silver gray. He inched forward. And a soft voice floated into the darkness. "Stop."

Blakely's hand clamped down on his arm. Slowly, Kinley materialized out of the shadows as she moved forward into the watery light. "Don't come any closer."

Gray held up his open hands in the universal sign that he meant no harm. "I'm not here to hurt you."

"That's a lie. Why wouldn't you be here to hurt me? I ruined your life."

"You know who I am."

"Of course I know who you are."

Gray took a deep breath, pulling in air and holding it for several seconds before slowly letting it out on a warm stream. Some of the tension that had been tightening his shoulders flowed out with it.

"All I want is to talk."

"Bullshit. You want to make me pay for what I did to you."

Gray tilted his head sideways, really studying his sister. She didn't look a thing like their mother, but that didn't mean she wasn't just as beautiful. In fact, she was even more striking. Her inky hair hung in long, thick curls down her back, contrasting with her creamy skin, making it glow in the moonlight. He couldn't tell their exact color, but her eyes were dark, as well—probably brown. She was tall—he'd guess only a few inches short of six feet. But her body was lean, a runner's build.

Gray wasn't sure what he'd expected, but it wasn't this beautiful, strong woman standing before him. Maybe he'd expected a child. The sixteen-year-old teenager who had influenced his life. Kinley was hardly that. Gray knew within seconds that she was fully capable of taking care of herself. Because she'd had to do it for the last eight years…or even longer than that.

In that moment, Gray realized they had much more in common than a shared parent.

"I want to understand what happened. Yes, I have questions. But I don't want you to pay for anything. I know you were only sixteen when our mother convinced you to steal that money."

Kinley took several steps closer, coming even farther into the light. "Wait, what?" Her dark eyebrows winged down into a deep V of confusion. "*Our* mother?"

Oh, hell. She didn't know.

Gray's mouth opened and closed. Of course Cece had never told Kinley. Why would she?

The job had been about his father, not about him. Kinley had accidentally framed him, pulling him into the mess. Without that mistake, none of it would have touched him, so there'd be no reason to tell his sister that he existed.

Blakely's soft hand landed on his shoulder. She squeezed and then took over when he wasn't sure he had the words to continue.

"Gray is your half brother. Your mother was angry with his father for refusing to give her more money. That's why she had you steal from Lockwood Industries. You were supposed to frame his father for embezzlement, but you put the money in Gray's accounts instead."

* * *

Kinley stared at the woman who'd just rocked her world, dumbfounded by the unexpected revelation. Her gaze jerked to Gray Lockwood, a man who had become as familiar to her as her own reflection. Hell, she'd spent hours watching him over the last several months. A lot more time than the cursory glances she'd taken in the mirror.

How had she missed it?

She'd dug into this guy's background. Read every piece of documentation she could find about his life. She knew he'd been a math whiz as a kid, but hated history. She knew he'd had his appendix out when he was eleven. She even knew the brand of underwear he preferred to buy.

"Not possible."

That was the only conclusion she could come up with. There would have been some paper trail. Some indication.

"I assure you, it's not only possible, it's the truth. My father had an affair with your mother. She got pregnant. My mother couldn't conceive so he paid Cece to give up the baby. My birth certificate was falsified."

Kinley let out a sharp laugh. "Money can buy anything, huh?"

"Something like that."

She stared at him. He was handsome and a little scary. Gray Lockwood reminded her of the men currently chasing after her. Despite the silver-spoon upbringing, he still carried an edge of danger that nothing could hide. He was big and broad and clearly possessed the skills to protect himself if push came to shove.

"Why should I believe you?"

Gray shrugged. "You don't have to. Yet. I'm happy to

get the tests to prove we're siblings…after we get you out of here. We have reason to believe the Russians after you will be here in less than twenty minutes."

Kinley swore under her breath. She'd always known her choices would catch up to her sooner or later. *You piss off enough powerful, vindictive people and eventually you pay the price.*

And she'd been okay with that. In theory. Now that the reality was breathing hot and heavy down her neck…

She'd done a lot of good for a lot of people. She'd righted a lot of wrongs. That was going to have to be good enough. The reality was, there was no one in her life who would give a damn if she disappeared. The Russians could kill her and her death wouldn't be a blip on a single radar.

Which was the life she'd chosen.

But she wasn't ready to give up just yet.

Spinning on her heel, Kinley headed back into the darkened house. She entered the room she'd set up as an office months ago, when she'd settled in Bali. She'd picked the house for very specific reasons, one of which was that despite the run-down appearance and out-of-the-way location, the house was wired like a high-tech ops center. Or at least it was now.

She started placing stuff into the open cases she'd abandoned when Gray had tripped her silent alarm. Most of her computers, servers, racks and equipment were already put away. She only had a few more, and packing them wouldn't take her five minutes. The issue would be getting everything loaded into her car in time.

Next time, she was going to invest in a heavy-duty cart so she didn't have to lug the awkward cases one at a time.

Her brother—she still wasn't ready to accept that—and the woman appeared. They stood in the doorway just watching, without saying anything. Clearly, they weren't there to hurt her, but the Russians would, so that danger was more pressing.

She'd deal with her brother and the woman later. Or not.

Grabbing the first box, Kinley tried to keep in the groan of effort, but couldn't quite make it.

Her brother shot forward, snatching it from her before she could protest. Lifting it like it was nothing, he spun on his heel and headed out the front door. Kinley started to chase after him—he was holding some damn expensive equipment and she really didn't want him to disappear with it.

But she stopped. There was no way she was going to win if they ended up in a wrestling match. Better to grab another box and get it into her car. She had the money to replace anything he took, even if it would be a huge pain in the ass.

Battles and wars and all that. She was picking and choosing.

Kinley headed out behind him, cognizant that the woman who'd come in with Gray had also grabbed one of the boxes stacked in the corner and was following. Great.

Ahead of her, her brother approached a Jeep idling in front of the house. He didn't pause, but lifted up the box and put it into the back. He motioned for her to do the same, but she was in no mood to comply. Instead, she started over to the small SUV she'd bought for ten thousand dollars when she'd arrived to the island.

The woman continued past her and dropped her box into the Jeep before silently returning back to the house for more.

Dammit.

It wasn't worth the breath to argue or try to stop them.

Instead, Kinley popped the door on her car and set the case inside. Gray came behind her and immediately pulled it back out again, then carried it over to the Jeep.

Fed up, she finally turned, put her hands on his back and shoved hard. "What do you think you're doing? Leave my shit alone!"

"Kinley, I'm not letting you deal with the Russians by yourself. Let us help you get out of here. I have a private jet at the airport waiting on standby to take us wherever you want."

Why the hell would he do that?

Kinley stared at the man in front of her, completely dumbfounded. "I ruined your life."

"No, you didn't, but we can talk about that later. Right now, we need to get out of here."

The woman came back with another case and stacked it on the others. Anger, fear, desperation and hope all mixed together in her belly, making her want to throw up. The two of them were certainly acting like they wanted to help.

The faint sound of an engine lifted into the air.

"Shit," Gray said. "They're here. Get in."

"But I don't have everything."

"There's no more time." Grasping her arm, Gray pulled her over to the Jeep, gripped her waist and tossed her into the back seat. The woman with him scrambled up into the other side as Gray vaulted into the passenger seat.

The driver, clearly a local, spun the tires as Gray urged, "Hurry up."

One of the other reasons she'd chosen the house was because there were two paths in and out, something the driver clearly already knew because he headed in the opposite direction of the approaching car.

Everyone was silent as they jolted into the overgrown

vegetation. Anxiety filled the air between them and they all waited to see if the car behind them would stop at the house or follow.

Kinley twisted so she could see out the back. And let out a huge sigh of relief when the wide circle of headlights stopped, shining straight onto the house. A handful of men jumped out of the two vehicles, swarming up onto the front porch.

That was all she caught before they took a hairpin turn and the house completely disappeared from view.

Turning around, Kinley stared at the back of her brother's head. Her world had just gotten very surreal.

The woman beside her leaned forward, catching her attention. Holding out a hand, she said, "Hi, I'm Blakely. I work with your brother."

The Jeep was silent and rife with tension. Blakely wanted to do or say something to cut it, but nothing would help. Gray was only in the front seat, but for some reason he suddenly felt very far away.

Not once since they'd gotten in had he looked back at her. Or at Kinley, for that matter. Blakely's stomach knotted with apprehension and uncertainty.

They pulled into the private entrance at the airport, racing toward the jet sitting on the tarmac.

Several people milled around. A few were loading luggage and cargo. Clearly, Gray had instructed someone to pack their things and bring them. She hadn't even seen him send a text or make a call.

But that was Gray, silently taking care of the things that needed attention.

They pulled up close to the jet. Several men raced forward, pulled Kinley's cases from the back and rushing them toward the plane.

"Wait," his sister protested, reaching for one. "I'm not going."

The man gave her a look like she'd grown two heads, shook off her hold and then proceeded to do exactly as he'd been instructed.

Gray approached his sister. "Kinley, we'll take you wherever you want to go, but I can't leave you here while the Russians are so close. It's not safe."

Kinley shook her head. "Why are you doing this? Helping me?"

A small smile played at the edges of Gray's mouth. "I know about what you do. You steal money from really bad people and give it to those that need it."

"I stole money from *you*."

"Yes, you did. Did you mean to?"

Kinley threw her hands into the air. "Of course not!"

Gray shifted, rocking on his feet like he wanted to reach out to his sister, but stopped himself before actually touching her. "Trust me, my bank account is fine."

"I have the money. You can have it back. I've been trying to figure out how to put it into your accounts without screwing myself or you even worse than I already did."

"I know."

"You know?"

Gray took another step closer to his sister. "I happen to know a hacker who's almost as good as you are."

"Who?"

Gray's grin widened. "Not my info to share. But I have a feeling you'll have an opportunity to meet at some point."

Blakely watched Gray tentatively reach out a hand to Kinley and set it on her shoulder.

Brother and sister faced off, Kinley with a perplexed

expression and Gray with hope. Blakely's chest tightened. It was a surreal moment, one she was grateful to witness.

Gray had lost so much. The only family he'd ever known abandoned him. He'd learned the woman who'd given birth to him never wanted him and didn't care what happened to him. Sure, he'd found two amazing friends that were as close as brothers, but at the end of the day it wasn't the same as blood.

God, she really hoped Gray was right and Kinley wouldn't screw him over, too. She was hopeful, but it was difficult for her not to let the cynicism of her childhood color that hope.

"I own a security company. We can always use someone with your skills."

"No." Kinley didn't even contemplate Gray's tentative offer. "I work alone."

"You still can. I'm just saying, if you ever want to freelance…" Gray pulled out a cell and handed it to her. "My number is programmed. Call me. Anytime."

"Just like that. You're going to let the twenty million dollars and everything else go?"

Gray shrugged. "It's not like I need it. Use it for something good, Kinley."

"You're not going to turn me in?"

Gray shook his head. "No."

Blakely took a step back. She wasn't surprised to hear him voice that decision, but it still made her heart hurt. He was giving up the one thing he'd been working so long and hard for.

Fourteen

Blakely had been quiet since they'd gotten onto the plane. A few hours ago, they'd made a fuel stop in Hong Kong. They'd also left Kinley there.

It had been difficult to watch his sister walk away. Not just because she was in danger, but because he'd just found her. And a huge part of him wanted the opportunity to get to know her better.

But that wasn't his choice. He'd made the offer of a position with Stone—from there it was up to her what happened next with her life. What he could control was what happened in his.

Gray watched the ground disappear beneath them as they rose higher into the sky. Soon enough, they'd be back in Charleston. He wasn't surprised when Blakely sat down in the chair next to his.

Since they'd boarded the plane, she'd been keeping a distance between them. Maybe she'd sensed he'd needed the space. Or maybe she was avoiding him.

He was so mentally and physically exhausted, at the moment he wasn't sure whether or not it mattered. The result was the same. There was this space between them that hadn't been there before.

"What now?"

Her question was simple. Unfortunately, the answer wasn't. Hell, he wasn't absolutely certain what she was really asking. But he could answer one thing.

"Nothing. We go back to the office and go on with life."

Leaning forward, Blakely put her elbows on her knees and dropped her head. "I was afraid you were going to say that. You're not going to tell the authorities or your father."

It wasn't a question. Clearly, she'd already figured out he wasn't. Not only had he said as much to Kinley, but deep down, he knew it was the right thing to do.

"It would put her in someone else's crosshairs and she's already got plenty of people chasing her."

"What about you?"

"What about me?"

"You deserve your life back, Gray. You didn't do anything wrong and you've lost everything."

Had he? Gray wasn't so sure that was true.

"Getting my life back would mean destroying hers." And he wasn't willing to do that. They might not have shared history, but they did share DNA. And at the end of the day, she was as much a victim in all of this as he was. He refused to punish her for her parents' manipulation and a mistake she'd made when she was sixteen.

"Not necessarily. She's really good at being a ghost. Just because you produce evidence that you were framed doesn't mean you need to give up her trail."

"Maybe, but it's a risk I'm not willing to take. My

father has means and determination. At the moment, he thinks I have twenty million stashed somewhere. If he discovered someone else was in possession of those Lockwood assets…he'd stop at nothing to find the person responsible."

"Kinley's willing to give back the money."

"And that might help, but it won't stop him. I know him, and he's relentless when he's on a crusade. No, it's better if he never knows. I've already paid my debt to society, Blakely. I can't get those years back, no matter what."

"No, but you can get your family back. Your reputation and legacy."

Gray laughed, the sound bitter even to his own ears. "I don't really have a family, do I? And I never did. My father doesn't give a damn about me. He cares about appearances. The woman I thought was my mother couldn't care less what happens to me. And the mother who gave birth to me is only interested in what she can get out of me. No, thank you. I'm perfectly happy with the life I have."

"What life? Gray, I've spent the last few weeks with you. Your existence has been entirely wrapped up in proving your innocence. The last eight years. All I'm saying is, don't make this decision in haste."

A tight knot cramped Gray's stomach. Blakely stared at him through those pale blue eyes that always cut straight through him. He'd seen them filling with passion and heat. Hope and frustration. Right now, they were awash with guilt and disappointment.

"Don't give up the chance to clear your name. Everyone needs to know you're not a criminal. You deserve the chance to shake off that stigma."

In that moment, Gray realized just how important that was to her. Images of her father standing in the middle of the office hallway, everyone staring at the spectacle he'd created, flashed across his mind. Her embarrassment and irritation at the precinct. The tired disappointment in her voice as she'd talked about growing up with a criminal as a father.

Clearing his name had become a crusade for her, as well, and not simply because of the guilt she harbored for her part in putting him in jail.

Blakely had a clear sense of right and wrong thanks to the gray world her father lived in. She'd lived with the taint of that stigma her entire life, and she'd done everything she could to distance herself from it.

And if he didn't clear his name, being with him would taint her once again.

He couldn't ask her to do that. But he also couldn't use the information he had to clear his name.

"I'll think about it." Although he wouldn't. Standing up, Gray gave her a weak smile. "I'm going to make a few phone calls and take care of a few things back home." And he walked back into the bedroom.

This day was about to get worse, but just like the fights he'd been in, sometimes he just had to take a punch.

Gray had spent the rest of their flight in the bedroom, only coming back out minutes before they landed. Blakely almost regretted what she'd said, but she couldn't quite bring herself to get there. He'd worked so damn hard to prove his innocence, she hated to watch him walk away from the opportunity to get back everything he'd lost.

Maybe he just needed time alone to deal with the disappointment of getting so close only to watch the redemption he'd wanted slip through his fingers. She completely understood the decision he was making...but that didn't make it suck any less.

It was late at night when the plane touched down. They disembarked and Blakely tried not to worry about the fact that Gray kept his distance and didn't touch her. He was just dealing with things.

That was, until they reached the tarmac. Two cars waited for them. Blakely caught a glimpse of her bag being loaded into one…and Gray's being put into the other.

Turning, she said, "What's going on?"

"What do you mean?"

"Why are we taking separate cars?"

Gray cocked his head to the side. "Because we're both going home."

Blakely couldn't stop herself, even though she already knew the answer. "Alone?"

"Yes."

"Why?"

He pulled in a deep breath and held it for several seconds before finally letting it out. "Look, Blakely. You held up your end of the bargain. You helped me prove my innocence."

"Even though you're not going to do anything with the information."

His mouth thinned. "Even though. I'm following through with my end. You should be receiving a phone call tomorrow from an accounting firm in town. They're going to interview you, but it's just a formality. You can start your life and career over."

Blakely stared at Gray for several seconds. An anxious pit opened up in the bottom of her belly. This wasn't what she wanted.

"That's it?" Her purse slipped through numbed fingers, dropping to the ground at her feet. She took several steps forward, right into his personal space. Gray didn't flinch—he just stared at her out of cold, remote eyes.

This was not the man who'd rocked her world and spent hours worshipping her body just days ago. The man in front of her was the aloof felon. The intense brawler hell-bent on victory.

"You're going to pretend the last few days didn't happen? That you didn't spend hours with your mouth and hands on my body?"

"No, why would I pretend it didn't happen? I enjoyed every minute of it. You did, too. But that was just proximity and chemistry, Blakely. We were physically attracted to each other."

"Were." The single word fell flat.

"There's no reason for us to see each other again. The job is finished."

"What if I want to stay at Stone?" She'd really enjoyed the work they'd done together. Being part of solving the puzzle had been exhilarating. And it didn't hurt that they'd been trying to find justice, something she prized highly thanks to her childhood. Being part of that had felt…purposeful and important.

"I don't think that's a good idea."

"Why? You're not this asshole, Gray."

His mouth twisted into a self-deprecating smile. "I assure you, I can be as much an asshole as the next guy. It was fun while it lasted, but it's over. Time for both of us to go back to our lives."

Blakely stared up at him, a mixture of hurt, pride, anger and pain making her physically ill. Heat washed over her body, and not the kind that normally filled her when Gray was near. Her stomach felt like she'd swallowed a cup of battery acid.

She refused to beg him, even if her brain was screaming at her to convince him he was wrong. She deserved to be with a man who wanted her, not someone who felt she was disposable as soon as she wasn't useful to him anymore.

Never once had she thought Gray was that kind of man, but apparently, she was wrong.

Taking two steps back, Blakely began nodding her head. "Normal. That's exactly what I need."

She spun on her heel and stalked away. It was either that, or let him see the tears she couldn't hold back silently rolling down her face.

"What the hell is your problem? You've been a right prick the last few days." Finn leaned back in the large leather chair, a single dark eyebrow winged up in that sharp, insolent and questioning way he had.

Gray fought the urge to reach across the table and punch him. Logically, he realized the reaction was way too much. But he was having a very hard time controlling his temper.

"Heartbroken fool." Those two words were Stone's contribution to the conversation.

"O-o-oh," Finn said, drawing out the single word. "Poor bastard."

Stone shrugged. "He did it to himself so I don't have a lot of sympathy."

Finn's lips tipped up at the corners. "Yeah, but you remember both of us had a stupid moment ourselves before we got our heads out our asses."

"Speak for yourself. I don't remember any stupid moments."

Finn scoffed, the incredulous sound echoing through the room and scraping against his last nerve. "Bullshit. Just because you don't want to admit it, doesn't mean it didn't happen. Besides, I'm pretty sure you had more than one."

"No reason to go there," Stone said with a pointed look. "Besides, we were talking about Gray."

"Any bets on how long it takes before he comes to his senses, goes after her and grovels?"

Stone tipped his head sideways, studying him like he was a specimen beneath a microscope. "I'm pretty sure he's close to the breaking point right now. I'd say…two days. Max."

"Nah, I'm going with tomorrow. I hear her dad's case is going before the judge then."

"No fair, you had insider information."

Finn grinned. "Always stack the deck, my friend."

Gray, tired of listening to the banter, growled, "You assholes can stop talking about me like I'm not here."

"Well, look at that, he is paying attention."

"Of course I am." His attention turned to Finn. "Her father's trial is tomorrow?"

This time both of Finn's eyebrows rose. "The high-priced lawyer you hired filed a motion to dismiss. The judge is hearing it tomorrow. Although, I would have expected you to know this already."

And he might have…if he hadn't told the guy who'd called yesterday about Blakely's father's case that he didn't want to hear anything about it. He just wanted the man to do his job. Period.

Dammit, but now he knew. His foot started tapping against the floor. The muscles in his shoulders tightened. Blakely must be stressed out over the outcome.

He needed to get out of here, before he did something stupid. Like call her and see how she was holding up.

Pushing back from the table, Gray said, "You guys will have to finish this meeting without me."

"Please tell me you're going to her."

Gray looked across the table at Stone. "No."

His friend groaned, closing his eyes. "You really are a fool." Waving a hand, Stone added, "Go, we've got this. Do us a favor, though, and don't come back in until you have your shit together. Amanda is afraid to come near you right now. She said you snapped her head off when she brought you some paperwork this morning."

"It was screwed up."

"Maybe so, but that wasn't her fault."

Stone might be right, but Gray wasn't in the mood to acknowledge it. "Whatever."

He was halfway to the door when Finn's voice stopped him. "Would you like some friendly advice?"

Gray paused for several seconds before turning back to his friend. "Not really."

"You're getting it, anyway. I don't know what happened between you. What I do know is that with her you were happier than I'd ever seen you. And that's saying a lot considering everything that was going on. I would have expected the last few weeks to have been some of the most difficult of your life."

And when Gray stopped to think about it, Finn was right. Aside from being convicted for a crime he didn't commit, finding out his mother wasn't really his, that his father had paid someone to cover it up and his birth mother had sold him...not exactly a happy time.

"Still, somehow, you managed to get through that experience without tearing apart someone or something. I saw you smile more often in those weeks than I have in the eight years I've known you. She makes you happy, man. And that's worth a lot."

Stone picked up where Finn left off. "It's worth doing whatever you have to in order to have that in your life.

Whatever the problem is…figure out how to fix it. All of us know, life is too unpredictable. You take the joy where you can find it."

"And when you find a woman worth having in your life, you do what you can to keep her there," Finn added.

Gray stared at both his friends. They watched him with matching earnest expressions, firmly believing what they were telling him.

And he had to admit, the last few days he'd been miserable.

"This is the right thing…for her. It'll get better."

"No, it won't," Stone said, his voice filled with certainty. "I let Piper go before I went to prison. And those feelings never disappeared. They were just as powerful years later. If you love her, tell her."

"Fight for her," Finn chimed in. "You're good at that, man. You know how to fight. So why are you walking away from the most important one of your life?"

Gray's gaze bounced between his two friends. Aside from Blakely, they were the most important people in his life.

What they said both scared him…and gave him hope. Maybe they were right. Stone had been noble, trying to do the right thing just like he was. But in the end, Piper hadn't wanted that sacrifice from him. She'd wanted the man she loved.

Walking away from Blakely was the hardest thing he'd ever done. And Finn had a point. He'd never backed down from a fight before. So why was he doing it now, when it mattered most?

"That's a damn good question."

Fifteen

Blakely sat behind her father. He was at the table in front of her. The lawyer Gray had hired sat next to him. She'd half expected the guy to drop the case, but he hadn't.

She couldn't decide whether to be grateful or pissed. Half of her had hoped Gray would pull an asshole move so she could be angry instead of hurt and heartbroken.

No such luck.

The bastard.

The judge walked into the courtroom and everyone stood. After he was seated, the bailiff instructed everyone else to sit. The registrar began detailing the order of cases. The hearing for her father's motion was first.

Everyone was shuffling papers and murmuring. Getting prepared. Blakely's stomach was in knots. Over the last several days, she'd spent some time with her father, really talking about what had happened. A few weeks ago, she would have gone into that conversation with a completely different mindset. But thanks to Gray…she'd truly listened to her father and decided for herself, and for him, that she believed him. He was far from perfect, but it was clear to her he'd been honestly trying to change his life.

Which made this hearing even more important.

Leaning forward, Blakely placed her hand over her father's shoulder and squeezed. He didn't turn, but brought his own hand up, covering hers. The pads of his fingers were rough with calluses, reminding her that no matter what, her father had worked hard all of his life to provide for his family. Maybe not the way she would have preferred…but the only way he knew how.

The hearing started, and the prosecution began with a brief outline of their case. Blakely listened to the evidence, her throat tightening with each word. They made him sound so guilty.

The defense was about to start when the door at the back of the courtroom opened. Blakely turned at the noise, nothing more than a reflex, but her world stood still when she saw who entered.

Gray.

What was he doing here?

Pausing, he looked straight at her for several moments. His expression was blank and impossible to read. A jumbled mess of emotions tangled into knots inside her already rolling belly. Anger, heartbreak, hope and frustration collided, so coiled together that she couldn't separate them enough to deal with any.

Clamping her jaws together, Blakely purposefully turned away from him, placing her focus back onto her father and the hearing.

She listened to her father's attorney decimate each of the prosecution's points, poking holes in their evidence and making a strong case for dismissing the charges altogether. He also made a compelling argument that her father had been turning his life around, distancing himself from the people who were bad influences and attempting to become a better citizen. He suggested no one should be judged based on their past behavior when they were clearly trying to make the right changes.

The experience was a roller coaster, but optimistic hope came out on top when her father's attorney finally sat. And in that moment, she was proud of her father. Something she'd never been able to say before.

When both sides were done, the judge sat back in his chair. He looked out over the courtroom, his gaze zeroing in on her father.

"Mr. Whittaker, I've heard from both sides. After careful consideration of the facts presented here, I find there isn't enough evidence to hold this case over for trial."

Blakely let out a huge sigh of relief. In front of her, her father sagged into his chair, his shoulders dipping with relief.

"I want to caution you, however. While it might be ideal not to judge people on their past mistakes, ultimately, we're all human and it happens. You have much to atone for in your past, but I'm a firm believer everyone deserves a second chance. So far, you've proven your willingness to make changes in your life. Keep it that way so I don't have to see you in my courtroom again." The judge paused for several seconds. "Because next time, you might not be so lucky."

Her father stood. "Thank you, sir. I understand and I'm so grateful for your decision."

Everyone around her seemed to move at once. Her father's attorney stood and began gathering his files and papers. He turned to her father and murmured several things before clapping him on the back and wishing him the best.

Her father turned to her, a huge grin stretching across his face. Blakely leaned forward, wrapping him in a hug. But she couldn't stop herself from whispering in his ear. "You're lucky, Dad. Please don't blow this second chance."

"I won't, baby girl. I promise not to let you down again."

Pulling back, Blakely looked deep into his eyes. "Dad, don't do it for me. Do it for yourself."

The smile on Martin's face dimmed a little, but he nodded and squeezed her shoulder.

Together, they walked out of the courtroom. Blakely couldn't stop herself from scanning the crowd in front of her, looking for Gray even though she knew she shouldn't.

But he wasn't there.

And for some stupid reason, her heart dropped into her toes when she realized he was gone. He hadn't come for her; he'd come to support her father. To make sure his money had been spent wisely.

In that moment, the last bit of hope Blakely had been clinging to disappeared.

Gray watched as Blakely and her father left the courthouse. Martin got into his car and drove away. His daughter stood for several seconds, watching him disappear.

Her hands were shaking. He wanted to go to her, hold her, and make it stop.

She was so strong for everyone, but for the first time, Gray realized that meant she had no one to be strong for her.

No, that wasn't true. She had him.

To hell with it. He didn't care if she wanted him to be there or not. Didn't care if she was angry with him, or if she didn't like his criminal reputation. They'd figure it out.

Walking out of the shadows, Gray crossed the sidewalk. Reaching out, he grasped her hands and squeezed.

She didn't startle or jerk away. But she also didn't turn to him. Instead, she stared straight ahead and asked, "Why are you here?"

"I wouldn't be anywhere else."

Blakely's head bowed.

Using his grip on her shoulders, Gray gently turned her to face him. Her face was drawn, unhappy and sad. Exactly the way he'd been feeling the past days without her.

"Blakely, I'm miserable without you." Those words were a hell of a lot easier to say than he'd expected. "I miss your laugh, the way you smell. I miss the way you burrow into me in your sleep, like you can't get close enough. I miss the way you argue with me and challenge me. I just miss you."

Blakely's mouth thinned. Her eyes glistened with tears she wouldn't let fall. "You pushed me away, Gray."

"You're right. I did. I was afraid."

"Of what?"

"That you were only with me out of guilt." No, it was more than that. And if there was ever a time to be completely honest with himself and her, it was now. "I was afraid I didn't deserve you. Blakely, I spent seven years in prison. And I might not have been a criminal when I went inside—"

Blakely cut him off, her voice hard and strong when she said, "You're still not a criminal."

And that was where she was wrong. "I've done plenty

of things that are on the gray side of the law. And I know you, Blakely. If you knew everything, you wouldn't be okay with it."

"That's bullshit, Gray. You say you know me, but I know you, too. I don't care what you think you've done. I have no doubt you had perfectly good reasons. Period. I don't need the details to know that, because I know you. Trust you."

Blakely's arm flung out, sweeping across the expanse of the courthouse steps. "I just spent the last hour in a courtroom with my dad. A few weeks ago, dread and disappointment would have sat heavy on my stomach. Because I would have been embarrassed and hurt by what he'd done. Instead, I was hopeful. And not just because you'd spent money on a damn good lawyer. But because I believe that deep down, he wants to change. I believe in him, in a way I never have before. You gave me that." She shook her head. "No, you gave *us* that. Because my support is going to help my dad be successful in making those changes."

Gray's chest tightened. "I'm really happy for you both."

"Then why won't you let me show you the same support you've given me?"

Blakely closed the gap between them, wrapping her hands around his face and bringing her body snugly against his. "I love you, Gray."

Everything inside him went silent at her words. Something sharp lanced through his chest and then warmth expanded, spreading throughout his entire body.

She loved him. Gray wasn't certain what he'd done right in his life to deserve her, but he'd take it. Because he wasn't strong enough not to.

Dropping his forehead to hers, he said, "I love you, too."

"There might have been a time I thought you were the worst kind of man, but I was clearly wrong. Gray Lockwood, you're one of the most honorable, selfless men I've ever met."

Gray's throat tight, he pulled her up until his mouth met hers. The kiss they shared was hot as always, but it was more. Connection, comfort, support and appreciation.

It was a beginning, one they were both anxious to start.

* * * * *

ALL HE WANTS FOR CHRISTMAS

KAREN BOOTH

For my aunt Judy,
who absolutely loved Christmas

One

Andrew Sterling had nearly forgotten how pleasant November in San Diego could be. As he descended the stairs of his Cessna, a soft breeze ruffled his hair and a strong dose of California sun warmed his face. If he had to guess, it was nearly seventy degrees today. This was a complete one-eighty from his adopted home of Seattle, where the cold and rain was a fixture this close to Thanksgiving. It crept into your bones and your psyche and made itself at home well past Christmas. San Diego was obviously a far better locale this time of year. But this city held too many unhappy memories for Andrew—dreams dashed, loyalties destroyed, love lost and, ultimately, two brothers forever divided. He wouldn't be staying here long, no matter how nice the weather.

Forever divided. That was the part Andrew was having the hardest time getting past. There was no repairing his relationship with his brother. Johnathon was dead, his life ended three short months ago at the too-young age of forty-one. It was a fluke accident—a line drive on the golf course, straight to the temple. There had been no time to say goodbye, not that it would have been an easy conversation. There would've been countless things to say, and even more things to apologize for, which could have only happened after getting past the state of their relationship that day—Johnathon and Andrew hadn't spoken in over a year. Even worse, Andrew was orchestrating a scheme to kneecap Johnathon's business, Sterling Enterprises.

He'd had good reason to embark on the secret venture, but that didn't matter now. Johnathon was gone, and Andrew had to stop the plan he'd set in motion. Defuse the bomb he'd built. Unfortunately, someone else still wanted to light the fuse—Andrew's one-time ally in the scheme, a man known only as Victor. Victor had been on the wrong end of a multimillion-dollar business deal with Johnathon and he was not the type to forgive and forget. Guilt and regret had made Andrew stop, but Victor didn't have family loyalty or even a conscience to constrain him. Victor was merciless. If he couldn't get his revenge on Johnathon, he'd destroy his legacy instead. Hence, Andrew's open-ended return to the city he could no longer stand.

Andrew strode across the tarmac to the idling SUV waiting for him at Gray Municipal, a landing strip so far south of San Diego it was nearly in Mexico. No one would expect Andrew to come into town via such a remote and admittedly unglamorous location. There were more than a dozen airports closer to the city, with better amenities and far nicer facilities to hangar his plane. But he wanted to slip into San Diego undetected. It was the best way to stop Victor at his game.

It was a half-hour drive to the historic US Grant Hotel, the five-star grand dame of downtown San Diego, but Andrew was not delivered to the front door. Instead, he was taken to the parking garage and used the private entry reserved for dignitaries and heads of state. Andrew was neither, but he did have a security detail and the money that afforded this level of preferential treatment. He and one of his bodyguards, Pietro, rode the elevator up to the presidential suite. It was pure luxury, with its tall arched windows, nine-foot ceiling and impeccable decor, not that Andrew planned to enjoy it. Pietro did a quick sweep of the living area, then headed up to the suite's second level for a full inspection of the bedroom and bath. Meanwhile, Andrew paced. He was eager to get to work, discreetly find out exactly what Victor was up to, and formulate his plan from there.

"Everything checks out upstairs," Pietro said. "Would you like me to head over to check on Ms. Sterling?"

"Yes. Just please be discreet. She doesn't know yet what's going on." Andrew swallowed hard, thinking about Miranda, his brother's widow. She'd played a crucial role in Andrew's decision to stop the plan against Sterling Enterprises. Only she didn't know it.

Andrew had gone to see her two weeks after Johnathon's death, and that visit had been nothing like what he'd expected. She'd had every reason to be angry with him or send him away. Andrew had missed Johnathon's funeral, too shell-shocked to deal with the avalanche of emotions that came with his brother's sudden death. Instead, Miranda had been welcoming, inviting him into her showpiece of a home. Not that she let him off the hook completely. She told him flat out that his absence at the service had hurt. Andrew did his best to explain, but it was complicated. Then Miranda did what very few people had ever done—she forgave him.

Once the air was cleared, Miranda happily spent time with him, telling him about her life with Johnathon and, most important, about her baby on the way—the child his brother learned of on his death bed. Andrew dismissed the too-shiny version of his brother in the stories Miranda told. Johnathon had always created his own reality, twisting things until he could not be considered at fault. But Andrew did listen carefully when Miranda pondered her future, the one in which her child would never know its father. That part of the conversation had stuck to Andrew like glue. When it was time to go, she hugged him, kissed him on the cheek and referred to him as family. She'd placed her hand on her pregnant belly and told him that she hoped her baby would be part of his life. Even now, over two months later, the entire experience haunted him. He'd always known that family was important, but he'd never seen it. Or felt it. Not like that.

That made his decision for him. He immediately returned to Seattle and told Victor that the scheme to hurt Sterling Enterprises was over. Johnathon was gone and any revenge to be exacted was his. He'd come up with the plan to prevent Sterling Enterprises from winning the bid on a project for San Diego, the renovation of the Seaport Promenade, a large public space overlooking the bay. Andrew had chosen that project for very personal reasons, as he was certain Johnathon had done the same. It had been the site of a particularly painful chapter in the long rivalry between the two brothers—the day Andrew was left at the altar, or more precisely, the Seaport Promenade wedding pavilion.

"Please let me know if you see anything out of the ordinary," Andrew said to Pietro, forcing himself to shake off the unpleasant memories threatening to take hold.

"Of course, sir."

"I'd like you and the team to continue surveilling Victor's home here in San Diego, his usual haunts and the airports, as well. Please let me know if he bubbles to the surface."

"You'll be the first to know, Mr. Sterling."

Andrew saw Pietro to the door, closed the door behind him and latched it, then pulled out his phone to call a woman named Sandy. She'd played a key role in the plan as a mole placed inside Sterling Enterprises to help run the Seaport project aground. Sandy readily agreed to stop when Andrew asked her, but then Victor managed to lure her away with a great deal of money, and she went right back to work. Andrew had never pegged Sandy to be a person who cared only about money, but apparently she was.

Unfortunately, Andrew reached her voice mail. "Sandy. It's Andrew. Again. This is getting old. You won't answer your phone and neither will Victor. We need to put this foolishness to an end. If I need to pay him off or buy out your contract, I'm willing to negotiate, but we can't do that unless one of you calls me back." He didn't relish the idea of drawing a line in the sand, but he was desperate to dictate at least a few rules of this game. "And I want to make sure that neither of you are entertaining any idea of retaliating against Miranda Sterling. If either of you harm a hair on her head, all bets are off. This is about business. Nothing else."

He pressed the red circle on the screen, ending the call. For a moment, he stared at his phone. Thinking. The late-day sun streamed through the window sheers and over his shoulder. His heart began pounding. Had he just made a mistake? Tipped his hand by letting on that Miranda meant something to him?

He sank down onto the couch and ran his hand through his hair. It would all be fine. It had to be. Pietro and his team had eyes on Miranda and her house. She would be safe, and he would fix the problem. Then he could get on with the business of forging a relationship with her and the baby. It might help him come to terms with the death of Johnathon, the brother he'd both loved and hated. It might help him bury so much unhappy history. Right now, it felt like the past was coming back at him, full speed, hell-bent on destroying him from the inside out. He wasn't about to let that happen.

After a long day at her interior-design company, MS Designs, Miranda Sterling was nearly home. She pulled her Range Rover into her La Jolla neighborhood, thoughts fixated on her most pervasive fantasy—a generous bowl of lobster ravioli prepared by her personal chef, followed by a leisurely bubble bath in her enormous soaker tub. Pregnancy had its perks. She was going to take advantage of every one.

She turned into her driveway when her phone rang, the caller ID lighting up the screen—Tara Sterling. Tara was a friend and business partner, but she'd also been the first wife of Johnathon, Miranda's recently deceased husband. Tara and Miranda shared controlling interest of Sterling Enterprises with Astrid, Johnathon's second wife. Johnathon had willed his shares of the company to his three wives, apparently as a testament to how much he'd loved them all. Johnathon had never been anything short of dramatic. "Tara, hey. I just got home. Is this important, or can we talk later? I'm starving and dying to take off these shoes." Miranda eased into the first bay of her four-car garage and killed the engine.

"I'm on my way over to your place with Astrid. We need to talk about Andrew."

Miranda hated the way she kept getting pulled into Sterling Enterprises' drama. Everyone was convinced that Andrew, Johnathon's brother, was somehow meddling in the business. Miranda wasn't convinced. Yes, he and Johnathon had reportedly had a lifelong rivalry, but Andrew didn't seem nearly as evil as people tried to portray him. "What now? We've already talked about this. I have serious doubts about your theory. Do you really think he's the reason there have been so many mistakes on the Seaport Promenade bid?"

"Yes, I do. Astrid and I are almost to your place. We'll talk about it more when we get there."

Miranda didn't love the way Tara and Astrid invited themselves over with very little notice. It was just another sign that everyone knew she had no life beyond work and the baby. Then again, she loved having people over. Tara and Astrid had become true friends, even if it was an unconventional sisterhood. "I hope you like lobster ravioli."

"Are you kidding? I love it."

Miranda made her way inside the house. She'd never get used to how big and empty it felt now that Johnathon was gone. Eight thousand square feet was a silly amount of space for two people to occupy, let alone one person, but she couldn't bring herself to part with their home. It not only had a breathtaking view of the Pacific, but Miranda had also painstakingly decorated every inch of it. The house brought Miranda comfort on the days when she found it hard to dig out from the depths of her grief, and it made her happier whenever she found the courage to simply look ahead to the good things on the horizon, like Thanksgiving, Christmas and, after that, the arrival of her baby girl.

Miranda popped three servings of the ravioli into the oven, thankful she'd had the foresight to ask for extra. Tara and Astrid arrived mere minutes later.

"Come on in." Miranda stepped aside as the two women entered the foyer. Tara, with her bright blond bob and determined stride, led the way, followed by willowy Astrid, the natural beauty and former model. As Miranda closed the door, she couldn't help but notice how she was the short one, especially since she'd kicked off her pumps, while Tara and Astrid were both in heels. At five-seven, Miranda was no shrimp, but the other wives towered over her.

Astrid stooped down and gave Miranda a warm hug. "How are you feeling? Everything good?" Astrid always showed great enthusiasm for the baby on the way, even though she'd suffered years of infertility with Johnathon. Now that she was engaged to Miranda's brother, Clay, Miranda wondered if they would pursue IVF, or perhaps Astrid would choose to focus on becoming a mom to Clay's daughter, Delia.

"I'm mostly just hungry all the time." Miranda waved them both through her spacious living room to the gourmet kitchen, where the heavenly smell of ravioli perfumed the air. "Thankfully, we should be ready to eat in about fifteen minutes. Can I offer either of you a glass of Chablis?" Miranda pulled a bottle from the wine fridge in the center island.

"I'd love one." Astrid perched on one of the barstools.

"Me, too. But I'd really like to address the Andrew situation right away if we can." Tara took a seat next to Astrid.

Miranda cut the foil from the neck of the bottle. "Okay. Shoot."

"He's back in town. I have a friend who saw him at the Grant downtown. I don't think we can wait around to see what he's going to try next," Tara insisted. She then went on to remind Miranda of the misdeeds they were sure he'd committed, including having someone at the city feed misinformation about the project specs to the team at Sterling. "We need to go on the offensive."

Miranda poured two glasses of wine, fighting the frustration she was feeling right now. She'd spent some time with Andrew when he'd come to San Diego a few weeks after Johnathon's death. He might not be perfect, but she didn't see any way he could be the force of evil everyone else seemed to think he was. "I fail to see where I come into all of this. I don't even work at Sterling."

"Exactly why you're the perfect candidate. He won't suspect you," Tara said.

"Plus, you have the best relationship with him. The rest of us don't know him well," Astrid added.

Miranda didn't know Andrew *that* well, but none of the wives did. Andrew hadn't really been a part of Johnathon's life during any of Johnathon's three marriages. Miranda did have the most recent experience with him, and she did like to think she was a good judge of character. There was a part of her that felt a need to clear Andrew's name. "What did you have in mind?"

"Call him and see if you can get together. Try to find out what he's up to."

"He told me he'd reach out if he came back into town," Miranda said. "He hasn't done that. Maybe there's a reason. Maybe he doesn't want to see me." Why that thought bothered her so much, she wasn't sure.

"Or maybe he's zeroing in on his plan. The city is weeks away from awarding the Seaport contract. If he's trying to meddle with it, he has to act now."

Miranda shook her head. "You all are crazy. I really don't see it."

"Maybe you don't want to see it," Astrid said, sliding her hand across the counter until her fingers brushed Miranda's. "I didn't want to believe it, either, but all evidence points in that direction. I know it's hard. He's our living connection to the man we all loved."

Miranda took in a deep breath. As far as she was concerned, that was a reason to give Andrew the benefit of the doubt. But was she being naive? Johnathon had told her stories about bad things Andrew had done. Vindictive and cruel acts. Of course, Miranda was certain that Johnathon had always countered every mean-spirited jab with one of his own. He'd not been the kind of man who let a punch go unanswered.

No matter what, Miranda wanted to put this topic to rest. If Andrew was innocent, she wanted to be able to say that with certainty. Ultimately, she wanted her child to know as much family as possible. Miranda and her brother, Clay, had no memories of their father.

She could not save her daughter that pain, but perhaps it would soften the blow if she was able to have a relationship with her uncle.

"Okay. Fine. I'll call him."

"You will?" Apparently, Tara had anticipated a much bigger fight.

"Yes. I'd like to put this question to rest so we can all move on." Miranda grabbed her phone from the center island and pulled up Andrew's information.

He answered after only a ring or two. "Miranda?"

A noticeable tingle ran down Miranda's back when she heard Andrew's voice. It must be her pregnancy hormones wreaking havoc again. She turned away from Tara and Astrid and wandered closer to the stove on the opposite side of the kitchen. "Andrew, hi. How are you?"

"I'm well. How are you? I'm surprised to hear from you." Again, his voice was warm and soothing, much like the bath she'd been longing for.

Miranda closed her eyes and pinched the bridge of her nose. What she was about to say was going to make her sound like a stalker. "I heard you're in town."

It was so quiet on the other end of the line that Miranda nearly wondered if the connection had dropped. "Who told you that?" His tone was cold and clipped, no longer so comforting.

She had to scramble for an excuse. She couldn't say that Tara and Astrid had provided her with the intel. "I have a friend who saw you. She's the nosy type. I think she assumed that you and I would be seeing each other." Miranda cringed at the sound of that. It was so presumptuous.

"I'm in town on business. I planned to call if I had any free time."

"Oh, of course." Miranda glanced over her shoulder at Tara and Astrid, who were both sitting on the edge of their seats, hanging on Miranda's every word. The pressure was on Miranda to produce. "How long are you here?"

Andrew cleared his throat, making it apparent that she'd put him on the spot. "Not long."

"Would you like to have dinner?" It was the logical invitation. Food was on her mind 24-7. "A man's got to eat, right?"

"I suppose."

"I recently did a full redesign of a steakhouse over in Harbor Island. It has a stunning view of the bay. I haven't had a chance to see the restaurant at night yet."

"Uh, sure. I can do that."

Something about Andrew's inflection made her wonder if he saw this as an imposition. Were Tara and Astrid right? Was Miranda deluded when it came to Andrew? Apparently, she was about to find out. "How about tomorrow night? Meet there at seven?"

Two

Miranda pulled her car up to the valet stand at Harbor Prime, her stomach in knots. Nervousness had been her default setting since she'd ended the call with Andrew yesterday. She was about to do a high-wire act without a net. Tara and Astrid were after answers from Andrew on some very difficult questions, while Miranda wanted to continue to forge a genuine connection with him. These objectives were diametrically opposed to each other. How was she supposed to extract sensitive information from Andrew when she would do anything to keep from burning this particular bridge? She had no idea, but she did know one thing for certain—she'd try her hardest to make everyone happy.

She walked inside, immensely pleased with how beautifully the renovation had turned out. Miranda didn't like to brag about her interior-design skills, but she could admit to herself that she'd done an exceptional job on Harbor Prime. The wood beams crisscrossing the high-peaked ceiling were now stained ebony, accenting the island architecture of the building. The booths were upholstered in a gorgeous fabric with a modern botanical print in shades of coffee-brown and grass-green. Of course, the most breathtaking feature of the restaurant was one that Miranda could not take credit for—the view. All along the far wall were floor-to-ceiling windows, which framed the magnificent evening vista of the bay with the city skyline twinkling beyond.

"Ms. Sterling." The hostess stepped out from behind her desk to shake Miranda's hand. "It's nice to have you join us this evening."

"I'm glad I had a chance to come out and see the renovation at night." Miranda scanned the dining room, but didn't see Andrew.

"We have a beautiful table for you this evening, with an exceptional view."

"I don't believe my dinner date is here yet." Miranda felt silly referring to Andrew that way, but it was the first thing that had come out of her mouth.

"Actually, Mr. Sterling arrived ten minutes ago. I went ahead and sat him at your table." The hostess swept her arm forward. "This way."

Miranda followed her through the dining room, which was abuzz with music, heavenly scents and the chatter of happy diners. As they rounded the central bank of booths, Miranda saw him in profile as he looked out over the water. A zap of excitement hit her, doing nothing to settle her nerves. Why would she feel this way? Pregnancy hormones? Or perhaps it was her heart, reminding her that he was so closely linked to the man she'd loved and lost.

Andrew turned and his intense eyes locked on her as he managed a reserved smile. He rose from his seat and she quickly drifted closer when he opened his arms, an invitation she was eager to take. "Miranda, it's good to see you," he muttered into her hair. His embrace was warm and comforting, and there was a part of her that just wanted to stand in his arms for a few hours. It had been so long since she'd felt this good.

"I'm happy to see you, too."

Andrew released and stepped back, noticeably eyeing her belly. "Baby's grown since the last time I saw you."

Miranda resisted the urge to smooth her hands over her stomach. She still wasn't showing much and didn't love the idea of fixating on the ways her body was changing. Being a widow was a vulnerable position, and the pregnancy made it even more so. "I'm just a little more than halfway."

"Pregnancy suits you. You look great." Andrew eased behind her chair and pulled it out for her.

Miranda appreciated the gentlemanly gesture and his kind words more than he ever could have known. It was so nice to be treated well. "Flattery will get you everywhere."

"I'll keep that in mind." Andrew punctuated the end of his sentence with an arch of one eyebrow, then took his seat opposite her. "I haven't ordered a drink yet, but I did ask them to bring you some water. But I don't know if it's filtered, so perhaps we should order something bottled. I know pregnant women need to watch every little thing they eat or drink."

He was so considerate. How anyone could ever suspect him of having unkind motives, Miranda didn't know. "This is just fine, but thank you." Miranda took a sip, her nervousness fading away. She smiled, unable to keep from admiring him. She couldn't help that her inclination was to notice the ways he was like his brother, and the many ways in which they were different. Andrew was remarkably good-looking, like Johnathon, with tousled chestnut-brown hair, but his eyes were a much more complex shade of blue-green. His facial scruff was more pronounced, stopping shy of being an actual beard. The biggest difference was that Andrew had a far more inward demeanor. Nothing about his manner suggested that he needed to be the center of attention, or, quite frankly, that he wanted it that way. That was a massive difference. Johnathon had always insisted on being the sun everyone revolved around.

The server appeared and took their drink orders—a cranberry juice with club soda and lime for Miranda, while Andrew ordered a bourbon neat, delighted that they had a brand called Michter's.

"You don't drink it on the rocks?" Miranda asked.

"Not this one. It's small-batch. Too delicious to water down."

"I see."

Andrew's sights settled on Miranda's face, and for a moment, she had the nerve to return the look, if only to peer into the storm of his eyes, hoping for clues as to who he really was or what he wanted. She'd heard so many stories from Johnathon, none of which cast Andrew in a positive light. Sitting here, just the two of them, it was hard to envision him doing anything evil or underhanded. But Miranda broke their shared gaze when she started to feel nervous again. She turned her attention to the water, just as the server delivered their drinks.

"Cheers," Andrew offered, raising his glass.

"To family." Her toast made her want to cast aside the true nature of her visit. This should be a time for building the bond between them, not extracting information.

He closed his eyes for an instant as he enjoyed a sip of bourbon, then swirled it in his glass as he again gazed at her with such intensity that it made her feel as though she was under a microscope. She had to wonder what he saw when he looked at her. Was she a friend to him? Merely his brother's wife, and therefore, an obligation? The fact that he hadn't called to let her know he was in town seemed to suggest she was an afterthought. And she couldn't ignore that he'd hesitated to accept her invitation.

Andrew opened his menu. "Any suggestions?"

Miranda snapped back to the moment and turned her thoughts to her favorite subject of late—food. "It's all good. They have an excellent wedge salad to start and they'll bring warm popovers to the table. Beyond that, the steaks are amazing and prepared to perfection. You seriously can't go wrong."

He nodded and closed his menu. "Perfect. Have you decided? We should order."

"Do you have somewhere you need to be?"

"I have some business to attend to later tonight."

That seemed strange. "That works for me. Food is a big priority right now." A breathy laugh left her lips. "It's all I think about. That and sleeping."

He turned to look over his shoulder, flagging their server. "Let's get you taken care of. My brother's not here to do it, so I will." A hush fell between them, even though the noisiness of the restaurant remained.

Miranda felt like she was adrift at sea, all by herself. It had been a familiar feeling since Johnathon's death, but she hoped she wouldn't have to live with it forever.

Andrew reached out his right hand for Miranda's left, which was resting on the table. His warm palm blanketed her fingers, including the one where her wedding rings still sat. "I'm sorry. I shouldn't have said that. It was incredibly insensitive."

"Andrew. It's fine. My loss is your loss. There's no way around that."

Their server arrived at the table. "Are we ready to order?"

Andrew dropped his head ever so slightly, seeking Miranda's approval. "Ready?"

"Yes. Absolutely." She rattled off a few favorites, her mouth watering at the idea of the meal ahead. Andrew followed.

"Perfect," the server said. "I'll put this in right away."

They were left alone again, and that meant Miranda's nerves returned. She wanted the uneasiness to go away, so she and Andrew could enjoy their meal together. Which meant she needed to move forward with her objective, get her answers and put the whole thing to rest. She was unsure of how to bring up the subject of Andrew meddling in Sterling Enterprises, but thought the direct approach was best. "Now that we're able to chat in person, there's something I'm curious about." She shifted in her seat, struggling to utter the question she had to ask. *Just come out with it so you can get past this.* "Did you come back to town because you have an interest in the Seaport Promenade project?"

* * *

Michter's twenty-year bourbon was not meant to be slugged back. It was meant to be savored. Still, Andrew considered downing it in one gulp, if only to take off the edge of the moment and calculate his next move. Unfortunately, Miranda's question put him on unsteady ground, while her beauty was a distraction that knocked him off his feet. Her warm brown eyes, while painted with uncertainty, were mesmerizing. Her dark, glossy hair softly framed her flawless face and fell across her shoulders in a luscious cascade. No wonder Johnathon had been drawn to her. It was impossible to look away. And yet, Andrew had to. She wasn't his to admire.

He couldn't ignore what she'd asked and he had no business expressing surprise that she'd figured this out. She struck him as incredibly smart and she was reportedly quite tangled up with Sterling Enterprises business now that she had a direct stake. Part of him wanted to brush aside his misdeeds for now, hide them until he'd had a chance to make everything better. But another part of him was exhausted from living under the guilt of secrets.

"How much do you know?" he asked, buying himself more time.

"How much do you want to tell me?"

Andrew could literally be here for hours, detailing every little thing that had happened between Johnathon and him that ultimately led to the decision to interfere with Sterling. But he wasn't about to air his grievances over dinner. "I did take an interest in the Seaport Promenade project. Specifically, an interest in preventing Johnathon from landing the deal."

"I see." She took a sip of her drink and ran her slender fingers around the base of the glass, then she set it back down on the table. Everything about Miranda was beautiful, but something about her hands was particularly enchanting. "And does that mean you took an active role in keeping it from happening?"

"Yes. I did. It was my idea."

She drew a breath in through her nose and her jaw tensed. She didn't seem like a woman who might make a scene, but in that moment, he could see the possibility. "Why would you do that? To your own brother?" Her voice wobbled ever so slightly, but her posture remained determined. She wasn't going to back down until Andrew gave up more of the information he'd worked so hard to hide.

"Surely he told you about our relationship. Surely he told you how little he liked me."

"He told me that you two never got along. He told me you were capable of being underhanded, which I really didn't want to believe once we'd finally met and had a chance to talk."

It confounded him that she had any inclination to give him the benefit of the doubt. No one did that. He didn't even do it for himself. It was a foolish pursuit. "It's true, though. I've done bad things."

"And I've been defending you to people at Sterling. Please don't tell me I made a mistake."

So it wasn't merely Miranda's suspicion that he was interfering with the Seaport project. The powers that be at Sterling were apparently aware of his scheme, as well. "I never gave you any reason to have any faith in me."

"That's not true. We had an amazing conversation that night you came to see me a few weeks after Johnathon died. I didn't know what to expect, but you were truly torn up about his death."

Memories of that night, which was the first time he and Miranda had met, flooded his brain. Little else had occupied his thoughts since then. He'd gone to her house expecting the worst—screaming and yelling and possibly kicking him out. After all, he'd done the unthinkable and skipped his own brother's funeral. He'd been unwilling to face their history, or the reality that this person who had consumed so much of his life, his brother, was gone.

But he'd ultimately let guilt dictate his actions and had reached out to Miranda in person. Everything hit him at once that night—she was pregnant with his niece or nephew, a child who would never have a relationship with his deceased brother. And Andrew was making an innocent baby's predicament worse by trying to drag Johnathon's business and reputation through the mud. That was the moment when he'd known he had to put a stop to his plan.

"I heard it in your voice that night when you talked about Johnathon," Miranda continued. "Whatever happened between you two, I believe you loved each other. I know it. That's all I care about."

Was that really true? Andrew wasn't sure. Right now, he was more concerned with a man at the bar who'd glanced over his shoulder in Andrew and Miranda's direction. The situation with Victor had him on high alert. "I'm sorry for having a plan in the first place. I had my reasons, but none of that matters now." He sat back in his seat and took another generous sip of his bourbon. "If I could do it all over again, I would never have set these particular wheels in motion."

Miranda sucked in a deep breath, seeming to run through everything he had just said. Meanwhile, their salads were delivered, along with the fresh popovers. She tore apart the yeasty, puffy bread as soon as she could, adding a dollop of butter. She popped a bite into her mouth then licked her bottom lip, where a drop of butter had been left behind. The vision left Andrew stuck. She was beguiling. And he needed to stop looking.

"Thank God there's food. This conversation is making me anxious." Miranda dabbed at her mouth with a napkin.

Indeed, the popovers were warm and comforting, and a welcome respite from the topic at hand. "I agree."

"Look, I'm not trying to get you to tell me everything about your issues with Johnathon. It's obvious that it's not something you want to talk about, and the truth is that he's not here to answer for any of it. I think it's most fair to you, and to him, if we just let it go. But I have one thing I want. I want you to stop."

"I want to, but it's not that simple." Again, the man at the bar stole another glance at them. He was tempted to ask Miranda if she knew him, but he didn't want to draw attention to what might potentially be a problem. If things got dicey, he'd keep her safe.

"From where I'm sitting, it's incredibly simple. You're the only living connection I have to Johnathon. You're the baby's only biological relative on her father's side. You should be a part of her life. But that can't happen if you're threatening her birthright with this scheme."

"Her?"

"Yes." A smile bloomed across her stunning face. "A little girl."

Every passing minute with Miranda brought Andrew's misdeeds into sharper focus. In his mind's eye, he could see his future niece. Hurting her was unthinkable. And here was her mother, with every reason to be angry with him, and she was inviting him into their life. The idea stole his breath away. "That's why I'm here in San Diego. To stop the plan." *I have to.*

Miranda's cycs narrowed on him. "Then just do it."

Their entrées had arrived, but Andrew didn't have much appetite anymore. "I had a partner. A man named Victor. You have to understand that Johnathon had a lot of enemies, and I'd put Victor near the top of the list. He jumped at the chance to take part. But after Johnathon died, I told Victor we had to stop. Unfortunately, he didn't agree. So now he's gone rogue and I have to track him down if I have any chance of convincing him to end it."

Her face clouded with confusion. "If he's here in San Diego, you should just let me talk to him. I can be pretty persuasive."

Andrew had zero doubt about that. Andrew nearly laughed at her willingness to trust others. It struck him as brave, but horribly naive. He wasn't going to let her within fifty feet of Victor, especially while she was pregnant. "I'm the only one who can stop him." Andrew again saw the man at the bar look in their direction. There was no way he was merely another customer. Something was going on.

"That sounds like something Johnathon would say. You should let me help you. This is in my interest, too."

"Please. Miranda. This is between me and Victor."

And the ghost of your dead husband. "It might require a few concessions, but I'll get it done. I promise."

Miranda shook her head while enjoying a bite of her steak. "I will never understand the games men play in business, especially when you get to be as rich as you are. You've already won. Can't you just be satisfied?"

She was so right. If only he'd had a Miranda in his life to steer him straight. Things might have turned out differently. But love hadn't been kind to Andrew. Not like it had been to Johnathon. "We're ridiculous, aren't we? We hoard our toys and don't want to share with anyone."

She pointed at him with her fork. "Exactly. That's how Johnathon was. Always on the lookout for the next kill. He took entirely too much pleasure in beating others."

Andrew knew that very well. He'd been on the receiving end too many times to count. "My brother was very good at it. It's hard not to keep going when you excel at something."

Miranda shrugged. "I guess. It still doesn't mean I understand the need to be ruthless."

"Of course you don't. You're a kind person. You clearly have a generous heart. I appreciate that you want me to be a part of your life and the baby's. It means more to me than you know."

"Family is incredibly important to me, and I don't have much. I have to hold on to everyone I can."

She was so beautiful and pure of heart. He wasn't sure he deserved to sit at the same table with her, let alone be part of her life. "I understand. I'm in a similar situation."

"Right. Which means you and I need to stick together. And that starts right now. You should not be staying at a hotel. It isn't right. Family stays with family. You should come stay with me."

His pulse picked up, pounding in his ears. He had no business getting physically closer to Miranda. She'd only distract him from the task at hand. "No. Thank you."

"You're turning me down?"

I'm keeping you safe. "I don't want to be an inconvenience."

"It's no trouble at all. I'm in that big empty house by myself all the time. It gets really lonely. And boring. You'd be doing me a favor. It would be so nice just to have someone else there."

Andrew scrambled for another argument to make. He was already fighting an attraction that was all wrong. Spending more time with Miranda would only make it worse.

Their server appeared at the table. "Are we still working on the meal?"

"Wow. I pretty well polished that off, didn't I?" Miranda asked, then pointed to Andrew's plate, which was still half-full. "Is everything okay?"

"I'm fine," Andrew said. "Just too caught up in our conversation."

"I have a piece of Mississippi mud pie coming out from the kitchen for you in a moment," the server said. "The gentleman at the bar sent it over." She turned and gestured in that direction, but then her expression fell. "Oh. I guess he left."

"Did you see someone you know?" Andrew asked Miranda, desperately hoping the answer was yes.

She shook her head. "I don't think so. But dessert sure sounds good."

The hair on the back of Andrew's neck stood up. He'd thought that man was suspicious. Was this Victor's way of letting Andrew know that he was close by? He wasn't about to let on about his suspicions. "It does."

The server left and Andrew took the chance to finish his bourbon. He had to remind himself that he could handle this. He could take care of Victor. So why was he feeling so especially nervous about it? Probably because of the pregnant woman sitting across the table from him.

"Well? What do you think about my offer? Coming to stay at the house?" Miranda asked.

Andrew knew this wasn't a good idea. He was already saddled with unbearable guilt over the plan he'd set in motion. Having to fight his attraction to his dead brother's wife was only going to make setting things right a more complicated proposition. But he couldn't worry about his own internal struggles. He was stronger than that. Bottom line, he had to keep Miranda safe. Johnathon would expect it of him. "It sounds great. I'd love to accept the invitation."

Three

"Moving in? With you? Into your house?" Tara asked Miranda, her voice booming over the phone line.

Miranda winced at the line of questions. Everything about them was bad. The tone. The substance. The volume. "He's not moving in. He's coming to stay with me for a few nights. People do that, you know. Families." Miranda peered out the window, waiting on Andrew's arrival.

"He's not your family."

"What are you talking about? He's Johnathon's brother. He will be biologically related to my child. That's family." She tugged the curtain back into place and wandered into the living room, plopping down in a chair.

"Family sticks around. Family goes to the funeral when someone passes away."

"He and Johnathon were estranged. That happens.

I could spend my entire life resenting Andrew for his mistake, or I can move on with my life. I'm inclined to do the latter. This hasn't been easy for me." It was the truth. Losing her husband while expecting their child had been one of the most difficult things Miranda had ever endured. It was a never-ending tug-of-war between the grief over what was lost and the hope over what was to be. She had to lean toward the more optimistic side of her circumstances. It was the only way to stay sane.

"Well, Grant and I are very concerned." It came as no surprise that Tara's fiancé, Grant, didn't like this idea. He'd been Johnathon's oldest friend. "Not only are you letting the man who was secretly sabotaging Sterling Enterprises into your home, he accepted the invitation. What is he after?"

Miranda sighed. She trusted Andrew. If that made her a fool, so be it. At least she could say that she'd tried to build a bridge to him. "I told you. He's in town to track down this Victor person."

"Grant doesn't know who Victor is. That seems highly suspicious. Grant knew about all of Johnathon's business dealings, and he knows everyone who hated him. I think Andrew is lying."

Miranda was not the sort of woman who convinced herself of things that weren't true, but she did feel as though she saw qualities in Andrew that no one else did. Perhaps it was her charge to show others the light. "Andrew didn't try to hide his plan from me. He came right out and owned up to it. He apologized. Why would he do that if he had ulterior motives?"

"That's the thing about hidden agendas. They're hidden."

Miranda choked back a grumble of frustration. "I

really don't think he was being dishonest, okay? Can we leave it at that?"

"What does your brother think?"

Clay had shown some reservation, but that was normal for him. He was immensely protective of Miranda, just as he was of his daughter, Delia, and now his fiancée, Astrid, the second of the Sterling wives. In the end, Miranda had convinced Clay that this was the right thing and that he had nothing to worry about. "He's fine with it."

"Really?" The incredulity in Tara's voice was unmistakable.

"Yes." Miranda heard the sound of a car door closing outside. "I have to go, Tara."

"I hope you know that I'm only being a pain because I care about you and the baby. You're like a sister to me."

Miranda felt utterly stuck between the people she cared the most about—Tara, Clay and Grant on one side, and Andrew on the other. "I know your heart's in the right place. You have to trust that mine is, too."

"Please tell me you'll call me if there's a problem."

"I will." She ended the call and got out of the chair, taking her time ambling to the front door. She didn't want to appear too eager. She wasn't sure how she was supposed to feel about his arrival. She was excited by the prospect of having some company and no longer being alone in this house. But she was unsure what their dynamic would be like. Between the things Johnathon had said and Miranda's own experiences, Andrew was still an unknown quantity.

She turned the latch and opened her front door just as Andrew was climbing out of a big black SUV. She couldn't help but notice the way her heart flipped at the sight of him in dark jeans, a black dress shirt with the sleeves rolled up and black sunglasses. He might be an enigma, but he was wrapped up in a far-too-appealing package. Andrew was more than handsome. He was ridiculously hot. Smoking. Was she just supposed to ignore that while they were living under the same roof?

"I didn't expect a welcoming committee." He waved to Miranda as he strode up to her front steps, toting a brown leather men's overnight bag.

"I wouldn't want to be a bad host." She was proud of herself for speaking, fighting her true inclination to bite down on her lower lip.

Andrew cupped her shoulder and leaned down to kiss her cheek, leaving behind a warmth that radiated through her body. "How are you?"

Dizzy. "Good. You?"

"Glad to be out of the hotel. I'll tell you that much."

"Good. Come on in." With a deep breath, Miranda composed herself and made her way inside. Andrew followed, closing the door behind him. "I'll show you up to your room so you can drop your bag and get settled," she said.

"Please. Lead the way."

She traipsed through the wide central hall, past the living room and kitchen to the left and her home office on the right. When they reached the stairs and started the climb to the second floor, she was overcome by a heightened awareness of his presence behind her. With each step, they were venturing closer to privacy and solitude, where absolutely anything might happen. The realization set off a conflict between her body and brain. She was undeniably attracted to Andrew. Her immediate physical reaction could not be questioned.

But he was her dead husband's brother. It wasn't right for her to have desirous feelings toward him. It was wrong, bad, and terribly inappropriate. How would she ever reconcile the battle between her wants and what was sensible?

Stop it. You're thinking like Tara. Miranda was not going to let worry rule her life. With a baby on the way, there was already plenty to feel unsure of. Andrew was a wonderful man, but totally off-limits. The time had come for her to strengthen their relationship—to get close, but not *too* close.

Down the hall, she arrived at one of her three guest rooms. Johnathon had always liked having people around, and there had been many times when the house was fully occupied by various friends from all over the world. Those memories were part of what made the present state of her home so unsettling. It was entirely too empty and quiet.

"Here you are," Miranda said, stepping inside and flipping on the light.

"It's perfect." Andrew set his bag next to the dresser. "Did you design this room? It's spectacular."

Heat rose in her cheeks. She was proud of the job she'd done on this room. It was the most masculine of the guest spaces, with charcoal-gray bedding and a faux parchment treatment on the wall behind the bed. Over each of the dark wood bedside tables was a dramatic pendant light fixture hanging from the ten-foot ceiling. This room was magnificent at night. "I did the whole house."

Andrew set down his sunglasses on one of the tables, then turned and offered a faint smile. "I'm duly impressed."

If anyone was blown away, it was Miranda. Everything about Andrew was a deluge to the senses—his warm and citrusy smell, his affable grin and the genuine mystery of his eyes. It made her appreciate his presence that much more, but she reminded herself that this was temporary. It was best not to fixate on his many selling points. "I'm glad you're here."

"I'm thankful for the invitation."

"How long do you think you'll stay?"

"Not too long. A few days? A week? I'll head back to Seattle as soon as I wrap things up with Victor."

"You won't be able to stay for Thanksgiving? It's less than two weeks away." She heard the disappointment in her own voice and knew she had to dial it back. It wasn't her place to put expectations on him. "I mean, it would be nice if you could be here for it. I'm hosting. My brother will be here with Astrid and his daughter. Grant and Tara."

"I doubt I'll need to be here that long."

Perhaps holidays weren't important to Andrew the way they were to Miranda. She clung to them because they signaled the normalcy she hadn't always had in her life. "Sounds like you're ready to get to work then. Will you need an office space? I could set you up in Johnathon's study."

He cleared his throat and his posture stiffened. "I don't know if that's a good idea. I wouldn't want to intrude on your memories of him. I'm sure that room means a lot to you."

"Honestly, I haven't stepped foot in there since he died. I'm sure that sounds crazy, but I couldn't bring myself to do it. I think it would be nice if someone actually used it. Then it wouldn't have to be a place for thinking about loss. It could just be a functioning room."

Andrew stuffed his hands into his pants pockets. "I don't know."

Miranda didn't intend to push Andrew to do something he didn't want to do, but she also sensed that he hadn't come to terms with Johnathon's death. Perhaps this would help him along. "Come on. I'll let you check it out."

"Okay. If nothing else, I'd like to see it."

Together they walked to the very end of the hall and to Johnathon's study. Miranda wasn't quite sure why she hadn't ventured inside after Johnathon was gone, aside from her fear of sinking into the depths of a sadness from which she might never return. She'd had her days of running her hands through Johnathon's clothes in the closet or smelling his cologne. Doing those things hadn't made her feel any better, and certainly hadn't brought him back. So why make it worse by going into the room where he'd spent so much time?

The office was exactly as Johnathon had left it—neat as a pin. Not so much as a stray piece of paper had been left out. There was the mahogany desk Miranda had spent months hunting for, an impossibly heavy antique, and a collection of vintage maps of San Diego and Southern California, to remind him of his love of the area. And, of course, there was an entire wall devoted to the many awards and pieces of publicity Johnathon had earned in his relatively short time on earth—businessman of the year, philanthropic accolades, magazine covers.

"It's a stunning room," Andrew said, noticeably not

venturing past the threshold. "My brother was a very lucky guy."

"He definitely had a way of bending the universe to his will, didn't he?" Miranda stepped inside, hoping that would make Andrew come along, but he remained in the doorway. She could see the trepidation on his face, the way he was unsure of himself, which was such a stark contrast to his usual confident stance. Was it because this room was as close to a confrontation with his brother as he might ever get?

"He sure did."

"Do you want to tell me more about what happened between you two? Or are you going to stay vague about it, the way Johnathon did?"

Before he answered the question, Andrew had to remind himself of the entire reason he was back in town and now found himself in Miranda's house. He was here to keep her safe and to meet the opportunity she'd put before him—to become a part of her life and her daughter's. This was a delicate proposition and he wasn't about to mess it up. He wanted to be closer to Miranda. But she was his brother's widow, and if ever there was a woman he needed to see as off-limits, it was her. He would not step into his brother's shoes.

Still, he'd gotten sucked right into Miranda's sweet disposition as soon as he'd walked through the door, and now he was having to deal with that while confronted with an uncomfortable presence—the specter of his brother. It was all around him, this entire room a testament to his accomplishments and the many ways he'd triumphed, with Miranda at the heart of it all.

"You're about to have his baby, Miranda. You were

his wife. I don't want my past with him to color the way you see him. It's not fair to him. And it's not fair to me, either, to be honest. I wouldn't exactly be a good houseguest if I came in and told you stories about how Johnathon and I were rivals, or how he always seemed to get everything right and I was the one who made the mistakes."

"He wasn't perfect. There's no need to worry about keeping him on a pedestal."

He still wasn't convinced. "Speaking ill of the dead is never a good idea."

"I understand what you're saying, but I've learned things since he died that were a total shock to the system." Her eyes darted from side to side as if she was searching for something, but eventually she seemed to put it all together. "Wait a minute. You already know what I'm talking about, don't you? The secret he hid from me?"

"No. I don't know a thing."

"But you orchestrated it. The email I got. The Sterling Enterprises IT department traced it back to your company. It was all part of the plan to disrupt the business at Sterling, wasn't it?" Much like she had at dinner last night, she was becoming more and more upset. The color rose in her cheeks, while her eyes were full of pain he didn't fully understand.

"I didn't send any email, Miranda. I honestly don't have any idea what you're alluding to."

"I got a message from Johnathon's work account. It said he slept with Astrid, his second wife, after he and I got engaged. It was written like it came from Johnathon, but that part was just a cruel joke. Unfortunately, Astrid confirmed that it was all true. I think the information was leaked by a woman named Sandy, who worked at Sterling. If you don't know about it, does that mean she's connected to Victor?"

Andrew felt the blood go cold in his veins. This was a lot to unpack—his brother had betrayed Miranda, but the news had been delivered by Victor, courtesy of his heartless ways. It made one thing very clear for Andrew—his true loyalty needed to be to Miranda. She was the person with the most to lose, who had been hurt the most. "I'm so sorry Johnathon cheated on you. I had no idea." He took no pleasure in seeing this chink in his brother's perfect facade. It had come at too high a price for Miranda.

She wrapped her arms around her middle, as if she could shield herself from the world. "There's nothing I can do about it. What's done is done. I've come to terms with it."

"It's still a terrible betrayal."

"It is, but it's also an instance in which your brother was not perfect. So whatever it is that you think you need to live up to, I promise you that you can stop trying to compete."

Andrew sighed and finally found the nerve to step into the room. It felt a bit like he was confronting the spirit of his brother, but right now, Andrew's most important task was to comfort Miranda. He pulled her into his arms and held her tight. "It's not about me right now."

"So it wasn't you who orchestrated the message? The email?"

"No." He stood back slightly and peered down into her flawless face. Her eyes were watery, like she was on the verge of tears. No, he hadn't been responsible for this, but he'd put the actors in place. "But I did hire the woman who leaked the information. Sandy. I put her in place at Sterling. It's just that she went to work for Victor after I tried to put an end to the plan."

"And what was her role in all of this?"

"She was the mole inside Sterling."

"She was hired as Johnathon's new assistant. You put her right in the lion's den."

Go big or go home. "That was a lucky break. It could have gone a different way. The plan was always to have someone there to interfere with Sterling's bid to redevelop the Seaport Promenade. She was there to create mistakes so they couldn't land it."

"Why that project? From what I understand, there are plenty of deals with far bigger profits. It seems like it's all about bragging rights."

Andrew wasn't about to answer her question fully, but he could at least give her the framework for his theory. "It was significant to me, and that made it of importance to Johnathon. The fact that there's so little profit to be made only seems to prove that he pursued it for personal reasons. To not only put a knife in my back, but to twist it."

"What could possibly be so important about the promenade that it would cause this much trouble between you?"

"It's a symbol of the city. This is where we grew up, and where we both tried to make a life for ourselves. Johnathon succeeded at building an empire here. I didn't." Andrew sucked in a deep breath and forced himself to stop. He didn't want her pity, and he didn't want to crack open his own heart in front of her, either. "Johnathon and I were engaged in a lifelong game of

king of the hill. It felt like this was his attempt to per-
manently plant a victory flag on top of the mountain."

Miranda shook her head slowly, seeming unsatisfied
with his answer. "Why do I feel like you still aren't telling me everything?"

Because I'm not. "Did you ever know him to be petty
or vindictive?"

She bunched up her lips like she was having to think
very hard about this. "Not toward me, but I heard stories."

"Some of those stories were right. That's why Victor wants to carry out the plan. He and Johnathon had a
bad business deal. Victor feels that he bore the brunt of
the loss. He doesn't care at all about the Seaport project,
but he does care about damaging Sterling's reputation
and sabotaging the company."

"But Johnathon's gone. He'll just be hurting innocent
people. There's no more revenge to get now, is there?"

Miranda saw it so clearly, but it hadn't been that
simple for Andrew. Even in the shock of Johnathon's
death, he'd been blinded by the memories of his brother,
a lifetime of conflict that had shaped nearly every cir-
cumstance of Andrew's existence. "I know. You're right.
But there's no telling Victor that." Just thinking about it
made him even more eager to fix the mess he'd made.
He had to redouble his efforts to reach Victor and get
him to pull the plug.

"Maybe I should be grateful for it. It brought you
back to San Diego. We wouldn't have had this time together otherwise."

What made Miranda so trusting and pure of heart?
Andrew couldn't imagine what it might be like to go
through life like that. He wasn't sure if he was wired

this way, or if it was the result of a lifetime of betrayal, but he felt destined to never put his faith in anyone. "That's a very sunny way of looking at the situation."

"Or it's desperate. I'm clinging to everything and everyone I have."

The idea of her holding on to him made him that much more resolute to fix the problem he'd created. He would not leave her with anything less than what she deserved.

"You must be hungry. Would you like some lunch?"

"You've already done so much. Let me cook for you?"

Miranda cocked an eyebrow at him. "Seriously? I don't think your brother knew how to operate the stove."

"You must realize by now that we're very different people."

"I'm starting to see that, but there are similarities. I see him in you."

Andrew needed to continue to set himself apart. He didn't want his identity and that of his brother too closely linked. "If it's all the same to you, I'd like to focus on the differences."

Four

Andrew had made it through his first week living with Miranda without doing anything stupid. That felt like a big win. By day, he worked out of her house, utilizing Johnathon's study. By night, they enjoyed time together. They even managed to largely avoid the topic of Johnathon, even though his brother was a looming presence in the house. Andrew seemed to make Miranda happy by preparing dinner every night, and that, in turn, filled him with a satisfaction that was growing by the day. But he knew that the pleasure he took in being around her was ultimately not good. He couldn't afford to get too comfortable. His life in Seattle was waiting for him—a lonely existence, but one in which the only risks he took were with business.

Unfortunately, he'd made no progress on the Victor front. He'd left countless messages. He'd sent Pietro on several trips to various locales around the city where they might be able to find him. Victor was hiding, lurking somewhere in the shadows, and that could only mean bad things. Andrew had also attempted to reach Sandy with a similar result. He suspected that money was at the root of her loyalty, and if that was all it would take to get her to end her involvement, he'd give her whatever she wanted.

It was late Friday afternoon when Miranda's doorbell rang, and Andrew went to answer it. A burly delivery guy was waiting outside, with a truck parked behind him.

"I have a delivery for Miranda Sterling." The man handed over a clipboard.

Andrew looked at the shipping order. It was from a furniture company, which made little sense. Wouldn't she have that shipped to her office? "Before I sign for it, I need to call Ms. Sterling and make sure this is okay." How was he supposed to know this wasn't Victor sending another signal that he was watching Andrew and Miranda?

The man grunted. "I have other deliveries to make."

"I'm sure you do. One minute." Andrew turned his back and pulled his cell out of his pocket to call Miranda.

"Hey there. Is everything okay?" she asked.

"Yes. Everything is fine. I wanted to see if you were expecting a delivery from a company called Bella Furniture."

"Oh, my God. That's the crib. It wasn't supposed to arrive until the middle of December. Yes. Please sign for it." The excitement in her voice was unmistakable, and it gave him a lift he hadn't expected.

He cradled the phone between his ear and shoulder while turning back to the front door and signing for the shipment.

"You want me to bring it inside?" the driver asked.

"Yes. Please." Andrew returned his attention to Miranda, but he watched as another delivery person began wheeling the crate to the door. "It looks like a flat box. Does it need to be assembled?"

"It does, but I'll have one of the guys from my warehouse come to the house and do it."

"Why don't you let me handle it?" He waved the deliverymen inside, and they hauled the oversize box into the foyer.

"That's not necessary. You're busy."

He didn't want to tell her that he felt utterly useless since he'd been unable to achieve his primary objective while in San Diego—stopping Victor. "I'd really like to do this for you. And the baby. Please."

"Okay," she said. "If you insist."

"I insist." He found himself smiling. It felt so damn good to make her happy.

"While I have you on the phone, I wanted to let you know that my brother, Clay, is coming by the house in a little bit. He has his own key, but I thought I should give you a heads-up. His daughter, Delia, left one of her favorite books at my house the last time they were over. She's been asking for it for over a week."

"Okay. Great. I look forward to meeting him."

"Sounds good. I'll see you when I get home."

Andrew ended the call, overcome by the feelings of comfort Miranda gave him. He reminded himself not to become accustomed to this. This wasn't his life.

The box was simply too big to carry upstairs, so Andrew cracked it open and began ferrying the parts up the stairs and to the nursery. With every trip, he thought a bit more about what was ahead for Miranda, raising a baby on her own. He supposed that she would have the help of her brother, so it wasn't like she'd be without a safety net, but it still made him wish there was a place for him somewhere in the midst of that. Perhaps more regular visits would be in order. But only if that was what Miranda wanted.

After six or seven trips upstairs, the doorbell rang again. Andrew answered, coming face-to-face with Clay, Miranda's brother, for the first time.

"Miranda told me you'd probably be here. Clay Morgan." Clay extended his hand. He had the same dark hair as Miranda, but a decidedly more intense demeanor.

Andrew shook Clay's hand and opened the door wider. "Please. Come in."

"I won't be in your way for long. I think the book I'm looking for is in Miranda's office," Clay said.

"You're welcome to stay if you want. I'm just unpacking the crib Miranda ordered for the nursery."

"Really? Can I help?"

"Yeah. Of course." Who was Andrew to say no? Plus, he relished the chance to get to know Miranda's brother. "Just grab whatever you want. Most of it is already upstairs."

Between the two of them, they were able to bring up the final pieces in a single trip. "Are you planning on putting it together?"

Andrew surveilled the pile of parts, wooden panels and hardware. "Believe it or not, yes."

"I assembled my daughter's crib when she was born

and let me tell you, it's much easier if you have two people. I'd be happy to help."

"You sure you don't need to go? I don't want to keep you from your family."

Clay consulted his watch. "I'll help you for an hour. Astrid is at work and Delia's with the nanny, so I definitely have time."

"Great. I'd appreciate it."

The pair went to work, Clay organizing the parts and Andrew reading the instructions after gathering some tools from Miranda's utility room.

"How long are you in town?" Clay asked as they started the assembly.

"I'd originally thought only a few days, but my work project isn't quite coming together the way I thought it would."

"You mean dismantling your plan to take down the company I work for?"

Whoa. Andrew hadn't quite expected that, but he admired Clay's candor. "In a word, yes. I don't know how much Miranda told you."

"She gave me the highlights. For what it's worth, I appreciate that you're willing to fix your own mess. Not enough people are like that. Most people hide from their mistakes."

Andrew was starting to think that kindness might just run in the Morgan family. Clay seemed as generous as his sister. "Don't give me too much credit. I still messed up pretty bad."

"I don't have a brother, so I can't really relate to whatever rivalry you had with Johnathon, but I do understand how intense a relationship with a sibling can be. I can see how it might motivate you to do some crazy things."

"You love your sister a lot, don't you?"

Clay looked right at Andrew. "I do. Absolutely. Which is why I'm rooting for you to be able to save Sterling Enterprises from any ill effects of whatever it is this Victor person plans to do. If you hurt the company, you hurt her. And the baby. It's the glue that brings us all together."

Andrew felt the weight of the moment squarely on his shoulders. He would not let Miranda down. He couldn't. "Don't worry. I've already promised Miranda that I won't let anything bad happen. Nothing at all."

Miranda had a hard time concentrating after she got off the phone with Andrew. The fact that he'd offer to drop everything and assemble the crib? Well, that was just too much. Once again, she failed to see the bad person others seemed to think he was. In fact, quite the opposite. She saw only good.

As a result, she found herself unable to focus as the rest of the workday ticked away, all in anticipation of the moment she could leave the office and spend the weekend with Andrew. She knew she shouldn't be getting attached, but she couldn't help it. After their first week together, it was clear that Andrew and Miranda had little trouble coexisting. They had breakfast together each morning, then went their separate ways, Miranda to her office and Andrew into Johnathon's study, where he managed his development firm from a distance, all while trying to track down the mysterious Victor. In the evening, they were drawn back together for dinner, which Andrew insisted on making. He enjoyed cooking. He said it relaxed him and that he liked doing something nice for her.

Every minute they spent together made Miranda doubt the opinion so many people seemed to hold of Andrew. He was not conniving, nor was he vengeful or even mean-spirited. It even had her questioning the picture Johnathon had painted of his brother. Perhaps they had been different together, although she'd never know. That opportunity was gone now. It saddened her to think about what might have been if the brothers had found a way to reconcile before one of them was gone.

She arrived home from work a little after 6:00 p.m. A last-minute panic from one of her clients meant that she'd left later than she wanted to. Just as she pulled into the garage, she got a text from Clay. I met Andrew. Super nice guy. Talk soon?

She was relieved to know that someone else liked Andrew. She wasn't imagining things. Great. And yes. We need to talk about Thanksgiving.

I'll call you this weekend.

She tossed her phone back into her bag and walked inside. "Hello?" she called out into the house.

"Up here in the nursery," Andrew shouted back.

She cast aside her purse and hurried down the hall and up the stairs. As soon as she reached the landing, she spotted Andrew wearing jeans, a T-shirt and a big smile, standing outside the baby's room. He looked good enough to eat. And she needed to stop seeing him that way. She considered trying to convince him to wear baggier clothes, but she wasn't sure that was going to

help. *Enjoy it while you can. He's not here forever.*
"How's it going?" she asked.

"It's done," he announced with more than a hint of excitement in his voice.

"It is?"

"To be fair, your brother helped me."

She couldn't ignore the way his shirt clung to his strong shoulders and sculpted chest. "I can't wait to see it." She tried to take a peek inside the nursery, but Andrew stopped her with both hands on her shoulders.

"Hold on. You don't get to look yet."

"Why not? My baby, my house, my rules."

Andrew shook his head with a hint of mischief in his eyes. "Indulge me. I'd like you to be surprised by my hard work."

"I thought my brother helped."

"Okay. I guess it's our work. Now close your eyes."

She did as she was told, which made the anticipation of this moment that much more urgent. She was dying to see what the baby's room was going to look like. She'd seen it in her mind's eye many times, but it was all about to become that much more real. Andrew held on to one shoulder and she sensed him moving. Sure enough, there was a hand on her other shoulder a moment later. He was standing behind her, close enough that she could feel his body warmth.

"I'm going to walk you inside. It's just about three steps, straight ahead." His voice was soft against her ear, sending tingles through her body.

"Okay." She took the first step and Andrew began to count.

"One…"

Another two steps.

"Two. Three."

"Can I open my eyes?"

"Yes. Go."

She did it slowly, the room coming into focus and then just as quickly going fuzzy from tears. Ahead sat the crib, in exactly the spot where she'd envisioned it, which was amazing considering she hadn't told Andrew where it belonged. It was even more beautiful than she'd remembered from the catalog, painted white with scrolled sleigh ends and exquisite wood carving along the bottom.

"You can't cry," he said, coming to her side. "This is supposed to be a happy moment."

"It is. I am happy." She heard the trepidation in her own voice. The truth was that this was all happening at lightning speed, and even with her usually optimistic worldview, it was hard to not be overwhelmed by the weight of what was ahead. Motherhood was the great unknown and she was barreling toward it.

"This is a good thing, isn't it? A baby's gotta have somewhere to sleep."

"Of course. I'm just surprised, that's all. And things seem to be moving so fast. I'm starting to feel overwhelmed, just thinking about everything I have to do for the nursery and the holidays on the way. It's a lot to think about." She hated unloading on Andrew. Like he cared about all of her problems.

"I don't want you to worry. Just enjoy this moment, okay?"

"Okay." She turned and sought the comfort of his arms. It was such an appealing escape that she didn't question the repercussions of what this physical closeness meant. He didn't hesitate to wrap himself around her, pulling her close. He was so solid and firm, and she felt safe there, like nothing could ever hurt her or the baby.

He caressed her back slowly, bringing up feelings that went beyond comfort. She fought back her own desires to touch him, to have him touch her. They were all alone in this big house with nothing less than an entire weekend stretching out before them. It would be so easy to lean forward and kiss him, but she feared his response. Would he recoil? Push her away? Leave town? There was too much of a potential stigma standing between them—a widow and her husband's brother should not become physically involved. Even if she wanted him badly.

"Thank you so much for this. It's wonderful." She didn't let go of him, resting her head on his chest and selfishly curling her fingers into his muscled back. "The fact that my brother helped you put it together really means so much to me. It makes the whole thing very special."

"I really like him a lot." He continued his lazy passes up and down the channel of her spine with his fingers. It was putting her into a trance, one where she was lulled into thinking everything would be okay. Even if she decided to act on her impulses.

"I'm so glad. He's a wonderful person. I don't know what I would've done without him over the years."

"He's great. But I think the real reason I like him is because he reminds me of you."

For a moment, Andrew's words hung in the air. At first, she thought that it was only natural that he would like her. Of course he did. She liked him, too. "That's sweet of you to say."

"It's the truth, Miranda. I know we've only been in the same house together for less than seven days, but it's been one of the best weeks in recent memory. That's all because of you."

"It's not just me," she said, finally lifting her head from his chest so she could look him in the eye. His face was painted with its usual serious expression, but she saw the vulnerability there, that he seemingly hid from other people. "You're half of this equation. You've cooked for me this week and been my companion. It might sound silly, but it's meant the world to me. I haven't been this happy in a while."

"Since before Johnathon passed away?"

Something about his statement struck a chord, and that made her stomach sink. Yes, she had happy memories of Johnathon, but she couldn't remember simply being happy on the days that were normal. There was always an air of discontent with Johnathon, a need to have more from life. Tara had once told Miranda that she'd felt like that the entire time she'd been married to Johnathon. Miranda hadn't thought much of it at the time, but now she got it, only because she'd seen a glimpse of what it was like to have more, even when there was no romance between her and Andrew.

"I don't think I could put a date on it," Miranda said, deciding that was enough information. "I only know that I'm happy right now."

A smile played at the corners of his tempting mouth. She wanted nothing more than to kiss him right now— or even better, have him kiss her. Have him show her that he wanted her. She wasn't sure he ever would. He might just be a fantasy right now. And perhaps that was for the best. Keep these crazy ideas of hers tucked up inside of her head.

"I'm so glad." He gripped her shoulders and pressed his lips to the top of her head. It felt like confirmation of the role in his life—sister-in-law or friend. "So, I wanted to tell you that I made a decision today while I was talking to your brother."

"Decision?"

"Yes. You'd mentioned Thanksgiving the day I moved in and Clay told me how much it means to you. Since things aren't quite wrapped up with Victor and Thanksgiving is next week, I just wanted to let you know that I'll be here for it. I'm happy to help with whatever you need."

Miranda was a lucky woman, and she needed to be grateful for the way things were. That meant she needed to stop making wishes about things that would never be. "Sounds perfect. I'm glad you decided to stay."

Five

Thanksgiving had never been a big deal in the Sterling household when Andrew was growing up. Their father had been injured at work when Johnathon and Andrew were young, which left their mom as the sole earner. Not a lot of money and a mother who was already pushing herself to the very limits of her abilities meant that big celebrations or big meals never took place. Often, Thanksgiving day meant burgers wrapped in paper from a drive-thru. Andrew couldn't blame it on anyone. It was simply a confluence of bad circumstances. And now he was the only one left on earth who recalled any of it. As far as he was concerned, it might be time to make new memories, starting with today.

Andrew and Miranda had spent most of the night before baking pies and planning out the Thanksgiving menu. Like all time he spent with her in that house, it brought him nothing less than pure happiness. They had forged a bond, especially since the day he put the crib together with Clay's help. But Andrew was haunted a bit by the scene in the nursery after the big reveal. Having Miranda in his arms brought too many good feelings that he wasn't sure he deserved. He'd wanted to give in to the cues his body was sending during those quiet moments, the ones that said he should cup her jaw and kiss her. That he should sweep her into his arms, carry her off to the bedroom and make love to her.

What had stopped him? The overwhelming presence of his brother and the sense that he wasn't entitled to someone as lovely and sweet as Miranda. So he'd kissed her on the head, made a promise to stay for Thanksgiving and taken thoughts of her to bed that night. He wasn't proud of what had gone through his mind while he imagined her asleep right down the hall...the way he'd fantasized about touching her beautiful body and bringing her to her peak again and again. Even now, those thoughts were pervasive. They followed him wherever he went.

"I think we're all set," Miranda said, adjusting one of the place settings at the table in her dining room.

"Absolutely. It's beautiful," Andrew said. "Just like everything you do." *Just like you, period.*

The doorbell rang and Miranda jumped. "Somebody's here." She practically squealed like a little girl on Christmas morning. Her enthusiasm was infectious as she traipsed off down the hall and Andrew followed. "If Grant and Tara aren't being nice, just ignore them," she said before flinging open the door.

Fortunately for Andrew, it was Astrid, Clay and his daughter, Delia.

"Aunt Miranda!" the little girl exclaimed, then flattened herself against Miranda's legs, wrapping her arms around her.

Miranda leaned down and kissed Delia on top of the head. "Hi, sweetie. Happy Thanksgiving."

Clay handed Andrew a bottle of wine. "Andrew, I'd like you to meet Astrid."

A former model, Astrid was just as stunning as the photographs Andrew had seen. One thing was indisputable—Johnathon had been a very lucky man. "It's so nice to meet you, Andrew. It feels strange that you were once my brother-in-law, but we never met."

Of the many things that were going to be awkward today, that detail might be pretty high on the list. "Better late than never, right?"

Clay slid Andrew a look of solidarity. He and Andrew had discussed the contentious nature of Andrew's relationship with Johnathon. Clay seemed to understand that it had been messy and complicated.

"Come on, everyone. Let me make some drinks," Andrew said, waving everyone into the great room. Just as the five of them arrived, the doorbell rang again.

"I'll get it," Miranda said, flitting off for the front door.

Andrew went to work, pouring glasses of wine for Clay and Astrid, and making a Shirley Temple for Delia.

"It's so fancy with a cherry in it." Delia eagerly sucked on the straw.

"Not too fast," Clay offered. "We don't need you bouncing off the walls."

Delia rolled her eyes. "Okay, Daddy."

"Look who's here," Miranda said, entering the room with Tara and Grant in her wake.

Tara went to hug Astrid while Grant shook Clay's hand. Andrew felt like the odd man out here, and it was no surprise. The last time he'd seen Grant and Tara, it had been at a party in downtown San Diego a few weeks after Johnathon's death. That had been Andrew's first attempt to stop the plan to sabotage Sterling Enterprises. It was also when Grant and Tara confronted him about the fact that he hadn't been to the funeral. That ultimately led to Andrew's visit to see Miranda and apologize. If he had to admit it, it was also when his fascination with Miranda had started. But he would keep that to himself forever.

"Andrew," Grant said. He offered his hand, but everything in his tone was clipped and curt.

"Grant," Andrew countered. "Nice to see you."

The look on Tara's face said she wasn't really buying it. "I see you decided to stay for Thanksgiving," she said. The subtext, of course, was that Andrew had no business being there.

"Miranda asked me to stay. It's her first Thanksgiving without Johnathon."

"And are you thinking you're a substitute?" Tara asked.

Andrew's stomach lurched. He so greatly disliked the suggestion. "No. I'm not."

Thankfully, Miranda appeared, which made both Tara and Grant relax. Apparently, they were saving their contention for only him. "Andrew, it's about time to take the turkey out of the oven."

He consulted his watch. "So it is."

"I'll come with you," Miranda said.

Andrew had never looked more forward to a trip to the kitchen. At least he and Miranda could be alone.

"Tara and Grant aren't happy I'm here," he said as he read the temperature readout on the digital thermometer. He grabbed the oven mitts and turned off the oven, then opened the door. The aroma of roast turkey filled the room, reminding him of what he was really here for—not to please Tara and Grant, but to make Miranda happy.

"I hope you know that I don't care what they think," Miranda said as she got out the carving knife and large cutting board.

"But I think you *do* care. You're so thoughtful. You care about everyone."

"Not at the sake of someone else's feelings." She turned to Andrew and grasped his forearm. "You're here because I want you here. This is one of my most favorite days of the year and I can't imagine it without you right now, okay? So let's just get a few glasses of wine into Grant and Tara, sit down to a fabulous meal, and try to forget everything else."

She had such a way of calming him. It was incredible. "Sounds perfect." He leaned forward and kissed her on the temple. It was only a peck, but how he wished he could have lingered longer with his lips. He wanted a touch that was more than fleeting, a whiff of her intoxicating fragrance that lasted longer than a heartbeat. Those unfulfilled desires left a hot ache in the center of his chest that echoed the regret he felt at not being able to clutch her nape, raise her chin, and deliver a real kiss.

The pair were soon joined by Astrid, who helped them ferry dishes of decadent mashed potatoes, green beans with crispy shallots, and herb stuffing to the sideboard in the dining room. Buttery dinner rolls, sweet potato casserole, turkey and gravy soon followed. It was quite a production, but you never would have known it was any work at all judging by Miranda's sunny mood. Andrew had suggested days ago that she consider hiring some help for the occasion, but she'd been strictly opposed to the idea. She wanted this to be about family.

As they sat down to the table, with Miranda at the head of the table and Clay at the opposite end, Andrew was struck by two things. First, it was sad that this was such an unfamiliar setting for him. He'd seen it in movies and, yes, he'd been to a few fancy Thanksgiving celebrations, but nothing as family-oriented as this. Second, he still felt like the interloper. Miranda may have said she wanted him here, but Johnathon's absence was omnipresent. It was all around them. And the logical deduction from that fact was that if Johnathon had still been alive, Andrew wouldn't have been sitting at this table at all.

The meal was wonderful, and everyone seemed to enjoy themselves, even Tara and Grant. Perhaps Miranda had been right. Maybe they'd just needed some wine to smooth away their rougher edges. After dessert, which was an array of pies—pumpkin, pecan, and apple—Clay and Astrid went to play with Delia in the backyard, leaving Andrew and Miranda with Tara and Grant.

"So, Andrew, how long do you think you'll be staying?" Tara asked.

"As long as he wants," Miranda quickly answered. "It's great to have someone here at the house with me."

"But the plan is to go back to Seattle, right? After you sort things out with the problem you created?" Grant asked.

"Yes. I have made Victor an offer to stop with what

he's doing. I'm just not sure he's received it. That's been the hard part. Getting a hold of him."

Grant nodded but seemed entirely unconvinced. "You know what's interesting?"

"What?" Andrew replied, sensing something bad was about to be lobbed in his direction.

"Things at Sterling have been remarkably quieter since you arrived. We've had zero problems." Grant sat back in his chair and crossed his legs.

"Maybe that means Victor is backing off," Miranda said.

Tara shook her head. "Or maybe it means that there is no Victor."

Andrew drew a deep cleansing breath through his nose. He would not lose his cool. He deserved this. He'd created the problem in the first place and he was going to have to fix his own mess. "If I could prove to you that he exists, I would. But for the time being, you're just going to have to take me at my word."

Miranda's heart was in her throat as she listened to the back-and-forth between Andrew, Grant and Tara. He explained that Victor was a man who did as much of his work as he could off the books, using offshore accounts and holding companies. Victor liked being invisible and that would make him much harder to stop.

It all sounded unreal to Miranda, but she had faith in Andrew. Her only disappointment was how much she hated the acrimony, especially on a holiday that she'd so looked forward to. Perhaps it was best if this all came out now so it could finally be gone and she could stop thinking about it. If that could be her reward, she felt a need to play a bigger role in putting it all to an end.

"I believe Andrew. One hundred percent. There's no doubt in my mind." Miranda sat a little straighter, as if she could convey her conviction with her body language.

Andrew turned to her, his eyes full of surprise, when really she'd expected him to be feeling hurt. Tara and Grant had said some terrible things. "Thank you. I appreciate your confidence in me."

"Miranda, can you and I talk in the other room?" Tara asked, getting up from her chair.

Miranda wasn't about to split this up until it was settled. "Whatever you have to say to me, you can say in front of Andrew. I don't see any reason to go in the other room."

Tara shot her a look that suggested Miranda was crazy. "I really think it would be good if we had some privacy."

Miranda felt her anger growing by the minute. "No. Tell me now. Whatever horrible thing you have to say, just come out with it."

"Guys, can we cool down for a minute here?" Andrew asked. "Miranda has been looking forward to today for a very long time. She worked her butt off and I don't think it's fair that we're robbing her of this moment."

Good God, he was such a sweet and thoughtful man. If Tara and Grant couldn't see that, they weren't paying attention. "Thank you, Andrew. I appreciate that."

"Neither of us is trying to ruin Thanksgiving," Grant said. "But, Miranda, I would be remiss in my role as Johnathon's best friend if I didn't say that I think Andrew is taking advantage of you." He turned to Andrew. "I don't know what your endgame is here, but none of this adds up. I don't know Victor, and I knew all of Johnathon's business deals. I knew everyone he dealt with. And more than anything, I have a deep familiarity with everything that went bad at Sterling Enterprises. That's why I don't believe there's a Victor. I think you're using it as a front to hide the things you did, or at the very least, as an excuse to get out of apologizing for trying to kneecap your brother's business."

"You're wrong," Andrew said. "I've already apologized. Victor is very real and it's only a matter of time until he does something to hurt Sterling. That's why I'm here. To stop that from happening. So I don't know what else to tell you, but you're wrong."

"That's not good enough," Tara said. "I want to know what's really going on here. Are you cozying up to Miranda because you're hoping you can get your hooks into Sterling Enterprises that way?"

Andrew pushed back from the table and tossed his napkin onto his plate. "That's enough. I'll excuse myself now." He turned to Miranda, nearly shaking with rage. "I'll get to work on the kitchen. I don't want the rest of your evening to be ruined by having to listen to this." He walked out of the room with determined strides.

Miranda's heart was currently residing in her stomach. How had everything gone so wrong? "What the hell, you two? Did you seriously just blow up my Thanksgiving dinner?"

Tara reached for Miranda's hand, but Miranda wasn't about to play at that game and she yanked it back into her lap. "Miranda. I'm sorry, but I just don't understand what he's getting out of this whole equation. Living in your house, chasing around some guy who we're pretty sure doesn't exist. I don't think the company is in trouble anymore. I believe that he put a stop to his plan, and I suppose he deserves credit for that, but otherwise, I think he's lying to you."

Miranda did her best to compose herself, but she could feel her blood about to boil. Why couldn't Tara and Grant take off their blinders about Andrew and accept that she was enjoying having him in her life? "Look. Here's the deal. I believe him. I believe him with every bone in my body. And you have to understand that he's not only my connection to Johnathon, he's the baby's connection, as well. If you can't imagine why that might be important to me right now, then I don't know what to say." She nearly gasped for breath when she finished. It had come out as a long string of words, but at least it had come from the heart.

Tara's head dropped to one side. "Miranda. Grant and I want the best for you. We're trying to protect you. All we know is that if Johnathon knew what was going on right now, he'd go through the roof. That's why we had to say something. We couldn't let it go."

"You can guess all you want about how Johnathon would've reacted to this, but the reality is that he isn't here right now. The rest of us are. And if we can't find a way to come together, this baby isn't going to have a family."

"Are you including Andrew in that?" Grant asked.

"Yes. I am."

For a moment, no one said a peep, and Miranda was thankful for the silence, but what she really wanted was for everyone to go home so she and Andrew could be alone and she could tell him how deeply sorry she was that this had happened. She was disappointed that her

Thanksgiving had been ruined, but much more than that, she hated that he had been so hurt in the process.

"I'm going to help Andrew in the kitchen." Miranda rose from the table and collected a few plates.

"Here. Let me help," Tara said, getting up from her chair.

"No. Please. Don't," Miranda said. "I can do it. If you want to spend time with Clay and Astrid, feel free. But otherwise, it's probably best if you go home."

Grant's face fell. "I don't want to leave knowing that you're so upset."

Miranda shrugged. "I'll get over it. I still love you both. But it's best for me right now if you just go." With that, she made her exit from the dining room. When she arrived in the kitchen, she spotted Andrew and Clay talking. They were smiling. Laughing even. This was what she'd hoped for today. Family and togetherness. She'd take this tiny moment and tuck it away in her head for later. The holiday wasn't a total loss.

"Everything okay in there?" Clay asked.

"Tara and Grant are leaving. They were being a pain in my butt." Miranda placed the stack of plates on the counter, then began filling the sink with hot water.

Clay came up to her. "I'm sorry. Honestly, I think the stress of planning their wedding is getting to them. I think they've been fighting about it. Grant has a huge family and they're all coming. I think Tara thought they wouldn't show up and she could have something su-persmall."

Tara and Grant were getting married right before Christmas. If that was the problem, at least it would eventually go away. It still didn't make Miranda feel any better. "Maybe."

Astrid and Delia came in through the French doors just off the kitchen. "Are we ready?" Astrid asked. "I'm exhausted from running around the backyard."

Clay grinned wide, his expression so full of love it was hard for Miranda to wrap her head around it. Her brother had found happiness. Not everything was terrible.

"Speaking of weddings," Miranda said. "Have you two thought about setting a date?"

Clay and Astrid looked at each other. "We haven't. We're too busy having fun," Astrid said. "We'll worry about that later."

How Miranda loved that attitude. Taking the good in the moment and not stressing about the rest.

"Thanks for hosting," Clay said, offering Miranda a hug.

"Thank you so much for coming." She stepped out of her brother's embrace and wrapped her arms around Delia and Astrid, who were standing together. She watched as Andrew bid his farewell. There was already a genuine warmth between Clay and Andrew. That had to count for something. Andrew wasn't a bad guy. He simply wasn't.

The happy little family unit of Clay, Astrid and Delia made their departure, leaving Miranda and Andrew all alone with a messy kitchen.

"I'm officially regretting my choice to not bring in any help." Miranda swished dish soap in the sink full of hot water.

"I'm sorry," Andrew said, stepping closer to her and trying to make eye contact.

"Don't be. It was your suggestion. I was the dummy who didn't listen."

He shook his head and laughed softly. "That's not what I'm talking about. I'm talking about the scene with Grant and Tara. That wouldn't have happened if I hadn't been here."

Miranda held up her finger. "No. Don't say that. It's their problem, not yours."

He pursed his lips and leaned against the counter. "I heard what you said after I left. I went back to grab some dishes and I overheard. I want you to know that I appreciate everything you said on my behalf. You shouldn't have to stick up for me."

"I had to say something. They were in the wrong. I couldn't let it go." Even with the heavy subject of their conversation, Miranda did feel a weight lifting. It was just her and Andrew now. She didn't need to worry about everyone else and their agendas.

"It meant a lot to me. Truly. Everything today did." Andrew reached for Miranda's hand. "The last two weeks have been some of the best of my whole life. I'm sure that sounds stupid, but it's the truth."

Her heart fluttered when he squeezed her fingers, making her feel equal parts excited and foolish. "It's not stupid. I feel the same way. I love having you here." She scanned his face for some sign of what he meant by holding on to her hand so tightly, but then he licked his lower lip and her knees nearly buckled. His mouth was way too gorgeous. His shoulders were too broad and his hair too touchable. She wanted nothing more than to thread her fingers through it, curl her fingers into his scalp and wrap her leg around his hip.

Before she knew what was happening, Andrew locked his gaze on her. There was an actual jolt to her system—a connection made. They drifted closer, the space between them slowly disappearing and time becoming elastic. Miranda struggled to keep up. Logic told her to look away, but she couldn't. It felt like the key to tomorrow was in his eyes and she had to find it.

His hand went to her jaw, his fingertips giving the lightest imaginable touch against her neck. "I'm afraid I'm going to make a mistake, Miranda."

Her heart was beating so fast it was either going to burst or give out. "What do you mean?" She was desperate for the answer, but it was a terrifying prospect. If he pulled away from her, it would take a long time to recover. She'd spent too much time over the last few months trying to get past unwelcome truths. Today, she wanted her reality to have at least a sliver of good news.

"I want to kiss you. But I worry that it's wrong." His warm palm rested on her jaw, his heat pouring into her.

Her mind scrambled for an elegant answer, but she didn't have a clever or witty reply. She was too relieved that they'd both been thinking the exact same thing. She didn't know how long he'd felt this way, but time didn't matter right now. The only thing she cared about was hurrying down this path he'd just set them on. "Maybe you should just try it and see how right it feels."

Six

The air in the kitchen was charged with anticipation.

"If I kiss you, Miranda, there's no going back." Andrew dropped his chin, working his way into Miranda's psyche with an intense flash of his eyes. His one free hand went to the other side of her face.

Miranda was all too aware of her breaths, her galloping heartbeat, the rotating sway of her body in his presence. This wasn't that different from the moment up in the baby's nursery, when she'd so desperately wanted him to touch her. Everywhere. "I don't see the point in going back, Andrew. I'm only interested in moving forward." Why wasn't he kissing her? Was he waiting for her to do it? She wished she'd come up with a sexier reply, but words seemed so useless now. She was too busy managing urges, like the one that said she'd finally be happy if he wasn't wearing that shirt. Or those pants.

"I need to be sure." He leaned even closer and kissed her cheek. "Absolutely positive that this is what you want."

If he didn't kiss her for real, she was about to explode. She popped up onto her toes, gripping his shoulders to steady herself. "I'm positive."

She closed her eyes and went for it—her lips met his in a kiss that made it feel like she was floating. There was only the slightest hesitation before his tongue slipped along her lower lip. Every atom in her body celebrated in a chorus of delight and relief. She shifted her forearms up onto his shoulders, dug her fingers into the back of his thick hair. His lips—soft and warm and wet—became more eager, seeking her jaw and neck. His arms wound tightly around her, pulling her against him, nearly lifting her off her toes.

His hand snaked under the back of her sweater, confirming what she'd been so unsure of before—he wanted her. He wanted clothes to come off as badly as she did. His fingers fumbled with her bra clasp, which was more than a little adorable. Andrew was always so sure of himself. It made him so human. And it made her feel ever so slightly closer to him.

"Here. Let me," she muttered. Now flat-footed, she lifted her sweater over her head, then clutched it to her chest. She could admit to being unsure of what he would say when he saw her pregnant form.

"Are you hiding from me?" he asked.

"No. I mean, yes. Maybe a little. Have you ever had to have sex with a pregnant woman?"

"Had to? I want to." He plucked the sweater from her hands and placed it on the kitchen counter. Leaning closer, he hooked his finger under one of the straps of her white silk bra, then popped it off her shoulder. "Everything about your body is luscious and beautiful. I can't wait to see every inch."

His words didn't merely prompt a wild wave of goose bumps—they were about to become a permanent memory, etched in her mind. She bit down on her lip. If this was going to happen, it would be good. She reached behind her and unhooked her bra, but left it for him to take it off.

"Keep going." He kissed the curve of her neck, the most sensitive spot, the one that made her arch her back and nearly call out from the pleasure.

She took his direction and slipped the garment forward from her shoulders. He helped by pulling it down the length of her arms. His vision sank lower and her heart picked up in anticipation. Gripping her rib cage with both hands, his thumbs caressed the tender underside of her breasts as he lowered his head and gave one nipple a gentle lick.

The gasp that rose from the depths of her throat sounded like weeks of frustration being cut loose. She dropped her chin to her chest when he did it again. She loved watching him admire her this way, knowing that she turned him on. "I want you, Andrew. Now."

"Upstairs," he answered.

Before she could take a single step, she was off her feet and in his arms, feeling like she weighed nothing at all. Considering her pregnant state, it was an amazing feeling. He marched down the hall and up the stairs as she clung to his neck, desperate to kiss him again.

"Your bedroom or mine?" he asked. The weight of the question was impossible to ignore. Her bedroom was where she'd slept with Johnathon.

It was too much to think about right now, so she gave the simplest answer. "Yours. It's closer."

He grinned. "I like the way you think."

They reached their destination, his beautifully appointed room. He set her down gently on the king-size bed, smiling again. He stood back and began unbuttoning his shirt. The soft evening light showed off the incredible contours and definition of his chest and abs. He had a lovely patch of dark hair in the center and a most enticing narrow trail extending from his belly button that disappeared behind the waistband of his pants. His shoulders were even better than she could've imagined. Not even a well-tailored suit coat did them justice. They were square and broad. They begged for her touch.

He stepped closer to the bed, and she sat up, flattening her hands against his firm chest, his skin warming her palms and fingers. With her arms raised, he cupped her breasts, making her drop back her head for a moment. It felt so good that it made her head swim. She forced herself to straighten, only because she was desperate to have his mouth on hers again. As if she'd spoken her desire, he leaned down and gave her a long, deep kiss. The sort of kiss that made a woman lose her mind.

She would've been lying if she'd said she wasn't eager to see the rest of him. She unzipped his pants and pushed them to the floor, then dipped her fingers beneath the waistband of his black boxer briefs, tugging them down his trim hips. He kissed her again, and she wrapped her fingers around his erection, loving the deep moan that went straight from his mouth to hers.

He gently pushed on her shoulder, urging her to lie back, then he kissed the bare mound of her stomach.

He was so tender and sweet, it took her breath away. She watched as he unbuttoned her trousers and wiggled them down the length of her legs. His eyes roved all over her body, full of admiration that made her heart swell. Everything between her legs was begging for his touch. Her whole body froze with the anticipation.

He tugged down her panties, casting his dark eyes up toward hers as his fingers met her center. She couldn't let go of her grip on his head as he artfully rocked his hand back and forth. It felt impossibly good to be at his mercy. To be wanted and desired the way she had been thinking of him so often over the last few weeks. Their gazes connected, and it was as if she saw more of him, parts that he expended so much energy to hide. The parts of him that were hurt.

The pressure was building, the peak upon her, but she wanted more. She wanted a deeper connection. She needed him. Inside her. "Please make love to me, Andrew," she said. She disbelieved the words as soon as they left her lips. This was such a crazy, inexplicable situation they were in, and yet it was the only thing that seemed right.

He pressed more soft kisses against her stomach. "Do you want me to use a condom?"

She giggled a bit. "You do know I'm pregnant."

"And I want to be sure you know that I'm clean. I haven't been with anyone in a very long time."

She loved that he showed such utter care and concern, but she was confounded by what he'd said. He was so damn handsome and sexy. It seemed improbable that he didn't have women vying for him constantly. Perhaps that was a topic for another time, when she didn't have such urgent needs. "We're good then."

He stretched out next to her, a truly magnificent male specimen, strong and muscled, but nimble and lean. He dropped back his head when she coiled her fingers around him and stroked his length. She could hardly believe how much tension his body was holding. When their eyes connected, he looked as if he wanted to consume her, which was a good thing. It was exactly what she wanted.

"Is it better for you and the baby if you're on top or the bottom?" he asked.

She hadn't thought about this. She'd never had to worry about her pregnant belly before, but it was still a very modest pooch. It wouldn't get in the way. "I want to be on the bottom this time. I want to feel you weigh me down."

"And that's okay with the baby?"

"Right now? Yes. She's the size of a tennis ball."

Andrew positioned himself between her legs and she arched her back to meet him, welcoming him as he sank into her. He took things slow and careful, with a patience she relished. Her mind swam as their bodies met and she began to experience each delightful physical sensation. She'd hadn't taken the time to let her fantasies about Andrew venture this far, but nothing could have prepared her for how good he felt.

He rolled his hips when his body met hers. It built the pressure at her apex quickly, her breaths coming faster now. Her hands roamed over the muscled landscape of his back, trailing down to his spectacular backside. His kisses were deep and passionate, matching the steady and satisfying rock of their bodies. She wrapped her legs around him, wanting him closer. Deeper.

She placed her hands on the side of his face, keeping

his lips to hers. She wanted to be connected with him when she came apart at the seams. She kept her mind focused on the here and now, waiting only for the bliss awaiting her, without a worry in the world.

Miranda was close—he could feel it. He sensed it in every sexy movement of her body. He was fighting off his own orgasm, which was a near impossible task. Concentrating on her breaths and the grip of her hands on the side of his face was the only way to do it. They were a beautiful distraction from the pressure coiling tight in his belly.

Her breathing was ragged now. Every pleasurable sound she made was a boost to his ego, but he wasn't prepared for the moment when she called his name, clutching his back and digging her nails into his back. The pain was such a delicious counterpoint to the pleasure as she tensed around him, her body holding on to his as if she'd never let go.

Tension had him wrapped up so tight that rational thought was gone. Pure instinct took over as a smile spread across her face and he took a few final strokes. The pressure finally relented and his body gave in to the pleasure. It rocketed through him, setting every nerve ending on fire.

He was quick to roll to his side, not wanting to put any unnecessary weight on the baby. Miranda rolled to her side and curled into him, resting her head in the crook of his armpit. He struggled to catch his breath, but part of him never wanted that to happen. He knew that as soon as his heart rate returned to normal, logical and difficult thoughts would walk right into his brain.

"That was amazing." She tangled her fingers in his chest hair, then craned her neck to kiss him.

Their lips met and there was more to it now than there had been before. He should've known he would feel this way now that the ice had been broken between them. He wanted her even more than he had several hours ago. He feared that he would never get enough.

"You're the amazing one, Miranda. Truly."

She laughed quietly and kissed his chest. "You're spoiling me."

"There's no such thing. You deserve to be spoiled. Rotten. Absolutely showered with affection and praise and expensive jewelry. Real estate. Yachts."

She popped up onto her elbow and looked him square in the face. "I never asked for a boat."

Now it was his turn to laugh. "My point was that I'll give you whatever you want." As soon as the words had left his lips and he'd had a second to absorb the ramifications, he worried that he'd gone too far. But just as quick, he decided that he'd wasted way too much time worrying about the things he'd done. There was nothing wrong with that statement. It had been uttered in the moment and it had come from the heart. He meant it. Every last word.

"I don't need much," she answered. "I really don't."

"Then tell me. Tell me what you want."

She was quiet for a moment and the stillness seemed to take over the room. He would've paid anything to have a glimpse inside her head, to know her innermost thoughts. He worried that she might not share what was truly there.

"I want life to be good and normal. I want to be

happy." She settled her head back on his shoulder. "I know that sounds stupid and boring, but it's the truth."

He rubbed her lower back with his hand, relishing the velvety touch of her skin. "It's not boring. I think it's beautiful in its simplicity. Plus, those are things you can't buy. I have to appreciate that."

"They also feel like the hardest things to come by."

We could be happy. The thought flew into his consciousness lightning-fast. He knew from experience that those instantaneous ideas that crop up in one's head were the most real. The ones that came from the heart. "Also the things worth fighting for, right?"

She nodded silently. "Can I tell you something? Something that I'm not very proud of?"

"A confession?"

"Yes. I suppose."

"I find it hard to believe that you have a single thing to be ashamed of or to confess."

She draped her hand across his belly and pulled him a little closer. "It's not something I did so much as it's something I thought. That day when we were in the nursery. After you surprised me with the crib. When I said that I was happy you were here."

He couldn't imagine what she was about to say, and part of him was scared to know, but he also didn't have it in his heart to tell her no. "Tell me, Miranda. I won't judge you."

She let go of a heavy breath. "It occurred to me then that I might not have been truly happy when I was with Johnathon."

This wasn't exactly a topic he was eager to explore, but he did want to know what she meant by that. "Were there problems?"

"No. There weren't. In fact, we were still sort of in that honeymoon phase, where everything seems easy. Do you know what I mean?"

"Actually, I don't. I've never been married." He'd come close once, but that wasn't something he cared to reveal right now.

"It's not even about marriage. It's just that giddy stage where the other person can do no wrong. But I don't know that we had any truly deep feelings between us. Everything with Johnathon was a whirlwind. Dating, our engagement, the wedding. It all happened so fast and I wonder if I just got carried away with it."

Andrew had heard women tell similar tales of being swept off their feet by Johnathon. It wasn't Andrew's style. It never had been. He wanted something deeper. He always had. "Do you think you're feeling this way because you found out that he cheated on you?"

"Maybe." She drummed her fingers on his chest, bringing every nerve ending in his body back to life. "I guess that's probably it. You're so smart."

He'd just slept with his brother's widow. He wasn't sure that applied to him right now. "I don't know about that, but thank you." He wanted to set them back on a happier course of conversation, one that hopefully didn't include Johnathon. "Are you sure you don't want to add anything to your list of what you want? Not a diamond necklace or a fancy car?"

"Honestly? No. But I'm a little afraid to tell you what I really want."

He reared back his head and looked down at her. He loved seeing her lovely face peering up at him. "Don't be afraid. Just tell me."

"I want to decorate for Christmas tomorrow."

"You're kidding me."

She shook her head. "Nope. I love the holidays, Thanksgiving was a semidisaster, and as far as I'm concerned, the Christmas season starts at midnight tonight. I don't want to waste a single minute not celebrating, and for me, that means transforming the house into a winter wonderland."

"In Southern California."

"Yep."

He grinned and pulled her closer. "You got it. We can decorate all day if you want."

"Great. But now you have to tell me what you want."

Did it really need saying? He supposed it did. "What I really want tonight is you."

Seven

In the light of day, waking up in Andrew's room, Miranda's first thoughts were decidedly more conflicted than any she'd had the night before. Her evening with Andrew had been both unexpected and incredible. In fact, it had been so amazing that guilt was threatening to eat away at the otherwise pleasant state she was in. She wouldn't allow the bad feelings to swallow her whole, but they were there, circling above her head and threatening to swoop in.

Andrew wasn't there with her in bed, but that was no big surprise. He didn't seem to sleep much. He certainly hadn't last night. In fact, he'd worn her out. But she'd needed that level of pure physical exhaustion. It had cleared her head after a difficult and crazy day. She sat up in his bed and let her feet dangle over the edge. Maybe it was the afterglow, but making love with Andrew had been transformative. She felt different this morning. More alive.

She tiptoed into her bedroom and grabbed a short, sexy nightgown, plus her silk robe. Taking a minute in her bathroom, she brushed her teeth, tamed her hair and spritzed on a bit of perfume. She wanted to look and smell good for Andrew. She wanted him to want her, like he had last night. A taste of him simply wasn't enough.

When she walked back through her bedroom to the hall, something stopped her—the picture of her and Johnathon on her wedding day, perched on top of her dresser. The gravity of what they'd done hit her. It was a little more than three months since Johnathon had died. Had she given herself enough time to grieve? How long was that supposed to be, anyway? She wasn't sure of the timeline, but she had to think it was longer than that. What would people say? Especially if they found out that the person she'd become tangled up with was Andrew, her dead husband's brother?

Nothing about this was fair. She'd endured more pain than she'd thought possible when she lost her husband, but despite that, she was still here, with a beating heart and desperate to give and receive love. Andrew was a kind and compassionate man. He was sexy and strong. He was also forever tied to someone she'd loved immensely. Of course she was going to have strong feelings for him. That part was baked into the mix. What harm was there in them expressing affection for each other?

None, she decided. What had happened last night had not hurt a single person. And she truly failed to see why it was of any concern to anyone in the first place. She deserved a sliver of happiness just as much as the next person. So did Andrew. Anyone else's preconceived notions about right or wrong in this situation were not her problem. No one else knew her soul, her innermost thoughts or the realities of her life. No one else knew what could make her happy.

It wasn't easy, but she forced herself to push past the moment, look beyond the photograph, and walk out the door and into the hall. With every step, she felt more determined. Meanwhile, the pleasant aroma of fresh coffee teased her nose. That brought a smile to her face and a flush of heat to her cheeks in anticipation of seeing Andrew. She'd been limiting herself to one cup a day since she learned she was pregnant, but she'd had a hard time giving up that little bit of caffeine. How nice it was to have someone else brew a pot, just as Andrew had done every morning since he'd moved in. It was a surprising bright spot in her day. Even when he'd come on a mission that was decidedly not sunny, he'd brought happiness into her home.

When she stepped into the kitchen, she was greeted by a breathtaking sight—Andrew in pajama pants and no shirt, busy cooking. She'd known last night that she was a lucky woman, but this morning was proving the theory again. The pj's were a dark navy plaid with a drawstring he hadn't bothered to tie, leaving the enticing contours of his hips and lower abs on full display.

"Good morning," she said, drifting into him, drawn to his bare chest the way a duck wants to be in the water.

"Good morning to you." Andrew pulled her into his arms and wrapped her up tight, kissing the top of her head again and again.

She closed her eyes and soaked up his touch. She

could get used to this, but that might not be wise. Andrew had been clear—he planned to return to Seattle as soon as the situation with Victor was resolved. Miranda couldn't leave San Diego. Her ties here—to her brother, niece and Astrid, and even to Grant, Tara and Sterling Enterprises—ran deep. For now, she couldn't bring herself to think about that. She would enjoy her time with Andrew and deal with life and logistics later.

Reluctantly, she opened her eyes and spotted the roasting pan from yesterday. "Oh, my God. We completely forgot to clean the kitchen last night."

He started laughing and released her from his warm embrace. "We were pretty distracted, weren't we?"

She surveyed the kitchen, which was nearly spotless. "How long have you been up?"

"Since seven."

A quick glance at the clock said that it was 9:15 a.m. She helped herself to a cup of coffee, adding a splash of cream and a spoonful of raw sugar. "I'm so sorry. Why didn't you wake me?"

He cast her a disapproving look that suggested she needed to have her head examined. "Are you kidding me? Nobody wakes a pregnant woman. It's like poking a bear."

She disliked the comparison to a large, hairy mammal, but he wasn't far off base. "You're my guest. You shouldn't have to clean up such a big mess in the kitchen. Especially when you did half of the cooking yesterday."

He arched both eyebrows at her and picked up a dish from the sink, wiping it dry with a towel. "I think I moved beyond being a guest last night. At least I hope I did."

She felt like a heel. "That's not what I mean. I'm sorry. You're definitely far more than a guest. Really, I'm so sorry."

"Don't be. We're both in unfamiliar territory right now." He put the plate in the cabinet, then grabbed his mug from the counter and took a sip. His observation was spot-on, but as she thought about it, she took the chance to admire a few of his appealing features, like his slightly messy bed head and the flex of his forearm as he held the coffee to his lips. Even the questioning look in his eyes was beguiling, and that did nothing but fill her with doubt.

"You aren't wrong." Their journey from strangers to brother-in-law and sister-in-law, to friends, housemates and now lovers was not a typical trajectory.

"How are you feeling about things?" he asked. "I'm not the type to push heavy conversations, but I think we need to recognize that our situation is not the norm. Not even close. There are a lot of complicated feelings involved and as near as I can tell, there aren't any rules for this. That could be good, but it could also be bad."

His admission, although dismal at first glance, brought an overwhelming sense of relief. So she hadn't overreacted upstairs when she'd seen the photo of Johnathon and her. The many thoughts that had gone through her mind, all clashing with each other, were understandable. "I'd be lying if I said that I didn't feel conflicted."

"Good."

"Good?"

"Yes. I think it's good." The kitchen timer went off and Andrew sprang into action, grabbing an oven mitt and pulling a pie tin out of the oven.

Yet another amazing smell hit her nose—bacon and cheese. "You made quiche?"

He shrugged and set the pan on the cooktop. "I cook when I'm stressed. It helps me think."

Now she was starting to understand what he meant by "good." "So it's weighing on you, too."

"Of course it is. We crossed a line last night. Or at least I did."

"No. We both did. They're just different lines."

He drew in a breath, pursing his lips and seeming deep in thought. "I have to wonder how I'd be feeling right now if we hadn't given in to temptation."

Was he regretting their choice? Because as much as she felt at odds with her own moral compass, she refused to look at last night and express remorse. She'd needed more than the physical release—she'd craved his touch and tenderness. She'd needed to feel less like a vessel for a baby and more like a woman. Plus, she couldn't deny that her attraction to Andrew had grown so much over the last few weeks as they'd become closer and closer with each passing day. "I think I'd be feeling frustrated."

He nodded in agreement and reached for her hand, pulling her close until they were standing toe-to-toe. That one gesture meant the world to her right now. It was a lifeline. She'd been feeling adrift for the last few minutes as he grappled with the ramifications of the fact that they'd made love. "You're right. I'd be feeling the same way. My problem is that I've been struggling with my attraction to you since the day we met. And that was definitely not the right time to be feeling that way. In fact, it was absolutely wrong."

"You can't help the way you feel, Andrew."

"But I have to wonder if that's maybe the real reason I came back to San Diego. I probably could've dealt with Victor from Seattle. I'm worried that part of me wanted a chance with you. And that's not right. The guilt of that is squarely on my shoulders this morning."

She sighed, looking up into his handsome face. Again, she felt like she could see shades of his past in his eyes. His history. The pain. "You came here with good intentions. And you've been nothing but wonderful to me. I've needed you this whole time and you haven't hesitated to help."

"That still doesn't lighten the load on my conscience."

"Then what will?"

"Honestly? I don't know. It's too wrapped up in my feelings about my brother and how everything went wrong between us. It makes me sad just to think about all the time we wasted being at each other's throats and knowing that I can't make any of it right. It's too late."

"From everything you've said, it was both of you. You can't take all of the responsibility."

"I know. But I do. I'm here. He isn't." He shook his head and looked off in the distance for a moment, his forehead crinkling with worry. She hated seeing the physical manifestation of this burden. "I think they call that survivor's guilt. I probably need a therapist."

"Well, I'm no psychiatrist, but I'm a good listener. We have the whole day ahead of us, and the weekend beyond that. If you feel like sharing, I'm all ears."

"While we decorate, right?"

She scrunched up her nose, hoping he wouldn't change his mind. She'd been looking forward to this since they'd talked about it in bed. "If that's okay. It's just one of my absolute favorite things in the whole world. When I was a kid, a big fancy Christmas was the one thing I always wanted, but never got. Now that I'm an adult, I don't miss the chance to get everything I couldn't have then."

"Totally understandable." He kissed her tenderly on the cheek. "It all sounds good to me."

Andrew couldn't help but question what he was doing, or more specifically, what he'd done when he'd gotten physically involved with Miranda. He felt a bit better after their conversation. At least they were on the same page, equally pulled between loyalty and love, attraction and desire, and, more than anything, the past and the future. If he had to continue to grapple with his history with Johnathon, at least he had a partner in all of this, one who understood for the most part where he was coming from.

After breakfast, he and Miranda got distracted from dishes yet again. He managed to say something that made her laugh, and the minute the happy sound hit his ears, he was overcome with his desire for her. He eased out of his chair and kneeled at her side, reaching for her face and pulling her lips to his. Their kiss was so soft and sexy he couldn't wait another minute. He tugged at the tie on her robe and peeled it back to reveal a silky black nightgown. With both thumbs, he pulled down the straps, freeing her full breasts. He cupped them in his hands, licked her nipples, flicking at the tight buds with his tongue and tasting the sweetness of her skin.

He slipped one hand between her legs, finding her wet for him. He moved his fingers in steady circles against her apex and she gasped for air between fiery hot kisses.

"I'm going to come," she blurted, breathless and frantic.

"I want you to," he said.

She grasped his wrist and looked him right in the eye. "So do I. But I want you inside me when I do."

She scrambled to her knees and he pulled off his pajama pants in a flash. With the silky nightgown around her waist, she straddled his hips, reached down for his erection and sank down onto his length. Her heat all around him, pulling him in, felt so good it boggled the mind. Meanwhile, the vision of her above him, the gentle bounce of her gorgeous breasts with every thrust, was nothing short of pure beauty on full display.

"I'm so close. Are you?" she asked. Her voice had a sexy rasp and he loved the fact that she'd been reduced to single-syllable words.

If only she knew that he nearly exploded as soon as he was inside her. "Yes. Just tell me and we'll come together."

She smiled and nodded, placing her hands flat on his chest and rolling her hips into his with determination, eyes closed and her raven hair splayed across the creamy skin of her bare shoulders. He nearly went blind as the pleasure circled and threatened to strike, but he focused on her face and the soft moans that came from her parted lips.

In one swift movement, she dropped her head forward. "Now."

He was so thankful for the go-ahead, and within fractions of a second, he was giving in to his release just as she called out, arched her back and whipped her long hair to the side. The waves kept crashing over him as he felt her body tighten and relax around him, over and over again.

She collapsed against his chest and kissed him softly. "That was one heck of a breakfast."

He laughed and pushed her hair back from her forehead, peering up at her stunning face. He wasn't sure he'd ever felt more lucky or more torn. She was more than everything he'd ever dared to wish for—she was a dream come true. But that meant he was going where he'd sworn he never would. He was falling for his brother's widow.

Eventually, they managed to peel themselves off the floor, and Miranda told him she'd take care of the kitchen if he wanted to shower. Andrew wanted to extend the invitation for her to join him, but he also knew he probably needed to slow things down at least a little. They had all weekend, after all. By the time he was dressed and headed back downstairs, she was on her way up.

"I'm going to throw on some clothes real quick, but if you want, you can bring out the boxes of decorations. Do you know where the storage area is? It's the door at the back of the utility room."

"Yeah. I got tools out of there when I put the crib together."

"Perfect. There are several stacks of red and green plastic tubs. They should all be together. I'll be back down in a minute to help." She popped up onto her toes and kissed him softly. "I'm excited, just so you know."

He laughed quietly to himself and proceeded with following orders, heading down the rest of the stairs and around to the utility room near the back of the house.

The door to the storage space creaked when he opened it and he reached inside for the light switch on the wall. Several bare bulbs lit up the space, which thankfully had a full-height ceiling. The bins were immediately obvious, but there were a lot of them. A quick count told him more than twenty-five. He wasn't about to complain. This would be an adventure and it gave him this time with Miranda.

He quickly went to work, running two or three bins at a time into the living room. There was more than enough space next to the soaring fireplace to stack everything. By the time Miranda arrived back downstairs, he was nearly done.

"Wow," she said. "You work fast."

He didn't have quite so many words right now—she was breathtaking in a creamy white sweater, which showed off her collarbone, and jeans, with her hair pulled back in a high ponytail. Her cheeks were flushed with pink, a beautiful afterglow, and he took a certain amount of pride in knowing that he'd put that color there.

"I aim to please," he said. "If you want to start digging through everything, I'll get the last load."

"Sounds like a plan."

When he returned to the storage space, something caught his eye—several old cardboard boxes labeled Baseball Cards. Both Johnathon and Andrew had collected them for a while when they were young. Although their generation was well beyond the golden age of collecting, it made it a very cheap hobby, which was a good thing since there was very little money around the Sterling household. They had no problem scoring shoeboxes full of cards at yard sales, often hundreds for only a few bucks.

Andrew peeled back the flaps of one of the boxes, spotting the cards in neat stacks. There was no telling how long they'd been sitting there, or whether Johnathon had even looked at them in recent years. But it was a potent reminder of the life they had once shared and one of the few endeavors they enjoyed together. Once again, the guilt wound its way into his consciousness, but he would not let it ruin today. He closed the box, gathered the final crates for Miranda and made his way back into the living room.

"Are you okay?" Miranda asked as he set down the bins. She'd already pulled out garland, lights and big boxes of ornaments. "You look like you've seen a ghost."

Apparently, he hadn't quite shaken off that moment in the storage space. "I spotted a few boxes of baseball cards. It made me think of Johnathon."

"In a good way or a bad way?" The tone of her voice was so tentative it nearly broke his heart.

"I don't want to talk about it if it's going to upset you. This is supposed to be your day."

"Are you kidding me? I've been dying to know more about what you were like as kids. I could never get Johnathon to tell me." She put down a bundle of lights and stepped closer to him, looking up at him with her big brown eyes.

He surveyed the room, needing a break from that earnest expression on her face. It was a lot of pressure to have someone care that much about the countless memories he was holding on to so tightly. "Christmas was nothing in our house. Did Johnathon tell you that?" he asked, finally able to look at her again.

She shook her head. "No. He never said anything about it. Then again, we really only had two Christmases together between the year we were engaged and the year we were married."

"Our dad worked construction and he was injured when we were young. He got some disability and benefits through his union, but it was never enough to make up for the loss of income. That meant our mom had two jobs just to put food on the table. Between working and having to deal with two boys who were constantly fighting and roughhousing, there was no way she had enough energy to think about Christmas."

Miranda took his hand and led him to the couch. "Tell me more."

He felt the hesitation inside him, but there was something deeper, urging him to keep going. Miranda deserved to know these things. She deserved to understand some of what had brought him to this moment, and Christmas was the perfect illustration. "Our dad was no help. He was horribly bitter after his accident and it only got worse over the years. He spent most of his days watching the news and yelling at the TV. I honestly don't think he expressed any affection for our mom in the final years before he died."

"When was that?"

"Johnathon and I were both in high school."

"It's so sad."

"It is, but it's just the way things were. Everyone has parts of their past they don't like to think about." He shrugged. "But you can probably imagine what the dynamic in our house was like. Johnathon and I spent every minute walking on eggshells. Our dad had an explosive temper and our mom was just worn-out. That's how we ended up in such fierce competition. Johnathon was the oldest, so it was easy for him to manipulate me. I wanted his approval so desperately."

"Manipulate you how?"

"If he did something wrong, he always blamed it on me. Even if it was something that was so obviously his fault, like failing a test at school. He'd make up some story about how I'd distracted him while he was trying to study. He could never stand to be at fault or have anyone look at him in a negative light."

Miranda pressed her lips together tightly and nodded. "I saw that in him all the time. He always wanted to be the life of the party, and never the heavy."

"Exactly. And I took it because he was nicer to me when I did. He'd even say thank you for taking the heat. Only if we were outside or in our room, of course. Never in front of our parents."

"And that continued as you grew up?"

"Oh, no. It got worse. The older we got, the higher the stakes were. He got busted with pot, he drove our mom's car into a light pole. You name it."

"Wow. He really messed up a lot."

"Well, I was no angel. I got into trouble, too. But from where our parents were sitting, especially our mom after our dad died, I was the bad one and Johnathon was good. He used that to his advantage. It was sort of hard to blame him. I let him do it."

"Why?"

Andrew had asked himself this question countless times. He always came around to the same answer. "Because I loved him." He heard the crack in his voice as clear as day. It was an unwelcome sound. He didn't want to break. He never did.

"I'm so sorry."

He shook his head—if nothing else, it helped to ward off the sadness. "Does that help you see how we ended up the way we did? How fighting against each other just became our only dynamic? And because he seemed to care more about me the more I fought, I never managed to find another way to be with him."

"That's why you went after the Seaport. It was another fight to pick."

"Yes. Although I think it was Johnathon who started that. He knew exactly what he was doing when he went after that project. He knew it would hurt me."

"Because it was your hometown?"

Andrew swallowed hard, still not ready to tell her this. Then again, he wasn't sure how much time he and Miranda would have together and he was tired of living with regrets. "Because the wedding pavilion at the Seaport was where I was set to get married. And it didn't happen. Johnathon knew that. The whole idea of wanting to beautify that space and make it new again just felt very personal. It felt like an attack."

Miranda clasped her hand over her mouth. "I had no idea. What happened? With the wedding? With your fiancée?"

He took in a deep breath for strength. Rehashing this was not fun, but he did feel safe in sharing it with Miranda. "Oldest story in the book. She ran into an old boyfriend a few weeks before our wedding and she left me for him, but she didn't make that decision until the morning of the ceremony. I had to call the whole thing off. I never went back to the Seaport after that. And Johnathon knew how painful it was for me."

"That's why you felt so betrayed when you found out

he decided to pursue the project. That's why you felt like you had to prevent it from happening."

"Yes." Now that he was admitting these things out loud, he wasn't sure if he should feel relieved or ashamed. There was a very big part of him that could look back and admit that he'd made some stupid choices. He had no direct knowledge that Johnathon had gone after the project to be cruel. It had only seemed like something he might do.

"I'm so sorry."

Andrew didn't want to let his sad story ruin their day. It was a good thing that he'd shared this with her. At least she could better understand his thought process and the events that had brought him to this moment. "Don't be sorry. It's in the past. I'd rather think about today." He got up and beelined for the mountain of storage boxes, opening one and pulling out a long strand of silvery garland. "I think it's time to get going on your decorating project."

Miranda hopped up from her seat. "We really don't have to if you don't want to."

"I wouldn't miss this for the world. All I ever wanted at Christmastime was some cheer and happiness."

Miranda lifted the lid from another bin and peered inside. "I don't know how cheery you'll be after we untangle all these Christmas lights."

He laughed and put his arm around her shoulder, leaning in to kiss her cheek. "I get you and the holidays today. I don't see how I end up being anything less than happy."

Eight

The Monday after Thanksgiving should've been like any other start to Miranda's workweek. She climbed into her car and headed to the office. The stereo was set to her favorite satellite radio station, playing a mix of pop and hits from her youth. The music was soft and in the background as she tried to focus on the day ahead. But today, she wasn't thinking about paint colors or special-order designer sofas. She wasn't ruminating over floor plans or deadlines. All she could think about was Andrew.

There was part of her that wondered if the events of the last few days had actually happened, even though she knew in her heart that they had. The echoes of his touch still warmed her skin, and the words he'd muttered into her ear still rang in her head. *If I kiss you, Miranda, there's no going back.* It was more than what he'd said, but how he'd said it that had really taken her breath away. The subtext was heavy. He wasn't about to make love to her then go back to simply being friends. But as for where that left them now, she wasn't sure.

She had never imagined this could happen. When she'd lost Johnathon, she'd thought that there would never be another man in her life. She'd seen herself becoming a mom and finding a way to parent on her own, but there would be no more romantic love. She simply couldn't have fathomed it in the aftermath of that tragedy. But with each passing day, things got a little better. She started to look ahead. Her grief changed from moment to moment, and it certainly wasn't always a straight line. But for the most part, she'd found the strength to move forward, in part because of those around her who loved her—Clay, Astrid, Tara and Grant.

But then Andrew had turned up and changed everything yet again. He'd awakened something in her, a part of her that she'd put aside as no longer viable. He'd made her feel like a woman again—desired and needed. He likely didn't understand the sheer scope of what he'd done, the switch that he had flipped, but it was no small thing. Right now, it meant the world to her.

She knew very well that she was playing a dangerous game with him, though. She needed him in her life. For her little girl, Andrew was more than an uncle. He was the only living extension of her father. Miranda would not deprive her child of knowing him. Which meant that she had to let Andrew know that she didn't expect anything of him. She couldn't saddle him with her feelings. What she had with Andrew was not a romance, even when her body believed it, her soul yearned for it, and there were tender and caring moments when she thought it was moving in that direction. It was…well, she struggled to put a label of any kind on it. And perhaps that was for the best. Labels came with expectations and that only led to disappointment.

She arrived at work and strode through the parking lot, noticing that Astrid's little silver convertible was already there. Miranda was really glad that she'd decided to hire her future sister-in-law. She was not only a hard worker, and eager to learn the business of interior design, but was also a positive presence in the office. Everyone on Miranda's team loved her and that gave Miranda a real sense of peace. Astrid could shoulder a lot of the workload in the weeks after the baby arrived. As for what the rest of Miranda's life would look like at that time, she didn't know. Could she count on the help of those around her? Would Andrew make his presence known? The uncertainty made her especially thankful for Astrid. She knew she could count on her.

"Good morning." Miranda popped her head into Astrid's office.

She looked up from her desk, a warm smile crossing her face. "Hello. How are you after the big Thanksgiving awkwardness?"

Miranda had been so horrified in the moment on Thursday evening, but it almost seemed like an afterthought now. If that situation hadn't happened, emotions wouldn't have been running so high that night. She and Andrew wouldn't have ended up kissing in the kitchen or even making love. Miranda gestured to one of the chairs opposite Astrid's desk. "May I?"

"Yes. Of course."

Miranda took a seat and crossed her legs. "That was something, wasn't it?"

"I wasn't there for the truly ugly part, but it's pretty obvious that Tara and Grant don't trust him. At all."

"So much of it seems like it should be water under the bridge, but obviously that's not the case."

"Andrew was well out of Johnathon's life when we were married," Astrid said.

"Same for me," Miranda said. "He talked about his brother, but it was all stuff that had happened in the past."

"It's really hard for me to say whether Andrew should be trusted, but he seems like a good person. Clay likes him a lot."

That counted for a great deal, as far as Miranda was concerned. Her brother was an excellent judge of character. "It doesn't really matter though, does it? Andrew will be here for a short while and then he'll return to Seattle and that will be it." Miranda drew in a deep breath through her nose. "The problem is that I want more than that. I want him to be part of the baby's life. He'll be one of her few living relatives."

"Do you think you can count on him for that? Johnathon always said Andrew was erratic. He might seem solid right now, but you don't know for sure, right?" Astrid picked up a pen and tapped it on her desk. "I don't want to be pessimistic, but I also don't want to see you get hurt."

Miranda appreciated Astrid's intentions, but she hated the misgivings these questions stirred up inside her. Andrew had been nothing less than rock-solid over the last few weeks. He'd been caring and attentive. "I'm pretty sure that Johnathon was letting other things color his opinions. Like the history between the brothers. Andrew told me some stories over the weekend."

"Like what?"

"He talked about how Johnathon was the golden boy of the family. He was the one who could do no wrong. Andrew really looked up to him, but from everything he said, Johnathon used that against him. He blamed things on Andrew, but he'd later say that it was just part of their rivalry and that if Andrew didn't want to be in trouble, he should learn how to turn the tables on Johnathon."

"Was he ever able to do that?"

"Not to the degree he wanted to. Johnathon was always a step ahead."

"Until the Seaport Promenade project came along."

"Exactly. That was when Andrew finally saw his chance to get even." Miranda decided against sharing the details of Andrew's broken engagement. It was deeply personal and he'd kept it from Miranda for a while, even when he'd had chances to tell her and bring his motives into focus. "But then we lost Johnathon and Andrew had to try to stop his plan."

Astrid nodded slowly, as if she was still digesting all of this information. "Maybe Tara and Grant need to hear more of this. I don't think anyone can discount the fact that Clay likes him. That has to matter a lot, especially to you."

That was a silver lining, for sure. Her brother was deeply skeptical of most people. If it was Clay's gut instinct to trust Andrew, Miranda felt that she could, too. "And what do you think?"

"He's incredibly handsome and smart and kind. What's not to like?"

The corners of Miranda's lips twitched, threatening a smile, and heat flooded her cheeks. She couldn't have stopped if she'd wanted to. There wasn't a single thing not to admire about Andrew. Or at least not a thing that she'd seen.

Astrid narrowed her gaze on Miranda. She was incredibly perceptive, which made Miranda nervous. "Why do you have that look on your face?"

"What look? I don't know what you're talking about." The tone of her voice betrayed her. It was high and squeaky, like a little girl who was terrible at keeping secrets.

Astrid sat back in her chair and crossed her legs, pivoting left and right. "You don't have to tell me if you don't want to."

Miranda wanted to tell someone what had happened, but she also feared sharing it, especially with Astrid. What if she thought less of her? What if she thought Miranda hadn't let enough time transpire since Johnathon's death? "I'm afraid to tell you. If I'm being perfectly honest."

"You can always confide in me. I won't tell a soul. Not even Clay."

"I slept with him." The words practically shot out of Miranda's mouth.

Astrid's eyes grew impossibly wide with surprise. "With Andrew?"

"Who else would I possibly be talking about?"

Astrid stared off, nodding as if she was adding this all up. "I did notice you two flirting."

"You did?" Miranda was horrified. She'd thought that any connection between her and Andrew was undetectable. Hidden.

"It's not a bad thing. I liked seeing it. I know how hard it's been for you. Dealing with Johnathon's death."

"Sleeping with his brother was probably not the healthiest way to chase away my grief."

Astrid shrugged. "You two have a very unusual connection, and you're living in the same house. It's not a big surprise to me that you were drawn to each other."

But where did all of that lead? Miranda had no earthly idea. And with a baby on the way, it was impossible for her to not think about the future. To fixate on it. Would it be okay if she and Andrew ultimately decided that they'd had a little fun together? Would she be able to maintain a relationship with him moving forward? Or would it always be uncomfortable and awkward, with sex as the elephant in the room?

Monday morning, soon after Miranda left for work, Andrew caught a break.

"I've found Sandy," Pietro said when Andrew answered his cell phone.

The relief that washed over him was immense. He had to get to Victor, and Sandy, Victor's foot soldier and one-time mole at Sterling Enterprises, was the best path. "Where is she?"

"She moved into an apartment downtown. It's a brand-new building. Not a lot of residents yet, but they have major security."

"Do you think we have any chance of getting to her?"

"Yes. We have found a way to access the garage and my guys have a good sense of her schedule. I'm outside the building right now."

Andrew grabbed his car keys from the desk. "I'll meet you."

"I have it under control, Mr. Sterling. I don't know that it's safe."

Andrew admired Pietro's dedication to protecting him, but Andrew was done caring about himself. He had to get to Victor. He had to find a way to convince him to stop. Andrew cared deeply about undoing the harm he'd done by setting the plan to destroy Sterling's chance at the Seaport Promenade project. But much more than that now, Miranda and the baby were the most important thing. He would not let them be hurt, physically or financially. More than that, he would not fail with the promises he'd made.

"I'll be fine," Andrew said. "Just ping me your location, okay?"

"Of course, Mr. Sterling."

Miranda and the baby were front and center in his thoughts as Andrew climbed into his car and zipped out through Miranda's gate. His heart was racing as he realized what it would mean if he got to Sandy and she was able to convince Victor to stop. He would have fixed the problem he'd created. He would also have no more reason to stay in San Diego with Miranda. The last few weeks had been incredible, a taste of the life he'd wanted so badly but couldn't help but think wasn't ultimately meant for him. It might be best to resolve everything, move on and leave Miranda to her life. But if he did that, it would be the hardest thing he'd ever done. There was a nagging sense that it wasn't the answer, but it was certainly the simplest solution—get through the pain and move past it.

He found Pietro on a side street. "Any sign of her?" Andrew asked as he climbed out of his car and met him on the sidewalk.

"She should be pulling out of the garage soon. We have surveillance that says she just left her apartment."

"What are we waiting for?" Andrew asked, starting across the street.

"I was waiting on you." Pietro jogged behind him to catch up.

At the garage entrance was a keypad. Pietro punched in a code and the metal door rolled up. Andrew made a mental note to give the man a raise. He never failed to amaze him. Inside, it was evident the building was both brand-new and for only the most well-heeled. Everything was pristine. It was more like a waiting room for cars, with no evidence of smells like motor oil or gasoline.

"Put on your sunglasses," Pietro suggested. "It'll be harder to ID you on tape."

Smart. Pietro was on it, as usual. Andrew did as he was told and the men strode through the concrete structure until they reached the elevator. Sure enough, a mere moment after they arrived, the lights above the door indicated that someone was heading down.

"I don't want to scare her," Andrew said. He'd been the one to hire Sandy. He did know her pretty well and he couldn't help but think that she had become a pawn in a game that was far outside her control.

"Of course not. It's merely my job to put you in a position to speak to her."

"Perfect. Thank you."

Seconds later, the door dinged and rolled open. Sandy took one look at Andrew and her already pale skin lost all color. Her eyes went wide and she jabbed the button. Pietro was one step ahead and stuck out his foot, preventing the door from closing and causing it to open again.

"I have nothing to say to you," she blurted at Andrew

as he stepped closer. Her dark hair was styled in a new way, cut in a sleek and sophisticated bob.

"Fine. You don't need to talk to me. I just need you to relay a message to your new boss."

"That's it?" She seemed unconvinced.

"That's it."

Sandy rolled her eyes and breezed past him and Pietro, into the garage. The door slid shut behind her. "Then what's the message?" She turned and faced him defiantly. She had a very large designer handbag hanging from her elbow. Victor was obviously compensating her well.

"Tell Victor that I will pay him ten million to go away. That's twice what he lost in his deal with Johnathon."

Sandy did not appear impressed by that number. "Where does that leave me?"

"Victor's the person who should answer that question. I'm no longer your employer."

"And if you really want me to deliver this message, you should probably pay the messenger her own fee."

"Fine. An extra million straight to you."

"I could spend that in three months. This building is ridiculously expensive. Try harder."

"Two?"

She pressed her lips together tightly, but everything in her eyes said she wasn't stressed. She was calculating. "Four."

This was becoming absurd. "If I give you four and Victor finds out about it, he'll only ask me for more."

"You're a very rich man."

"Twenty to Victor. Five to you. Final offer."

Sandy swallowed hard. Finally some sign that he was getting somewhere. "I'll take it to him. No promises."

"Please let him know that I'd like to hear from him today."

"I will." She clicked a key fob and the lights on a shiny black Audi flashed.

"So he's in town?" he asked.

"Nice try. I'm not telling you where he is." She put her sunglasses on, then reached for the car's door handle. "And please don't do this little act again. I don't appreciate you showing up where I live."

"Fair enough."

Andrew and Pietro watched as Sandy got into her car. They waited for her to leave before following through the open garage door and back outside. Moments later, they were at their vehicles across the street.

"Only thing we can do now is wait," Andrew said.

"You'll let me know if you hear anything?" Pietro asked.

"Absolutely." Andrew climbed into his car and pulled away from the curb, heading back to Miranda's. He was nearly there when his phone rang. The caller ID popped up on the screen on his dash. *Unknown caller.* He took the call, anyway. "Hello?"

"You must be getting desperate," the voice said.

Victor. "What makes you say that?" Andrew did his best to maintain his composure.

"You're trying to bribe me. Which I can only guess means that you are getting close to your brother's widow. Miranda, right?"

Andrew's stomach turned. Waves of nausea rolled over him. He didn't ever want to hear Victor utter Miranda's name again. "That's not why I made the offer. I just want this done."

"You must realize that money does no good. I couldn't spend everything I already have if I tried."

Andrew needed to focus on this conversation, which meant he needed to get off the road. He flipped his blinker and took the next exit, pulling onto a side street. He put the car in Park and killed the engine. "It's not about the money. It's about making up for my brother's mistake. It's the principle."

"Mistakes. Plural. It was more than the five million I lost in that deal that you know about. That was the final insult. There was another forty or fifty before that. And the lies. Your brother left a wake of destruction wherever he went."

Andrew was looking at paying a small fortune if he wanted to appease Victor, but he would do anything to finally have it resolved. To have a chance to look at his future and see some possibilities for happiness. "What do you want? Name your price."

Victor laughed. "What I want, you can't give me. Unless you come back to my side."

Andrew pinched the bridge of his nose as a headache sprang up right behind his eyes. "I don't know what you're talking about."

"I want Sterling Enterprises destroyed. Over. Erased."

Andrew blew out an exasperated breath. "Johnathon's dead. What's the point?"

"The point is that Sterling is going to land the Seaport project and Johnathon's picture is going to be all over the place. His firm will win accolades and awards. They're hoping to get the new playground at Seaport named after him. It will be like he never did a single bad thing and that's not right."

"But you're only punishing the people he left behind."

"You mean like his wives? And his business partner, Grant Singleton?"

"Well, yes. That's exactly who I mean." He wasn't about to mention the baby, but Andrew's niece would also be a victim. He was sure Victor knew that Miranda was pregnant, but Andrew didn't want to call attention to it.

"This way, they will all know that Johnathon wasn't the perfect man they all think he was."

Andrew's frustration was growing by the minute. "Why do you care so much? This just seems like it's about more than money and ego."

"Johnathon seduced my daughter when she was only twenty years old. He broke her heart. He made promises to her and he didn't keep a single one. I can't forgive him for that. Never."

Andrew stared straight ahead at the city scene before him—a busy Mexican restaurant and people milling around on the sidewalk—but it was like he wasn't truly seeing any of it. He was too busy grappling with this revelation. "When did this happen?"

"He was married to the second wife."

"Astrid."

"That's her name."

Andrew shook his head in disbelief. There was a very big part of him that was so tired of cleaning up his brother's messes. But he knew that this one wouldn't simply go away. "I'm sorry. I don't know what to say about your daughter. I didn't know that happened. Why in the world did you keep working with him after that happened?"

"I kept hoping that at some point, I would have a

chance to get back at Johnathon with one of our deals. Screw him over. Unfortunately, he always seemed to be a step ahead of me. I don't like it when that happens. I don't like being made to look like a fool."

Andrew felt like he was out of options. "What do you want me to do, Victor? This needs to end. I'll give you whatever you want. You can have every last penny I have in the bank."

"I have a few tricks up my sleeve. If they pan out, I'll go away. I just want to see a few people squirm. If I can't bury Sterling Enterprises, I can at least hurt them badly."

The line went dead. The display on Andrew's dashboard said "call ended."

Andrew could've easily sat there and felt sorry for himself, but one word wouldn't stop echoing in his head—*them*. That sounded personal. Andrew had to warn someone at Sterling about what might be coming down the pike. The logical person was Grant. Maybe Tara. But after the scene at Thanksgiving, Andrew wanted to speak to someone whom he knew would actually listen. He needed some help from Clay.

Nine

Andrew raced to Sterling Enterprises feeling uncertain but determined. He'd had a hopeful conversation with Clay, one that made him feel as though he had a true ally at the company. That would be important as he found a way past this.

Andrew's central concerns always revolved around Miranda and the baby—keeping them safe and happy. He couldn't make peace with his brother, but he could take care of the people Johnathon had left behind. Part and parcel of his duty would be finding a peaceful way to stay in Miranda's life. At the very best, he couldn't let his relationship with the people in Miranda's life get any worse. He had to keep Clay and Astrid on his side, and he had to find a way to make Tara and Grant trust him. They didn't have to like him. That might never happen. But Andrew did not want his existence in her world to bring pain or stress to Miranda. She'd been through enough.

"Andrew Sterling for Clay Morgan," he said to the receptionist when he arrived at the Sterling offices, near the top of a downtown skyscraper.

"Andrew," Clay called, emerging from a corridor to the right. He offered a handshake, followed by an inquisitive look. "You doing okay? You look rattled."

Was it that obvious? "I've been better. I'd like to catch you up on everything."

"Yeah. Of course. We'll talk in my office." Clay led Andrew through the serpentine maze that was Sterling Enterprises, the empire built by his brother. The specter of Johnathon didn't feel as overwhelming here, and for that, Andrew was grateful. "Here we are," Clay said.

"Thanks." Andrew was glad they'd reached the safe haven of Clay's office without encountering Tara or Grant. He didn't want a scene. He'd had his fill on Thanksgiving.

Clay closed the door and rounded behind his desk. "Please. Have a seat."

Andrew sat at one end of a black leather sofa and decided to get right to it. "I spoke to Victor. I attempted to pay him off to keep him from his attempts at sabotaging Sterling, but he refused to listen. My guess is that he'll make another run at messing with your chances on the Seaport project, but there's a chance he'll try something else."

"Like what?"

If only Andrew knew the answer to that question. It would make life so much easier. "No idea. I only know that he's really out for vengeance. He lost quite a bit more money to Johnathon than I ever knew. North of fifty million."

"Ouch."

"And it gets worse. There's a personal aspect to his mission." Andrew hesitated to offer more. This news would impact Clay because of his relationship with Astrid.

"What kind of personal?"

Andrew cleared his throat and decided the most direct approach was the best. "Johnathon seduced Victor's daughter when she was twenty. He broke her heart. This was several years ago, but Victor's still very angry about it. His daughter seems to mean the world to him."

Unmistakable concern was painted all over Clay's face. "I understand. I feel the same way about my daughter."

"Of course." Andrew's thoughts were drawn to Miranda's baby. She hadn't even been born yet and he already felt extremely protective of her. He could imagine the fierce anger that would crop up if he discovered that anyone had hurt her in the same way Johnathon had hurt Victor's daughter.

"Okay. I get it. He's out for blood. Or as close as he can get to it."

"Exactly. But you should know there's one more important detail to this story. Johnathon did this while he was married to Astrid."

Clay sucked in a sharp breath. It was like he'd taken a punch to the gut, but of course he felt that way. He loved Astrid. Anything that hurt her, hurt him, too. "Wow." He set his elbow on his chair's armrest and ran his hand through his hair, shaking his head in disbelief. "She will be so hurt when she finds out. Or we need to think about whether she needs to know at all."

"I won't say a thing. That's up to you to decide."

"What do we do now?"

Andrew sincerely wished he had a plan that went beyond waiting to see what Victor might do next. "We have to be hypervigilant. And since his primary target is Sterling, that means watching everything here very closely."

"I can't do that on my own. I simply don't have involvement with every project we're working on."

Andrew knew what came next. "Right. Which is why we need to put Grant and Tara in the loop. The problem is I doubt they'll listen to me."

Clay rapped a knuckle on his desktop. "All we can do is try." He picked up his office phone and pressed a button. "Grant. Hey. It's Clay," he said. "Can I steal a few minutes with you and Tara? It's important."

Andrew's stomach wobbled with uncertainty, but he had to get past this. Ultimately, he was on the same side as Tara and Grant. He just needed to prove it to them.

Clay nodded. "Great. We'll be there in a sec. I have Andrew with me." He dropped the handset back into the cradle like it was a hot coal. "I decided not to give him a chance to yell at me now."

"Smart." *Might as well let him save his ire for me.*

Clay and Andrew headed over to Grant's office. That meant crossing a large open area of people working at desks, a bullpen of sorts. Andrew attracted curious glances with every step. His resemblance to Johnathon had to be the reason, but that realization did nothing to calm his nerves. It was yet another reminder that he'd spent his life in his brother's shadow, and getting out from behind it might never be possible.

Clay hesitated at the doorway to Grant's office, but they were quickly welcomed in. Tara was already there, perched on the arm of an upholstered chair opposite Grant's desk. Her posture said she was ready for battle, her arms crossed defiantly. Grant was settled in his high-backed leather chair, like a king overseeing his domain. Silence fell as Clay closed the door behind him and he and Andrew ventured farther inside. Neither Grant nor Tara invited them to sit, and that was probably for the best. Andrew did not want to stay.

"Okay, then." Clay clapped his hands together once. "Andrew has some developments regarding Victor."

Tara was already shaking her head. "I hope this is going to be quick."

Andrew's patience was already gone, but he wasn't about to lose his temper. He'd deliver this news in as cool and dispassionate a manner as he could. "You don't have to listen to me. But I hope you will." He launched into everything he'd just told Clay, but he kept the detail about Astrid to himself. He wanted that information kept to the smallest circle possible. When he was finished, Grant and Tara remained unimpressed.

"What exactly do you want us to do?" Grant asked.

"That's up to you, but I suggest you keep tight control of everything. No new hires. Brief your security team. Your IT department, as well. Watch who's coming in and out of the office, and who's getting access to the company's computer servers. More than anything, keep an eagle eye on the Seaport project. That's still his most likely target."

"Once again, we have to wonder if this is all a cover for you pursuing a scheme that you started," Tara said.

"What do I have to gain from lying to you? I want this to be done as much as anyone."

"So you can leave town?" Grant asked.

Andrew's stomach sank at the thought of that. He might not be welcome in this room, or in other parts of Miranda's life, but when it was just the two of them, alone, he felt like he had a glimpse of the life he'd always wanted. He didn't want to turn his back on that, but how could he ever prove himself in these circles? For years, Johnathon had poisoned Grant and Tara to the very idea of Andrew. That was a fact. It would take time for Andrew to turn this ship around. He couldn't expect that to happen overnight, and it certainly wouldn't happen until he could prove Victor's existence. That might mean a painful outcome and waiting until Victor pounced.

Andrew looked at Clay. "I've said all I needed to say. I'll show myself out." He turned to Tara and Grant. "Thanks for your time." He had to find a way to be above it all.

Andrew marched through the bullpen, trying to ignore the repeated stares. He'd nearly crossed the space when Clay caught up with him.

"Wait. Hold up," Clay said. "Are you okay?"

Andrew kept walking until they were in a quiet section of the hall. "Yeah. Fine. It's just more of the same."

Clay clapped Andrew's arm. "I'm sorry. Don't worry. It'll all get worked out."

If only Andrew could be so sure. "Thank you. I appreciate that you have any confidence in me at all."

"Of course. Thank you for being there for my sister."

That made Andrew feel one hundred times better. Miranda was the reason to fight. "No need to thank me. I'm happy to do it."

Outside on the street, Andrew pulled his phone out of his pocket and immediately called Miranda. It wasn't that he wanted to dump all of this on her. He just needed to hear her voice.

"Hey there," she answered. "This is a nice surprise. Everything okay at the house?"

Andrew strode down the city sidewalk to his car, which was parked near the corner. It was chilly being in the shadow of the tall buildings around him, but thoughts of Miranda kept him warm. "Everything at the house is fine. I actually just came from the Sterling offices."

"You did? Why?"

Andrew clicked the fob and climbed into his car. "I didn't have a choice." He gave Miranda the abbreviated version of his morning, without the detail about Astrid. "So that's where we stand. It looks like I'm going to be in San Diego indefinitely. I hope that's okay. I'm happy to move back into the hotel."

"Andrew. Don't be silly. I want you staying with me. I need you there."

Heat rose in his body, especially his face. "Good. Because that's where I want to be."

"Maybe you can stay through Christmas. That would be nice."

The idea of that made Andrew incredibly happy, but he didn't want to get too far ahead of himself. *One day at a time.* "If that's the way the calendar works out, I will try to stay."

"So you weren't able to make any progress with Tara and Grant? Mend any fences?"

"No. I'd say things are pretty much the same."

"Oh." She sounded nothing short of disappointed, making Andrew feel as though he'd failed.

"Are you surprised?"

"Not necessarily. I guess I was just being hopeful."

Andrew laughed. He couldn't help it. At this point, the idea was absurd, but Miranda often wore rose-colored glasses. "What about that situation would give you hope?"

"Maybe it was more wishful thinking."

"Why's that?"

"Because I'm hoping you'll be my date for Grant and Tara's wedding."

"Really?" Andrew would have gone anywhere with Miranda, but attending Tara and Grant's nuptials was the absolute last thing he wanted to do.

"Yes, really. Astrid and I are the bridesmaids and I don't want to go by myself."

"You don't want a pariah for a date. It'll be like Thanksgiving all over again."

"Oh, shush. You're perfect. And I love the thought of being on your arm."

Something inside him melted. How could he say no? He couldn't, even when the list of his reservations about attending Grant and Tara's wedding was a mile long. "Okay, then. I guess I'd better rent a tux."

Miranda nearly didn't answer the phone when Tara called on Friday. Between Andrew's unpleasant chat with her and Grant at Sterling earlier this week, and the lecture she'd given Andrew on Thanksgiving, Tara was not her favorite person. But Miranda had been home from work for an hour now and was looking forward to a relaxing weekend with Andrew. She hoped that Tara was ready to let cooler heads prevail.

Miranda answered the call on speaker. "Hello?"

"Everything is ruined," Tara blurted. "Absolutely everything." It almost sounded as if Tara was crying, which really put Miranda on notice. Tara did *not* cry. "The wedding has been cancelled."

"Did something happen with Grant?"

"No. We're fine. It's not that. It's our plans. Everything I've spent months working on is ruined."

That made no sense, but Miranda was sure this was normal bridal jitters. It was two weeks until the wedding. Perfectly understandable that Tara would be worked up about it. "Take a deep breath. Tell me what happened."

"Someone phoned the venue and said we'd called off the engagement. Same thing for the florist and the caterers. Even the tuxes were canceled."

"What? How does that happen?"

"I don't know. It happened some time on Monday, but nobody bothered to tell me. We'd already lost our deposits, so I guess they didn't care? I tried to reach the caterer to give them the final numbers for entrées, and that's when I found out. Then I started making other calls and it turns out that the whole thing is ruined. I don't know what I'm supposed to do."

"There has to be a way to fix this. I'll help."

Andrew walked into the room and looked at Miranda inquisitively. She pushed the mute button on her phone to prevent Tara from hearing what she was about to say. "It's Tara. Someone canceled her wedding. How weird is that?"

Andrew stuffed his hands into his pants, shaking his head. "I don't have a good feeling about this."

"Hold on. I'd better get back on the line or Tara will freak." Miranda turned off the mute button. "Once again, take a deep breath. We can fix this." As to why any of this was Miranda's problem, she wasn't sure, but it was her inclination to help.

"What if Andrew did this?" Tara asked.

Miranda deeply regretted leaving Tara on speaker. Andrew was still standing right there. "I know you're upset, but that's ridiculous. Why would he do that when he's been trying everything he can to earn your trust?"

Andrew threw up his hands and bounded out of the room. Now Miranda had two sets of ruffled feathers to smooth, but at least she had an excuse to take Tara off speaker.

"Because it's affecting the business. There's a big story on one of the business-news websites saying that Grant and I have called off our engagement and the company is in trouble because the two most senior people are at odds. Our shareholders have been calling Grant nonstop."

"Does that really sound like something Andrew would do? Because I don't think it does."

"You're blind to all of this, Miranda. You two are sleeping together, aren't you?"

It had only been a matter of time before this news got out, but it still didn't make it a more comfortable topic of conversation. "How do you know that? Did Astrid tell you?"

"So you *are* having sex." She said it in such a deeply accusatorial tone. "I was just guessing. There's entirely too much solidarity between you two. I sensed that at Thanksgiving."

"Solidarity? We're helping each other through a difficult time. If that's a crime, then I guess I'm guilty as charged, but I'm not going to apologize for it. I'm a grown woman and this is my life."

"Do you have any idea how much this would upset Johnathon?"

Miranda's heart skipped a beat, and not in a good way. It was like being plunged into ice-cold water. That was an *extremely* low blow. How dare Tara ask that question? "Of course I know, Tara. I was still his wife when he died. You were not."

Several moments of silence played out on the other end of the line. It seemed like an eternity, and Miranda already felt bad for what she'd said, but she was tired of being on the receiving end of so much disrespect. Either directly or indirectly, so many people had suggested to Miranda that they'd known Johnathon better than she had. Yes, their marriage had been a short one, and Miranda hadn't been around long enough to know every detail of Johnathon's life before her, but that didn't mean they hadn't been close. She might not have been privy to every shred of his history, but she'd known what he had in his heart for her.

"Oh, God. I'm so sorry, Miranda. I don't know what got into me."

"I need you to understand something. Every day, I deal with the ghost of Johnathon and the question of what he would have wanted or not wanted. I want to honor him. I do. But I'm also the person who's left on earth after him. I want a life, Tara. It might have felt like I died the same day Johnathon did, but that's not permanent. I don't have the luxury of staying in that frame of mind. This baby is going to be here before we know it. She needs me to look forward. To the future. And try to see the possibilities."

"You're so right. And I'm truly sorry. Can you forgive me?"

"Can you start putting a little faith in Andrew? Because I know with every fiber of my being that he would not cancel someone's wedding and he certainly wouldn't plant some fake, gossipy story. That's just not him."

"You really do trust him, don't you?"

Just then, Andrew walked back into the room. He was wearing that look of deep concern, the one that was so often painted on his face. She truly hoped that one day soon, the weight of all of this could be off his shoulders. He didn't deserve to carry the burden.

"I do trust Andrew," Miranda said, catching his eye. "One hundred percent."

For a moment, the expression on Andrew's face lightened, his eyes flashing with their deep brilliance. "Thank you," he whispered.

"Tara, I need to go. What can I do to help with this wedding fiasco? I have to think the venue is your first concern. Can't you or Grant put some pressure on them? Surely you know someone over there."

"It's not a matter of pressure. This close to Christmas, the space is in high demand. It's gone. But maybe that part of it is for the best. I never wanted a big wedding, and we kept the guest list small. I think I've convinced Grant that we should just get married at the house."

"That's a wonderful idea. You couldn't ask for a more beautiful setting. What about the flowers? Other decorating and rentals? You'll need chairs. Have you thought about a tent? I'm happy to handle any of that. I have contacts through my design business."

"Really? After what I said about Johnathon?"

Miranda wasn't sure if she was being naive, but something was telling her to keep pushing her agenda of mending these ties for Andrew. When this baby arrived, she wanted her world to be harmonious, or as close to that as she could get. "Yes. I really want to help."

"If you could tackle the flowers and rentals, that would take a big weight off my shoulders. I can deal with the caterers and everything else."

"That works. Can you send me some details about what you wanted? I'll make a few phone calls to let people know we need them on that date. December nineteenth, right?"

"That much has not changed. You're wonderful, Miranda. Thank you."

"You're like a sister to me, Tara. Sometimes you're a pain in the butt, but that doesn't mean I don't love you and care about your happiness."

"I love you, too. I want you to be happy, too."

"Good. Because I need you to know that Andrew is my date for the wedding. And I need that to not be a problem, okay?"

Tara sucked in a deep breath. Miranda could hear it over the line. "Got it."

"I'm serious. I want you to tell Grant, too."

"I'm on it. Believe me, I don't want that day to be anything short of perfect."

"Me, too, Tara. Me, too." Miranda ended the call and tossed aside her phone. "Well, that was an ordeal."

"I only heard part of the conversation. Tara and Grant's wedding plans were canceled?"

"Yes. And there's a gossipy story on the internet

saying they've split up and it's making things bad at Sterling."

Andrew wagged his head from side to side. "It has to be Victor. He said that if he couldn't destroy Sterling, he wanted to hurt them."

"You mean *it*."

Andrew again shook his head. "I specifically remember him saying *them*. That's personal. You don't get much more personal than ruining someone's wedding."

"And it's Grant and Tara. The two most senior people at the company."

"It's a twofer. A direct hit. One more reason I have to stop Victor."

"Any ideas?"

"When you were on the phone with Tara, I was in the other room trying to reach Sandy. I had to leave a message. No telling when or if she'll call me back."

"So we wait?"

"We don't have a choice right now. I told Tara and Grant to be watching everything, but I was talking about the company. It's understandable that they weren't focused on the wedding plans they thought were firmly in place."

Miranda got up from her seat on the sofa, drawn to Andrew, like always. "I told her you're my date. And I was very specific that everyone needs to be on their best behavior."

He gazed down into her eyes and once again, she felt as though she might never understand the complexity hidden behind them. "That shouldn't have to be said. You shouldn't have to defend me. I hate that it demands anything of you at all, other than to RSVP *yes*."

"I can't help it. It just comes naturally to me. And I know they'll come around. They will."

He gripped her forearm and tugged her closer, combing his fingers into her hair. "What makes you the way you are, Miranda Sterling? You have every reason in the world to be bitter and angry, but you never give in to it. I could learn a lot about generosity and forgiveness from you."

"You're sweet." Her heart felt like it was jumping around like a droplet of water on a hot skillet. She wanted him to take her upstairs and take off her clothes, so she could feel his hands all over her body. She needed him. She wanted him. And it would happen. But she had to make a few phone calls first. She'd promised. "If you want to learn some more about generosity, you can help me fix Tara and Grant's wedding."

Ten

Miranda was on wedding-repair duty, but Andrew was trying to help. He was on his laptop in her home office, sifting through the lengthy emails Tara had forwarded to Miranda, detailing everything from flowers to something called swags. He didn't want to be a guy about it, but he was in a bit over his head.

"That's the last call." Seated at her desk, Miranda jabbed at her cell phone once, then put it down. "Did you get anywhere with Tara's wish list?"

"I don't even know what half of this stuff is."

"Like what?" There was a flirtatious edge to her voice that took him by surprise. She got up from her desk and walked over to where he was sitting, on the small love seat in her office.

"Like a swag." He pointed to the email on his laptop. She pushed down the screen until his computer was closed up. "Remember how we hung the strands of silver bells and garland above the doorway in the living room when we decorated for Christmas? That's a swag. For the wedding, it'll just be some fabric. It softens the rough edges." Her grin was equal parts come-hither and shy. Her cheeks flushed with a breathtaking shade of pink, a lighter color than her lips. It was hopelessly inviting. All he could think was that *she* softened *his* rough edges.

"No more volunteer work for Grant and Tara."

She stood before him in the same blue dress he'd seen her in when she'd left for work that morning, but somehow he hadn't taken the time to really notice the way it hugged every inch of her gorgeous body, or the way it brought out her deep brown eyes.

"You look absolutely gorgeous," he said, craving her touch. Their gazes naturally found each other and the electricity between them was hard to fathom, like an entire year of a power plant's output encapsulated in that moment. He was shocked that the current arcing between them wasn't visible.

"Thank you." Her head tilted to the side, only a fraction of an inch, but he loved seeing the way she was willing to show him the subtle hints that he'd said the right thing. "You don't look half-bad yourself." She stepped closer, peering down at him. She was conveying a most intriguing mix of business and play. If she wanted to get serious about playing with him, he was up for that.

She tugged on his hand and he stood. Her hands pressed hard against his chest, smoothing the fabric of his dress shirt. He watched her, smiling, their eyes again connecting. It looked as if there was a fire blazing behind hers—wild and intense. Which one of them would give in to the kiss first? He had no idea. He only knew that he would win either way.

"I want things to be good between us, Miranda. I don't want us to be lugging around so much baggage. It doesn't feel fair." He felt a burning need to bring up the state of their relationship, however much it was tenuous and defied definition. This was the price of wanting to make love to a woman who had once been married to his brother. He was treading on hallowed ground.

"I agree. I don't want anything else between us." Her lips parted ever so slightly and a gentle rush of air passed from them. It was the sound of pressure being released. "Including clothes." Her hands hadn't left his chest. She leaned into him, and her fingers played with the buttons of his shirt. "I vote that we don't worry about anything more than you and me and the evening we have stretching out before us."

He grinned again, this time much more eagerly.

"You're smiling," she said.

"Of course I am. It's impossible to not be happy around you. Even when it's been a terrible day, you bring it out of me."

He snaked his hand around her waist and settled it in the curve of her lower back. Her lips traveled closer to his, but she stopped shy of a kiss, humming instead, the vibration sending waves of anticipation to his mouth. She flicked open one of the buttons of his shirt. Only one. This was quickly turning into a game of undressing, and as much as he loved a slow seduction, he wanted her naked. He reached up for the zipper of her dress, then pulled it down the center of her back as she finally started to rush through his shirt buttons. He longed to see the stretch of her skin revealed by the open zipper, so he turned her around, admiring her creamy skin as it contrasted with a black bra. He continued with the downward motion of the metal closure, his breath catching when he caught sight of her lacy panties. He eased the dress from her shoulders, savoring every sensory pleasure—her smell, the heat that radiated from her, her smooth skin as he dragged the back of his hand along the channel of her spine. Her presence didn't merely have him primed. He was already perilously close to the brink.

The garment slipped down the length of her body to the floor and she cast a seductive look back at him, her eyes deep, warm and craving. "A lot less between us now."

Oh, yes. He grasped her shoulders and pinned her back to his chest, then wrapped his arms around her waist. He reached down and caressed the soft roundness of her belly as she craned her neck. He kissed her with some force—enough so that she would never question how much he wanted her. He cupped one of her breasts, the silky fabric of her bra teasing his palm as her skin tightened beneath his touch. Their tongues tangled and Miranda turned herself in his arms. He wrangled himself out of his shirt and pants with some help from her. It was a frantic and hurried blur. They were both eager to get to the main event. He pulled her close when he was naked and kissed her again. Miranda cast aside any sweetness for a demanding edge he wanted to satisfy.

With a pop, he unhooked her bra and quickly teased it from her body. He took her breasts in his hands and Miranda's eyes fluttered shut as his thumbs rubbed back and forth against her dark pink, firm nipples. The gasp that came from her when he flicked his tongue against her tight skin was music to his ears.

She bent to one side to step out of her panties. Her beautiful bare body heightened his awareness of how badly he wanted to claim her. There was no way they'd make it upstairs. At least not until later. He sat on the love seat, half-reclining, and reached out his hand.

"Come here. I need you."

She smiled and cocked an eyebrow, taking his hand. "No bedroom?"

"Not this first time. We have all night. For upstairs."

"Are you that impatient?"

"In a word, yes." The breath caught in his chest as he watched her carefully set her knee next to his hip and straddle him. The sky outside had fully fallen into darkness, but the glow from the lamp on her desk was just bright enough to show off the dips and hollows of her delicate collarbone. He traced his fingers along the contours.

She smiled, dropping her head to kiss him. Her silky hair brushed the sides of his face. He was almost sorry he didn't have the visual of the moment she took him in her hand, guided him inside and began to sink down around him. A deep groan escaped his throat as her body molded around him, warm and inviting. He couldn't think of another place on earth he'd rather be.

She settled her weight on his and they moved together in a dance he wanted to go on forever. He couldn't believe that this beautiful, sweet woman would ever want him. She rocked her hips into his, again and again, as they kissed and his hands cradled her velvety, perfect bottom. He was already in such ecstasy that it felt as if his body was floating, but he would've been lying if he'd said that his heart wasn't heavy. This happened every time they made love. Every time she gave of herself like this. He'd done the unthinkable. He'd fallen for his dead brother's wife. There was no unringing that bell.

Miranda's breaths quickened and before he knew what was happening, she was gathering around him in steady pulses. It was enough to pull him out of his more serious thoughts and mercifully push him into the moment. She sat back, their eyes connecting for an instant, then she gave in to the sensation fully, closing her eyes and knocking her head back. He shut his own eyes and the relief shuddered out of him. Either he was dreaming, or each passing wave brought them closer.

Miranda felt worn-out, yet light as air. She collapsed against Andrew's chest, still struggling to catch her breath as a few echoes of the pleasure washed over her. There had been a moment in the midst of their lovemaking that he'd slipped away from her. He'd seemed disengaged. It probably only lasted for a second or two, and it was insignificant in terms of what they'd just done together, but it still made her concerned.

"Are you okay?" She sat back and cradled both sides of his head, peering straight into his eyes.

He laughed quietly, his eyes not quite open all the way. "Are you kidding me? I'm better than okay. I'm magnificent. You're amazing."

He brought his lips to her bare shoulder and it reminded her body of the things he could do to her with just a single touch. Her nipples grew hard again. Her center ached for more of him, even when she was straddling his lap and there were no clothes between them.

"Okay. It's just that there was a moment when it felt

like you weren't here. It's not a big deal. And maybe it's my pregnancy brain. I swear it doesn't work the way it used to. I just wanted to be sure that everything's okay."

"Sure."

"You can tell me anything, you know."

He grinned. "You love to push it, don't you?"

She shrugged. "I don't like leaving things unsaid."

He nodded and pulled her closer until she had no choice but to settle her head on his shoulder. Perhaps this was easier for him, when they didn't have to look each other in the eye. His fingers traveled gracefully up and down her back, lulling her into peacefulness. Still, she sensed that there was something between them, and she'd just told him that she didn't want that to be the case.

"This isn't easy, Miranda, but I feel stupid even saying that. It's not like you don't already know that. It's not like you don't experience that every day."

She sensed what he was about to say next, and it brought a tear to her eye.

"Like it or not, the reality of our situation is that Johnathon brought us together. He's the reason we're here alone. It's difficult for me to come to terms with that. I have to wonder if the guilt will always be there."

Miranda pushed back so she could see his face. She wanted him to understand that she was just as torn as he was. "I know. There are times when I can look beyond it and moments when I can't. But I don't want guilt to dictate what happens between us." She felt foolish for saying that, but the truth was that she was a widow who was expecting a baby. Her life was flat-out serious. That was all there was to it. She could act like things were of little consequence, but that wasn't where she was.

"I don't want it to, either. I'm just telling you that's the struggle I'm going through right now. But I don't want to burden you with that. You have enough to worry about, between the baby and work and now having to deal with Tara and Grant's wedding."

"How did I get sucked into that, anyway?"

"You're too nice. That's how."

"Um, not entirely true. I stood up to Tara today. She knows we're..." She waved her hands around. "Doing this."

"Having sex?"

"Yes. I asked her if Astrid told her, but it turns out that she guessed."

"Astrid knows, too? How did that happen?"

Miranda felt the heat rise in her cheeks. "I couldn't help it. We were talking about all of the Thanksgiving drama on Monday and it just sort of slipped out. Are you mad?"

"I'm assuming this means your brother also knows."

Miranda shrugged. "Probably." She hadn't given that too much thought, but it was logical. Astrid and Clay were very open with each other. "It's a good thing, if you think about it. He still likes you."

Andrew let loose one of his unguarded laughs. They didn't come often, but Miranda loved it when they did. "He said he likes me because I take care of you."

"He's right. I was not a happy camper before you moved in."

"I find that very hard to believe. I mean, I know you're still in mourning, but you're so upbeat."

Miranda thought about the many days where it was nearly impossible to roll out of bed, or the mornings where she sat at the kitchen table and couldn't bring herself to go back upstairs, take a shower, get dressed and go to work. And then there had been the many, many days when she couldn't function in the office for more than a few hours before she was exhausted and had to go home. On those nights, she usually curled into a ball and cried herself to sleep. She'd felt it was a necessary part of grieving, to simply give in to the things her mind and body craved, but the reality was that ever since Andrew had come along, those inclinations had started to fade. Just feeling life in the house again made her happy. But once she'd discovered what it meant for that life to be from Andrew, everything had started to change. He was strong and selfless. Warm and caring. Everything she'd always been told he wasn't.

She loved Johnathon, but damn him for portraying his brother in such a negative light.

"Let just say that things have gotten a lot better since you've been here. And not just because you cook for me and make coffee in the morning." She smoothed back his hair. "And it's not because you've done so many things for me around the house or you've listened to my problems or worries. It's because you've never once judged me. Not even for a minute."

"When you've felt the weight of others' judgment, it's hard to want to inflict it on anyone else. Especially someone you care about."

She gazed into his eyes, taking note of the warmth that radiated from the center of her chest. Her heart was putting itself back together, piece by piece, simply because this amazing man had walked into her life at the most inopportune of times. She was falling. She knew it. But she had to be careful. Because she wasn't sure

Andrew would ever allow himself to be happy. And that meant she wasn't sure that Andrew would ever stay.

"Will you make me a promise?" she asked.

"What's that?"

"You're already staying for Tara and Grant's wedding. Promise me you'll stay through Christmas."

"Is that what you want?"

She didn't want to think about the alternative. "Yes. Absolutely."

Eleven

Andrew heard Grant's voice plain as day over Miranda's speakerphone. "Can you and Andrew come early today? We have something we need to tell you both."

Miranda cast a curious look at Andrew. They were both still getting dressed for the wedding. And they were already expected to arrive an hour before the rest of the guests. "Is everything okay?" Miranda asked.

"Yes. Everything's fine. But I owe Andrew and you an apology. If you come early, we can set it all straight."

"Okay. We'll be there as soon as we can." Miranda ended the call. "What do you think that's all about?"

"I have no idea, but the thought of an apology sounds pretty good." It sounded better than good, and at least made Andrew slightly more optimistic about attending this wedding. He'd been dreading Grant and Tara's big day. Not because of his date. Going with Miranda was the only reason to put on a tux. But he wasn't thrilled about the idea of facing another virtual firing squad in the form of the bride and groom. It was one thing to be chastised at the Thanksgiving table, and quite another to be given the evil eye over wedding cake and champagne.

"Ready?" he asked Miranda after he'd worked his way into his shoes. "I'm going to save my jacket for after we get there. I don't want it to wrinkle."

Miranda emerged from the closet in her bridesmaid dress, a strapless burgundy gown that nearly made his jaw drop to the floor. "Do I look like a beach ball?"

He went to her, wishing they didn't have to rush out the door. He caressed her silky shoulders. *You look like everything I ever wanted.* "No. You don't. You look absolutely gorgeous and full of life."

"Is that code for beach ball? Because I have to stand next to Astrid, who pretty much has a perfect body and will be wearing the exact same dress. This doesn't bode well for my self-confidence."

"Don't compare yourself to Astrid. You're the most beautiful woman I've ever seen."

She bunched up her lips and narrowed her gaze. "That's not true."

"But it is. Part of that is knowing what's in here." He tapped a finger on her forehead. "And here." He pressed his hand where her heart was, watching as that skeptical look on her face morphed into a smile.

"That's sweet. I don't entirely believe you, but that's okay. You've armed me with enough courage to stand next to Astrid. That's all I needed." Her expression changed again, into one of sheer delight. "Baby's moving," she muttered, reaching for his hand and flattening it against her stomach.

Miranda had told him how active the baby had been, but the movement never seemed to happen when Andrew was around, or when it did, he wasn't able to detect it. He still couldn't feel it now, and he really wanted to. "I just don't feel it."

"A little harder." She pressed his hand even more firmly against her belly.

"I don't want to hurt—" He didn't manage another word before he felt little taps and flutters against his palm. Miranda's pregnancy was mysterious and wondrous, but this was a whole new frontier. Her eyes sparkled when her gaze connected with his. "I feel it," he whispered, dropping his eyes to her belly. "Wow. She's really going for it, isn't she?"

Miranda giggled. "Amazing, isn't it?"

"It really is." He was so in awe that he didn't dare move until the baby decided to stop making her presence known.

"We should go or we won't be there early at all," she said.

"Okay."

Miranda stopped on her way out of the bedroom to grab her handbag and a wrap for her shoulders from the dresser. Downstairs, they gathered their coats. The ceremony was set to happen in Grant's backyard, which overlooked the Pacific, and although there would be heaters and, later, firepits, it would be chilly by evening.

Outside, they climbed into Miranda's car, with Andrew behind the wheel. She pulled up the address for Grant's house on the GPS. Andrew wasn't entirely sure of the way. As he drove, he could feel his shoulders tighten up. He'd spent so much time worrying about what Grant and Tara would say to him today, that he hadn't taken the time to think about the fact that he hadn't been to a wedding since his fiancée left him. *It's nothing*, he said to himself, but it was eating at him. It was yet another reminder of the many times he'd come up short. Could he ever be enough for Miranda? The fact that he was competing with the memory of Johnathon, the one person he'd always come in second place to, didn't help.

He was in love with her. He couldn't deny himself that label for his feelings, even if he kept it tightly contained in his head and had done so for weeks now, especially since the night they'd made love in her office and had such a heartbreakingly frank conversation. Despite the sensitive subject matter, Miranda brought so much naked honesty to the equation, it stole his breath away. Before he'd met her, Andrew had existed in a world built on fast moves, dubious motives and sleight of hand. Miranda was a complete one-eighty from that, and it fed his soul in a way he hadn't counted on.

He kept looking for moments where he could chalk up his feelings to lust or infatuation, but every time, his thinking led back to one word—*love*. Whenever they were around each other, she'd do or say something that made him want to say it. Even the simplest of smiles from her was enough to make it sit on his lips, but there was always something that made him choke it back.

Victor was the obvious reason. He wouldn't feel right about even broaching the subject until that slate was wiped clean. He needed to fix the problem. But Johnathon was also lurking in the back of his head, telling him that he was treading where he didn't belong.

"Is everything okay?" Miranda asked when they pulled up to Grant's palatial modern home. "You've been quiet."

Now was not the time to unspool everything running circles in his head. "I guess I'm just curious about what Grant has to say to us."

"Nothing else? Because I was thinking about it last night and I have to wonder if it's hard for you to attend a wedding because of your fiancée." Miranda was so in tune with him, it was uncanny. No, she hadn't touched on everything that was bothering him, but she'd keyed in on part of it.

"Maybe a little. I'm fine now. Let's go." He climbed out of the car and helped her with her things.

"Okay. But let me know if you want to talk about it," she said as they walked up the driveway. "Or if it becomes too much. I don't want you to think I'm insensitive by bringing you here."

"Don't worry. I don't."

The front door was wide open, with the occasional person ducking in or out. They stepped inside and asked one of the caterers, "Do you know where Mr. Singleton is?"

"The last time I saw him, he was in his office. Right off the living room. Across from the kitchen."

Miranda and Andrew walked through the wide expanse of the living room, which had been tastefully decorated for the holidays with a tall Christmas tree next to the fireplace, decorated with silver and white ornaments. The house was unbelievable, with stunning views through many windows, all of them leading the eye to the lush landscape and the ocean beyond.

Tara emerged from a door near the back of the house

and waved at them. She was wrapped up in a fluffy white robe. "I'm glad you guys are here," she called as she padded toward them in bare feet. "Grant is right in here." She came to a stop outside his office.

Miranda stopped to kiss her on the cheek. "I thought it was bad luck for the groom to see the bride."

"That's just if she's wearing the dress. Hence the robe. Plus, I don't really believe in bad luck. Bad actors, maybe." Tara then turned her attention to Andrew, shocking the hell out of him by offering a hug. "I'm glad you're here."

You are? This was all too bizarre, but Andrew wasn't about to argue. Today was her wedding day. She was entitled to act however she wanted, even if Andrew was thrown for a loop. "I'm happy to be here."

The three stepped inside Grant's home office, tastefully decorated, but it could definitely have benefited from Miranda's deft touch. Grant looked up from his desk, then rounded it to hug Miranda and shake hands with Andrew. He wasn't dressed for the occasion yet, either, wearing jeans and a T-shirt. "Thank you both for coming early. Please. Sit."

This felt a bit like a meeting at Sterling Enterprises, but again, Andrew went with it. He made sure Miranda had her first choice of seating option—the middle of the sofa. He sat next to her while Tara stood next to Grant, the pair holding hands.

"So, I'm sure you're both curious about why we wanted to say this in person, but after everything at Thanksgiving, and then again a few weeks ago in the Sterling offices, Andrew deserves a full-fledged in-person apology. Tara and I are both deeply sorry that we doubted you."

"About Victor?"

"Grant thinks he figured out who he is," Tara said. "His true identity."

Miranda shot a look at Andrew. "Oh, my God. Can you believe this?"

"I'm curious to hear what you learned." Andrew nodded. After all, he'd been the person shouting loudest that Victor was a real person.

"One of the first times Johnathon and I partnered with another developer on a building project, it was with a man named James Bloodworth," Grant started. "This was early days of Sterling Enterprises, after Tara had left the company."

"I remember the Bloodworth fiasco, though," Tara said. "Everyone talked about it."

"Johnathon had been interested in trying a project outside of San Diego, so we partnered with James on a high-rise in Toronto. In short, the deal was a major disaster for him and for Sterling. Everyone lost a pile of money. We underestimated the timeline and the building costs, and we grossly overestimated the market at that time. It was the one and only time we worked outside this city."

"I don't understand. Where does Victor come into this?" Miranda asked, mirroring what Andrew was thinking.

"Victor is James Bloodworth's middle name. Of course, I never knew that," Grant said. "He was terrible to work with. A real hothead. Johnathon and I agreed that we would never partner with him again. At some point, Johnathon went behind my back and cut several deals with him directly, using his own money."

This had been the missing piece of this puzzle—

Johnathon's initial partnership with Victor and how Grant could've been left in the dark. Grant did know Victor. The names just weren't right. "This is all starting to make more sense. How did you figure this out?" Andrew had to know how this had come together.

"I've been going through Johnathon's files since his death. Just making sure there wasn't anything crucial tucked away in them. He wasn't always the best at sharing information." Grant cast Tara a knowing smile. "I had a box of them here at the house and Tara needed me to move them into my office for the wedding. I only had one more file to go through, so I did it this morning. It was the last file. Under *V,* for Victor. As near as I can tell, he stopped using his full name after that first failed deal."

Andrew drew a deep breath in through his nose, letting it bring some much-needed oxygen to his brain. Yes, this all made sense, but it was still a lot to take in at one time.

"What does this mean moving forward?" Miranda asked.

"Hopefully, destroying our wedding was the extent of his malicious actions," Tara answered. "We find out who landed the Seaport project on Wednesday, right before Christmas Eve."

What a relief that will be. It almost sounded too good to be true. In fact, Andrew couldn't escape the idea that it likely was. He simply didn't trust Victor to stop or to simply go away. Then again, maybe he was just giving in to old thinking and needed some time to adjust to the idea of not being in constant crisis mode.

Grant extended his hand to Andrew. "I'd like to apologize again. Johnathon definitely left a few surprises behind for us, didn't he?"

Miranda placed her hand on Andrew's knee. "I'm just glad we can all move forward," she said. Her touch was a comfort. It felt like permission to take a deep breath and relax. He hoped he could do that today.

"A wedding seems like a good start," Grant said, taking Tara's hand.

A look of panic crossed Tara's face. "I need to get ready." She shot Miranda a sideways glance. "Do you want to come help me?"

"Sure."

Miranda knew all along that the situation with Grant, Tara and Andrew had been bothering her, but now that it was resolved, she could hardly believe it. Perhaps that was because Andrew still seemed on edge, forcing smiles and being quiet as she kissed him on the cheek before going to help Tara. "Sit up front. So I can see you."

"I don't feel comfortable doing that. Those seats are for family."

She realized then that she was practically throwing him to the wolves. This wasn't set to be a big wedding, but most guests had known Johnathon, which meant they likely did not have a good opinion of Andrew. "Sit wherever you want. The ceremony will be super short. Then we can spend the rest of the day together."

He unleashed another of those unconvincing smiles. Miranda felt torn between the things she'd promised to Tara, and what she truly wanted to do, which was hold on to Andrew and not let go.

"I will be fine, Miranda. I promise." He pressed a soft kiss to her cheek. "I'll see you after the ceremony."

She admired his strong silhouette as he walked away in the direction of the living room. A heavy sigh came from her lips. She was smitten. But she needed to focus on the task at hand. She turned and rushed down the hall to Grant and Tara's bedroom, where Tara was getting ready.

"If you can just help me get into my dress without getting makeup all over it, that would be great," Tara said.

"Hold on." Astrid slipped into the room, shutting the door behind her. "I'm an expert at this. Let me help." Astrid was a former model. She'd likely done this sort of thing countless times.

"You're here," Miranda said, unable to tear her sights from how incredible Astrid looked in that dress. Andrew's words echoed in her head. *You're the most beautiful woman I've ever seen.* It might not be true, but he at least knew the right thing to say.

"If you could help, that would be amazing," Tara said, easing the robe from her shoulders.

Feeling useless, Miranda stepped aside, leaving Astrid to the job of wrangling the dress. She removed it from the hanger and threaded her arms up through the skirt and bodice, then lifted it above Tara's head. Astrid was tall, and in heels, so she did it with ease. "Raise your arms straight up, but put your chin to your chest," Astrid instructed.

Tara did as she was told. "Won't this mess up my hair?"

"A little. But we'll fix it." Astrid lowered the gown while Tara's torso emerged through the top. Astrid helped her ease the straps over her shoulders, then went to zip her up. "See? No makeup, and your hair looks perfect."

Tara turned around in her dress, a simple but striking winter white satin gown with thin straps, a deep V-neck and a graceful trailing skirt. Astrid and Miranda raced to deliver the good news—she was a beautiful bride.

"It's incredible," Astrid declared.

"Absolutely gorgeous," Miranda added. "Grant's going to flip."

"I'm so glad you're both here. You really are my closest girlfriends. Which is strange, isn't it?"

"I wonder what Johnathon would have thought if he'd ever lived to see this day," Astrid wondered aloud.

"I'm guessing his ego would've been out of control," Tara said. "We look amazing."

Miranda laughed, but she was a little tired of entertaining questions of how Johnathon would've felt about anything. Yes, she'd loved him, but guesses about his wants and desires were looming as too big a presence in all of their lives. "I think it's more important we acknowledge everything the three of us have done to find common ground and work together. It's pretty astounding if you think about it. We could have easily walked out of the lawyer's office after the will was read and gone our separate ways."

"I think that was the money talking," Tara said, walking over to her bureau and checking her makeup in the mirror hanging over it.

"No. Miranda's right," Astrid said. "The money might have been the starting point, but it was still up to us to keep it all together. That wasn't easy. There were secrets looming and we had to ride it out together." She reached for Miranda's hand and gave it a squeeze.

"And now we have a wedding to celebrate, a baby who will be here in a few months and, hopefully, if everything goes right, Sterling Enterprises will win the Seaport contract."

Miranda sighed. It would be nice if that last part happened, but she was also preparing herself for the idea that it might not, and how that might impact Andrew. It could end up being a big blow to his sense of self and the guilt he wrestled with on a daily basis. "Let's all hope for a happy ending."

Astrid's phone beeped with a text. "It's Clay. Grant is down there and Clay is waiting to walk you down the aisle. Delia's with him."

"Sounds like it's game time," Miranda said.

After a last-minute spray of perfume and hairspray for Tara, Miranda checked to make sure the coast was clear in the hall, then they wound around to the back staircase, which led to Grant's lower floor. This house was built into a slight hill, with two thirds of this level still above ground. At the back of the house was a wall of accordion windows that were open today, with the wedding guests in white wooden folding chairs on the expansive lawn. Beyond that was the arch, covered in a blanket of white roses. That had been Miranda's touch. Luckily, Grant had a tall solid wood fence on one side of his property, which gave them privacy and a break from the wind.

"Ready?" Clay asked, approaching the three of them. Delia was holding tight to his hand, but broke free when she saw Miranda.

Miranda crouched down and kissed her niece on the head. "You look very pretty in your flower-girl dress."

"Thank you. These shoes hurt my feet, though." She

rocked one foot from side to side in her white patent Mary Janes.

"Yeah. I'm afraid that's one of the prices of being a woman. Wearing shoes that hurt."

"It's time to go," Astrid said. She arranged everyone in order—Delia first, then Miranda, Astrid and finally Tara on Clay's arm.

Moments later, the music started and Delia did a wonderful job, tossing flower petals as she started down the aisle. The guests stood, and that was when Miranda spotted Andrew, sitting in the second-to-last row, at the very far end. Would he ever feel a part of this? She hoped he would. She hoped he would want to. As she took her turn to march up the aisle, she stole the chance to lock eyes with him, finding that familiar mix of sad and tender emotions in his expression.

As promised, the ceremony was short and sweet, and after a rousing round of applause from the attendees and the happy couple's walk down the aisle, the caterers swooped in to rearrange the chairs for the reception as guests left their seats. Miranda found her way to Andrew right away.

"It was nice," he said.

"It was, wasn't it?" She took his hand. "You positive everything is okay?"

He pulled her into his arms and pressed a kiss to the top of her head. "You can stop asking me that. Just enjoy yourself. That's all I really want."

That didn't bring her much comfort or encouragement, but she didn't want to dig deeper. "Let's get you a drink."

"I'll have whatever you're having. I heard something about a spiced Christmas cider."

"You want bourbon in yours?"

He shook his head. "No, thank you."

"You should have a drink if you want one."

"Think of it as a sign of solidarity."

She grinned and popped up onto her toes to kiss his cheek. "You're the best." "I love you" played at her lips, but she didn't want this to be the moment when she blurted it out. She'd wait until she was more sure that there was a chance he would return the feeling. And if that day never came, and he ended up leaving, she'd say it then. Just so he'd never doubt her true feelings. Just so that he could look back on their time together in a happy light. Things between them would never be simple, or cut and dried. Never. He was her dead husband's brother. That was never going away.

They happily made it through dinner and the start of the reception without incident, although Miranda definitely noticed that a few of Johnathon's friends had cast disapproving looks in their direction when she and Andrew were holding hands or dancing. *It's none of their business*, she thought, but she knew it had to bother Andrew. She couldn't shake it off completely herself.

They were in each other's arms on the dance floor when a slow and romantic song segued into a much more raucous one. Guests popped up from their seats and began to move in Miranda and Andrew's direction. She took that as their cue to leave.

"Come on. Let's go steal a minute alone before we sneak out of here." She grabbed his hand and pulled on it.

Andrew took a few steps, but looked out over the party, which was now in full swing. "This is showing signs of lasting all night. Are you sure it's okay if we leave?"

"I'm sure. The cake has been cut. Toasts have been made." She tugged a little harder on his hand. "I want us to have the moment alone that we didn't really get all day."

He grinned. "I can't deny that's an enticing invitation."

They rushed away from the party, out of the light, and into the deep blue night air. The wind whipped, chilling her face and arms. Miranda had a fleeting thought of a wish for her coat, but she didn't want to ruin the moment. When they got to the farthest reaches of Grant's property, they were less than fifty feet from the precipice, the cliff that overlooked the tumult of the ocean below.

"Come here," Andrew said, pulling her into his arms and wrapping her up in his warmth. She didn't need a coat—all she needed was him. "You're shivering."

"It's okay. I just wanted to soak up this view. With you." She snuggled against his chest and gazed out over the water. The moon, hanging low in the sky, glowed bright, the light glinting off the whitecaps. "Did you enjoy yourself today? I know it couldn't have been easy with so many of Johnathon's friends here."

He tightened his embrace, making her feel like nothing could ever hurt her. She didn't know what she was going to do if he left, but she wasn't going to waste time worrying about what might happen.

"It's not anything I'm not used to, Miranda. I've spent my entire life contending with my brother. Even in death, he casts a long shadow."

"At some point, you have to find a way to let that

fall away. But that's easy for me to say. I've never had to do something like that."

"It's hard when other people foist it upon you. But today was a first step away from that. Tara and Grant finally seeing the light was a good thing."

She eased back her head so she could peer up into his handsome face. She was so glad for a blip of positivity from him. "See? It will just take time."

His hand rose to her cheek, his thumb brushing her skin tenderly. "Speaking of time, I think it's time I get you out of here, into the car and back to a warm house."

"And a warm bed?"

"It will be when we're done with it."

Twelve

On the Monday morning after Grant and Tara's nuptials, Andrew was shaken from his sleep by a terrible thought. He sat up in bed, his breathing labored. What if the wedding cancellation had been a distraction from Victor's true plan to go after Sterling?

"Are you okay?" Miranda muttered, rolling over in bed. "You were talking in your sleep."

Andrew didn't want to share his theory. He wasn't quite awake and hadn't had a chance to think this through. Leaning down, he kissed Miranda's shoulder. "I'm fine. I'll go put on some coffee."

She snuggled her pillow closer. "I'll be down in a little bit. My alarm isn't set to go off for another half hour."

Andrew took his time getting downstairs, thinking through his last conversation with Victor. Victor had suggested that he might interfere with the personal lives of those involved. That explained the problems with the wedding. But it didn't account for the Seaport project, and that was one thing Victor had always fixated on. It was, after all, Johnathon's last chance to be held up as a pillar of his community.

Andrew ground the coffee beans and leaned against the counter as the carafe filled up, drip by drip. The more awake he was, the more likely his idea seemed, but Grant and Tara felt like they were in the home stretch of the Seaport Promenade project. Nothing to worry about. He didn't want to go to them with his theory. It might set them back to right where they'd been before, at war, and with Andrew out in the cold. The person he really needed to broach this with was Clay. But when? It was 7:10 a.m., and Andrew really didn't want Miranda to overhear this conversation with her brother. Hopefully, Clay would understand that Andrew had a good reason for calling.

Clay answered after only one ring. "So I'm not the only one who's an early riser?" he asked.

Andrew managed to grin, despite the worries on his mind. "I don't sleep a lot."

"Me, neither. What's up?"

Andrew could hear Miranda walking around upstairs. She must not have been able to get back to sleep. This would have to be quick. "Can you do me a favor and check in with the city today about the submission for the Seaport?"

"They've made it clear that they don't want us doing that. They're supposed to issue their final decision on Wednesday. December twenty-third."

"I understand, but I'm worried that what Victor

pulled with Tara and Grant's wedding was a distraction. It forced everyone, especially Tara and Grant, to focus on things other than work over the last two weeks." Andrew really hoped that this conjecture would all end up being nothing. "This is just a precaution. You guys are so close to the finish line. I'd hate for anything to mess that up."

"Okay. Sure thing. I'll do it as soon as I get into the office."

Andrew heard Miranda's footsteps on the stairs. "Let me know what you learn."

"Will do."

Andrew ended the call and tucked his phone into the back pocket of his pajama pants just as Miranda was walking into the room. Seeing her always brought up a firestorm of feelings. He was tired of living on this edge, where he was in her life but not all the way in. Where his affection for her had been expressed physically, but never in words. He wanted to put everything on the line, but he was terrified of where it would leave Miranda. If he ended up going back to Seattle, he had to know that she'd be okay. That he hadn't made everything she'd been through so much worse, by stirring up trouble and leaving it unresolved.

"Coffee?" he asked.

"Please. You know how I feel about Mondays."

He poured her a cup of coffee, adding a healthy splash of cream. "I'm hoping this will make it ever so slightly better."

"Exactly the way I like it." She took a sip, then smiled warmly at him.

Moments like this really got to him—the seemingly insignificant glimpses of everyday life. He couldn't fathom leaving San Diego once everything with Victor was resolved. *If it's resolved*, he reminded himself. The reality was that he wouldn't feel good about professing his feelings, or his desire to stay, until he had redeemed himself. Grant and Tara's forgiveness had been a big step forward, but he wanted a clean slate. Miranda deserved a fresh start that came without conditions.

"I've decided not to go into the office for the rest of the week after today." Miranda reached for his hand. "It'll give us some time together. A few days before Christmas to relax."

Andrew hadn't wanted anything so badly, ever. "Great."

"I ordered some artwork for the nursery a month or so ago. It's due to arrive tomorrow. We could hang that. Maybe watch a Christmas movie." She shrugged. "I don't know. That probably sounds pretty unexciting."

It sounds like everything I ever wanted. "I'm sure it'll be more fun than work."

"That reminds me. I need to check my email. There's a chance my only client meeting today is going to be moved up. I'll be right back." She traipsed off into the living room, presumably heading for her office.

Andrew went to work on breakfast—some eggs, sausage and fresh fruit—and tried to clear his head. There was a distinct chance that everything was fine—Clay might very well call him sometime after nine and proclaim that all was good with Sterling's place in the final round for the Seaport project. Miranda would come home after work and he'd make a fabulous meal for her. Hopefully, they'd make love and he'd hold her in his arms while she slept. They'd spend several days together, tucked away in this house, and ultimately spend a beautiful holiday together. His first truly happy Christmas.

If all of that could happen, it might be the right time to tell her his true feelings. He'd put it all on the line. And if he was fortunate, Miranda would say that she felt the same way. Could he be that lucky? He wanted to believe he was due, but he was smart enough to know that the world didn't always work like that.

Miranda joined him in the kitchen and they sat down to breakfast together.

With her first bite, Miranda moaned. "You're spoiling me." She always expressed her sincere appreciation for his cooking skills, and this morning was no different.

He soaked up every second of the attention. "Not possible."

She grinned. "I like watching you try."

And I love trying. After breakfast was done, Miranda went up to shower while Andrew cleaned up the kitchen and prayed that his phone would ring soon. It didn't happen before Miranda was out the door for work, so Andrew got cleaned up and dressed for the day.

The caller ID lit up with Clay's information a little after ten. "You were right. Our bid has been withdrawn. Completely taken out of the running."

Andrew's heart began to hammer. He took no pleasure in seeing his hunch proven right. "What happened?"

"Apparently, a woman with a letter on Sterling Enterprises letterhead showed up at the planning office on Friday morning. It was a formal request to withdraw from the competition."

"The day before the wedding."

"Yes. Grant and Tara weren't in the office at all that day. And neither was I because they had the Christmas pageant at Delia's school that morning, then I went with Grant to pick up their rings."

"Can you undo what's been done?" Andrew's mind was running a million miles a minute as he thought about what his next move might be.

"Yes. We've already begun the process. The clerk was annoyed at first, but I think I sweet-talked her. That's not really my forte, but I think we're going to be okay."

Finally, Andrew could exhale. Clay had set things back on track from the Sterling side of things. Still, this had been entirely too close a call. Andrew needed Sterling to get across the finish line on Wednesday. They might not win the bid, but at least it would be because everything had played out the way it was supposed to. "Okay. I'm going to get to work on tracking down Victor and finally putting an end to this."

"Andrew, you know I believe in you, but I've heard you say that so many times. What's different today?"

All Andrew could think about was the prospect of spending the next few days with Miranda. Beyond that, maybe more? It felt like his future was lying at his feet, but he was going to have to wrap it all up. He had to redeem himself. "I have an idea."

"Maybe there's just no stopping this guy and we have to ride it out until he gets bored and walks away."

"I've thought about that, but I don't want us all existing under this dark cloud. It's no way to live."

"Us all? That almost makes it sound like you're planning on staying. Have you and Miranda talked about this?"

Andrew hoped he wasn't overstepping. "We haven't. I haven't felt right about saying anything until the Victor situation is resolved."

"But you want to stay?"

"How would it make you feel if I said yes?" Andrew wanted to believe that he and Clay were close now, that it was okay for him to ask this question, but he wasn't sure.

"I'd say that it's an amazing idea."

Andrew couldn't contain the smile that crossed his face. "Good. Just don't tell your sister. I'm not going to bring it up until this is all put to bed."

"Don't worry about me. Mum's the word."

Andrew's phone beeped with another call. It was an unknown caller, but Andrew had an irrational hope that it might be Victor. "Clay, I need to go. Keep me posted if anything changes."

"I will." Andrew hung up and answered the other call. "Hello?"

"Mr. Sterling?"

Andrew was shocked as hell. "Sandy, are you okay? You sound terrible."

"Were you serious about the offer you made me before?"

"Of course I was. Why? Are you thinking about flipping on Victor?"

"He just called me. He's enraged. Someone at Sterling called the city and got them to put Sterling back into the bidding process. He thought he'd successfully pulled the company out of the running."

Andrew didn't want to tip his hand. He had little faith in the idea of trusting Sandy. "Oh, wow. I didn't know."

"He's furious."

Andrew's stomach soured. "Look, Sandy. I'm happy to give you what I promised you, but at this point, I'm not sure you can help me. It sounds like Victor's going to forge ahead, with or without you."

"I have something that can help you take him down. Audio recordings."

"Of what?"

"Every conversation he and I ever had. Everything he ever asked me to do. And it's not just the Sterling Enterprises plan. Victor had me doing other corporate espionage. Scary stuff with very big players."

Andrew's thoughts were moving fast. "Will you give them to me? My offer still stands if you will. Five million."

"The money's not enough anymore. I need to disappear. I need to get to somewhere where he'll never find me. I know too much and if the recordings come out, he'll know that I double-crossed him."

"One of my private planes is in a hangar down at Gray Municipal. I can get you to Mexico. Pietro, my security chief, can go with you. Once you're in a safe place, you give us the audio recordings and we'll transfer the money."

"I want *you* to do it. I want you to come with me."

"What? Why?"

"Because I trust you more than I trust Pietro. You have more to lose. You're the one who's been chasing Victor this whole time."

Andrew's thoughts hung on Sandy's words. He *did* have everything to lose. If this all went down the drain with Sterling, the company would ultimately be fine. They'd find a way to move forward, make millions and Johnathon's reputation would most likely remain intact.

Yes, they would suffer the embarrassment of not landing the massive public contract they were expected to win. Miranda might ultimately forgive Andrew for things he'd done. But he would not have made peace with his brother's memory, and he would never feel right with the world until he did that. He had to know deep in his heart that he'd done everything possible to save what Johnathon had built. "Okay. I'll take you."

"I don't want you to just fly me over the border and drop me off. I need you to take me somewhere remote. Somewhere that's safe."

Andrew had traveled all over the world, but one locale he'd visited years ago had struck him as the perfect place to disappear—a tiny village tucked away in the mountains of Costa Rica. "I have an idea. I can tell you on the plane. Ping me your location? I'll pick you up myself."

"Okay. Please hurry."

Andrew ended the call and rushed upstairs. He did not want to leave, but what choice did he have? He'd put Sandy in this situation at the very beginning. Yes, it had been her choice to side with Victor, but he couldn't blame other people for their poor choices. He'd made too many of his own.

Upstairs, he called Clay, and put him on speakerphone while he packed up the suitcase he'd wheeled into this house weeks ago.

"Hey, Andrew. What's up?" Clay asked.

"I need you to keep an eye on your sister for the next few days."

"Going somewhere?"

"Yes. I need to take care of our big problem. I think

it's best if I don't tell you where. No idea who might be listening."

"Is Miranda in danger?"

"No. I'll have my head of security stay in San Diego. We'll have someone with eyes on the house the whole time, but I'd feel better if you were checking in with her, too." Andrew's phone screen flashed a notification from the number Sandy had called from. It was her location. "I have to go. I don't plan on checking in. I don't want to leave any lines of communication open, okay?"

"Got it. Good luck."

Andrew zipped his bag shut and thundered down the stairs, but he came to a stop when he saw the array of beautiful holiday decorations in the living room. The fireplace mantel had the lovely scene Miranda had designed—with pine boughs, red velvet ribbon and twinkly white lights. Over the doorway into the foyer was what Andrew now knew was a swag, of silver Christmas bells in various sizes and glittery garland, all artfully arranged. In the corner sat the Christmas tree, looking like something out of a magazine, with its array of carefully chosen ornaments. These things had brought Christmas spirit with Miranda's skilled guidance, but she was what made those warm feelings come to life. He hated the thought of missing out on the next few days with her. He was supposed to be here. They'd made plans. He intended to return, but he'd had so many intentions over the years that hadn't turned out. He really hoped that wouldn't be the case this time. Regardless, it was time to let her know he wouldn't be here when she arrived home from work.

He waited until he was pulling his car out of Miranda's driveway to make the call.

"I feel like I just saw you," Miranda answered. "Are you sure you're okay?"

"I am, but I have to leave town for a few days."

"Wait. What's wrong?"

The distress in her voice made his task that much more difficult. "I'm within striking distance of fixing my problem."

"Victor? Seriously? I thought that was over."

"It's not. Not completely, at least."

"This is starting to feel like a wild-goose chase. Is this really necessary? Can't someone else deal with him?"

"I started this. I have to finish it."

Miranda grumbled. "You don't have to. You've tried everything imaginable. You're the only one expecting this of yourself. You hold yourself to a standard that's impossible to meet."

He knew he was being stubborn. It didn't change his determination to follow through. "I know."

"Just this morning, we talked about spending the next few days together. You said it sounded like fun. That's not enough to make you stay?"

"Don't make this harder than it already is, okay?"

Miranda didn't immediately say anything in return, but he could hear her breathing. "You're definitely coming back?"

"That's my plan. Yes."

"When?"

Andrew didn't want to give definitive answers, but he also didn't want to leave her hanging. He'd already saddled her with so much uncertainty over the last month or so. "I'll be back by Christmas, okay? I promise." He hoped like hell that nothing bad happened and that he didn't have to break that promise. It would crush her visions of a happy holiday.

"Will you also promise me that you'll be careful?" Her voice was starting to crack.

"Of course."

"Because I want you to come back, Andrew. I hope you know that."

He managed half a smile, but his heart was aching. There were so many things he wanted to say, but once again he was overwhelmed by the need to wait until the time was right. "I want to come back. I hope *you* know that."

"Okay. 'Bye. Be careful."

"Goodbye, Miranda." He hit the red button to end the call before he could say what he longed to tell her... *I love you.*

Thirteen

By late afternoon on Wednesday evening, Miranda was starting to lose hope. Andrew had been gone more than forty-eight hours. Where was he and what could he possibly be doing? She picked up her phone and pulled up his number in her contacts. It rang and rang, as it had the other times she'd called since he'd left on Monday. It then went to his voice mail, just like before. The sound of his voice made her ache for his presence. *"This is Andrew Sterling. Please leave a message."*

"Hey. It's me. I'm just calling because I'm worried and this makes me feel better. Please call or text me to let me know that you're okay. Even just a thumbs-up emoji would be a big help." She ended the call and tossed her phone to the other end of the couch. She was tired of feeling so helpless. The last time she'd felt like this was during the first month after Johnathon's death, when she'd had to get used to being all alone in this big house. In some ways, she felt as though she was reliving that loss. It wasn't a pleasant feeling.

Her phone rang and she scrambled, crawling on hands and knees across the cushions and grabbing it without looking at the caller ID. "Hello? Andrew?"

"Sorry to disappoint. It's Tara."

Miranda slumped back against a pile of throw pillows, her heart practically in her throat. "Oh, it's okay. What's up?"

"The city just made the announcement. Sterling landed the Seaport project."

Miranda struggled to understand why her first reaction was tears. Perhaps it was stress. Perhaps it was closing this chapter when Andrew wasn't around. Sterling had made it through despite Victor's interference. If Johnathon was still here, he would've been so pleased. "Congratulations. You all must be so excited."

"Everyone is. There's a fair bit of relief, too."

"How are you going to celebrate?"

"We'll do it in January. After the holidays. After pulling a wedding together in two weeks, I'm trying to take a break from party planning."

"Makes perfect sense."

Tara hesitated on the line, which made Miranda wonder if there was more she wanted to say. "I take it you haven't heard from Andrew?"

"You know that he left?"

"Yes. Clay told Grant and me. Don't worry. We haven't told anyone."

"Okay."

"I'll be honest. I'm worried. Grant and I wanted him to take care of the situation with Victor, but from a distance. We never thought he'd get on a plane and go after him."

Miranda felt her blood go cold. Yes, she'd believed Andrew all this time, but it somehow made it worse that everyone else now knew that Victor was real. "Do you think he's in danger? No one has heard from him since Monday afternoon. I don't even know what to do now. I'm so consumed with worry."

"Do you want Grant to do some asking around? See what we can find out?"

All Miranda could think about was that Andrew had wanted this all kept quiet. "No. I don't want any of us to do anything to jeopardize his safety." Speaking of which, Miranda probably needed to stop leaving him messages. There was no telling what sort of circumstances he was in.

"Okay. Will you please call us when you hear from him? Andrew was right all along, and Grant and I will never stop feeling bad about it. We also feel indebted to him. His quick thinking on Monday morning kept us in the game. We got the Seaport project. Everyone gets their happy ending."

Except me. Miranda hated that her mind would go to such a negative place, but she couldn't help it. "I'm so glad. Hopefully I'll get to tell him soon."

"Please keep us posted."

"I will. 'Bye, Tara."

"Goodbye."

Miranda hung up. All this good news and it still didn't make her feel any better.

She worried that the obvious was staring her in the face—Andrew might not come back. She had to distract herself, so she went into the kitchen and made herself a mug of cocoa, then settled on the sofa to watch a movie. *It's a Wonderful Life* was on the TV, and it had just started, showing snowy scenes in black-and-white of quaint Bedford Falls. Miranda turned the volume low. The movie was so familiar, she could recite nearly every line, but she couldn't focus enough to watch it. Maybe Andrew was going back to Seattle and he simply couldn't bring himself to tell her.

That would've been the Andrew of old, the fictional one constructed by Johnathon and sometimes Grant and Tara. Miranda knew that wasn't the real Andrew. The real Andrew kept his promises. He made good on everything he said he'd do. As night fell and the clock ticked closer to Christmas Eve, she continued to waver between hope and disappointment. He'd said he'd be back in time for Christmas. There weren't many hours left until Christmas Eve would be upon them. The thought of him not showing up, in time or at all, reminded her of the many times she'd defended him. She'd always wanted to believe that he would never lead her astray or let her down. Although he'd always been thankful to have her confidence, he'd also told her that she didn't need to do it. It had always been a gut instinct. A reflex.

This was her connection to Andrew—immediate and visceral. Something she couldn't explain. They'd had an invisible bond from the moment they met. Yes, it all started with Johnathon, and that fact still ate at her from time to time. How she wished she could talk to her dead husband, explain to him that her feelings for Andrew didn't mean that she wouldn't always love him. When the baby arrived, that feeling would likely grow. But Miranda had a big heart, one meant for giving, and also receiving. She hadn't planned it, but she'd fallen. In love. With his brother. And she should have been smarter about it. She should have told him before he took off.

Miranda's phone rang. She jumped just as she had every other time over the last two days. She fought the disappointment when, once again, it wasn't Andrew. She loved talking to her brother, but it wasn't quite the same.

"You don't have to keep checking up on me," she said without offering a hello.

"Oh, but I do. I promised Andrew. Why don't you come over and hang out with us? Delia would love to see you. We're baking Christmas cookies. I'll come and pick you up."

"I think I'll stay put. Thank you, though." The invitation truly sounded lovely and she sure could have used the distraction, but she wanted to hold on to hope, even when she wondered if her optimism wasn't about to bite her on the butt. Sometimes things didn't turn out okay. "I talked to Tara a little while ago. Congratulations on the Seaport project."

"Thanks, but it's not really my victory. It was the whole team. And frankly, it was the wives. You three were the ones who pushed the hardest."

"I guess we did."

"You sound tired."

"I am. Although I don't know why. I've basically been puttering around the house for two days. I haven't done much more than worry."

"That can be draining in its own right," Clay said.

"I suppose." Miranda took another sip of her cocoa and set the mug on the end table. "You haven't heard from him, have you?"

"You know I would've called you right away if I had, right?"

"I know." Of course she did. It still didn't hurt to ask. "I think I'm going to go to bed."

"It's so early," Clay noted.

"I know. I'm super tired."

"Okay. We'll see you on Christmas morning for brunch at our place?"

"Absolutely."

"Sleep well."

Miranda didn't have the energy to walk all the way upstairs. She clicked off the TV, grabbed a throw blanket from the end of the sofa and arranged a few pillows until she was comfortable. She tried to think good thoughts as she closed her eyes and felt her body slowly giving in to sleep. How she hoped she wouldn't be spending this Christmas alone. How she hoped she wouldn't have to face her future without the man she loved.

Andrew's plane touched down on the private landing strip at the San Diego airport, smooth as silk. He took his new phone off airplane mode. His old one had died an untimely death in Costa Rica, falling out of his pocket and into the small plunge pool of the cottage he'd found for Sandy. He still didn't have the message he'd been waiting for from Pietro. He wasn't going to tell Miranda that the coast was clear until he was absolutely certain that was the truth.

He'd left his rental down at Gray Municipal when he'd left town with Sandy, so he had a driver pick him up. "Mr. Sterling. I believe you're expecting this." The driver handed over a small black velvet box as he held the door.

Andrew popped it open. It was exactly as he'd remembered, even though he hadn't looked at it in years. "Thank you." He dropped it into his pocket and climbed inside the car. Excitement bubbled up in his body at the thought of seeing Miranda. He was nervous, too. He could imagine relief at confessing his feelings, but he could also picture several different types of rejection. She might want to wait. It was awfully soon. Her husband hadn't been gone very long.

Finally, Andrew's phone buzzed in his hand. It was Pietro. "Well?" Andrew asked when he answered.

"I'm sorry I'm a little late in calling you. His flight was delayed, but he's off to Munich. I watched the plane take off myself." Andrew had instructed Pietro to buy a ticket for the flight, just so he could accompany Victor through security and down to the gate.

Andrew had never breathed such a big sigh of relief. He had a promise from Victor that he would stay in Europe for the next twelve months. Andrew had plenty of insurance to make sure Victor would keep a safe distance. Forever. "Thank you so much. I couldn't have done this without you."

"Are you on your way to Ms. Sterling's?"

"I am."

"Good luck," Pietro said with a glint of mischief in his voice.

"Thank you for having one of your guys track down the ring in Seattle and sending it down. I just got it."

"No trouble at all, sir. Is there anything else I can do for you?"

"Now that we have everything wrapped up, you and your guys are welcome to head back to Seattle."

"And what are your plans?" Pietro asked.

"I don't know. But I'm hoping that I get to stay here in San Diego."

"If you do, what does that mean for your operation in Seattle?"

"I don't know, exactly, but I do know that you'll always have a job. Don't worry about that."

"Good to know, sir. I can't imagine working for anyone else."

Andrew smiled. "Good. And good night, Pietro. Job well done."

"Good night, sir."

Andrew hung up the phone. That call from Pietro had been the last thing he was waiting on before he called Miranda. They were only ten minutes from her house, but he didn't want to hold out for even a second more. Unfortunately, the call went to her voice mail. Was she in bed already? It was only nine-thirty. None of that made sense. Hopefully, everything could be cleared up once he arrived.

As soon as they arrived at Miranda's, Andrew grabbed his suitcase and beelined for the front door, then put in the security code for the electronic lock. Inside, the house was so quiet. "Miranda?" he asked, setting down his bag. There was no answer.

He spotted a soft ray of light beaming into the hall from the living room. He went to investigate, and spotted Miranda all curled up on the sofa, asleep. He crept closer, finding emotion welling up inside him. She was everything. His whole world. And he'd been tormenting himself, waiting to tell her.

He kneeled down next to the couch and stole a moment to look at how truly beautiful she was in serene slumber. Her amazing mouth was slack, her eyelids pale and her lashes dark against her skin. Her gorgeous hair tumbled across her shoulders. He braced himself by placing a hand on her upper arm and leaning in to kiss her on her forehead. "Miranda?" he whispered as he moved back.

Her eyes drifted halfway, then suddenly popped open. The look of surprise on her face made him wonder if he'd scared her. "Oh, my God. You're here."

He sat back as she pushed herself to sitting then lunged for him. They landed in a heap on the floor. She kissed him at least ten times. Maybe more. All he could think was that if this was his reward for all of the pain and misery he'd been through, it was absolutely worth it.

"You're back. You're here. I was so worried."

"I'm sorry I didn't call. My phone died and it took some time to get a new one in Costa Rica."

"That's where you went?"

He nodded but held his finger to his lips. "Yes. But we can't tell anyone. That's where Sandy is. I got her relocated. It took some doing with setting up offshore accounts and getting her into the country in the first place. But she's good. She should be safe. From Victor."

"Sterling got the Seaport contract. Tara called me earlier today."

"I heard."

"Does that mean Victor is gone? For good?" Andrew was going to spare Miranda the details, but it was safe to say that Victor would not be coming back. Andrew had hours of audio of Victor detailing his various schemes, most of which were illegal. Andrew's only ask for not handing them over to some of Victor's more notorious partners was that Victor disappear.

"He is. He's gone, darling. Nobody has to worry about him anymore."

Miranda sat up, her legs curled up under her body. "Darling? You've never called me a pet name before."

Andrew pushed himself to sitting. "Huh. I guess I haven't."

She smiled wide. "I like it a lot."

His heart began to hammer again. "Good. Because I need to ask you something."

She shook her head. "No. Hold on. There's one thing I need to tell you first. If that's okay."

He laughed quietly. She was so adorable when she was being pushy. "Of course. Whatever you want."

"I realized when you were gone how much I need you. And how many things I left unsaid while you were here. About what you mean to me. About the void you've filled in my—"

He shook his head wildly. "Hold on. I feel the same way, Miranda."

A tear rolled down her cheek. "Can I finish? Please? I've got this all rehearsed in my head and I don't want to forget a word of it."

"Yes. Of course." How could he say no when she was crying?

"I can't lose another person in my life, Andrew. I can't lose you."

"I love you," he blurted. "I'm sorry. I couldn't wait anymore."

Now the tears were rolling down her cheeks even faster. "You do? Because I love you, too. Please tell me you won't leave."

"Please tell me I can stay."

She nodded and he slipped his hands into her silky hair, pulling her face to his. They drifted into the kiss and Andrew let fanciful thoughts swirl in his head, even when he was normally not inclined to give in to such things. This felt like the start. A fresh one. Full of bright promise. Even with everything that had gone wrong in his life, he still felt lucky. He had love and good fortune. He was about to have a family if she answered his question the way he hoped she would.

He reared back his head and pulled the box out of his pocket, opening it for Miranda. "Will you marry me, Miranda? Will you be my wife?"

He wasn't sure exactly what her reaction would be, but he hadn't expected how eagerly she would wipe away her tears and thrust her left hand forward. "Oh, my God. Yes. I would love to marry you."

Andrew removed the ring from its safe spot and slipped it onto Miranda's finger. "It was my mom's, and it belonged to my dad's mom before that. It's quite literally the only Sterling family heirloom that exists. I had Pietro get it from Seattle while I was getting Sandy settled."

"You did that? For me?" She admired the ring with a flutter of her lovely fingers.

"Do you like it? Be honest. You can tell me if you don't."

"I love it. I absolutely love it. It's beautiful. It has so much character."

"Good. Because the other person I tried to give it to thought it was ugly and wanted something else."

"That should've been your first sign."

She might be right. "Probably."

Her gaze returned to his face. "I know this couldn't have been easy. Proposing a second time in your life."

A breathy laugh escaped his lips. "You want to know what's funny? I never even thought about that. I was nervous, but only because it was you. I wasn't anxious about the actual question."

"Why would I make you nervous? We've grown so close. You can tell me anything at all. I will not judge you."

"It's precisely that. You always believe in me. Even when you had reason to not feel that way. I worry a bit that I'm not worthy, but I think that's normal. You are pretty amazing."

"You're the one who's amazing." She leaned closer and gave him a soft kiss that warmed him from head to toe.

He couldn't wait to get her upstairs. He got up from the floor and reached down for her hand. "Come on. Time for bed."

"Sleeping or bed?"

He laughed and gently pulled her along toward the stairs. "Bed, if that's okay with you. I want to make love to my fiancée."

Miranda stopped before they started their ascent. "I'm so excited you made it back in time for Christmas."

"I told you I'd be back. I wouldn't have missed it for the whole world."

"I can't wait to subject you to all of my favorite Christmas Eve traditions tomorrow. Baking cookies. Lighting a fire. Listening to Christmas music."

He wasn't sure what to say. What sort of words match the moment when you realize you have it all?

"I'm sure it sounds like a lot," she said.

He didn't hesitate. He swept her into his arms and started up the stairs. "Honestly, it sounds like all I ever wanted."

Epilogue

Four months later

Baby Chloe was crying. Miranda knew it was just a ploy, but she watched as Andrew totally fell for it.

"Shh. Shh. It's okay." He scooped her up out of the baby carrier and gently placed her over his shoulder. "There's no need to cry."

"You don't have to pick her up every time she cries, you know." Miranda walked up behind him and lowered her head to get the baby's attention. Chloe's eyes lit up and she unleashed her new, toothless grin when she spotted her mom. Miranda's heart swelled to twice its size. This was a regular occurrence. It happened several hundred times a day, especially since Chloe started to smile a few weeks ago.

"It kills me when she cries. I can't help it." Andrew

turned so he could look Miranda in the eye. Damn, he was sexy with a baby in his arms. "You can tell me to stop it, but I doubt I ever will."

"I forgive you. I just don't want her to get spoiled." Miranda glanced at the clock on the wall. "Oh, shoot. We'd better pack up the car or we're going to be late."

Andrew grabbed the diaper bag from the kitchen counter and began sifting through it with Chloe still in his arms. "Plenty of diapers. Change of clothes. Wipes. Pacifier. Oh, no." He turned to Miranda. "Where's her inchworm?"

Chloe had a stuffed inchworm sewn of soft fabric in a rainbow of colors. It was small enough for her to wrap her tiny fingers around and hold on to it. "I think it's on the sofa."

"I'll get it."

"I can do it," she said. "You can put her in her carrier."

"I'd rather wait until the last second. She's just going to start crying."

Miranda shook her head, grabbed the diaper bag and walked around to the other side of the couch, finding the inchworm. "This is the last second. Tara will be furious if we're late."

"So much buildup to this thing. You'd think someone was getting married or having a baby." He nestled Chloe into her seat, and sure enough, she started to wail the second he had her strapped in. "We'd better hurry up."

They hustled out to the car and Andrew clicked the carrier into its base in the back seat of Miranda's SUV. He rushed to start the car. As soon as the engine rumbled to life, Chloe stopped crying. He was visibly relieved. "Next stop, Seaport Promenade?"

"Hard to believe the day has finally come to break ground on this thing. I don't know about you, but I'm relieved. And ready to stop hearing about it."

"I swear it's all anyone talks about lately," Andrew said.

Of course, Miranda knew very well that Andrew was relieved. In many ways, today was about him facing Johnathon one more time, but this time, he was armed with vindication and the knowledge that he'd done right by everyone, even himself. Johnathon's legacy would be sealed, but Andrew had a life ahead of him with Miranda and Chloe. It didn't need to be said that Andrew knew he was the lucky one, after a lifetime of feeling like he'd been on the losing end of that relationship.

They arrived downtown a few minutes later and Andrew found a spot near the convention center, which meant a short walk to the promenade. He unloaded Chloe's stroller and tossed the diaper bag into the storage basket while Miranda put in her seat. They were a well-oiled machine by now, nearly two months after Chloe's arrival, but it hadn't always been like this. The first three or four weeks were rocky, all three of them operating on too little sleep because Chloe had been colicky. She'd arrived on February fourth, so at that point, Miranda and Andrew were still in the honeymoon phase of their relationship, even though they hadn't yet tied the knot. There was nothing like sleepless nights and too few showers to test a partnership. But they got through it and Andrew took to parenthood like a fish to water. He might be strong, and sometimes stolid, but he'd been putty in Chloe's hand from the minute he laid eyes on her in the delivery room, and they both cried their eyes out at the miracle before them. It still felt like a dream some days. A beautiful, perfect dream.

They strolled down the sidewalk, enjoying the warmth of this sunny April day. They reached a break in the city buildings, one of the walkways to the place where the old Seaport development had once been. The demolition began in January, right after Sterling landed the project, and was completed in short order. Included in that was the destruction of the wedding pavilion, the one where Andrew would've gotten married if his fiancée hadn't left him. Andrew had a bit of an epiphany that day, wondering aloud if perhaps Johnathon hadn't had nefarious intent when he'd wanted to pursue the Seaport. Maybe he'd wanted to see it erased and brought back to life in a new form, one that wouldn't have to cause Andrew so much pain. It was a lovely thought, and although no one had any way of knowing, he and Miranda had decided that would be the story they would tell the baby. For Johnathon's many faults and missteps, he had been a good man with a big heart. And he'd been part of bringing the two most important people in Miranda's life, Chloe and Andrew, to her.

When they emerged on the other side of the buildings, they spotted the construction site, ringed in chain-link fence with an enormous sign that read Sterling and Singleton Enterprises. That was another development since Christmas—in February, soon after the baby was born, Grant invited Andrew to merge his development firm with Sterling Enterprises. It was a natural pairing, plus Andrew wasn't going anywhere and it seemed foolish of him to branch out into San Diego development and attempt to compete with the company his brother had started.

In turn, Andrew felt it was only right that Grant's last name finally go on the company letterhead. Andrew kept the Seattle office open, but only went up once a month or so, and only overnight. He never wanted to be far away from San Diego or Miranda and the baby. *I need my family*, he'd say whenever he decided that he couldn't bring himself to be gone for more than twenty-four hours.

There was a small crowd assembled, upwards of fifty people, most of them Sterling-Singleton employees or the press. To the far side stood Astrid and Clay. They were in the midst of planning their wedding, which was set for June on the beach in Coronado. They'd wanted to wait until Delia was out of school so they could take her to Norway for a month and introduce her to Astrid's homeland. Miranda had never seen her brother happier, and that, in turn, made her own happiness that much brighter and more complete.

"Hey there," Clay said, when Andrew and Miranda rolled up with the stroller. "Where's my beautiful niece?"

Andrew pulled back the sunshade a fraction of an inch and peered inside. "She's sleeping."

"Well, can I see her?" Clay asked.

Miranda and Astrid laughed, hugging each other. "They're so funny," Astrid said.

"That's one word for it," Miranda added.

"Folks, we're ready to start," Tara's voice announced over a loudspeaker. She and Grant were both standing with hardhats on and shovels in their hands. Alongside them were the mayor and several members of the city council. Andrew had been invited to participate in this part of things, but he'd decided against it. Andrew said it didn't matter that he was the Sterling part of the company name now. He'd rather stand with his family.

"We'll keep this short so everyone can enjoy this beautiful day," Tara continued. "With that, I'll turn it over to Grant Singleton to make the dedication."

Grant took the microphone from his wife and kissed her on the cheek. "Sterling Enterprises has been fortunate to be a part of this community for more than fifteen years, but it's always been in the private sector. Yes, we've built some beautiful, state-of-the-art buildings in this city, but this project is the one that will ultimately mean the most. It is my sincere hope that this will be a place for the citizens who live here, and those who travel to visit our amazing city, to gather for years to come. And with that, let us break ground."

Grant, Tara and several members of the city council poised their shovels in the artfully arranged mound of dirt at the entrance to the construction site. After a count to three, they all dug in, officially breaking ground on the redevelopment of the Seaport Promenade.

The crowd erupted in applause, which noticeably put Andrew on edge. He peeked inside Chloe's stroller to check on her. "Okay. Good. She's still asleep."

Miranda laughed quietly, then leaned in for a kiss. "I love you, Andrew."

"I love you, too."

They both looked on as Grant, Tara and the other local dignitaries shook hands. "You know, I've been thinking," Andrew said. "What if we got married here? When it's all done?"

That was the one piece of their happy ending that hadn't happened yet. Miranda hadn't wanted to walk down the aisle at eight or nine months pregnant, and they were still adjusting to Chloe's arrival. Ahead of them was Clay and Astrid's wedding. Perhaps Christmas would work well. It *was* Miranda's favorite time of year.

"Really? You want to do that?" she asked. "This place holds some bad memories, doesn't it?"

He shook his head and looked over at her, shielding his eyes. "Miranda, darling, you need to know something."

"What's that?"

"With you in my life, there are no more bad memories. Only happy ones."

* * * * *

COMING SOON!

We really hope you enjoyed reading this book.
If you're looking for more romance, be sure to
head to the shops when new books are
available on

Thursday 12th November

To see which titles are coming soon, please visit
millsandboon.co.uk/nextmonth

MILLS & BOON

MILLS & BOON

THE HEART OF ROMANCE

A ROMANCE FOR EVERY KIND OF READER

MODERN
Prepare to be swept off your feet by sophisticated, sexy and seductive heroes, in some of the world's most glamourous and romantic locations, where power and passion collide.
8 stories per month.

HISTORICAL
Escape with historical heroes from time gone by. Whether your passion is for wicked Regency Rakes, muscled Vikings or rugged Highlanders, awaken the romance of the past.
6 stories per month.

MEDICAL
Set your pulse racing with dedicated, delectable doctors in the high-pressure world of medicine, where emotions run high and passion, comfort and love are the best medicine.
6 stories per month.

True Love
Celebrate true love with tender stories of heartfelt romance, fro the rush of falling in love to the joy a new baby can bring, and a focus on the emotional heart of a relationship.
8 stories per month.

Desire
Indulge in secrets and scandal, intense drama and plenty of sizz hot action with powerful and passionate heroes who have it all: wealth, status, good looks…everything but the right woman.
6 stories per month.

HEROES
Experience all the excitement of a gripping thriller, with an inte romance at its heart. Resourceful, true-to-life women and stron fearless men face danger and desire - a killer combination!
8 stories per month.

DARE
Sensual love stories featuring smart, sassy heroines you'd want a best friend, and compelling intense heroes who are worthy of th
4 stories per month.

To see which titles are coming soon, please visit

millsandboon.co.uk/nextmonth

JOIN US ON SOCIAL MEDIA!

Stay up to date with our latest releases, author
news and gossip, special offers and discounts, and
all the behind-the-scenes action
from Mills & Boon...

 millsandboon

 millsandboonuk

millsandboon

't might just be true love...

MILLS & BOON

MODERN

Power and Passion

Prepare to be swept off your feet by
sophisticated, sexy and seductive heroes, in
some of the world's most glamourous and
romantic locations, where power and
passion collide.

Julia James
Heiress's
PREGNANCY
SCANDAL
MILLS & BOON
MODERN

Jennie Lucas
Chosen as the
SHEIKH'S ROYAL
BRIDE
MILLS & BOON
MODERN

Kim Lawrence
A WEDDING
at the
ITALIAN'S DEMAND
MILLS & BOON

Sharon Kendrick
The
SHEIKH'S
SECRET BABY
MILLS & BOON
MODERN

Eight Modern stories published every month, find them all a

millsandboon.co.uk/Modern

MILLS & BOON
True Love
Romance from the Heart

Celebrate true love with tender stories of
heartfelt romance, from the rush of falling
in love to the joy a new baby can bring,
and a focus on the emotional
heart of a relationship.